ROYAL WILLIAM

Royal William

The Story of a Democrat

DORIS LESLIE

HEINEMANN : LONDON

William Heinemann Ltd
LONDON MELBOURNE TORONTO
CAPE TOWN AUCKLAND

First published 1940
Reprinted 1941 (three times)
Reprinted 1943
Reprinted 1945
Reprinted 1949

This edition first published 1966

043441803X

Printed in Great Britain
by Bookprint Limited
Kingswood, Surrey

This edition is dedicated
to the beloved memory
of my husband,
Sir Walter Fergusson Hannay

All we have of freedom—all we use or know
This our fathers bought for us, long and long ago.

KIPLING.

Contents

Foreword

ALTHOUGH the story of this obscure and much maligned
English King is presented here as fiction, no character or
name of a character is fictitious. The main events in the
private life of William IV have been closely followed, and if
doubt is cast upon the authenticity of his early romances, those
who care to verify them will find ample proof in the authori-
tative sources quoted at the end of the book.

Thanks to Greville and Creevey whose observations of
Royalty were tempered by the amount of favour they received,
and since from King William—who had not much use for
toadies—they received no favour in his reign at all, posterity
has been handed the malicious caricature of a vulgar buffoon,
of whom, however, investigation produces nothing worse
than that he liked to walk the streets of London incognito
and unattended, that he hob-nobbed with old shipmates and
that he said 'God damme' in the presence of his wife.

That he set his sign and seal upon reform, that he was the
first democrat to sit upon a throne, and that he kept his throne
in the face of revolution, has been entirely ignored by the
Grevilles and the Creeveys.

But in spite of the calumnies hurled at him by these arch-
gossips and by a certain latter-day biographer of Mrs Jordan
who depicts her as an angel of virtue and him as a monster
of vice, there are two men whose good opinion of this prince
who never thought to be a King is worth noting: Horace
Walpole, who knew him as a boy, and Nelson, who knew him
as a sailor.

To Mr Roger Fulford whose admirable books, *The Royal
Dukes* and *George IV*, have provided much valuable information; to the Navy Records Society for kindly permitting me
to reproduce Prince William's letters from the *Journal and*

xi

Letters of Admiral Sir T. Byam Martin; to the Clarendon Press, Oxford, for permission to quote from Horace Walpole's correspondence, some extracts of which are incorporated in the dialogue; to the officials of the London Library who have so willingly aided my research, and to my husband, whose advice and criticism helped me to write this book, I am deeply and most gratefully indebted.

DORIS LESLIE.

BOOK ONE

The Sailor

Chapter One

ON a sultry day in June 1779, a post-chaise containing a man and a boy drove along the London road to Portsmouth. Notwithstanding the elegance of its appointments and the Royal coat of arms upon its paint, the chaise, with windows sealed against the dust, was airless, hot, and stank of the vinegar with which Mr Majendie, who travelled ill, had refreshed himself throughout the journey.

The other occupant of the carriage, his flaxen hair streaked dark with sweat, and who sat unhappily clutching to his chest the Bible his father had given him as a parting gift, was hard put to it to hold his tears. Even Mr Majendie and his megrims were more supportable than the dreaded end of this long drive.

He wore a brand new midshipman's uniform, white duck trousers, a coat of navy blue, and boots too tight for him. His hat, which for comfort's sake he had discarded, lay on his knees. And how he loathed his uniform, his ridiculous slouched hat, his pinching boots, himself, and all the world!

Yet, when, on the eve of his departure not two days since, he had been summoned to the presence of his parents, wearing for the first time this very uniform, William's pride had almost burst its buttons. Why then this swift revulsion?

The cause of it was not far to seek.

It lay in the person of Mr Majendie who in suffering silence at William's side, sat clothed in nightmare repetition of William's dress, a hybrid suit, half-mid-

3

shipman's, half-cleric's; the selfsame cloth, but navy trews instead of white, the same round hat slouched down upon his nose, and under it a parson's collar. And this by order of King George III who had appointed the Reverend Henry Majendie as gentleman-in-waiting and tutor to his son aboard the gallant battleship *Prince George*.

For weeks William Henry had joyfully anticipated this fifteenth day of June. With the most fervent attention – and Mr Majendie – he had mastered the use of the globes. He had the map of Europe in his heart. In spirit he had charted the Atlantic Ocean. As Lord High Admiral of the Fleet he had sailed the seven seas and dealt damnation to the French and Spanish. He had held George Washington at bay. His Papa had covered him with glory. He, William Henry of England, had won the American War.

And now . . .

Mr Majendie, yawning and heaving, and dabbing vinegar on his forehead, Mr Majendie of whom William had believed himself well rid, was destined to be his shadow on this greatest of adventures, habited to shame him in a suit of navy blue.

There could have been no boy in Britain in more wretched case than his. By all laws of common decency such tutorship should certainly have ceased when William was gazetted to the Navy. Bad enough indeed to embark on a career with the odium of Royalty upon you – William Henry had no illusion on that score. As the King's son he started with a handicap among his fellows, a handicap he might have battered down were it not for Midshipman the Reverend Mr Majendie in his pietistic juvenile dress

William's ears burned red. A fine beginning! A fine entry he would make with such an object on the deck behind him. He'd be a butt – a by-word in the cockpit.

If his brother George had laughed to split his sides at
William in his uniform, he'd laugh to kill himself had
he seen *this,* which spectacle had happily been spared
the Prince of Wales. George had not, however, spared a
parting thrust.

'You'll have Majendie near at hand to rock you in
your hammock and hold the basin for you when you
spew.' And, 'At any rate your worsted work's not
wasted. You can tie yourself in safety to the rigging with
the wool.' There again! . . . William's ears burned
redder. Wool and worsted. It had been his curse
although his mother's wish, that he should ply the
needle under supervision of the Lady Charlotte Finch,
who had been his nursery governess at Kew.

Kew! . . . With a furtive finger William rubbed a
tear out of his eye. A nostalgic longing filled him for the
red-bricked house upon the Green that for as long as he
remembered had been home, shared until recently with
his brother Frederick whom he loved a great deal more
than he loved George. Frederick had given him a silver
compass and some sound advice.

'Forget your rank. The son of a whore amidships is
as good as the son of a King,' and, 'Punch the head of
any fellow who deserves it.'

Which was all very well, but William fancied he'd be
punching heads all day if the fellows once got wind of
old Majendie, whom William wished might drown or
be too turned in the stomach to attend him. If he sickened on a carriage drive who knew but what he might
not *die* of sickness on the sea? One could but hope.

Peering at the window Mr Majendie spoke. 'I think
we are about to enter Portsmouth. Your hat, Sir, if you
please.'

William Henry braced himself and put it on.

He sat with Mr Majendie in the stern of the barge

and gazed under his hand at the *Prince George* where she stood, all sails set, manned fore and aft awaiting him. Diamond pointed, dazzling, the waters of Spithead danced in the last of the sun. A slight breeze had sprung up with the afternoon to dishearten Mr Majendie.

William's eyes searched the barge's crew; one officer, a twinkling fellow with a jolly brown face slit by a wide white grin (was that grin for Mr Majendie?), and four men whose faces were as wooden as their oars.

William's mouth went dry. He glanced at his keeper, sitting straight and pale green, clasping his bony knees. Why had he not suggested that the fool wear a 'kerchief round his neck to hide it?

'Sir, do you not feel the wind a little sharp?' asked William Henry.

Mr Majendie answered wanly that it certainly was sharper than he had thought from shore.

'Then pray muffle your throat, sir, or – turn up your coat collar,' urged William, unwontedly solicitous.

Mr Majendie thanked His Royal Highness. He would have more to bear aboard, he said, than a cool breeze.

'Indeed, yes,' said William, eagerly. 'I've heard of men who die at sea being bad sailors.'

'I have no doubt,' answered Mr Majendie hollowly, 'that I shall find my sea-legs in good time.'

'You would not care to stay ashore, sir?' persisted William spurred by the officer's grin. 'This boat will take you back. My father would excuse your duty, sir, if he could know you were given to indisposition. It would be asking too much of your duty, sir, to enforce on you the perils of the sea.'

'I obey His Majesty's commands and know my duty, Sir,' uttered Mr Majendie faintly, and subsided, overcome.

But not even this disgrace could quench the thrill of

sheer excitement that surged through William Henry as the barge drew alongside Digby's flagship.

The rope ladder was lowered; red and perspiring William clambered up. Officers and men saluted him, and William drew a breath.

They saluted him because he was the King's son, but one day they would salute him as an Admiral of the Fleet.

And ignoring the tottering Majendie William answered the salute and came aboard.

*

A hundred and fifty years ago the cockpit of a man-of-war was of all places not the most inviting, and the conditions of a midshipman's life therein, according to accounts of those who lived it, scarcely enviable.

When William first entered the service, his berth and that of his fellows had not been changed to the gun-room, which transition at a later date was found to be imperative since the air of the cockpit was never renewed by ventilation.

Although Prince William is said to have received from his Papa an allowance of a thousand a year table money, there is no indication that he fared better than his mates. Perhaps the fear lest such advantage would render him unpopular among them, prompted him, as much as native generosity, to share his ample mess provision with the berth.

One may well believe that the splendour of his house at Kew and the squalor of a midshipman's cabin, presented a melancholy contrast to the new cadet, even though his introduction to the mess was modified by the absence of Mr Majendie. He, for some reason, either by command or from *mal de mer* was in no attendance on his prince that night.

At table, before the barrage of eleven pairs of eyes

whose silent inquisition was more embarrassing than speech, the King's son, acutely conscious of hostility, dumbly sat, and with misery reviewed his future residence.

He found in his survey nothing much to reassure him.

The air was stifling. One meagre oil-lamp lit the darkness on which daylight never shone and revealed the faces of that staring company, who, owing to the heat had removed its jackets and sat, regardless of Royalty, in its shirt-sleeves; so fearing to be fussy, William sat in his.

The lingering effluvia of red-herrings, bilge-water, and fried onions, together with the airless stench of the place, dispelled what little appetite he might have brought to the repast spread upon a greasy tablecloth, and consisting of small-beer, mouldy sea biscuit and beefsteak. In every corner reigned confusion; a heap of soiled clothing, naval half-boots, wet towels, a mahogany writing desk overturned and scattering its contents on the floor, a box of carpenter's tools and the fruits of some young amateur's experiments therewith, evidenced in a half-sawn beam, a pile of sawdust, and a trickle of glue from a broken pot. On the shelf that ranged the walls was a miscellany of plates, glasses, books, cocked hats, dirty stockings, tooth-combs, a litter of white mice and a caged parrot.

This agreeable apartment which might have uncomfortably accommodated three young gentlemen, now housed a dozen.

At length, the silence proving unendurable, William found his tongue. He had already decided to offer an apologia for Midshipman the Reverend Mr Majendie, and to explain away as plausibly as possible that uniform, to assure his colleagues that his tutor would not inflict his classics or his company on them; that he, in

8

fact, and no one else was victimized. He knew his speech all pat, he had it ready, but its pronouncement which did not gain by incoherence, was interrupted by a brusque inquiry from Sturt, the senior cadet.

'By what name are you rated in the books?'

William's blushes deepened; a leading question this, and his answer may have turned the balance of approval in his favour.

'I am entered as William Henry, but my father's name is Guelph. I hope you'll call me by it – if you please.'

Sturt stood and raised his glass. 'We'll drink to that,' he said, 'and here's to Guelph!' They drank it, shouting. The blushing William grinned and blinked the water from his eyes. He was accepted. . . .

That same evening the Admiral interviewed him in his cabin and read an extract from a letter written by the King to Hood, who passed it on.

'I have sent an hair trunk, two chests and two cots done up in one mat to be delivered unto you for the use of my young sailor. I flatter myself you will be pleased with the appearance of the boy who wants neither resolution nor cheerfulness. . . .' Here Digby paused, to emphasize: 'Both necessary adjuncts, Sir, for all who enter this profession, in especial at this time which is no time of peace. Any hour after sailing you must be prepared for an engagement.'

This news may have come as something of a shock to one who till that day had never trod the deck of a battleship before. From under lowered brows Digby shot a keen but not unkindly glance at the pop-eyed youngster.

The King was not self-flattered too unduly. Cheerfulness enough – but resolution? The trained eye doubted, though what it saw did not at all displease. Sturdy, if small for his fourteen years and girlishly complexioned, with tousled flaxen hair on a head like a pineapple,

William Guelph bore comparison with many worse and better.

'You said,' piped William, startled, 'an engagement?'

'You are here in no ornamental office, Sir. Britain,' Digby told him sternly, 'is at war.' But he hid a smile as he added, 'Your Royal Highness will go short of Latin. Mr Majendie takes a chaplain's duties in this ship. He'll have more to do than wait on you, Sir; so you must learn to wait upon yourself.'

At which decision William's dreams that night were undisturbed, despite the novelty of sleeping in a hammock to the tune of the cockpit's snores.

Digby had not exaggerated the possibility of immediate encounter with the enemy. Three days after William went aboard, the *Prince George* weighed anchor for Torbay, there to join the Channel fleet under command of Sir Charles Hardy. They were then to sail westward with a view to intercepting the French and Spanish squadrons, who with two fleets amounting to more than sixty sail of the line and an almost equal number of frigates and smaller vessels, were heading straight for the Channel in the mouth of which was Hardy cruising with thirty-eight ships. The allied enemy having each double that number, vauntingly crossed the Channel and came in sight of Plymouth just as a British convoy was entering the port. For some reason unexplained the enemy ignored the convoy and permitted it to pass unmolested up the Sound. The sight, however, of the Spaniard in that vicinity raised a panic on the coast. A second Armada and only Digby's flagship and Plymouth's guns to meet it! . . . No Drake this time with his bowls.

The enemy was so close in that the watchers on the shore could read the names upon the prows of all the Spaniards, each called after saints and saintesses, while the Spanish Admiral, struck through his telescope with the beauty of Mount Edgcumbe, decided to claim it for his own. The Frenchman had already in his mind annexed the town, when he saw the fortifications bristling with cannon, and Hardy's cruisers putting in from sea; so, thinking to be caught between two fires, he and his ally sheered off down midstream to the wonder and delight of the whole garrison and Guelph, who on the deck of the *Prince George,* cheered himself hoarse at the sight of that retreat and drank to its damnation in the cockpit.

So far so good, but not good enough for William, who, having viewed the enemy so near and unattacked, was hot as any pirate for blood.

He had not long to wait.

At the end of November Digby's division under the command of Rodney was sent to throw supplies into Gibraltar.

William meanwhile had been learning more than naval tactics. He learned to hold his own among his messmates, to take an order or a punishment and not to question why. He learned to read the heavens and a brave ship's moods, and the chartings of an ocean on white paper. He knew the savage fury of great seas, and the lash of wind-whipped spray on his flesh when he clung to the rigging half-naked. He knew the long night-watch, the vast grey dawns, the mornings clear and splendid, with the taste of salt on his lips and the scream of gulls in his ears above the rattle and creak of filled sails. He knew the still gold evenings, the brooding calms, the lowered clouds that cast their storm on heavy waters. He learned to steer by the stars with his head in the sky, and the ship plunging like a stallion to the rhythm of the waves. . . . And he learned to laugh at danger for the joy of all of these, that are the same for cabin-boy or admiral or King.

He toughened. His girl's face peeled, he grew a skin

11

burnt to a fierce brick-red; his hair was bleached white at the temples. And Mr Majendie troubled him no more.

It may be that Rodney at Digby's instigation pulled a string or two; or it may be that William on the leave which he was granted before sailing for Gibraltar, appealed – as man to man – to his Papa, and gained a fatherly indulgence not devoid of pride in 'my young sailor'.

He had grown a good half inch, and in his bell-bottomed trousers trod the floors of Windsor with a roll. If this exhibition was a trifle overdone for the admiration of his sisters and the swelling heart of his Mamma. it may also have induced his father to believe that the offices of a gentleman-in-waiting were redundant to a mariner at sea.

But no matter what may finally have moved the King's decision, the fact appears that Mr Majendie was cloistered at Windsor when William rejoined the *Prince George*.

Two months later came from Rodney the following despatch:

SANDWICH AT SEA,
CAPE FINISTERRE.
January 9th, 1780.

Yesterday at daylight, the Squadron of ships under my command, discerned twenty-two sail of the line in the North-East quarter. We immediately gave chace, and in a few hours the whole was taken. This proved to be a Spanish convoy which sailed from St Sebastian the 1st of January and was under the protection of seven ships and vessels of war, belonging to the royal company of Caraccas.

Part of the convoy was laden with naval stores and

provisions for the Spanish ships of war at Cadiz . . .
As I thought it highly necessary to send a sixty-four
gun ship to protect so valuable a convoy I have commissioned, officered and manned the Spanish ship of
war, the Guipasciano, of the same rate, and re-named
her the Prince William, in whose presence she had
the honour to be taken. . . .

There are no records other than this laconic statement to tell how William stood his first experience in
action, but one may credit him with a steady head and
courage enough to keep it when a few days later off St
Vincent he again faced the enemy's guns.

'Won't we give these haughty dons a thrashing!'
William gleefully remarked when the Spaniards were
sighted through a fog which delayed the 'chace' till
night and a rising gale dispersed it.

Rodney's ship, the *Sandwich*, led the fleet and sank
the *San Domingo*. The *San Eugenio* got upon the rocks,
the *San Julian* was run ashore and lost, but her crew
were saved and taken. In all the British gains amounted
to three Saints, a Princess, and a Phœnix – this latter
with the Admiral, Don Juan Langara, haughtiest of
dons – aboard her.

The British ships escaped without much damage,
although they suffered casualties enough among the
men, and William had his fill and more of blood. He
lost his taste for mock heroics; he knew reality for what
it was and found it grim.

He had his favourites among the crew, and was particularly attached to one jocular old tar who told
hair-raising yarns of the pirates, sea-serpents, mermaids
and monsters he had encountered here and there. His
name was Adams, but William dubbed him 'Commodore' and hung upon his words, and when this
veteran had a leg blown off in action, he visited him in

sick-bay, brought him tit-bits from his own supplies, and found his hero's greeting very touching.

'Well, my Royal William, me starboard timber's gone. I'll go no more aloft – I'm now a hulk.'

'I'll see you get a comfortable berth,' said William stoutly, and on arrival of the ship in port, he made immediate arrangements to have his 'Commodore' removed to hospital at Greenwich, where he allowed him a pension of five shillings a week which was punctually paid until he died.

Behind his back the cockpit called him 'Snotty', for that inelegant trick of his, which never left him, of wiping his nose on his finger; the first inception, surely, of the word, since all tradition flourishes on trifles.

And if tradition be accepted in the sum of his account, William fought his way to popularity. His love of practical joking was a nuisance and often led to combative retort. His chief antagonist was Sturt, who said: 'It's lucky for you that you're the son of the King or you'd get what you deserve.'

'Son of the King be damned!' William said, and offered to fight him over a chest in the way they had in the Navy.

Sturt, however, having the advantage in weight and seniority declined. But the son of the King was not always so easily let off. When on another occasion he cut down a hammock with its occupant snoring inside it, who woke to find his feet in the air and his head on the ground, there was a regular to do which was only settled by the intervention of an officer. And there is, of course, the tale of Moodie, a marine, whom William ragged till he was given a black eye: and 'You know how to fight if you *are* a marine,' was Guelph's reply to that.

Such incidents are trifling, but if also they are true, they may have served their purpose in fostering the first seeds of democracy in the first of England's democratic kings.

The friend of his bosom was Beauclerk. With him at Gibraltar, William went ashore, inspected the fortress, was received by the Governor and came to grief in a brawl in the town.

Too young to seek the pleasures of the alcove, and less flattered than embarrassed by the glance of Beauty's eyes, William visited a tavern to sample Spanish wine in the company of Sturt and his friend Beauclerk. There fired by the grape, and always slightly paranoic, William chose to take offence at the remarks uttered by some natives in his hearing, levelled he supposed at him, and detrimental to the British Navy.

It was Beauclerk who demanded an apology and got hit in the jaw for his pains. Sturt offered substantial assistance, and William, not to be left out of it, though the smallest in the fray, entered the contest with a kick in the pants of Sturt's opponent, a fat and greasy Spaniard who turned and snatched a knife out of his belt. He might have done some damage had not Sturt caught the fellow by his upraised arm and wrenched the weapon free.

A general row ensued with the three youngsters in the midst of it, blood flying in all directions and everybody hitting out at everybody else. William's nose was bleeding, he was too small to use his fists to any purpose, but nothing daunted he went on kicking at the shins and the behinds of the assailants.

The noise of the disturbance brought officials to the place. The townsmen dispersed, vowing they had been assaulted. The midshipmen were taken into custody, and all very much subdued, spent the night in jail.

Rodney and the Fleet were scandalized. No matter what the provocation, an insult had been offered by a horde of Spanish curs to British naval officers, and one of them the King's son! Instant liberation of the prisoners must be secured and an apology demanded. Digby was sent to do it, and after much palaver managed to obtain release for his errant three. On their return to the ship the adventurers were severely reprimanded and had all leave suspended during their stay at Gibraltar.

Shortly after this affair – perhaps because of it – Digby received his orders to sail for England. And on 8 May William arrived at St James's, having been away a year.

＊

London gave him an ovation; flags flying, cheers from the crowd, the ballad-mongers bawling his name in the street and the cartoons depicting him in warlike attitudes against a background of sea and sail. Prints damp from the press were dangled in your face at every corner, and Mr Pye, the Poet Laureate, put him into verse.

> Now last not least in love, the muse
> Her William's name would fondly chuse
> The British youth among.
> Still may the sailors love thy name
> And happy wealth and blooming fame
> Awake the future song.

The tale of his exploits was in everybody's mouth and William in a fair way to have his head turned. He paid a visit to Drury Lane with his Papa and his Mamma and brother George.

The audience, touched by his smallness and his flaxen hair, rose to a man and yelled for him. He stood in the box in his middy's dress, bowing and saluting right and left. His mother shed tears of pride, and his father beamed approval, and the exquisite George, in powdered wig and brocade, sat in the sulks, disregarded.

Though not his favourite, for Frederick was that,

William had the greatest admiration for his elder brother with his lordly airs, his graces, his good humour. During William's leave, George exerted himself to entertain him. George was kind, amusing; no longer did he patronize and tease. William was his slave and followed him instead of Frederick, watched George's indiscretions and applauded, and learned much that was not good for him to know.

He decided that Buckingham House, the home of George, the heir-apparent, was a gayer *ménage* than his home at Kew. Having lived most of his young life in a village and the latter year of it at sea, William found the precincts of St James's and the society of those elegants who made up his brothers' circle and took their pleasures with such devilment and daring, a welcome change from the cockpit and the ministrations of Majendie or the Lady Charlotte Finch.

He was not, however, much at ease in Court dress. He detested wigs and powder, lace and foppery. He left all such to George and Frederick, who wore them with an air he never could acquire, and accompanied those dashing two on their revels, in his uniform, unless at a ball, which bored him. He had not yet learned to dance. He much preferred to walk the streets of London attended only by one gentleman, and see the life lived there, not as onlooker, but as participant. The beautiful red-bricked city never failed to enchant him with its gaudy signs hung out above shop doors, and the contrast of its gaiety and squalor.

He liked to watch the comings and goings of ordinary people about their ordinary work: the street-criers, the old women with their barrows: 'A groat a pound black-heart cherries – round and sound cherries!' the black-faced sweep with his 'Sweep Ho! Soot Ho!': the news-vendor with his trumpet and his prints. 'Extraordinary news! Great news in the *London Gazette*—' and the painted chairs and groups of chair-men at their stands. William had never ridden in a chair and would have been glad to do so but that his gentleman restrained him, 'A public conveyance, Sir! There might be vermin.'

With George and Frederick he watched, incognito, the hanging of a man who had stolen a sheep from a butcher. William sat in the front row, rubbed shoulders with the rabble, ate oranges and thoroughly enjoyed himself. He saw a harlot whipped at the cart's tail from Leicester Fields to Newgate, and a fellow in the pillory at Charing Cross with a blue face and his tongue hanging out. George held a handkerchief soaked in amber to his nose to keep away the smell of the common people, and Frederick was sick, but William did not flinch. He had seen worse. As for whippings, he had seen men thrashed with ropes till their backs were like raw beef. He had seen men blown to bits by gunfire, and rags of flesh flying through the air. He had seen the decks run red with blood, and a man's brains plastered to the rigging. He had seen a man without a head get up and walk – yes, truly, he'd seen that. He had seen war. His brothers took these tales with a degree of salt, but his sister Augusta, who was a year younger than himself and his confidante, screamed and covered her ears and thought her dear William a hero.

In mask and domino he was taken by George to Vauxhall and the Rotunda at Ranelagh Gardens. His childish treble deepened to a harsh distressing croak. He no longer feared the ladies.

Once he got drunk and was scolded by Frederick, who at the age of seven months had, by the King, been created the Very Reverend Father in God, the Bishop of Osnaburg. There were times, not often, when Frederick endeavoured to remember his calling and read pious lectures to his younger brother who told him to practise what he preached. It was Frederick who introduced him to the gaming tables and taught him dice and faro, and to him William lost three hundred guineas at his first sitting, had no money to meet the debt, and gave a promissory note for the amount, which it seems he never paid.

At last these goings-on were reported to the King. William was commanded to the presence. The King received him with a brainstorm and though accustomed to the Royal fits of temper, William stood and trembled. The violence of his father's rage was more alarming than the Spanish guns. There was something very shocking in the glare of those bloodshot eyes, those swollen veins, those hysterical gesticulations. His Papa, who could, when he chose, show the kindest affection, sang hymns, and had musical tastes, was now transformed into a fury. He raved and shouted till his vocal chords gave out, and whispering, he called upon his God to subdue this wilful spirit, bade his son go and pray, and sat down at his harpsicord, exhausted.

The knowledge of the sort of life his 'young sailor' had been leading under the auspices of his elder brothers induced the King to curtail William's leave and hurry him back again to the *Prince George*.

The Channel Fleet was assembling at Portsmouth, but no longer under Hardy. He had died on 19 May and was succeeded by Admiral Geary, who shortly afterwards resigned his command, and gave a dinner to the captains of the Fleet when he struck his flag on board the *Victory*.

William was invited, and when the King's health was drunk, to the surprise of everybody, since none had asked him for it, he got up and made a speech.

Blushing, but unabashed, he began in his cracking boy's voice:

'Admiral Geary and Captains of the Fleet. You may

perhaps deem it presumptuous in me to present myself to your notice on this occasion, to return you my most sincere thanks for the Royal manner in which you have drunk my Royal father's health. As a father I can only speak of him with all the fullness of filial affection and I am certain that there are few beings who have swayed the – swayed the sceptre of these realms who has been more of a father to his people than my father and to whom the title of father is more justly due—'

Here he paused for his words, beamed round with the greatest good humour on the grinning captains, rubbed his nose with his finger and started off again.

'Involved as the nation is at present – involved at present as it is in a most unnatural war, for it cannot be considered in any other way than that of a child fighting against its parent or a son against its father single-handed as we are against our enemies – and should I ever be called upon to lead his Fleet I should consider that day the proudest in my life if I were called upon to shed my blood for the flag' – and so on and on until: 'I am certain I have spoken with all the sincerity of a sailor's heart who glories in the profession to which his father has appointed him and who sincerely hopes he will never be induced by any dishonourable act unworthy of a British sailor or the flag under which he fights to do – to do anything dishonourable. Gentlemen, I hope I am not out of order in asking you to fill your glasses and drink – to Admiral Geary!'

Then he sat down and they roared for him. He had written it out beforehand and had spent all day learning it by heart, but none of them knew that, and none but himself could have made head or tail of it. That, however, mattered not to William. It was his first speech, forerunner of those many with which, half a century later, he electrified his ministers, and already marked by that trick of repetition which became in after life much more pronounced; but still it was and still remains on record – his first speech.

*

For the next three months William's life at sea was spent in uneventful cruising in the Channel with an occasional glimpse of an enemy ship, but no deliberate encounter. In December the *Prince George* returned to Spithead and William was given leave again for Christmas.

In January at St James's and in celebration of her birthday, his mother gave a ball. This was to prove for William an event.

He had not looked forward with much pleasure to that evening. He couldn't dance. He hated his elaborate Court dress. In a stuffy wig and velvet coat, with the lace of his ruffles pricking his chin and his feet squeezed into satin shoes, he stood apart and watched his brothers lead their partners in the minuet, and glowered at their antics. All very well for landlubbers to point the toe and strut on polished floors, but let them try and walk the quarter-deck of a man-o'-war in a gale! Huh! that would be comical. Very droll indeed that sight would be.

It must be owned these meditations were not un-mixed with envy. He had made some vain attempt to learn his steps under guidance of Augusta, but she said he was a centipede with at least a hundred feet, and poked fun at him until he gave it up.

So, standing aloofly in his corner, William surveyed the jewelled splendour of the pageant with a misan-thropic eye. The sparkle and the glitter, the rustle of brocade, the dazzle of a myriad candles reflecting rain-bow points of light from crystal clusters, the music, the magnificence, roused no response in him. He despised it as he despised those bowing persons around his mother's chair.

At her side the King, with the Star and a galaxy of orders blazing on his chest, sat sunk in a melancholy dream, wagging an absent finger to the fiddlers' tune and listening to the whispers in his head.

The Queen, so William dared to think, was painted far too high and monstrously bewigged. His elder sister, Charlotte, was something of a gawk. Yellow, he decided, ill became her. Augusta, he allowed, looked very well in white, her head dressed high with flowers; she stepped daintily in red-heeled shoes, and when she passed him on the arm of her cavalier she waved a hand and cried out: 'William! Join the dance!' He shook his head. Who in that room would dance with him? He knew no girls and every one of them looked alike in powder, patched and rouged, all wearing those enormous hoops that hid the figure. You couldn't tell the shape of any one of them, or the colour of her hair or her complexion.

And then. . . .

She was standing by a marble column near the door, guarded and almost entirely extinguished by the prodigious hoop of a lady in violet brocade, with an incredible denture, and a 'head' surmounted by a ship in full sail.

Behind this apparition William glimpsed a sprig of a girl whose hair, unpowdered, hung in curls on her neck. She had soft brown eyes and the quick timid glance of a squirrel. She wore a little silver hoop festooned with flowers. Her eyes encountered William's; she blushed and so did he. Her lashes drooped, and William's heart bounced under his velvet coat. He looked for his gentleman, General Budé. He must know her. She was pretty.

Budé, as usual, was fawning on the Queen. William watched his opportunity to sidle up.

'Over there – next the one in purple – with the teeth. Who is she?'

Budé raised a quizzing glass. 'The teeth? In purple? Ah – hah! Yes. The teeth!' Budé cackled to his prince's humour. 'She, Sir, is Mrs Fortescue.'

'Mrs!' echoed William with a falling lip. 'Is she – is that young lady married?'

'Young?' Budé's glass went up again. 'That *young* – ah! now I see! Delicious! No, Your Royal Highness, that is *Miss* Fortescue – Miss Matilda Fortescue, I think.'

Matilda! The name was music.

'Present me,' muttered William, very red. Budé hemmed and thumbed his chin. There was none present whose rank and calling were unworthy of the honour, but to take upon himself the onus of responsibility without the sanction of – he hesitated, glancing at the Queen.

'Present me,' insisted William, glaring.

Budé hemmed again. It would not do to have an argument with the Prince before the Court. There was also that appointment with the Bishop of Osnaburg to be considered when Prince William returned to his ship and the Bishop paid a visit to his relatives in Germany. Their Royal Highnesses were hand in glove together. To offend one would offend both.

So Budé bowed.

Madam's curtsy was a thing to wonder at. Miss Fortescue dropped her lids. Her lashes were stupendous. As she bent to the bob her silver skirts floated round her like the petals of a rose.

'I fear I am a clumsy dancer,' William croaked. His breaking voice would play the strangest tricks. Sometimes it squeaked and sometimes descended to the deepest bass, and always it abashed him. 'But if Miss Fortescue would care to—' His look unwillingly commanded Madam's for consent. The teeth, in ever widening exposure of their gums, approved the Royal favour.

The group was now attracting some attention. Budé, hovering and anxious, Madam with her smiles and her ship so much a-nod that it seemed it might go sailing any minute; Miss with her blushes and young Royalty, all eyes, leading out Miss Fortescue to dance.

Fans fluttered and whispers flew behind them; those persons round the Queen's chair raised their eyebrows.

Miss Fortescue danced three, four times, with Prince William. He danced the minuet. He danced in paradise. He stumbled in the *chassée* and trod upon her toes, and was cast in purgatory, scarlet with confusion.

'I am accustomed to the sea – one has no opportunity – I have not yet acquired – pray forgive—'

'But, Sir, your step goes well with mine – I think.' He hardly caught her whisper. He could scarcely see her eyes. They were hidden by those lashes that lay like crescent moons upon her face. And what a face! White as a flower, with a mouth as ripe as strawberries and as tempting. And to think that such perfection could be the daughter of that ogress with the teeth! Miss Fortescue had teeth like pearls – adorable small teeth, and when she smiled she showed dimples. William squeezed her hand.

The music stopped.

'Will you – could you – do you care to take refreshment?' stammered William.

Miss Fortescue's lips moved faintly to effect that she would care to do whatever His Royal Highness pleased.

He led her to a buffet spread with golden plate. Flunkeys in gold and scarlet served them with syllabub and bon-bons. They drank mulled wine. Miss Fortescue sipped hers in bird-like sips and nibbled sugared violets and cherries drenched in brandy. William had no appetite for such. He asked her age. She was fifteen. His age, too. Miraculous!

24

'Do you,' he inquired, 'live in London?'

It seemed she did. In Piccadilly, opposite the Park.

The Park. His father's park! 'So near,' dared William, 'yet – so far,' and he dared further. He hoped he might be permitted to see Miss Fortescue again.

Her blushes gave an answer to that hope. Her lashes lifted. Her eyes returned his ardent look and bereft him of all speech. Dreamily she bit a brandied cherry, while William floundered, lost.

'Hem!' Budé was at his elbow. 'Sir! Her Majesty desires—'

'May I,' urged William in a frenzy, 'see you again? Will you walk in the Park in the morning?'

'Your Royal Highness – hem!'

'In a minute, in a minute! . . . I must,' muttered William, 'see you again. I shall be in the Park by the gate in Piccadilly at eight o'clock. . . . I will wait till . . . *Yes*, Budé!' He handed the General his wine-glass. 'Pray, Miss Fortescue, excuse me.'

Miss Fortescue rose and curtsied. Deliciously her cheek bulged with a bon-bon. And while Budé fidgeted and hemmed, William bowed as though she were the Queen. He wished he could have kissed her.

It might have tasked a greater strategist than William to evade the watchful eye of Budé, but that the Court and his gentleman slept till noon after the night's diversions, and William was up and out of the Palace before even his valet waked.

The day was cold and raw, but the weather is no deterrent to a sailor. And William was in love.

He waited, stamping his feet and blowing on his hands, though his blood ran in a fever. Would she come? Was it possible the ogress would release her? He doubted it. If he had known her house he would have stood upon her doorstep, gained admission, braved the teeth, carried her away. None would dare forbid him entry. Let them try!

He walked up and down wrapped in his cloak with the collar turned up to his chin and his hat pulled well over his eyebrows. It would not do if he were recognized. He would be followed, and politely, taken prisoner. A king's son had no liberty. Life for such as he was nothing but a jail. He envied Sturt and Beauclerk. They were free to meet a girl and love her as they pleased. He fussed and fumed. God send that she would come. She *must*! Of course she wouldn't. Her abominable mother would never let her out.

He was mistaken.

Madam had scored a triumph with her daughter. No girl had made a more successful *début*. She was the gossip and the envy of the Court. Miss Fortescue had captured young Prince William. True, it would have been a greater triumph to have caught the Prince of Wales, but he was already much *épris* with Lady Sarah Campbell, to say nothing of that actress Mrs Robinson, so Matilda must make do with second best. Blood Royal, after all, is still – Blood Royal.

So in this fashion Madam may have reasoned, and similarly, confidences may have been received, perhaps extracted. For who knows what intimacy – under pressure – may not be divulged in the privacy of her chamber, by a well brought up young lady to her Mamma? And since there is no evidence to tell us how Miss Fortescue escaped that hawk-like vigilance, we must draw our own conclusion, for escape Matilda did, attended by an abigail who kept her distance and an eye on the encounter. Madam must be furnished, no doubt, with a report, or she may have watched the proceedings from her window. History does not say. All we are permitted is the fact that 'Stolen interviews took place in the Green Park'.

One can well imagine that Matilda at her tryst was
overcome with shyness, and that the eyelashes were displayed to even more advantage on cheeks pinkened
from the cold and cosily enshrouded in a fur-lined hood.
Her hands were in a little muff. There must have been
some charming palpitations.

'Oh! Sir! Your Royal Highness! If Mamma could
know! Pray, Sir, I must not stay a moment more. I vow
I shall be punished, Sir. . . . Oh, dear!'

'Don't,' panted William, 'call me Sir.'

'Oh, Your Royal Highness—'

'Call me William.'

'Oh! Sir—' The brown eyes, timid as a squirrel's,
peeped from the fur-lined hood. 'I must not take the
liberty.'

''Tis no liberty. I'm human. I'm a man.' He stuck
out his chest to prove it, breathing down his nose. 'I
have a heart like other people.'

'Yes, Sir, indeed.'

'Then let me hear you call me by my name.'

It was the merest whisper of a 'William. . . .'

'And may I say Matilda?'

'Yes, Your Royal Highness, if you please.'

'Matilda!' ejaculated William in an ecstasy. 'Matilda,
I adore you. I adored you at first sight. Do you read
Shakespeare?' Shades of Majendie and his schooling
urged him on. ' "Whoever loved that loved not at first
sight." '

She trembled. The concession was too much. What
would Mamma say to this? Mamma had said already to
effect that: 'Kings have married commoners. Play your
cards. You may be Her Royal Highness yet.' Was ever
girl so honoured? Her head was in a whirl. She tingled
with delicious queer sensations that owed nothing to the
promptings of Mamma. William was at that age of a
Prince Charming with his bright hair, his rosy cheeks,

his sturdy shoulders. They walked together, speechless.

The Park was empty, their own universe, containing nothing but themselves. The rime-frosted grass crackled under their feet. A robin hopped and peered at them and flew away. The abigail at their heels shivered and rubbed her chilblains. It began to snow. Flakes dropped on Matilda's hood and sparkled on the curls that strayed beneath it. Matilda's pearly teeth were all a-chatter.

'Are you cold?' William slid a hand inside her muff and found her fingers. 'So small – your hands!' He lifted one and held it to his lips and stared at hers. Yes! Strawberries. If one could eat them! 'Adorable Matilda. . . . You must go home. . . .' It would never do to let this lovely creature die of chill. 'You will come again to-morrow.' It was half plea and half command. She must obey it.

She glanced this way and that, and then at him whose eyes were popping and whose face was red with fond emotion.

'My . . . mother, Sir,' faltered Matilda.

'Damn your mother!' quoth William, like a sailor. 'Until tomorrow then. . . . Goodbye.'

Tomorrow and tomorrow. . . . A succession of to-morrows. Stolen meetings, interchange of vows. He, grown bolder, extracted from his lady a confession. 'Do you love me as much as I love you?'

'As much. . . . Oh! yes, Sir.'

The faint admission spurred the panting William to fresh conquest. 'Not *Sir*! . . . Loveliest Matilda, I must kiss you. I shall go mad if I don't kiss you. Can't you get rid of your woman? Why should she follow us? Send her away.'

The handmaiden was beckoned. 'Fetch,' Matilda said, 'my reticule.'

28

For the first time in their acquaintance they were alone.

They found a holly bush beside the water. There, screened, they stood spellbound, trembling with magic and the sweet surprise of touch. They spoke in whispers. 'In six years' time I'll be of age,' breathed William. 'Will you wait for me?'

She would wait for him for ever. Her mother's odious hints were all forgotten. She loved him for himself, for his fair hair, his clumsiness, his stolid sailor's ways. He was no courtier. He had no manners. He wiped his nose on his finger, no lace-edged handkerchiefs for him! His hands were roughened from hard work, like any common person's. He wore no rings save one, and that a signet with a Royal crest. He took it off and gave it her.

'A keepsake. Wear it when I'm at sea, and – and when you look at it you'll think of me . . . perhaps. My hands are so red and yours so white.'

He measured her hands with his and laughed to see how hers was dwarfed beside it. She loved him all the more for his red hands. She kissed his ring. Yes, she would always wear it, all her life. . . . Oh! He was brave. He had fought the Spaniards, had sailed the high seas. He had faced death. He did not tell her so. He did not boast to her as he had boasted to his brothers and Augusta. There was no time to talk of anything but love.

And oblivious of a hundred eyes that watched them and a hundred ears that overheard, those two vowed their vows and kissed in the Green Park.

The gossips of the palace were enchanted. Here was a tale. A pretty how d'ye do! Budé in a panic hurried to the Queen. To warn her first was to forearm himself. Too shocking! His Royal Highness all unknown to him had stolen out each day to meet Miss Fortescue, and the young lady had similarly evaded her Mamma.

The scandal was up and down the palace in an hour.
The Queen heard it with dismay. William? *Das Kind!*
Disgraceful! Was there perhaps more in it than calf-
love? These sons! What with George and his actress,
and William and this girl, a mere child from all
accounts. . . .

His Majesty must be consulted

The King was in his moods. He would see no one. He
sat all day at the harpsichord singing and playing hymns,
in a world of fantasy that to him was more alive than
life itself.

Dragged from his whimsies to attend to fact, the story
of his son's transgression caused the King another brain-
storm. It caused also the expulsion of Matilda's mother
from the Court, and her fair young daughter with
her.

Once again was William summoned and harangued.
The King violently referred him to the Royal Marriage
Act. William learned that he might never marry without the King's consent, nor by any possibility could he
marry one who was not of Royal blood. Thus the law,
the King's own law. No son of his should dare defy it.

In silence William heard his parent out. Marriage!
He had not thought of marriage. He had thought only of
the lovely lips of sweet Matilda. If to marry her meant
that he could kiss her all day long, then certainly he'd
marry her when he grew up, law or no law, Royal rage
and all. . . . But at fifteen, six years is an eternity. He
had not looked beyond it, if he had looked as far. And
while his father roared at him of commoners and princes
and the issue of the Blood, William saw the breaking of
a dream. His secret had been snatched, his romance
mangled, tossed from ear to ear. The whole Court knew.
He'd be a laughing-stock. His heart swelled. What of
Matilda? What had they done to his Matilda? She had
been torn from him. O cruel injustice! She had done

no harm, and he had meant no wrong to her – his own Matilda. She must not be punished for his fault.

Faltering but undaunted by parental fury William made attempt to stem the flood.

'Sire, pray do not blame Miss Fortescue. She, Sire, I promise you is not to blame. . . . It was I, Sire, who persuaded her to. . . .'

'Silence!' his father thundered. 'You will rejoin your ship tonight. Now leave the room.'

Thankfully he left it and sought his brother George for consolation. The Prince of Wales was in similar case. Both loved where love, by law, must be forbidden. George said for him it was the greater blow. His heart was honestly engaged. His desired marriage with his 'Perdita'. As for William – such idea was ludicrous. 'For you,' George told him cuttingly, 'are still a child.'

Child! It was too much. Was insult to be heaped on injury? William doubled his fists, but even that small satisfaction was denied him. Brother or no you could not hit the Prince of Wales. You could not walk in the Park with the girl of your choice without creating a disturbance. You could not marry whom you pleased. You had less freedom than any beggar in the street. Better be dead than the son of a King. He was sick of the Court and of landlubbers' ways. . . .

He was glad to go back to the sea.

Chapter Two

AND now he was to visit the New World. America. The
West Indies. The Fleet conducting convoys to Gibraltar
was joined again by Digby's flagship in the Channel.
The Spaniards, intent on the reduction of the fortress,
seemed to have no other object in the war, and the
Prince George on her voyage out encountered no worse
enemy than equinoctial gales.

But although foul winds delayed the course of the
Channel Fleet, they did not sweep from William's mind
the vision of Matilda.

By day, at night, she haunted him. It was she and not
the stagger and roll of the ship that swung his hammock.
Her face appeared in flashes in the wake of the churn-
ing wash, to dissolve on the white foam circles. He
heard her whisper his name above the yell of the storm
and the constant groan and creak of bolts and beams
and gear, and the scurry of waves against portholes. She
stood beside him in the midnight watch, and her lips
were cold and sweet against his face when the wind
dropped and the snow whirled from an ice-grey sky, and
the dawn crept up through the dark like a ghost.

He wrote her letters by the light of a tallow candle
when he should have been asleep and when his messmates were. He gave them to Beauclerk to despatch
under cover of his own in secrecy. Whether or no they
ever reached their destination is not proven, but it is
recorded that write he did, and that he yearned and
suffered as only youth can suffer – to forget. For young
love comes as the storm and as the storm, it passes.

And while the great ship, rocking like a drunkard, ploughed her way through the Atlantic, William took his turn at the maintop and at the topmast-head. The cockpit worked to a man and William no less than any. He played, too.

Before sailing, the midshipmen had stored some ladies' gowns for the purpose of charades and play-acting. They acted Shakespeare, Snotty was asked to have his choice and plumped for Romeo. (Was not he a Montagu and she a Capulet – as cruelly parted?) His suggestion was received with negative howls, and put to the vote which threw it out in favour of *The Merry Wives of Windsor*. They appointed William stage director, and cast Lieutenant Storey for Falstaff because he was fat. They stuffed him with pillows to make him fatter. William and Beauclerk played the Wives and the stage was the orlop deck.

Rehearsals went apace. The performance, to which all officers and men had been invited, was timed for the last night of the voyage. Each actor was perfect in his part. The fat lieutenant took his very seriously, and was seen at all hours walking the main deck repeating lines aloud – with gestures – to the amazement of the tars.

A hammock was to be the bucking basket, and William devised a special bit of business. The 'muddy ditch' must, he said, be realistically displayed. Mud there was not, but pitch there was in plenty. With Beauclerk's co-operation and unknown to other members of the cast, buckets full were poured into a heap of junk for the scene in the Garter Inn.

The audience took its seats; the play began. Mesdames Page and Ford were in excellent high humour, so merry that their giggles did, in fact, hold up the play and put Sir John's lines out. They pummelled the fat knight in his pillows and in more vital places. They tumbled him and rolled him and tossed him in the

33

'muddy ditch' where he stuck head foremost, to emerge spluttering and furious, and black from top to toe.

The cockpit held its sides and roared: 'He has mistook his part. He plays the Moor! Three cheers for Othello!'

Vowing vengeance the unfortunate lieutenant went to scrape himself and wash, and the frolic ended in feasting and hot rum to each man of the crew. . . .

The winds dropped and the fleet came to anchor in a fog. The convoy was safely landed, the garrison relieved, and by the beginning of the summer the *Prince George* was back again at Spithead, but this time William did not leave his ship, for no sooner had she come to port than she was off again hunting the French in the chops of the Channel, but not one of them was to be found.

And Digby had his orders to turn westward, bound for Sandy Hook.

This was the first time a member of the Royal Family had set foot on American soil, and William was received with an address from the loyalists and much fulsome adulation. It was even suggested that his visit might put and end to hostilities, but the wrongs of the Americans were too deep-rooted to be healed by the appearance in their midst of a scrubby youngster, son of the very King they had rejected.

To the speeches of the loyalists he made suitable reply, but this time one that had been drafted for him and not of his own composing.

It may be that he felt himself inflated. Hitherto, with the one exception of his return to London after his first year at sea, he had never appeared in public, or been cheered. And here he was with a great following – a viceroy! It had even come to his ears that if peace were declared he would be crowned King William the First of America. . . .

Accompanied by Digby with whom he lodged, he drove through the streets as his father drove through London, sitting straight and bowing right and left as though the crown were already on his head. His neck was stiff, less from pride than from his posture. Digby growled out a rebuke. 'Afloat or ashore, Sir, you're a midshipman first, before you're the son of a King.'

William sat corrected and reddened to the ears. He was giving himself airs above an admiral. . . . His hand went to the salute and Digby smiled. There was no more drives. The Prince walked out alone and unattended, to the consternation of his suite and Digby, who began to wish he'd held his tongue.

And William took to skating. It was an exceptionally cold winter and the lake outside the city was frozen over. There with Sturt and Beauclerk to support him, he slid and floundered, tumbled on the ice, lost his temper, and made an exhibition of himself. God damn the skates! He'd have a sled. . . .

According to an eye-witness's account:

> . . . As the Prince was unskilled in the exercise he would sit in a chair fixed on runners which was pushed forward with great velocity by a skating attendant, while a crowd of officers environed him, and the youthful multitude made the air ring with their shouts for Prince William Henry. . . .

Although the same observer assures us that 'the Prince when on shore showed a decided fondness for manly pastimes', he gives no indication that these included feminine interest. But if romance is lacking during William's visit to New York, intrigue of a less charmful nature certainly is not, for it seems that he was very nearly kidnapped.

The British Army was at that time in possession of New York City, while a division of the rebels commanded by Colonel Ogden was stationed in a winter encampment of wooden huts on the opposite bank of the Hudson. William's quarters on shore, which he shared with Admiral Digby were only slightly guarded, more for form than for security. It might not have been so very difficult for Ogden to have landed secretly at night and carry off the Prince and the Admiral and make for the Jersey shore.

The plan faithfully detailed in all particulars including the time of embarkation, 'The first wet night after we are prepared and the place to be agreed upon according to the tides' was submitted to George Washington, who replied:

To Colonel Ogden, of the First Jersey Regiment.

SIR,

The spirit of enterprise so conspicuous in your plan for surprising in their quarters and bringing off the Prince William Henry and Admiral Digby merits applause; and you have my authority to make the attempt in my name and at such time as your judgment shall direct. I am fully persuaded that it is unnecessary to caution you against offering insult or indignity to the persons of the Prince or the Admiral, should you be so fortunate as to capture them.

In the case of success you will as soon as you get them to a place of safety treat them with all possible respect, but you are to delay no time in conveying them to Congress and reporting your proceedings with a copy of these orders.

Given at Morris Town on this 28th day of March 1782.

G. WASHINGTON.

The enterprise remained 'conspicuous' in spirit only. Secret dispatches revealed that the 'plan' had been submitted to the British, never mind by whom or how. History does not enlighten on that score, but we presume that William, despite his solo promenades and skating exploits, was sufficiently well watched, and it is possible our secret intelligence was as equally effective then as now.

But although the plot miscarried it was deemed advisable to move the Prince out of the danger zone and he was transferred to the *Warwick*, which, commanded by Captain Elphinstone, sailed on a cruise of the coast to Virginia.

William parted from his messmates with regret. He had been happy in the *Prince George* under Digby. In the *Warwick* he was once more among a horde of strangers. He would have to feel his way.

Always supersensitive of his position he imagined he was detrimentally discussed and quizzed behind his back. He was well aware the fellows spoke of him as 'Snotty', but while in the *Prince George* he had ignored the appellation, in the *Warwick* his ears resented it and burned. Above all things he wanted to be popular, and in order to create a good impression he would overstress his affability, was inclined to be too boisterous and bubbling, too ready with his: 'You may call me Guelph.'

The request, so naïve and so spontaneous, that had broken down all barriers on his first day at sea, fell flat when repeated in the *Warwick*. The whole Navy knew he liked to be called Guelph.

The cockpit was too polite, too studiously careful of its manners. He had, of course, his satellites – those whom he was quick to sense were out for favours; none who was his friend. He missed the fun, the practical joking; he missed the jovial incompetence of Lieutenant

Williams who had been nautical tutor to the cockpit on board the *Prince George*. Lieutenant Lock was tutor in the *Warwick*. No laxity with him could be permitted. He held a dreary class from nine till noon, while William, bored, resentful, sat and picked his nose and thought about Matilda.

The *Warwick* did however see some action. Off the Delaware, she encountered a French frigate, *L'Aigle*, ran her into shallow waters, and captured her and her Commander, Comte la Touche; but he cut away her masts and bored the bottom out of her before he gave her up.

After this encounter life went slow. William had time enough for observation. It had occurred to him that the French ship they had captured had more speed to her than anyone of ours. Although she carried forty guns she had all but slipped the *Warwick*. Our men-o'-war could do with reconstruction. They were unwieldy, slow, their rate of sailing, he thought, could be increased. Also, the Frenchman's men and officers were smarter. He had been tremendously impressed with Comte la Touche who surrendered with a flourish. The men, too, were better cared for.

William had seen sights afloat to sicken him; now, of a critical mind, he looked for more.

He went below; he inspected the galleys and the servants' berths under the lower deck. He asked questions and heard something of the methods of the press-gangs.

He was received with looks as black as hell. Indeed, down there it was something, to his mind, of an inferno. The heat was insupportable. The pig-tailed crew worked in the dark, half naked. Squalor, discomfort, he had himself experienced but not conditions such as these, brutalized, sub-human. Beasts should live better. For men to live so was a sin against life – against God.

He saw one punished for a minor fault, lashed to the mast and flogged. He forced his eyes to watch but stopped his ears to the shriek of a man in his torture. He saw the blood – not now to boast of it – staining the knotted rope. He saw the raw hide ooze and burst. He looked till his sight was red, and he looked further. He saw the food thrown to these men who lived in his father's ships to fight his father's battles. He saw the pork crawling with worm, the biscuit grey with fungus, the stinking water. He remembered his old friend the 'Commodore'. Had he lived so?

His heart revolted but his tongue was tied. His rank had no significance aboard. He had less authority with these poor devils than the petty officer who flogged them *His* word was law. The King's son had no voice in it.

He brooded. The King should hear of this. The King must know. Through his son's eyes the King would see. The King's ships must hold no secrets that are shameful. . . .

When the *Warwick* came back to Sandy Hook William heard he was to be moved into the *Barfleur*. She was bound for Jamaica, and commanded by Hood, thanks to whom he made one lasting friendship.

Some days before the *Barfleur* sailed an officer from the *Albemarle* came alongside in his barge. William had the watch on deck and was called by Hood to be presented to the visitor.

He was, so William in after years described him as he appeared at that first meeting, 'the merest boy of a captain I ever beheld'. His lank unpowdered hair was tied in a Hessian tail of extraordinary length and he wore a full-laced uniform and an old-fashioned waist-coat with long flaps. Never before or since had William seen anything like it. Nor did his name enlighten. Captain Nelson. William had some difficulty in keeping a straight face as he saluted.

The 'boy of a captain' looked him in the eyes, very clear and steady. They were of one height, but William had not done growing and Captain Nelson had.

'Look you, Sir,' said Hood, with some pomposity, 'Captain Nelson knows more of naval tactics than any officer in the Fleet. If Your Royal Highness desires information you can do no better than ask him.'

There was much William could have asked him had he dared. There was something in that cool-eyed gaze and the twist of those lips that encouraged. He had a mouth too womanish for any man, yet hard, as though the skin of it were drafted on steel.

William would have liked to ask if Captain Nelson knew the life lived below deck in the Navy – or if those eyes had seen men flogged till their backs were bursting. Those lips could give an order. Had they ordered such things to cease? If he could talk to this oddly dressed young Captain one might drop a hint or two. William was sure he would listen. He had a listening face, but it was difficult to speak of the abuses of the men before the Admiral. It would – decided William, fussing in his mind and worrying the thought as was his habit – it would be too much of a presumption. Discipline had trained him. Who was he to criticize superior command? If the men deserved a flogging, flogged they'd be. In civilian life a man who stole a sixpence was put in the pillory; if he stole more he was hanged. The British Navy was no dames' school. Best leave it at that. So: 'Do you sail with the squadron, sir?' asked William.

The Captain glanced at Hood from under his eyelids. 'That's as the Admiral says, Sir.'

Hood stroked his chin, looking down his monumental nose. 'I presume,' said he, 'that from the length of time you were cruising among the Bahama Keys, you must be a good pilot there?'

'My second lieutenant,' replied Nelson, 'is a better.'

Hood raised an eyebrow and William subdued a grin. He had a fancy for this Captain who wore his uniform as though it were a rag-bag and didn't mince his words.

'I hope, sir,' said he, still standing at attention, 'that you will serve under this flag.'

'I second that hope, Sir,' Nelson said.

The Admiral said nothing.

But when the *Barfleur* left Sandy Hook for the West Indies, Nelson in the *Albemarle* went, too.

*

The Fleet approached Jamaica in the early morning. Looking landward as the *Barfleur* skimmed like a swan round the south-eastern point of the island, those on the main deck saw a haze of blue appear on the horizon, that was not sea, nor sky. It heightened, it took shape, it came striding out to meet the ship, a velvety sheer blueness, deepening to violet in shadowed slopes and ravines. High above the plumed masses of cocoa palms and the level thickets of mangrove, spreading westward rose those summits, crowned with the clear gold of the risen sun. . . . The Blue Mountains of Jamaica, rightly named.

It was William's first voyage in tropical seas; his first sight of tropical land.

The visit was a confused medley of impressions. As in New York he was fêted. He was addressed by the Council and House of Assembly. He held levées in Spanish Town. The merchant planters raised a corps of cavalry as his bodyguard. He drove through sun-swept streets under the broad leaves of palm that cast no shade. A multitude cheered, white faces and black, agleam. He saw slaves toiling in the plantations and heard the crack of the overseers' whips. Were all men flogged who worked? . . . On every glaring white wall clambered a

riot of strange flowers, sending down a heavy intoxicat-
ing scent to make him giddy. Black faces were merged
in white; heads dodged, peering and cheering, crowding
the dusty way.

All day the sun blazed in a cloudless sky. The sea
burned under it, a fiery sapphire, splintered into radi-
ant crystal gems on the wave-ribbed surface . . . William
looked with longing to bathe in those tinted waters that
revealed depth under depth of clear translucence down
to the silvery sea-floor where jewelled fish darted in and
out of coral places, and sea-flowers, stranger than those
on the white walls above, bloomed unfading in a dim
blue world.

But he was guarded. He had no freedom. He could
not now walk alone where he pleased, to explore. The
visit was official. Here indeed he was received as a
viceroy. He drove with Hood at his side, saluting right
and left till his arm ached and he was sick of it. His
sleep at night was disturbed by buzzing insects. He
found cockroaches in his bed. He rose unrefreshed and
heavy-eyed to receive more potentates, more merchants
and their ladies, hooped and powdered, curtseying . . .
Not one so sweet as his Matilda.

With the Governor beside him, he stood in the heat,
sweating from every pore, his mouth set in a polite fixed
grin, his voice repeating parrot-like, the whispered
promptings. He attended banquets and ate horrible
sticky food and had the stomach-ache. There was no
dancing. His messmates went to revels in the town, and
had tales to tell of their adventures, that did not lack
embellishment by repetition; but while they romped
with negresses and made love to the planters' daughters,
William was put to bed to rest for the exertions of the
next day.

There was reason for these flourishes and celebrations. The preliminaries of a peace treaty had been

signed. The Spanish troops at Cape François had surrendered, and their Commander, Galvez, presented the English King's son with a batch of British prisoners of war as a mark of his esteem. All had been condemned to death.

Will you be pleased, Sir, to accept their pardon and their lives in the name of the Spanish army and my King? It is, I trust, the least present that can be offered to one Prince in the name of another. . . .

To which, as one Prince to another, William made reply:

. . . It is the most agreeable present you could have offered me and is thoroughly characteristic of the bravery and gallantry of the Spanish nation. . . . Be assured that an action so noble as that of your Excellency will ever be remembered by

William Henry.

*

When Hood's squadron sailed back to England William was ordered to transfer to the frigate *Fortunée*, which, escorted by Nelson in the *Albemarle*, proceeded to Havannah.

The frigates arrived off Mero Castle on the morning of 10 May, and were received by the Spanish Admiral, Don Pedro Solano, in his barge. Royal salutes were fired; William reviewed the Spanish troops, visited the castle, the fortifications and the dockyards, and was the guest of Don Pedro in whose house he lodged.

And now at last he was allowed some relaxation from the exigencies of his officialdom. There was no longer a necessity to guard him with a cavalry of merchant planters. He went sightseeing with Nelson, unattended. He explored the narrow byways of the city whose poorer quarters stank to heaven, but for William it was a city of enchantment. The scent of the tobacco plant defied the odours of an open drain that flowed through the town to the harbour. Every villa had its garden, every garden had its fountain, every wall was splashed with colour from all kinds of flowers. The flat-roofed white stone houses, gay with paint and marble, held mystery in thrall behind their close-barred windows. He was given tantalizing glimpses of dark lustrous eyes, the flirt of a fan, the flash of a smile as swiftly veiled in the lace of a mantilla; he heard the silken twang of a guitar, gay laughter, and a girl's voice singing. . . .

And while William's eyes went roving, Nelson strode beside him and talked of this and that, but never at all of women.

'There is a feeling of a need for improvement, Sir, in those nations that stand first in power, whether by sea or land.'

'Improvement? Yes, I've seen men flogged,' said William, 'as one wouldn't flog a beast. Whew! This city don't smell of amber, Captain Nelson!'

'Poor drainage, Sir. As I was saying, there is the necessity among us always for perpetual change. The very steering of a ship is performed at the present time on wholly different principles than were adopted half a century ago. As for punishment, Sir, discipline is the first rule of the Navy. Your Royal Highness has already found it so.'

His Royal Highness was on tiptoe in the dirt of the road and pulling a wry face as he avoided it. 'Faith! The Thames Strand is no muddier! Discipline? Yes, sir, I agree, but not to thrash a man until he's raw! When I'm an Admiral, I'll change all that.'

'When you're an Admiral, Sir, you'll still be taking orders. A sailor is a servant all his life.'

'Then I'll be First Lord,' said William, 'and give the word myself.'

'And the First Lord, Sir, takes his orders from the King, and so *ad infinitum*. For the King takes his orders from the Parliament, and Parliament from the people – or so it should be if the people had the voice to speak. And God forgive me if I utter treason,' declaimed Nelson, kindling, 'but the day is not far distant when that voice *will* be heard.'

Such talk was Greek to William, if he listened, which is likely he did not.

The magic of the sun was in his blood, romance was in the air; it beckoned from behind wrought-iron grilles, it breathed from every balcony, but always guarded, screened.

'Will it please Your Royal Highness to visit the cathedral? The bones of Columbus,' Nelson said, 'lie there.'

His Royal Highness was not pleased to visit the cathedral. He cared nothing for a dead man's bones. He cared more for the scent of a rose. . . .

It came to him under his window when he took his siesta in the heat of the noon. It must have woken him out of a dream, for his thoughts were full of roses and the lilt of a woman's song.

And that evening Don Pedro Solano gave a banquet.

Tables were arranged on the terrace between a fountain and a flight of steps that stretched to the gardens. It was taper-time, but in those parts the twilight spreads no bridge of dusk between sundown and the rising moon. The sun still lingered in the feathering tops of cocoa palms, its warmth in the heart of some nameless yellow blossom that clambered on the parapet and spent its last breath in fragrance on the air. Then all light faded from a copper sky, and dark dropped like a curtain on the day.

The tall candles in their silver sconces revealed to the glowing tropical night a scene that was fantastically ornate. The British officers wore their uniforms, but the Spaniards were in elaborate Court dress. The ladies, exquisite in gowns of every hue, gemmed, befeathered, billowing with lace, adorned with flowers, scarves, outrivalled in their elegance the most famous beauties of the English Court; but of all those who bent her knee to him, William saw only one.

'*Con permiso,* Your R'yal Highness,' murmured Don Pedro in his ear. 'If Your R'yal Highness pleasse to perrmette that I shall pres-sent my daughter. . . .'

She was younger by a year than William, but she might have been ten years older. She wore a wide hoop of turquoise veiled in black gauze, and in the wings of her black hair, half hidden by the folds of the mantilla, was poised one crimson rose. Her mouth was not less crimson: she had a necklace of heavy silver, her earrings were of silver, too, not gold; but gold lay in her clear skin's undertones, and sparks of gold danced in her deep-fringed eyes . . . Doñ Maria Solano.

Goya may have painted her, but William knew nothing of Goya: he only knew that here was romance beyond imagination to conceive. Not all the eunuchs of a sultan's harem, nor those barred windows of the city could have guarded a more lovely secret. . . . She smiled, and the shy ghost of Matilda fled, forgotten.

There was that in the smile of Doña Maria to turn a boy into a man. A smile that was less a smile than a rounding of half-open lips, a gleam, an indrawn breath. . . . A smile. As a goddess might have smiled so did she; and curtsied formally.

William bowed.

His hands were clammy and his pulses throbbed. He had no voice to speak, for how should he address a goddess?

'Donna. . . . Madonna. . . .' Confound this foreign lingo! He was dumb.

A majordomo – a Malvolio in black and silver – marshalled the guests to table. Don Pedro Solano sat at the foot, William at the head, and next to him, Doña Maria.

He ate ambrosia; he drank nectar. His voice returned to him at last. He spoke: in English. 'Cuba . . . 'tis a beautiful island, Madam, a more beautiful island than Jamaica—' his tongue and his thoughts ran on beauty. 'Never in my life,' breathed William, staring at her eyes, 'have I beheld anything so beautiful as—' he curbed himself in time.

Doña Maria shook her head; her ear-rings tinkled to the movement, her smile gleamed again. 'Not spika Ingliss, Sirr.'

Confusion seized him. 'A thousand pardons, Señor – Señorita,' stammered William. 'You speak French? Vous parlez Frongçais, Mademoiselle?'

'*Mais oui, mon prince.*'

Her prince! Hers! He was: entirely.

'Parlong Frongçais then, Madame,' gasped William, whose knowledge of the language matched his accent. 'Vous et arrivay d'Espayne depuis long tong, Señorita?'

'*Comment?*'

William tried again.

'Combeing de tong est vous ici in Havannah, Mademoiselle?'

'*Ah! Je comprends! Depuis que ma mère est morte, mon prince. C'est à dire, depuis que j'avais douze ans.*'

'Dooze ans? Twelve years? You've been here – vous est ici dooze ans?'

'*Non, non!*' She shook her head, and rippled into laughter.

William laughed, too, such laughter was infectious.

'My French – mon Frongçais est très mal, il faut excuse moi – Donna – Donna Mar-ree-ah.'

'Il faut que votre altesse apprendre l'espagnol, n'est ce pas?'

'What? Oh wee. Certainly. If you – si vous—' floundered William hot in the ears, 'will l'apprenderay moi.'

'Avec le plus grand plaisir . . . Sirr.'

He saw the tip of her rosy tongue as she rolled the r upon it.

'And I – I'll,' declared William hysterically, 'I'll – j'apprenderay vous l'onglay, n'est par? C'est à dire comme we say on onglay – a bargain!'

'Barr-gin?' Again the ear-rings tinkled. *'Oh la la! Comme c'est drôle ça, enfin!'*

Droll indeed! Doña Maria may have found it so, not William whose words stuck in his throat while she laughed at him. 'Devil take my tongue!' he groaned, 'I'll buy a dictionary.'

After supper, when the tables were removed, the guests danced on the terrace, shielded from the invasion of flying insects by curtains of silver gauze. Musicians with guitars and castanets played a lilting melody. The Spaniards danced with the liveliest abandon, and Doña Maria with more liveliness than all.

Couples whirled in the dusty light of the candles; the coloured hoops of ladies swung like bells to the swaying movement of their hips. William envied the 'haughty dons' their grace and abandon. He was no adept in the steps of this fandango. Doña Maria laughed at his clumsy efforts as she had laughed at his French. He drowned in the laughter of her eyes

The music stopped; the company dispersed to take refreshment and to drink more wine; to wander in the gardens. William, guest of honour, was again partnered by the daughter of his host.

She led him to a marble seat in the shelter of a grove

of palms where moonshine lay like silver water on the close-clipped lawns, and shed a brilliant radiance on tall columnar tree-stems, and oddly patterned bark, on stunted hairy cactus, and the wide leaves of the mango outspread like a giant's hand. All shapes of vegetation had been bewitched, distorted. They stood unstirring, spell-bound, in that unearthly light. The humid pall of heat, the perfume of invisible flowers, those dark pools that were the eyes of Doña Maria, the curved shadow of her mouth alternately hidden and revealed by the rhythmic motion of her fan, the breathless silence – all, and all of her conspired to render William's head as giddy as though he had drunk too deep of wine; yet wine that evening he had scarcely tasted. She was drink enough: the sight and scent of her – that aching scent – of what? Of spices? Of a woman? Of the rose that faded in her hair?

'Teach me,' he whispered. 'Teach me your language . . . Mar-ree-ah.'

To that quavering appeal she turned her eyes but not her head, to look at him; he saw her eyelids drooping till they closed, and the gleam of her teeth between her parted lips; he saw her bared throat girdled by the heavy chain of silver and the stir of her breathing in the valley of her breasts; and then a madness seized him and his mouth reached, thirsty, for the fruits of hers, and his blood beat a wild torment in his ears till all sense perished.

This was her answer; this her language, spoken with subtle fluency of lips and sight-blind touch and warm sweet juice of tongue, and wordless sound. . . . He was not slow to learn.

Unlike others of his age and time, he had been allowed no licence. His sex-knowledge was limited to hearsay and the virgin kisses of Matilda. He had listened, envying, to the boastful sagas of his messmates,

49

all of whom had ventured into realms denied to him. The secrets of the alcove, the guarded balconies of Cuba, had revealed their mysteries to many younger than himself, but the tree of knowledge that is free to all of Adam's sons was denied to the son of the King. Only his Eden lacked an Eve where Eves were plentiful. At the entrance to those luscious groves stood gentlemen whose orders were as adamant as any flaming sword. And should he stray to hidden pastures, their footsteps followed him to track him down; to uncover him beneath the moon . . . and break a miracle.

One stood there, uniformed and bowing. 'Sir.'

'God damn you!' Adam, new-born, challenged this outrage to his manhood. White-lipped and blazing, he was up and on his feet to shield his woman. His voice, no boy's croak now, but a man's voice sharp as steel and colder, struck the silence. 'Why do you come here?'

'Your Royal Highness – I have been—'

'And you can go!'

'But, Sir – your pardon, Sir – but—'

Although the stammering lieutenant may have wished himself ten miles away he was commanded. 'Captain Nelson, Sir, sends me to request that you report at once – for duty.'

'Duty? What duty?'

His duty was to her whose bosom heaved with indignation, whose eyes, no longer laughing, held sparks of devil's flame, whose fingers closing with savage fury on her fan snapped it in two. She had been wooed before and many times, but never interrupted. Her very skirts hissed as she rose to pour out in a storm of Spanish her opinion of the *gauchierie* of Englishmen.

The lieutenant had no answer but to repeat his order and summon to his aid the privilege of rank above a midshipman. 'Captain Nelson, Sir, awaits you. Report at once.'

God's word to Adam: Nelson's to his underlings:
King's servant to King's son: the flaming sword.

Heels clicked; a hand was lifted in salute, not to the
Prince but to the lady. The moon's gleam on powdered
hair, on gold lace and the sword hilt. Then the world
darkened, for the moon was fled behind a cloud to hide
a man's resentment; a boy's shame.

Somewhere in the darkness stole a whispered laugh:
even in her rage she was not far from laughter. The rose
had fallen from her hair and lay at William's feet . . .
a scented death.

*

Doña Maria was a woman for her years and William
a boy for his, but with such refreshing naïvety, the lady
found no fault. The experience was new and quite
delightful. Her heart if not engaged, was doubtlessly
intrigued by the novel situation. Here was one, whose
country until recently the sworn enemy of Spain, had
called a truce. To Spain's colony of Cuba England sent
her son to offer friendship in the name of England's
King.

It would, so Doña Maria may have reasoned, be
impolite, if not undiplomatic, to spurn the homage of
an English Prince.

Moreover, he amused her. His uncouth gallantry, his
inarticulate surrender, were more acceptable than all
the honeyed phrases of the Spanish nobles whose impassioned declarations she rejected with a shake of her
head and ear-rings.

And, with her seal upon him, William was her slave
and her creation. She withdrew her favour from the
'haughty dons' to bestow it on himself, and he was
proud. In blissful unawareness of the jealousy he roused
among those whose privilege he had usurped, he ven-

tured clumsily where others, prouder and point-device in grace to please a lady, were denied. This red-faced princeling with his rolling gait, his roughened hands and his simplicity, took precedence where they stood by, discarded.

Resentment turned to spleen and spleen to venom. Their mutters reached the ears of those in charge, to whom His Royal Highness's infatuation had already caused anxiety enough. The boy was obstinate and mad in love, and the girl – a demon.

Motherless, she ruled her father and his household with a flick of her finger and thumb. The Spanish Admiral could well command his fleet, but not his daughter. The watchdogs found themselves between the deep sea and the devil with a vengeance.

The tactful hints they dropped to Don Solano were received with indignation. The bluest blood of Castille was offended. The marked attention of the English Prince was fitting homage to the reigning toast of Cuba. The suggestion that her presence be withdrawn from too-fervent Royal glances and kept in retirement while the British ships remained in port was, to say the least of it, impertinent. And the least of it, as said by Don Pedro Solano, with smoothest tongue but flashing eye, conveyed that the gentlemen had blundered.

William's watch-dogs, discomfited, retired to confer. Each one may have wished himself at the bottom of the Gulf of Mexico, and the Prince in safety – and a ship – upon it. He must be got away. These dagos might turn dangerous. They carried knives as well as swords, and all were practised duellists. If the Prince should be called out, there'd be no holding him. He'd fight. He had been all but kidnapped in New York. God send he'd not be stabbed to death in Cuba.

Meanwhile, William rhapsodically unconscious of the

hornets' nest about him, browsed in Elysium and
learned to conjugate the verb 'to love', in Spanish. He
learned other things besides.

From the wintry glades of the Green Park to the
perfumed moonlight of a Cuban garden is a lightning
transition, and might require a steadier head than
William's to take it in his stride and keep his balance at
the feet of Doña Maria. He could not; the odds were
all against him. He was lost, bowled over, prostrate, for
the hidalgos of Havannah and all the world to see.

Nelson saw, and seeing came to a decision.

The boy had made an ass of himself. This mawkish
ogling would have to stop. There must be no more
hanky-panky and meetings in the moonlight; no more
carriage drives to visit ruins with a duenna – be it noted
– in the background. Duenna be damned for a tale!
That black-haired minx dropped duennas overboard as
carelessly as she had dropped her suitors. But there were
more serious issues at stake. Relations between Spain
and England were strained enough, in spite of peace
treaties and celebrations and the hospitality of Don
Solano. A nice thing if the diplomatic apple-cart were
upset by a whisper, a word, a stab in the dark at the
eleventh hour! These grandees, dons, and what-not
were sufficiently provoked by the sight of this youngster
in his teens blundering where they might never tread.
He had trod far enough already. And how far, one
might ask, was that? Nelson had his own suspicions.

On duty the lad was in a flutter, burning to be off
again; shook when you gave an order, dreamed at his
work, kept dead roses in his pocket, and spent his spare
time in my lady's chamber. It had been whispered that
the Prince's bed was empty every night. That might be
rumour, though one could hardly blame the boy if it
were not. The witch had eyes to melt a sterner heart.
But . . . Nelson served his King before his sentiment.

His world as yet did not contain an Emma; and when it did he served his country before her.

So came the day, by William feared and dreaded, that brought the inexorable order: 'All leave cancelled. All officers and gentlemen belonging to His Majesty's ship, the *Fortunée*, return to duty.

By King's son or midshipman Command must be obeyed; and there must be no quarter asked, or given.

The frigate *Fortunée* was homeward bound.

*

At dawn on the main deck, William watched a blue mist that had been Cuba fade into the horizon. He watched till the first glow of morning deepened and the faint stars died on the edge of the world, and the last sight of land became a memory between the sky and sea.

Chapter Three

THIS homecoming lacked the celebrations that had greeted his previous return. The King's welcome at St James's was lukewarm. His Majesty had heard something of the reason of that hurried flight from Cuba, and was not disposed to greet the prodigal with open arms.

The gift from his son, however, of a captured Spanish flag, may have modified to some extent the tone of the reception and averted cross-examination if not worse. The King made a speech stressing honour above glory, and with laudable restraint avoided a more personal attack, dropped a chilly kiss on William's eyebrow, and dismissed him.

The Queen shed tears.

Doch! The King perhaps had been a little brusque – not? After so long away and in such danger. *Der Junge* was so brave, and so well-grown, so handsome. And the flag! How charming was this gesture, then, to bring the flag!

Sentimentally the King's eyes watered while he drummed impatient fingers on his chair-arm. 'Yes, all very well – all very well – the flag, but—'

'But! But!' With wary sprightliness the Queen insisted there must be no 'buts' today. No quarrelling, no scenes. Above all, pray, no scenes. Her *lieber* George, then, would so tolerant be, *nicht wahr*? Was he not always tolerant? The most tolerant of fathers. Yes, one knew that trouble enough already with these sons one had, but was it not that too much attention was been to gossip paid? 'Would not it sometimes better be to go so—' The Queen playfully covered her ears and as playfully uncovered them with palms outspread, 'than to go *so* to all these tales? Does it not say to speak no slander, no! Nor to it listen?'

'Hey? What? What?' A vein swelled on the Royal forehead. 'Do you insinuate that I– that *I* – speak slander?'

'Ach! Nein!' The Queen summoned to her aid her widest smile, keeping one anxious eye upon that swollen vein. Her dearest heart must not misunderstand. All she would say – to let us forget these tales, is it not? The Court was full of them. All lies and tittle-tattle. From the equerries to the kitchen-maids – everyone spoke slander. *'Ach!* Now! *Du lieber Gott!'* cried the poor lady in a tremble, for threateningly her dearest heart had risen and she feared he might break out. 'Let us calm and – and happy be to make a joyful homecoming for our dear William, *nicht wahr*? We will so charming a reunion tonight with music have. And Mr Papendiek's flute.'

If William found that the reunion – with Mr Papendiek's flute – was less charming than his mother fondly hoped, the music had charm enough at all events to divert the King's attention from himself. At a safe distance in the salon he sought the company of George and Frederick to hear the news of London and the German Courts, whence Frederick had recently returned, keeping a check on his own tongue, less from modesty than from discretion.

Those two were all agog to know the truth of *'l'affaire* Cuba', for thus did George with callous levity defile a deathless love. But William's secret was still too bruised with parting for exposure. He sat constrained and let them talk and felt superior. For though his brothers may have steeped themselves in gentlemanly vices and were *blasé*; though they may have plumbed the depths of amorous experience, he had scaled the heights, had climbed Olympus. He had loved! Had Frederick who jested bawdily of man's supremest moment ever loved? Had George, whose grinning cynicism attributed no motive but the basest or most worldly to a woman's yielding – had *he* loved? William doubted it, for all that George three years ago had raved like a lunatic to everyone he met of his obsession for the Robinson, and cost his father a cool five thousand to get the letters he had written her returned.

In his brothers William critically observed a change, not much to their advantage. George had grown handsome but he also had grown fat; was overdressed and Frenchified. He stank of scent. His hands were white and womanly and small. William had never before observed how small were George's hands, and always fluttering with studied gestures, lavishly gemmed. Ridiculous. His snuff-box must have cost at least a whole year's table-money. William was in uniform. He had broadened out of his old Court dress and had no other. He would have to see a tailor and get rigged up in a coat of cherry velvet and gold buttons bigger than crown pieces. Was that the latest fashion? And a lilac waistcoat and lace ruffles and silk stockings. . . . William rubbed his nose and fidgeted and eyed George with disfavour, but all the same he made some mental notes. A bag-wig! He'd be damned before he wore one. And rings and things and jewellery. . . .

Perspiring he began to fuss and wondered how much this foppery would cost, for he'd have to buy some clothes. Would George supply the needful if he asked him? And dammit! Why shouldn't he ask him? George was drawing twenty thousand per annum from the Government, or thereabouts.

He heard little of his brothers' pleasantries and none of Mr Papendiek's high notes.

George's face was like a mask. Exactly, William thought it – like a mask. Rouged and powdered – Faith! The fellow was half-girl and half-Apollo, and surely his eyes had never disappeared in pouches when he laughed. As fat as butter.

'Damme, George, you're fat!'

'Fat!' The blue eyes rounded; the moist red lips fell open in alarm. 'You find me fat? Then sink me if I don't live on a diet of raw carrots for a month.'

' 'Pon my life!' ejaculated William. 'Here's a pair o' macaronis! Fred in a satin coat as yellow as his face – Hey, steady! Don't spill good liquor, lad, it's wasteful.'

The Bishop of Osnaburg in truth was full of wine, and scarcely holding it. 'I was not aware,' continued William very solemn, 'that St James's Palace and Greenwich Hospital had so much in common between 'em.'

With a careful hiccup Frederick asked him, 'Why?'

William explained. 'Why? Look you! In Greenwich Hospital the penalty of drinking or any other form of misbehaviour is to clap the culprit in a yellow coat and dub him the Yellow Admiral. I take it complimentary, Fred, that you wear your yellow coat to honour me. I've sailed under the command of an Admiral of the Red, the White, and the Blue, but never one that's yellow. So here's to the Yellow Admiral. I salute him!'

George guffawed and registered the name which stuck to the Bishop of Osnaburg from that time forth, but Frederick scowled. He could never see a joke against himself and was too full to be cheerful.

'Our august father's eye,' drawled George, 'is wandering in this direction. Best get our Yellow Admiral out of here – before the deluge!'

And Frederick, expostulating, but only just in time, was handed over to his page and lugged to bed.

The next day the household moved to Windsor. William would have sooner stayed in Town to drink and gamble with the worst of them at Brooks' and seek Nepenthe. His heart was broken: three thousand miles of ocean lay between him and his love. The universe contained no other woman, but all the same he did not see why he should not be offered some amusement on his leave. Last leave he had been fêted. The whole of London knew he was at home and now – notwithstanding that he'd seen some hearty fighting, had captured Spanish flags and French commanders – what sort of greeting, eh? Not a soul outside the Palace and only half within it knew he had arrived. He'd been hurried up from Portsmouth and delivered to the King as though he were a parcel. And now, forsooth, he must be carted down to Windsor with the girls!

He could, however, find no quarrel with his welcome in that quarter. His sisters received him, in private, with embraces, and such a chattering and chirruping you'd have thought yourself among a brood of starlings.

Charlotte, the Princess Royal, had lost some of her gawkiness and when not overawed by the presence of Mamma, was quite a *raconteuse* and gave a comical imitation of Mr Papendiek playing his flute. Mr 'Pap' was married now, did William know? – to Miss Albert who had been used to reside at Kew. William *must* remember her – she was of his age and had been brought to visit in their nursery days. William would surely not forget an early flame, even though her name did *not* begin with M.

'M?' The blood rushed to his face. He knew no one whose name began with M.

'Oh, oh! Fie! Here's perfidy!' cried Charlotte.

'And she believed you ever faithful.' Augusta sighed and shook her curls.

'She? She?' quoth William, turning puce.

'Now, don't repeat us like Mamma's grey parrot. Is it possible you have forgot – *Matilda*?'

If truth be told he had. Matilda? Why, of course – Matilda. For one moment he had thought the hussies had meant . . .

'Hear him!' Augusta turned her eyes up. 'There was only *one* Matilda – none other in the world! And she, Miss Fortescue, alas! She is no more.'

'What! Miss Fortescue!' ejaculated William, fairly caught. 'Good heavens! Is she dead, then?'

'Aha!' Augusta's peal of laughter reassured him. 'So you do remember! No, she isn't dead. She's *married*, and so in truth she *is* Miss Fortescue – no more. She's Mrs Drummond now and lives in Stirling and her husband is a jealous Scot who never lets her out of sight. He keeps her shut up in a castle.'

William was relieved. At least his sweet Matilda had not died for love of him. A pretty simple child, but insipid. . . . He turned the subject, caring little for the trend of it. There was no knowing where this talk of 'M's' might lead. The girls were too inquisitive by far and had nothing else to do but sit and chatter, and peck at scraps of gossip as birds will peck at fruit. Hurriedly he steered to safer channels. Augusta, he remarked, had grown into a beauty, but she already knew it without telling. Elizabeth, whom he remembered in the nursery sewing samplers, was now a plump little madam in a hoop. She painted prettily in water-colours, and presented William with a view of Windsor Castle and a group of sisters in the foreground.

William declared in all good faith that Mr Gainsborough himself could not have done it better, if as well.

He paid a visit to the nursery that had recently sustained the loss of two little brothers: Octavius aged four, and Alfred, whom he had never seen; born and dead within the time he'd been away. Ernest, a fifth son, was almost in his teens, and resembling no one in the family; a dark-haired, long-nosed, slouching youngster, tall for his years with an eye that never met your own and a sneering unchildish mouth. Arrogant, too, with his orders: 'Bring me this – take away that.' His page was at it here and there all day to do his bidding. What a family! Twelve living and another on the way. This according to Augusta, retailed as a secret, although despite his Mamma's hoop, he'd had suspicions.

Then there was Edward who lived in William's old home on Kew Green. Edward, destined to be the father of Victoria.

Prim and pernickety, very well-mannered, he resided in spinsterish state with a staff of servants to attend him, two tutors to care for his mind, two pages to brush and comb him and his lap-dogs, and an aviary of love-birds in his garden. He was a prince indeed!

' 'Twould do you good, m'lad,' said William bluntly, 'to reef in the top'sle on a winter's night when the spray turns to ice on the deck; or to stand at the helm in a gale; or share your wash-basin with a dozen others – if you get the time to wash at all, which believe me you don't – in a battle. Or pick the bugs out of your blanket before you can turn in. 'Pon honour! It must cost your country ten thousand a year to keep you dressed and petted like a lady, not to mention satin cushions for your lap-dogs and seed for your canaries.'

Edward was too polite to tell his brother that he thought him intolerably coarse; or that he had no desire to exchange his comfortable existence for a life so depraved as that of the common sailor William represented: a life which Edward had no doubt was in all respects conformable with one of such low tastes: a boor, an oaf, a disgrace to the Blood with his quarter-deck gestures, rude speech, and his dreadful red hands.

'They are not canaries,' said Edward, holding himself in. 'They are called budgerigars. A breed of parokeet – charming little creatures, and the most devoted mates. Allow me to present you with a pair.'

'Now what in the devil,' replied William with a noisy guffaw that made Edward shudder, 'should I do with a pair o' bugger-what-you-may-call-'ems? Put 'em to roost in the crow's-nest?' But on second thoughts he decided to accept the birds. He could give them to Great-aunt Amelia.

The Princess Amelia, sole surviving child of George II, deplorably deaf, unmarried, and seventy-three, re-sided at Gunnersbury Park within an easy drive's distance of Windsor.

As William must have known her she was ugly, bad-tempered, and bronchial. She spoke good English in a guttural voice – her heritage from Germany – that seemed to rise, not from her vocal chords, but deeper, as though it had been dragged from her intestines.

She was a source of endless entertainment to that arch-mimic George, the Prince of Wales, who was wont to caricature her strong language and her accent for the delectation of his household.

Her teeth had fallen out and her mouth had fallen in, and she dressed outlandishly. She wore a 'head' so high that her face appeared to be in the middle of her body. Under this edifice, her eyes, surprisingly quick and bright for her years, gleamed between their wrinkled shutters like lit windows in a darkened house. Her claw-like hands were jewelled to the knuckles, but her nails were filthy and she smelled of age, of camphor and the aniseed she took in large doses for her cough.

If Amelia Sophia had been a beauty or a wife, had not been deaf or not been born a century too soon, her independence and her caustic tongue might have

changed the face of Europe, made history, or bred kings.
She was once engaged to Frederick the Great. Lacking,
however, these essentials, she makes history nowhere
save in Horace Walpole's letters, and notwithstanding
that he boasts of how she very nearly married him, she
died as she had lived, alone.

On the morning William called, he found his great-
aunt seated by the open window in her salon, playing
loo with a lady-in-waiting. The lady was bored, the
Princess cross, and although the day was blazing hot she
had her face and 'head' wrapped in a shawl and her
shoulders in a tippet.

'I haf der ear-ache,' she explained, as William entered
with Edward's love-birds in a cage. 'You – can go.' This
to her lady, but William thought she spoke to him, and,
greatly disconcerted, was on the point of backing out
when she offered him two fingers and her cheek. 'Sit
down. You've grown. And what in der name of fortune,'
the Princess asked unamiably, 'are d'ose?'

'Love-birds, Madam,' William said, presenting them,
'especially brought for you from – um – Cuba.'

'Cuba! Heck! Heck! You don't haf to tell me about
Cuba,' said Her Royal Highness with a splutter and a
leer. 'I may be hardt of hearing but I haf heardt all
aboudt you! Cuba! Dey sent you home – isn't it? You
almost broughdt aboudt anoder war from all accounts –
you r-r-rascal!' And the old lady subsided, coughing in
her handkerchief and with such a roguish wagging of
her head that the edifice upon it was in danger of
collapse.

Completely shattered by his great-aunt's misinterpre-
tation of his, approximately, innocent remark William
sat and burned, nursing the bird-cage on his knees and
a new grievance. So! The whole world talked of him –
and her! And somebody or other had come down here
to bellow it at Aunt Amelia.

'Parrots?' inquired the Princess, unexpectedly.

William started.

'Parrots? . . . Oh! yes. No. They are called Bugg . . .' Better not attempt it. 'Yes, Aunt, *parrots*,' shouted William, in Her Royal Highness's approaching ear. 'I bought 'em – I *bought them* in – Jamaica. They're for *you*.'

'For me?' echoed Aunt Amelia, astonished. 'My Gott, whad do I wandt wid parrots? Dey look extr-r-r-ordinarily schmall. Do dey screech? Or talk?' she seldom waited for an answer to a question. 'I hear already talk enough from Mr Walpole widout keeping parrots to do it. Talk, talk – mumble, mumble. He says dere will be a general election, and goodt time, too!' The Princess clawed at a pastille from a silver bonbonnière and munched it, rubbing her chest. 'Dat damdt old fool Lord Nordt wid his hums and his hahs – to see never an inch before his nose. He is losing his eyesight now dey say. He ought to lose his head for losing us America. Gott send your fader will turn him out and bring dat young Pitt in. He is a fire-brandt from all accounts. How is your fader? He never comes to see me. Der childer-r-en's deats' upset him. Not der baby. He said he didn't care aboudt der baby – but der oder – what-is-its-name? Octavius. Schmall-pox. Mr Walpole tells me died of an inoculation der schmall-pox. Murder! Your fader makes murder wid his nonsense. Inoculation! Fiddlesticks! Take d'ose birds away. Dey schtink. Pull der bell-rope.'

William obeyed. 'Do you not feel the weather very warm, Ma'am?' he inquired, mopping his face.

'Mr Walpole,' said the Princess, unsuccessfully attempting the removal of a pastille from her gums, 'is coming presently for dinner. You can go or stay – or what you pleass. Do you play loo? Not dat it matters if you don't. We can play widout you, or we can play whist.'

William said that he would like to stay. He had long desired to make the acquaintance of Mr Walpole whom he had heard was vastly—

'Take d'ose what-is-its-names outside,' said Her Royal Highness to the footman, 'and be careful der cats don't eat dem.'

'May I stay then, Aunt?' asked William.

'Very well. If you won't, you won't. No respect. Come and go. *Auf Wiedersehen*,' said the Princess, stonily, offering two fingers.

'I said *I'd like to stay*!' William repeated loudly.

'Pleass not to shoudt. Everybody shoudts,' the Princess fretfully complained. 'You may wait in der garten. I shall take a nap. I need all my wits for Mr Walpole.' The old lady leaned her monstrous 'head' against her chair-back; her eyelids closed. The shawl dropped from the edifice to the floor. 'I will haf it on my feet,' said the Princess as William stooped. 'Is it true dat your broder Frederick is always dr-r-ronk and dat George playss so deep he will haf to get a grant from Parliament to pay his debts? Parliament,' said Her Royal Highness sleepily, 'never paidt mine. Before you go will you pleass to close der window and pull der bell-rope twice – for Lady Mary.'

Punctually to the hour, Mr Walpole arrived in a lavender suit, and was presented by Princess Amelia to William.

Trim in his dress and lean in his person with small precise features, he looked considerably younger than his sixty-five years. His excessive pallor gave to his eyes a peculiar sombre alertness. His wig, lightly powdered, was tied in a queue and combed straight from his high unlined forehead. He walked mincingly, as if on tiptoe, and supplemented his speech with elaborate gestures of his womanish hands that were very much swollen with gout.

In a letter to Lady Ossory he tells how at that meeting with Prince William: 'I attempted at the risk of tumbling on my nose to kiss his hand but he would not let me. You may trust me, Madam, who am not apt to be intoxicated with Royalty that he is charming. Lively, cheerful, talkative, well-bred . . .' (the string of adjectives is inexhaustible) . . . 'You may judge how good-humoured he is when I tell you that he was in greatest spirits all day, though with us old women – perhaps he thought it preferable to Windsor!'

He did indeed.

The restraint and ceremonies of the Castle had soon palled. The Queen's middle-aged ladies-in-waiting were as handsome as a row of turnips and as dull. The chatter of his sisters was infinitely boring. He had no friend at Court. The Prince of Wales was in London preparing to take up residence at Carlton House. Mr Walpole's anecdotes and strokes of wit delivered with feline delicacy at the expense of famous persons, provided better entertainment than anything Windsor could afford.

Throughout the dinner Mr Walpole kept up a patter of amusing conversation. His naturally high-pitched voice penetrated even to the muffled ear-drums of Her Royal Highness, who alternately cackled and coughed at his quips whether she heard them or not, and offered her visitor his favourite white wine in a pail of ice.

'And so, Sir,' said Mr Walpole, pecking with dainty enjoyment at the food on his plate, 'I hear that the Prince-Bishop returns in the autumn to Germany. Is it true that you go with him?'

It was the first William had heard of it. 'It is likely, sir, that you have more knowledge of my movements than I have. I never know where I may be sent at any moment's notice. But Germany? I doubt it. There's no naval port of ours in that quarter. May I ask where you have learned this news, Mr Walpole?'

'You may ask, Sir, but I cannot guarantee an answer. How does news come? On the winds? On the air? I have been – and may be perhaps again – a prophet, though that is a profession never honoured in its own country.' A small twisted smile came upon his lips. 'It would be idle in me, Sir, in any case, to busy myself with speculations in the future, of which I shall probably have but a glimpse.'

'Who limps?' asked the Princess with her mouth full.

'I, Madam,' replied Mr Walpole gaily, 'with the gout in my left foot and right ankle which has attacked me since I left off, or kicked off, all my coverings last night. Although I confess I love to have summer in summer, I find this sultry season deals me more harm than good. But I have no doubt His Royal Highness finds this English tropical heat tolerable after the climate of Cuba, which they say—'

' 'Tis greatly overrated, sir,' William interrupted hastily. 'Is it true the Thames is running dry?' Confound the fellow with his smiles.

'I know, Sir—' said Mr Walpole airily, while with his napkin he gently patted the smile from his lips – 'nothing but my own disasters. Another is that all day yesterday I thought my goldfish stolen. I am sure that they are not, but they tell me they stay at the bottom of the water in hot weather. It is all to be ladled out tomorrow morning, and then I shall know whether they are gone or boiled.'

'What are you saying? Who's gone?' squawked the Princess.

Mr Walpole raised his glass. 'The last of your good wine, Madam.'

'Bring anoder bottle for Mr Walpole. . . . Der worst possible drink for gout. Do you not find Prince William grown?'

'I cannot tell, Madam, as this is the first time I have had the honour of—'

'Who haf you been entertaining lately?' asked the Princess taking up her chicken-bone to gnaw it. 'Give me some newss to make me laugh.'

'I have had no news of any laughing matter this month, Madam. There have been the deaths of two Irish peeresses, Lady Middleton and Lady Gage, but as Hibernian peers spring up like mushrooms, or *are* mushrooms, I suppose there will be as great plenty of ermine in that country as ever. Perhaps some of their own growth, without a drawback from *our* custom-house. . . . Your Royal Highness's very good health. And yours, Sir, and more new worlds to conquer, and the world's seas to command!'

So in some such fashion did the guest entertain his hostess and her nephew, who returned to Windsor in a fuss about Mr Walpole's hints. Could it be true that he was to be sent to Germany with Frederick? Mr Walpole would know if anybody did. He knew everything, even before those most concerned had any news of it. Cunning old bird, preening his feathers and pecking at his food and smirking at Great-aunt Amelia. . . . And what a tongue! As charged with poison as an adder's! Not his dearest friend if he possessed one would be safe from it. William would have liked to know what Mr Walpole had to say of *him*.

What Mr Walpole had to say of him has been already quoted. It may be that Mr Walpole protests too often and too much of his indifference to Royalty; or perhaps his unique powers of observation have penetrated deeper than youth's callow surface, to discern that gleam of solid worth, which, though unrecognized by his contemporaries and by posterity ignored, is none the less akin to greatness, and illuminates the character and the all too brief a reign of a King who ruled a hundred years before his time; or it may be that the dinner provided by his hostess, and some temporary surcease from the gout, may have rendered Mr Walpole's correspondence on that day more scrupulously critical than catty. Whatever the cause of it, however, the fact remains on record in those incomparable letters, where so much gall is mingled with the ink, that Prince William is exceptionally favoured, for Mr Walpole states he is impressed.

It appears, too, that he was not mistaken in his prophecy, or news, no matter where he gleaned it, of the King's plans for the Prince's future. Within a week of that visit to his aunt's, William was told that arrangements had been made for him to join his brother Frederick in Hanover.

He was not elated at the prospect. He had been looking forward to the expiration of his leave, and the possibility of promotion from midshipman to sub-lieutenant, and he resented this untimely interruption to his training. He was no landlubber to make the Grand Tour in a coach and four. He had no desire to attend the German Courts and bow and scrape to small Electors and great Prussians. But he knew better than to give voice to his objections. The King would never listen if he did.

It was the custom for young gentlemen – Royal Princes not excluded – to complete their social education on the continent under guidance of a tutor. William had two. A soldier and a sailor; General Budé and a Captain Merrick whom he had met in the West Indies while serving under Hood.

Having been thus furnished with attendants and some introductions to the German Courts, William proceeded to Greenwich where the Royal yacht, the *Princess Augusta*, awaited him.

Before embarking he had a duty to perform. The King had desired he should inspect the hospital. Sir Hugh Palliser, the Governor, received him with the other chiefs of the establishment, and was prepared to show him round, when William, with customary bluntness, electrified his audience by requesting to see John Adams before he saw anything else.

John Adams, accordingly, was sent for, and hopped up to the Prince with his crutch under one arm and his cocked hat under another. Oblivious of Sir Hugh Palliser's uplifted eyebrows and General Budé's 'hems', William stuck his hand out to have it wrung.

'Well, my Royal William! I am comfortably brought up at last. You promised me when I lost me starboard timber after that action with the lubberly dons that you'd find me a berth for life, and here I am, safely moored – thanks to you, my Royal William!' said the old fellow gruffly, with a moisture in his eye.

On inquiring how many were in hospital who had been in action in the *Prince George* when they captured Langara's flagship, William was told thirteen; whereupon he counted out thirteen guineas from his purse and gave them to Sir Hugh Palliser to be distributed 'among my old shipmates'.

'I'll drink your health in 'em tonight, my Royal William,' said the 'Commodore' saluting. And he did, with so much zest, that he wore the Yellow Admiral's uniform for the remainder of the week.

The passage across the North Sea was boisterous, but while General Budé groaned in his cabin, William and Captain Merrick took turns at the helm. The Royal yacht arrived at Stade on 2 August, and William, being the first of the Royal Family to visit that city, was invited to a masonic dinner where choristers assembled to sing him Schiller's 'Ode to Joy'.

The next morning he moved on to Hanover and was met by Frederick, who had been three years in Germany learning how to be a British soldier.

Although his tutors reported that they saw in him a future Hannibal or Alexander, the Bishop of Osnaburg's military education seems to have been confined to attending reviews in his uniform, and social functions in his cups.

With Frederick as his guide William lost no time in sampling the hospitality provided by a clique self-styled 'The Court Circle', although no Court was ever held in Hanover, of which city the King of England was Elector.

The daily programme of the brothers appears to have consisted of visiting the stables to inspect the famous cream-coloured horses from which the Royal stud at Windsor was supplied, and this occupied the better part of the whole morning; in the afternoon they reviewed the troops drawn up for their inspection in the market-place; after that they paid and received calls, when, for some inexplicable reason, Frederick was presented as Count Hoya and William as Lord Fielding. They then dined, wined and slept, preparatory to an all-night session at the gaming-tables.

Among the many undesirable acquaintances the brothers managed to collect between them was a certain Baron Hardenberg, a smooth-tongued, polished crook who took William on at faro, and finding here a novice and something to be fleeced, stood him drinks and connived that he should win, hoping to draw him on to higher stakes. But William, unlike his brother Frederick, preferred to play cold sober. He refused the offer of more wine, and having received a warning chit from Captain Merrick, who knew something of the Baron's methods of play, he had the sense to retire with his winnings.

The Baron, furious at this frustration of his plans by such unprecedented caution, expressed his disgust in a storm of abusive and defamatory remarks, which, uttered in the public rooms, reached the ears of William's gentlemen and caused a proper scandal.

Captain Merrick, loyal, hot-tempered and devoted to his Prince, as all who served him in the Navy were, called on Baron Hardenberg to demand an apology or satisfaction, rendered to himself on behalf of His Royal Highness.

But William did not at all approve of that. 'Damme, Merrick, what in hell? D'you think I'm white-livered?' he demanded, when he learned of Merrick's interference. Up and down the room he stormed, his hair on end, Budé at his heels striving to placate, and Merrick, hand on sword-hilt mumbling long-faced: 'Sir, Royal etiquette forbids—'

'Who gives a damn for Royal etiquette? An insult's been offered to my name and person, and God sink me!' roared William, 'I'll avenge it.'

Budé sidled up to him. 'We, Sir, are here beside you to take that satisfaction to ourselves.'

William swung round.

'You can stand my second. I'll fight my own man, thank'ee.'

Moistening his lips Budé prayed for patience. 'Indeed, Sir, you must consider—'

'Hold you your potato-jaw!' retorted William, inexcusably. 'You may talk till you're blue, you'll not alter my decision. This is my affair and no one else's.'

'If Your Royal Highness would permit I call it mine?' ventured Merrick concealing a grin at the sight of Budé's face.

'I've *said* that you can second me! And if you won't

I'll find a pair who will. My faith! You'd be better qualified to teach knitting in a dame's school than mind me!'

'Sir—'

'You waste your breath, Budé, and God knows you're short in the wind enough already,' was William's last word as he left the room.

The Prince's gentlemen were greatly put about. Such a breach of etiquette could never be permitted! The affair must be hushed up – but how? On what excuse? The wily Budé found one.

It appears that the General was on agreeable terms with a Countess von Solberg. This lady, now a dowager but once a beauty, had frequently attended the Courts of Berlin, and professed to know certain unsavoury details of the Baron's former life and that of his profession as a card-sharper, the least of them. It may have been a case of woman scorned: if so her fury seems to have been opportune.

Armed with the damning evidence extracted from the Countess, Budé waited on the Baron and gave him peremptorily to understand that unless he could, to the General's entire satisfaction, contradict the statements there produced, he was unfit to cross swords with a gentleman, let alone a Prince of the Blood Royal.

The ruse worked. The evidence was not without foundation. The General had been explicit and the Baron was alarmed. He was given six hours to clear his name or to clear out. He chose the latter course, thinking it were better to retreat than to be publicized; and William, protesting that a man with such a record deserved to have been slit, was hustled in a post-chaise to Berlin.

*

Not the least of the many well-meant but characteristic blunders the King displayed in the education of his sons, was to keep the third of them dancing attendance on the German Courts when he should have been qualifying for a commission in the Navy.

If George III's choice of a career for his 'young sailor' had been a happy stroke of intuition, this idea of sending a midshipman scampering across Europe to watch military reviews was idiotic; but the example of the Prussian Courts was worse.

The contrast between the bourgeois decorum of St James's, and the Saturnalian excesses offered by the German Royalties by way of entertainment in his honour, had already undermined what little stability of character the Bishop of Osnaburg possessed, and there is no doubt that similar indulgence had left its mark on William.

Although more temperate than his brother, he was frequently convivial, and made himself on those occasions quite ridiculous with his interminable speeches, and his endeavour to attract attention to his voice above the din, by hammering on the table in order to be heard, and leaving it in dudgeon if he wasn't.

William's impression in the land of his progenitors must have been as varied as colours in a tapestry; but woven through the threads of feasting and carousal, against the graceful background of Hanoverian plains and castled forests, of vineyards and of mountains and the green waters of the Rhine, the one central figure perpetually recurring in the pattern is surely that of Frederick, surnamed Great.

He, that aged misanthrope, shrunken in body but not in spirit, though nearing his end when William first knew him, feared death less than he hated mankind and his own existence. 'The sweetest day of life,' he wrote, 'is the day on which one leaves it for ever.'

With the Bishop of Osnaburg William accompanied

this veteran monarch to Silesia, when, in defiance of his doctors, it was his custom annually to review his troops in honour of past glories.

There astride his great white horse he sat, a frail, bent, but still impressive figure, his quavering voice shouting his orders, his seared eyes watching the soundless march of phantom armies – the hosts that he had conquered and commanded, and those spectacular defeats and ruthless victories that had won for him his niche in immortality and left him friendless, tired of living, waiting to die, half-poet and all despot to the last.

William had the misfortune to fall foul of the old King on his first introduction to him, when, on being asked if he had read *Candide*, he replied with more honesty than tact that he had not, but would like to know the author of the work. Whereupon, with a shrug of contempt for such deplorable lack of *Kultur*, the Great Frederick ignored him for the remainder of that and all subsequent receptions at his Court.

From Berlin, William was removed to Lüneburg, where he passed the winter and where for the first time the memory of Doña Maria was, if not totally, at least partially, eclipsed by a beautiful blonde.

His attentions to Fräulein Schindbach – whose name coincidentally also was Maria – soon became the talk of the town, and occasioned a good deal of malicious gossip among other young ladies who had not received an equally signal honour.

Every day the Prince, in a sledge drawn by the finest of his father's cream-coloured horses from Hanover, was to be seen driving through the snow-covered streets of Lüneburg or the moorland tracks beyond the town, with the golden-haired Fräulein beside him.

Nor was that all. He partnered her upon the ice; he couldn't skate, but what of that? He ran at her heels in fur-lined boots, to the consternation of his gentlemen and the amusement of the crowd. He honoured her house with his presence when her father gave a ball, and he danced with her four times and gave her a locket with his hair in it. What she gave him was of the least importance.

He called – with fruit and flowers: sometimes he was received and sometimes not. And then suddenly it seemed that Fräulein Schindbach could no more receive him, and when urgently requested in a note to explain why, the answer shatteringly came.

The Fräulein was betrothed – to Captain Merrick!

William was aghast, less at the heartlessness of her who had led him on to let him down, than at the double-faced behaviour of his gentleman! That Merrick – his friend – whom he had trusted with his confidence and had sent back and forth with notes and fruit and what-not (William wondered if his demonstrations had been delivered, since half the time he never got a 'thank you') – that Merrick should step in and steal a march, was treachery indeed. Besides which, he had been made to look a fool.

He fumed and fretted, imagined every eye was on him, as no doubt at all it was. Merrick – by God! He'd have the King dismiss the fellow out of office. He should be taught his place which was not within thieving distance of a Prince's pastime. Devil take all women – and to this one he was welcome. She had served her purpose as an antidote to boredom, but her charms had been too ample altogether. These German girls – they ran to fat at twenty. And a blonde. He never cared for one of his own colour. Black and hot as hell was more to his taste.

Old Budé coughed and grinned behind his hand and held his peace till William's ravings were exhausted. His Royal Highness would no doubt prefer to leave Lüneburg before the wedding.

76

The wedding? So it had gone as far as that! Merrick had made good use of his time, to say nothing of his opportunity. Fräulein Schindbach was an heiress and would be well endowed. William swore that he'd be sunk before he gave a present. He seemed to be unlucky with his 'M's'.

So that spring and all the summer was spent in travelling in Switzerland and Italy with Budé, before ending his grand tour at Prague.

It had been two years of his life wasted; he had learned nothing to his good and much to his undoing. He had known no discipline and little supervision. Wherever he went he had been fêted, spoiled, fawned on by sycophants, pampered, and poisoned. He had accepted the *laissez-faire* morality of German princelings as a Royal right. He had learned to gamble; he had learned to drink; he had learned about women of a sort – and at a price. And he had lost his boyhood.

Still flaxen-haired, but now a trifle plump, a trifle florid, it was a very self-possessed young man who passed down the gangway of the Royal yacht at Greenwich.

Chapter Four

WILLIAM returned to find the Court buzzing with a scandal that had filtered through the walls of Buckingham House to every trollop in the gutter, every tavern in the town and every ballad-monger in the street.

> 'I'd crowns resign
> To call thee mine
> Sweet lass of Richmond Hill.'

The blades of St James's hummed it on their way to Brooks's Club and Boodle's. They inhaled spicy tit-bits with every pinch of snuff. 'A thousand guineas to one he'll marry her! . . .' 'Five thousand to one he won't.' Mr Walpole's pen was scratching gleefully to all his correspondents. 'Oh, but the hubbub you are to hear and talk of, and except which, you are to hear and talk of nothing else. . . .'

The smoke that had kept alive the tales of the Prince of Wales's extravagance and debts, was consumed in the flame of publicity attached to a lady at Richmond.

Not all of England's victories, nor that recent mutilation the other side of the Atlantic that had split the English-speaking race in two; not Elliot's magnificent defence of the Gibraltar rock, nor the name of Warren Hastings who had saved India, had occasioned one tittle of the talk throughout the city from Newgate's hangman to the King himself, as that which centred around Maria Anne Fitzherbert.

A widow – and a papist! Both were enough to damn

her in the sight of every self-respecting Briton; her beauty had already damned her in the sight of British matrons, and every maid who hoped to be a wife.

The Prince of Wales was in love; no sordid intrigue this, no passing fancy, but a frenzied declaration that he would marry her or die. Rumour said he had suited words to action and stabbed himself and brought the lady to his side at Carlton House, where the sight of the Prince covered in blood had broken her resistance. Also, she was very badly frightened. Next time he might cut a vein and bleed to death and she'd have *that* upon her conscience.

Promises were made. A deposition was drawn up and signed and sealed and witnessed, but what it contained the poor lady, seeking only to placate her Prince, had not the smallest notion. She only knew that she had said that she would fly to Holland, where he could – if he would – follow her.

The King was frantic. At all costs the heir-presumptive must be kept at home. Once out of the country and travelling in pursuit of this . . .this harlot . . . The poor sick mind was near to breaking point, but the stubborn spirit that controlled it still fought for dominance: it was not broken yet. . . . Such conduct! Such lack of Royal dignity would blast the Prince's character for ever in this country and out of it – across the face of Europe.

The question of marrying the woman did not transpire in the fevered calculations of His Majesty, since no union with a commoner was legal. Moreover, any party or parties conniving at such marriage in direct contravention of the Royal Marriage Act were guilty of a felony.

So much for that, and too much for the Prince of Wales, who produced a formidable list of debts which he demanded the King or Parliament should pay. But he offered an alternative: that he should be allowed to live abroad in temporary retirement to economize, and pay for them himself.

The King, well aware of the reason why his son evinced this sudden desire for disbursement, declared that he should put aside ten thousand a year out of his income for that purpose, and made it clear that on no account would he be permitted to appeal to Parliament.

The offer from Pitt and the Government to increase the Prince's income to a hundred thousand pounds, one half of which should go to his creditors on condition that he stayed in England, had been emphatically rejected by the King. Whereupon his son resorted to a form of blackmail, and threatened to reveal state secrets, as, 'suffering as he did from the treatment at his father's hands, he was an object of suspicion and contempt to half the kingdom'.

Such was the state of affairs at home when William rejoined his happy family, and which continued unabated for a year until it reached its climax in the following December, with the return of the lady from the Continent.

The King had obviously little time for William, who as soon as he arrived was submitted to the Board of Admiralty for his examination prior to receiving his commission.

Having managed to scrape through, with, possibly, some lubricating influence to smooth the way, William was appointed third lieutenant in the *Hebe* and kissed his father's hand for the first time in the uniform of a commissioned officer.

He was given no leave, nor was he permitted to meet his brother George, who at his wits' end at the flight of his lady, was hysterically declaring to his friend Mr Fox, that he would forego the crown, sell his jewels, and escape with his love to America.

William was glad to be out of it, for although his sympathies were all with George, he knew better than to air them and turn fatherly attention to himself.

The King's congratulations were warm, and slightly tearful. Here, at all events, was a son who had not, as yet, disgraced the throne. William was entertained to supper in the Queen's House, on boiled mutton and turnips – the King's favourite dish – and hurried down to Portsmouth the next day.

And there he was put to lodge in the house of the Naval Commissioner, Mr Henry Martin, whose young son, Byam (afterwards Admiral Sir Byam Martin), was at that time a midshipman, and served in the *Pegasus* under William's first command.

Besides a son – or several sons – Commissioner Martin had a daughter, Sarah.

William had seen her first when he had visited the dockyards at Portsmouth while in the *Prince George*. She, a child then, lined up in the hall of her father's house with her brothers to receive the Prince, had been passed by him unnoticed, but when he saw her for a second time, he looked – to look again.

She was now seventeen, and from all accounts a beauty; her brother, in his memoirs[1] is not stinting of his praise.

> She was handsome, exceedingly attractive and interesting in her manners, with an excellent under-standing and a well-cultivated mind; but there was nothing at the time, or through life, which so marked her character and so endeared her to her friends as her exemplary propriety of conduct.

This paragon succeeded where Fräulein Schindbach failed, in securing a total eclipse of the Cuban sun and the light of Doña Maria.

[1] *Journal and Letters of Admiral Sir T. Byam Martin*, Navy Records Society.

Miss Martin, fourth in succession in that rosary of M's, needed no brotherly avowal of her virtues. She was every bit as good as she was 'handsome', though the word scarcely conveys the essence of her charm, that owed less to form and feature than to a ravishing look of child-like innocence in the grey eyes, widely set; in the faint colouring of rounded cheeks, in the closely folded mouth, and the slow, grave smile that drew William's susceptible heart out of his body at first sight of it. She wore no powder on her hair, no hoop or frills or fripperies, about her person. Her throat rose pale as a flower, from a fichu, demurely folded across the firm young budding breasts. She sat in cloistered silence at the table, while her father entertained the Prince with interminable talk of the dockyards and the shipping; of politics and Mr Pitt, quoting between gulps of his claret, the jingle of the day. ' "A sight to make surrounding nations stare – a Kingdom trusted to a schoolboy's care." '

In spite of which Mr Martin was willing to concede England's youthful premier: 'A sound enough young man, as witness this new policy of Free Trade and his commercial Peace Treaty with France, and certainly, as Your Royal Highness will agree, a better leader of the Government than the leader of the opposition – eh? This Fox – a fox indeed! A crafty and corrupt supporter of the traitor, Burke, whose proposed Economic Reform Bill is an outrage to the power of the Crown. . . .'

If the Commisionner's young daughter heard little of this discourse, it is likely that Lieutenant Guelph heard none. His contribution was confined to monosyllables, a lapse, that may have probably been disregarded, even welcomed by his host, who cared more for the sound of his own voice than any other.

So, while Mr Martin droned, with momentary intervals for mastication, William sat, entranced, and gazed at Sarah.

His only chance of seeing her was at the table; his only hope of speech with her, across it, and then merely to thank her for the passing of a dish, or the re-filling of his glass at a signal from her father. What sacrilege that she should wait on him who yearned to wait on her! She never uttered. And where she vanished when she left the room could only be conjectured, for he had no glimpse of her about the house. Divine, exquisite creature! All spirit, scarcely human. He imagined her in the virgin fastness of her chamber, upon her knees in prayer. A saint. . . . One hardly dared, knowing how base and evil was man's mind and his desires, to approach her. And *if* one dared, one could scarcely interrupt Mr Martin's monologue with an open declaration to his daughter, while accepting mutton-pie.

It might be possible by the distribution of a bribe among her younger brothers, to discover where she took her daily walks. If she walked at all, which was improbable. So angelic a being could not sully her feet in the refuse and dirt of a dockyard. True, the house boasted a good-sized garden, and there, between those yew-lined paths, or tending flowers, he might find her. Alas! the Commissioner was too cognizant of his duties as the host of Royalty to allow the Prince a solitary inspection of his grounds. When William expressed a wish 'To see your roses, sir', he was accompanied by Mr Martin, talking still.

And then one day he chanced upon her on the staircase. He was coming down as she was going up with flowers in her arms, a wide-brimmed hat upon her head, and a bunch of housewife's keys swinging from a girdle at her waist.

And what a waist! A man's hand might have spanned it. The impulse to do so was almost irresistible, and the effort at control where he stood above her on the staircase, nearly sent him crashing headlong down it. Clutching at the banisters to save himself, he babbled – of the weather. 'A lovely day, Miss – Miss Sarah.' Of her flowers: 'From the garden?' Of anything in order to detain her.

Yes, from the garden. She had that moment gathered them. Her slow entrancing smile seemed to linger in her eyes while it faded on her lips, and stole what little sense was left to him.

'The garden? Do you walk – that is to say – do you go – into the garden every morning at this hour – and – and – alone?'

'Alone?' Under her hat-brim's shadow the grey eyes widened. 'Oh, yes, Sir, to fetch flowers.'

To fetch flowers! Any dolt without imagination – and William had not much – might have guessed that she and flowers were inseparable. 'You are like—' words came and stayed unspoken. What need was there for speech while he looked down and she looked up – at him?

'And what,' asked William, 'is the name of – these?' His clumsy fingers strayed to touch the multi-coloured fragrance in her arms beneath her chin; it was as near as he dared come to touching her.

'The cottagers hereabouts,' for the briefest second only did she pause but long enough for him to see a glowing in her cheeks, 'call them Sweet William, Sir. Would Your Royal Highness please to have them in your bedroom? They do smell very sweet, Sir, and refreshing.'

Refreshing – yes, and sweet!

All the sweetness in the world was offered to his gaze in the candid innocence of those grey eyes, uplifted to his own. And it may be in that moment some new intangible emotion stirred him, not with desire, but

84

regret for all that he had lost until he knew her; and for those tainted pleasures that had left him, no worse, although no better than others of his age, and of all time.

'I – I am not worthy,' stammered William, 'of – a – flower to my name.'

Then, because he may have seen her startled wonder, and her shy response to something not yet born between them, something yet to come, he bowed, and stood aside to let her pass.

*

'I am not worthy.' That was the key-note of his passion for this child, of all his early loves the most sincere, and the only memory that left a lasting scar. He would have married her. It was his tragedy, and perhaps also it was hers[1], that he could not.

Summer faded: a cold breath crept through the dawns at sea. Great waves crashed over the *Hebe*'s decks, swept by October gales. The last of the Michaelmas daisies died in the Martins' gardens; the flame of scarlet creeper on the wall rusted and fell. The Commissioner sat longer at table with his guest, over his two bottles. In the parlour Sarah sat at her harpsichord and sang.

She was more often now about the house. William was given recurrent, tantalizing sight of her busy with her duties in the still-room, or sewing in a window-seat with a cold sunbeam on her hair making a halo round it, or going up and down the stairs with fresh linen – and no flowers – in her arms; and where she went a fragrance seemed to follow her. But he came no nearer knowing her save in imagination. Of what, he wondered, did she think, behind those grave clear eyes? Not of him who thought of her to the exclusion of all else.

It was a delightful new experience to be admitted to

---

[1] Sarah Martin died unmarried in 1826.

that household, and to live that homely life as innumerable other lives were lived around him, and he – outside of them. A home! He had never known, till then, a home ashore, only a palace. He had never known life within walls unguarded, rooms unwatched. Here you could laugh without a cackling echo from a courtier; could speak without a group of fawning mouths waiting to snatch the words from your lips in chorusing agreement. And yet you were not free. There was no freedom from the cursed fetters of your rank that denied you what was given for the asking to all the sons of man, except the King's. . . . A wife of your own choosing, and a home to keep her in and raise up children to your name – by her. Such thoughts were dangerous, and bitter-sweet.

The Commissioner drowsed in his chair over his second bottle. William had no taste for port, no need for wine to heat his blood. . . . In the next room a girl's voice sang like a chorister's in Heaven.

The Commissioner's head was nodding; his three chins dropped; and William, rising stealthily, pushed aside his chair and tiptoed out to creep across the hall that was in darkness, to a door ajar and a room lit only by the fire's glow on walls patterned with sprigged flowers, its red eye winking in the polished depths of mahogany, and one candle's flame, swaying, burning slowly down the pale wax, surely the most alive of all unliving things. A room of warmth and shadow, with one dim shape enshrined.

Her song ceased abruptly as he entered; her hands trembled on the keys and then were still. She bent her head; it was as though she waited.

What did he tell her in that quiet room, while in another her father slumbered, and his paternal spirit hovered like some heavy unseen chaperone, listening between winey snores to steal a secret?

'I am not worthy. . . . I have no right to speak, but I cannot feel it wrong to say – I love you. . . .'

Love? Hah! What! The Commissioner's last snore waked him; a coal dropped in the grate. There had been a sound of whispers – and a sigh: it may have been the wind among the dead leaves in the garden, or rain against the window-pane, or the passing of a dream that left behind it a flavour of the good roast pig that he had eaten, and had not yet digested – and his port.

But the Prince's chair was vacant, the room empty, and damnation cold with the wind sniffing under doors and down the chimney, and the fire gone to nothing and no servants here to mend it.

The Commissioner rose from the table to bang a fist upon it and call, 'Sarah!'

She came and her eyes were strange and shining.

'Papa,' she said, and went to him. 'I think it would be better that I leave here very soon. It is best I think,' she told him softly, 'that I go.'

For:

Although she felt the compliment, her brother says, of his [the Prince's] professions of attachment, she felt also and above every other consideration that the spark which had lighted this latent feeling must be instantly extinguished. It was therefore at once decided by my father and Sarah, that she should forthwith set off to an uncle and aunt in London.

Which brought matters to a head, and Lieutenant Guelph to the Commissioner, when, putting aside all questions of his rank, he formally demanded Miss Martin's hand in marriage.

Her father now was in a quandary. He had a genuine regard for this young hot-head who wore his heart so palpably upon his gold-laced sleeve, but at the same time the Commissioner was bound – as he at pompous length explained – 'By a deep sense of duty to my Sovereign and in view of recent difficulties relating to a similar – h'm – problem in the case of the heir-apparent—'

'My brother's case, sir,' William interrupted, 'does not apply to me. There is no smallest possibility of my ascension to the throne, and therefore no reason why I should not marry whom I please. If Sarah will accept me I'll be honoured. And she will, for she has promised – if the King will recognize her as my wife. And if he won't—'

'If His Majesty will not, Sir,' said Mr Martin smoothly, 'there is no law in the land to make the marriage valid. Would you, who profess to love her, condemn her to a life of shame?'

'There is no shame in honest love,' protested William, turning red, 'but before God, sir, I swear – my father *shall* consent!'

There was no holding him. He travelled post-haste to Windsor the same day to find on his arrival that the King was out hunting with the stag-hounds. Failing his father, he sent a message to the Queen and had to wait her pleasure to receive him.

It was not the most propitious moment he could have chosen, to implore his mother's intercession with the King on his behalf.

The poor lady's peace of mind had been disturbed enough by the breach between the King and their eldest son, due to the latter's mad infatuation for 'that Woman', and she was in no mood to hear that William had been similarly afflicted.

Du lieber Himmel! Was there an infection, then, of marriage? Were both these sons gone crazy – or would they drive their father so together with their wickedness? First one and then the other – and the King was

in bad health. He never slept. He had a fever. The
doctors had advised that he should hunt for exercise to
relieve his mind, and now so soon as he comes a little
better – God be thanked! – so must he be made again
ill with this talk of marrying. Who is it? Miss – Miss
Martin? . . . *Ach Ja!* Charming. *Wunderschön*. No
doubt. The Queen was ready to believe it, but the
young lady's personal attraction could not make possible what already was *im*possible – *nicht wahr?* Had
William not heard then of the Royal Marriage Act?

'Yes!' shouted William. 'And a monstrous wicked
violation of all natural—'

Aber! The Queen threw up her hands to cover her
shocked ears – that he should dare! Would he have her
ladies in the next room to hear him?

'Let them!' retorted William, inexcusably. Let the
whole world hear him. He had nothing to disguise. He
had come to plead his cause – an honest cause. Any
commoner – a cabin-boy – had the right to plead as
much. 'Pray, Madam,' William slithered to his knees, 'I
beseech – I implore you – speak to the King. Induce him
to see reason.'

Frenziedly he jogged his mother's elbow. She must
heed him. She must listen. She *must* speak to the King.
It meant his life, his love!

'Love! Love!' The Queen took her hand from her
ears to let one fall on William's tousled head. A sigh
broke and wavered in a smile. 'Always I hear this word.
What does it mean? Where, then, is this love of which
so much is spoken? You, my son, who have of love to
spare and give away, give none of it to me – your
mother. Not? Yes, yes, I will speak for you, *liebes Kind*.
It will do no good and may do harm, but still – yes – I
will speak.'

She did, that very night; and the King, in a rare state,
sat down and wrote to Howe.

On returning from hunting this evening the Queen desired to see me before I went to dinner. It was to communicate to me the arrival of William. I find it indispensably necessary to remove him from the Commissioner's house at Portsmouth. And therefore desire that either the Hebe may be removed to the Plymouth station or William placed on board the 32 gun frigate that is there. I merely throw out what occurs to me on a very unpleasant and unexpected event. . . .

Not so unexpected surely with marriage in the air, the Prince of Wales in disgrace, and William despondently covering the return journey to Portsmouth in a carriage. From Godalming *en route* he writes to Mr Martin:

Jan. 30th, 1786.

DEAREST FRIEND,

All is over . . . I shall be with you at breakfast tomorrow morning at ten, and then proceed to Plymouth, and from thence to another ship to America. . . . Say everything that is proper to the poor, unfortunate Sarah.

I am, dear sir,
Yours sincerely,
WILLIAM.

He found that Sarah had not yet left her father's house, but that Mr Martin remained adamantine in his refusal to allow a meeting between the two. William was frantic. To see her once to say goodbye was all he asked. A felon would be given that much grace.

The Commissioner, touched by the boy's genuine emotion, agreed to grant five minutes for an interview. Five minutes in eternity for William.

She came, composed but very pale, with shadows like

faint bruises underneath her eyes that were grey-washed, as though the colour had been drowned in them from weeping.

'I have to leave you,' William said below his breath. 'But I shall never leave the thought of you. Had I been different. . . .' His throat closed, and the living seconds fled before their pain. They were too young for this.

'I would not,' she whispered, 'have you different.'

That broke him: he gave a short cry and took her. 'God send you all the love that you deserve,' he blurted, agonized, 'and that I am not allowed to . . .'

They clung together, those two children, lost in misery beyond desire, seeking comfort in the moment's sight and touch, crushed by a destiny devoid of reason, coldly merciless to part them, who asked nothing of each other but to love.

Out of some far-off vacancy he heard the small, hidden sound of her tears, and felt her fingers light as moths upon his lips, and eyes. Her voice came, achingly, through the darkness. 'God save you, Sir. God bless and keep you . . . always.'

Then her father entered, watch in hand, and William went from her, blindly . . . .

Never to see her again.

He took with him her face framed in a miniature he had begged from her father, and to him he wrote since he must not write to her:

HEBE, *Feb*. 6*th*, 1786.

DEAREST SIR,

We are thus far on our way to Plymouth. Our cruise has been full of events. We sailed, you may remember on the Tuesday at noon. The next morning we found ourselves off Dunnose, and as it blew strong from the westward we bore up for St Helen's;

in the evening when we we were within a mile of the ledge the wind suddenly shifted to the N N W and we immediately hauled our wind and began to beat down. . . .

In a heavy squall as we were standing off, the main yard gave way in the slings, and we found it badly sprung. The only thing we then had to do was to bear up for Guernsey, where we anchored on Thursday at noon, and lay all the next day to repair our damage. We sailed again Saturday morning and found it necessary to take shelter here from the badness of the weather. We shall remain in Torbay till the wind shifts.

I hope a *certain person* is in good health and spirits. As for myself . . . God knows I have suffered enough in my own mind and do still. To my lovely girl, I leave it to you, sir, to say to her what you think proper. I love her from the bottom of my heart, and only wish I had been in the situation of life to have married her. My best wishes and prayers shall be always offered up to heaven for her welfare.

I once more beg your forgiveness, and hope you will ever consider that I am, sir,

Your most affectionate
but unfortunate friend
WILLIAM.

And two weeks later this:

To Commissioner Martin.

HEBE, OFF PLYMOUTH,
Feb. 19*th,* 1789.

DEAR SIR,

Upon my arrival at Plymouth, I found your first letter, and the morning we sailed your second came to hand. I am fully sensible of the friendship and regard with which you have always honoured me, and I hope to deserve a continuation of it. . . .

I find absence has increased my passion. What I feel on this unhappy subject is not to be expressed. Everything conspires to make me regret my most worthy friend at Portsmouth. Mr Laforey[1] is a proud, imperious fellow and on bad terms with everybody at Plymouth. Mrs Laforey a proper West Indian, which I think the most disagreeable character. I make their house a lodging-house and am as little there as possible. I shall never again find the comfort I did in your hospitable house . . . Had I been your son you could not have treated me with greater tenderness.

Nothing has yet transpired of my future destination. The *Pegasus* is ordered to be commissioned; most probably she intends to take me to America. The sooner the better. . . .

Do pray give my best wishes to the dear object of my heart, and tell her what you think proper. Love her I do, and hope to do so all my life-time.

'All my lifetime. . . .' It was none the less emphatic for long reckoning. He was not yet twenty-one.

The King's letter to Lord Howe did more than serve its purpose in the successful termination of an event both 'unexpected and unpleasant'.

It increased in his son the gloomy belief that he was the victim of some fatal persecution.

If the course of true love in the normal destiny of man was never permitted to run smooth, in William's case it was beset with cyclones, his hopes wrecked almost before they had ventured out of harbour.

So be it! Never again would he follow a star to find his course abandoned by its setting. His father's and the

[1] Commissioner of Plymouth Dockyard.

hand of every man, was turned against him. He was mocked. His shipmates – the whole Navy – must have heard of his removal from the house of the Commissioner of Portsmouth.

Knowing his tendency to exaggerate in the attitude of those around him any symptoms that could be construed into adverse criticism of himself, his state of mind almost induced him to abandon his career. He would quit the Navy – 'or at least,' he wrote to Mr Martin, 'refuse to serve with particular officers'. Those no doubt who may have chivvied him past bearing.

But notwithstanding this defiance, he had no choice in the selection of his shipmates, or his ship. The King had spoken, and in April 1786 he was appointed to the *Pegasus* – as Captain.

*

Promotion had been easy, or easy enough to cause a certain amount of jealousy among those who may have more deserved to be promoted than a Prince. On the other hand, Nelson, with whom William at this time renewed acquaintance, wrote in glowing terms of him:

> He has his foibles as well as private men, but they are far outbalanced by his virtues. In his professional line he is superior to nearly two-thirds, I am sure on the list, and in his attention to orders, and in respect to his superior officers, I hardly know his equal. His Royal Highness keeps up a strict discipline in his ship, and without paying him any compliment, she is one of the finest ordered frigates I have seen.

Whether this testimonial – since Nelson as well as 'private men' may have also had his foibles – was prompted by less regard for discipline than Royalty, is hard to say, but there certainly appears to have been an absence of any discipline at all on the occasion of Captain Guelph's twenty-first birthday.

This event was celebrated in the *Pegasus* on 12 August, 1786, off Halifax, Nova Scotia, when his brother officers in the ward-room entertained him to a dinner.

The cook that day surpassed himself in providing a sumptuous spread. The provisions which had been fetched from port the day before, consisted of stuffed goose, eel-pie, and half an ox roasted which the honoured guest insisted should be shared by every man aboard – creams, pasties, fruit of all kinds, and a pine-apple. William took his sword to cut a slice of it and shout: ' 'Ods blood! Why – here's me head! I'll wager I'm the first afloat to eat his head! Come! We'll eat me head! . . .' His sword went whizzing – slick! – to cut another slice and send a clean half of the pineapple flying to the beams. William caught it on his sword point, scooped out the juicy flesh, and solemnly crowned himself amidst yells of applause from his delighted hosts.

'Send for the cook! Come on, fellows! The cook! We'll drink to him!' They did. Then the cook, too, must return it; then every sailor had to have his tot of rum. 'And let there be no stinting!' roared the Captain as he rose – to make a speech. Nobody listened, every-body sang, and William gave a sentimental solo:

> Under floods that are deepest
> Which Neptune obey
> Over rocks that are steepest
> Love will find out the way
> Love will find ou-ou-*hout* the WAY.

And then they gave 'The King' with shouts to shake the wooden walls, and not content with that, they needs must roar in chorus:

Here's a health unto His Majesty
With fa la *la*
Conversion to his enemies
With fa la *la*
And he that will not pledge his health
I wish him neither wit nor wealth
But a good stout rope to HANG himself . . .

By that time half the company were under the table and William on top of it, dancing the hornpipe, and sending glasses, platters, pineapple, crashing – with him – to the floor. Whereupon those who had not yet passed completely out, hoisted him to their shoulders and carried him to the main deck where he was received by the sailors, who, having each had a treble allowance of grog, insisted on their privilege of carrying their Captain. Up and down the deck they ran with him to such a din of cheering as never had been heard at sea since the British beat the French. William had lost his pineapple and was in danger of losing his head which was barely an inch from the beams, and, at the rate they were going and the state they were in, might have been struck off his shoulders any moment.

This display of loyalty and devotion was watched by a group of giggling midshipmen who had been thought too young to be admitted to the party. One of them, Byam Martin, brother of Sarah, records it in his memoirs, as: 'altogether a strange scene, and one that would have astonished the members of a temperance society'.

It might also have astonished Captain Nelson, who heaps praise on further praise when he says: 'In short, he promises to be what we all hope and wish, the restorer of the ancient glory of the British Navy. . . .' Little dreaming – though Nelson had his dreams and his ambitions – that the glory of the British Navy was to be immortalized in him.

From Halifax the *Pegasus* sailed to the West Indies, and came to anchor at the British station of Antigua, where Nelson, the officer in command of the Leeward Islands, was busy introducing reform and innovations in the dockyards.

The friendship that had slackened off in the three years that had elapsed since the episode at Cuba, was now resumed to William's great advantage.

Nelson was at that time twenty-eight, as odd as ever in his dress, with the same long pigtail and shabby uniform, but thinner – a very pigmy of a fellow, who looked as if he were on the verge of a decline. It had been said he was consumptive, yet his physical resources were unlimited. He had twice William's stamina and would walk him off his feet on a tour of inspection round the islands. It was as though that emaciated body were fuelled by the nervous energy within it, that kept its spirit feverishly lit. He seldom stopped talking; he had a bee in his bonnet over the malpractices of the contractors and prize-agents connected with the naval service and the merchant traders, all of whom, he was convinced, had scandalously over-charged the British Government in the past, and would do so in the future, unless the trouble could be rectified. He must see to it. He must instil some law and order on this station.

In the noonday heat he tramped, waxen-faced, shining with sweat, his eyes in all places at once, and his boots white with dust, while William at his heels, gasped: 'Egad, sir! I'll melt in grease if you go on!'

'This slave traffic,' Nelson declared, unheedful, 'is a monstrous outrage, Sir. It must be stopped. By God, it must! It shall! As for those poxy thieves – their days are numbered. The fraudulent accounts have been sent home. We'll see what we shall see.'

William would have gladly seen a long cool drink and a seat in the shade, but the indefatigable little Captain kept him at it till the day's work was done.

Unfortunately with all the will in the world, and the King's son to support him, Nelson could not induce the Board of Admiralty to raise an inquiry with regard to foul dealing on the part of the contractors. By his zealous interference on the Government's behalf, he only succeeded in turning prejudice and criticism to himself, which lasted until a series of startling triumphs induced those in power to receive him, not only as a naval genius, but as a hero.

But in spite of his activities in various directions, Nelson must have allowed himself a certain time for dalliance, for it was on the Leeward Islands station that he met and became engaged to Mrs Nisbet, the young widowed niece of the President.

Confidence for confidence may perhaps have been exchanged between Captain Nelson and his junior, who, still smarting from the wounds of separation from his Sarah, possibly contrasted his own consuming passion with his friend's unsentimental attitude towards the lady of his choice, for – 'I never saw a lover so easy – or say so little,' William told him a day or two before the wedding.

'He says the least,' replied Nelson with his twisted smile, 'says the most – in love.'

'And the least – or the most – said by those who suffer it,' retorted William, 'is that 'tis a vapour – a disease. If you sicken of a fatal malady, either you lose consciousness or rave. You may have a fine esteem for your good lady, but damme, sir, it's not what *I* call – love.'

He who had raved but had not yet lost consciousness, could speak with more authority on that all-absorbing subject than could Nelson. He at that time had still some way to go before he, too, was star-crossed.

'I am married to an amiable woman,' he wrote to a friend on his honeymoon, 'and that makes amends for everything.' A not conspicuously fervent confession for a bridegroom.

William was best man, and if at that flower-filled altar he watched those two united with a tugging at his heart for all that might have been and was not to be – for him, he didn't show it. At the reception held afterwards at the house of Mr Herbert, the bride's uncle, he led the toasts, made speeches, and was the most cheery of them all.

When Nelson in command of the *Boreas* sailed in the autumn of that year, William greatly missed his friend. Nelson's successor was overbearing and unsociable. William had been accustomed to dine alternate days at Nelson's and his own table. All hospitality offered by the residents of Antigua had a painful similarity: dances, drawing-room card-playing at drawing-room stakes, dreary parties at some merchant planter's or official's house, when the *élite* of the island were invited to meet him and pay court. Antigua lacked the gaiety of Jamaica. It was as lifeless as an English market-town on a wet day. But even in the rain, William thought nostalgically, England could produce some pretty faces. Here there were none; the best of them were colourless and the worst of them were black. He was sick of the sight of grinning negresses, of simpering young ladies and their corpulent Mammas in hoops of the fashion of a dozen years ago. He loathed the heat and he disliked his new Commander; and above all he had nothing much to do.

But none of this was any reason why he should withdraw his ship from harbour and sail back to Halifax without instructions.

Not only was it a gross act of defiance, but his first intimation in the seven years he'd been at sea that the King's son could, and would, do as he pleased. He gave the authorities to understand as much, when as a punishment for disobedience he was ordered to Quebec, the least desirable of all ports in the winter. If Antigua had been too hot, Quebec was far too cold, so without any more discussion, and without a by-your-leave, he hoisted sail and set off in the *Pegasus* for Plymouth.

So much for one, who, a year ago had promised to be 'the restorer of the ancient glory of the British Navy'. Men had been court-martialled for less.

One can offer no excuse for his flagrant misbehaviour, as unaccountable as it was foolish, and for which in a few years' time he so dearly had to pay. It may be that Nelson's good opinion of him had been too often aired – to turn his head.

'Princes seldom find a disinterested person to communicate their thoughts to,' Nelson wrote with better sentiment than grammar. 'I do not pretend to be that person: but of this be assured by a man who I trust never did a dishonourable act, that I am interested only that Your Royal Highness should be the greatest and best man this country ever produced.'

What Nelson thought of his protégé's escapade has never been recorded, but the King thought enough of it to send an urgent message that he was to be held in Plymouth when he landed – in disgrace.

His brothers, George and Frederick, the latter now created Duke of York, seeing here an opportunity to annoy their father, who with his petty tyranny had so often anoyed them, hurried down to Plymouth to give the truant their support, and to paint the place red between them, with their welcome.

The King, in ordering detention for his son, had in mind a drastic punishment devoid of social contact in a dull provincial town; but with the arrival of two more Royal Princes, the dull provincial town woke to bustling activity. Flags flew, crowds cheered, and excited girls flung flowers as the brothers, arm-in-arm, paraded through the streets, while salutes were fired from any ship that carried guns whenever they approached the harbour.

It was a gala week: dances every night given by rival hostesses, each determined to out-do her neighbour in hospitality and entertainment; balls in the public rooms, masquerades, feasting, and fun.

It was at one of these assemblies that William met Miss Wynne, a merchant's daughter. True, her name did not begin with M – unless inverted – but she was the first who had succeeded in bringing him back to consciousness of any feminine charm since he had parted from 'the dear object of his heart'.

Miss Wynne was the antithesis of Sarah: a gay, highly-coloured girl, big-bosomed, boisterous. The ladies of Plymouth might perhaps have called her vulgar. She was jewelled like a begum; her caps were over-trimmed; her waist too big, her arms too fat, and what the Prince could see in her . . . And so on.

What the Prince saw in her, others had already seen before him. Miss Wynne was a young lady with dozens of admirers and a dowry to attract a dozen more. It was, however clearly not her dowry that attracted William. It must have been her wit, her capacity for telling yarns that were ever so slightly shocking, with the Devonshire burr in her voice and invitation in her eyes, to which William may doubtless have responded as any sailor would – or maybe not. At all events his attentions to the sparkling Miss Wynne were marked enough to be reported higher than the houses on the Hoe. The King's messengers plied back and forth in coaches along the Great West Road to London twice a week. The King's

ears soon heard the drift of all the gossip. 'What – what
– hey? William playing the fool again? Give him the
Andromeda and send him back to – Halifax!'

The King's mind though slowly sagging could control
an errant son.

So, out came the Royal mandate in the shape of an
Admiralty order.

It was a thunderclap to William. He was scarcely
given time to say goodbye.

But he sailed out of Plymouth Harbour in better case
than he came in, with drums and fifes and a crowd on
the quay, and Miss Wynne in a scarlet cloak, with a
laugh on her lips, tears in her eyes, and a damp handkerchief waving in the breeze, to see him off.

William in his cocked hat and gold lace, his hair in a
queue, his face a-beam, bowing and saluting in answer
to the cheers, paused, with one foot on the gangway to
look back as she came forward; and there for all the
world, and his grinning officers, to see, he took her
hands – damp handkerchief and all – and kissed her.

Well!

And as the *Andromeda*, all sails set, her white ensign
flying, and her Captain on the bridge drew bravely out
of port, the band struck up 'The girl I left behind me!'

Chapter Five

A MURMUR went about the Court. The King was . . .
indisposed. He had not been well for some time past.
His symptoms certainly were strange. He had grown
stout and florid; his eyes goggled, his face was a bright
brick red, its colour heightened by the white powdered
wig he wore, day in, day out. It was murmured that he
slept in it – if he ever slept at all. His gentlemen
reported that he didn't, but babbled half the night,
talking to himself, or reading, of all things, *King Lear*
aloud. And he also read *King Lear* to the Princesses,
and would tell them, 'You are all Cordelias – everyone
Cordelias. No Gonerils – no Gonerils or Regans – all
Cordelias.'

It began to be alarming.

His pages told, with giggles, of an incident that had
occurred in Windsor Great Park. The King out driving
with the Queen, had suddenly shouted: 'Stop! There –
there he is!' And got out of the carriage, went up to an
oak-tree, removed his hat, and ceremoniously bowed.
He then went through a show of shaking hands with
one of the lower branches. The poor Queen, almost
swooning in her fright, sent a footman to his side. 'If
you please, Your Majesty—'

'What – what! How dare you interrupt? Do you not
see I am engaged in conversation with the King of
Prussia?'

He was got home and put to bed, and purged and
cupped and plastered. The news flew: the King had
caught a chill, was in a fever. Nothing of a serious

account. . . . He was soon recovered and about again, strutting in the gardens down at Kew, dressed in the semi-martial uniform he had recently affected: a blue coat, red collar and cuffs, and a cocked hat with a rosette perched a-top of his white wig, chattering away with the utmost affability to everyone he met, the gardeners, his gentlemen, his wife's ladies.

There were three of these in constant attendance on the Queen: Lady Effingham, gentle, charming, but not over-burdened with wit: Mrs Schwellenberg, truculent, portly, and hideous, who had a peculiar passion for toads which she collected and kept under glass; and least of the trio, a demurely attractive young person whom the Schwellenberg greatly disliked. Miss wrote books, which no well-brought-up young girl had any right to do, and which to Frau Schwellenberg's Teutonic mind was a symptom of excessive immorality; Miss was too clever, and far too observant; she kept a discreet watchful eye on the King. She also kept a journal – to the advantage of posterity if not to Mrs Schwellenberg's.

And in her journal Fanny Burney writes: 'We are all here in a most uneasy state. The King is better and worse so frequently and changes so daily, backwards and forwards, that everything is to be apprehended . . . I dreadfully fear he is on the eve of some severe fever.'

And a few days later we are told that: 'The King went out in his chaise, with the Princess Royal, for an airing. I looked from my window to see him; he was all smiling benignity, but gave so many orders to the postilions, and got in and out of the carriage twice, with such agitation, that again my fear of a great fever hanging over him grew more and more powerful. . . .'

So we have it – one day better, one day worse. Some-

times he called for music. 'You play, Miss Burney? You
are musical? What? Let us have music. Send for Mr
Papendiek.'

Or he would demand to be alone, and play his own
music at the harpsichord, singing doleful hymns. Or
he would sit for hours, silent, plunged in melancholy,
brooding on the loss of his colonies. . . . His beloved
American colonies. A whole continent gone. Lost. . . .
Lost. There had been a war – a war of Independence.
America was independent. The Americans had severed
their connection with him and with his Government as
an axe fells a branch from a tree. The Americans, born
of the blood of his people, were now and for ever more
a race apart. Strangers, though brothers in root and kin.
. . . My colonies. America. 'Why,' he wailed piteously,
'why – why have I lost America? What was Lord North
about to let me lose America?'

The poor swollen body was shaken with weeping,
great rending sobs that turned in an instant to fury. He
was up on his feet in a passion, calling on God to witness the monstrous blunder of that madman North.
That madman. A man both blind and . . . and . . . He
stayed his clenched fists as they beat the air and dropped
them against his sides. A page, not giggling now,
listened behind a curtain and entered, trembling, to
ask: 'Did Your Majesty require—?'

'Nothing, I want nothing. Leave me – leave me in
peace – in peace.'

The King went back to his harpsichord – his kind
and soothing harpsichord. He played Handel. There
was surprising magic in those thick, clumsy fingers; the
notes rang like a tender voice that spoke quietly – of
danger! Danger – of what? . . . A flash, forgotten, re-
curred with ominous warning, startlingly clear, blaz-
oned white-hot across infernal darkness. Treachery! It
had been whispered – he could hear the whisper still,

that Burke – the traitor Burke had dared to say a word.
A strangely sounding word. Reform!

Parliamentary Reform.

A cold wind swept through the tortured brain to
cleanse it of confusion. The scattered thoughts were
disciplined as soldiers to command . . . *Parliamentary
Reform*. A deliberate insult to the King and the King's
'Friends' who had held rights of privilege since the
reign of Charles II. But what of *before* the reign of
Charles II – hey? What was it – what – what was it that
Junius – Junius – that damned, impertinent anonymous
scribe who dared accost the King's Majesty with scur-
rilous public letters what was it he had written?

'The same pretended Power which robs an English
subject of his birthright may rob an English King of his
Crown. . . .' So! One kept one's memory. And in keeping memory it were possible to keep one's – keep one's
reason. *'Who robs an English subject . . . and an English
King of his Crown.'*

An English King had been robbed of his colonies.
Yes! And of his Crown in those colonies. . . . Pretended
Power. Was that – was that why America and his own
sons defied him? George – and his Woman. It was
whispered George had married her – whispered, with a
buzzing that grew voluminous in sound until it seemed
one's head was full of bees – and Mr Fox. A fox – for
emblem. Good-lack-a-day! A pretty emblem – a good
sign to carry through the streets to lead the Whigs and
his own son George, the Prince of Wales . . . My son!
. . . My sons! What of my sons! What of William who
sailed the high seas against his orders? What of Frederick who had returned from Hanover demanding
favours? Frederick who asked that Turkish instruments
be introduced into the Guards' bands, with ornamental
tails. . . . 'Hey, Charlotte!'

His pale wife came hurrying. 'Frederick wants tails

introduced into the Guards' band and Turkish music.'

The poor soul thought he raved, but actually, on that point he did not. Frederick had insisted on Turkish musical instruments for the Guards' band, with crescents and ornamental tails by way of decoration. He had come without permission from Germany with this astonishing request, and was ordered back but didn't go.

Instead he stayed at Carlton House, played deep every night, drank deeper, and entertained his friends at Boodle's with an edifying imitation of his father in a brain-storm. Frederick was almost as good a mimic as George; nothing was lacking in that jocular performance to create side-splitting applause. The King's speech – his trick of repetition, his 'heys', his 'what – whats', his rolling eyes, his uncontrolled awkward gestures, all were caricatured by the Reverend Father in God the Prince-Bishop, the Duke of York, to the mirth of the blades of St James's.

Meanwhile at Windsor, doctors met in consultation on the health of the King and reported vaguely 'a disorder'.

*

The Prince of Wales in retirement with his lady in the Sussex village of Brighthelmstone began to wonder if his father's illness were likely to be fatal. For if so . . .

He looked with longing at his love . . . If so, he could acknowledge her before the world; he could repeal that inhuman Royal Marriage Act, and proclaim her his Queen – and England's. Why not? She had culture, charm, and beauty, she would make a better consort than some guttural German princess. True, she had not been received into the Church of England, she might not be willing to renounce her popery – but that could be arranged. There was nothing that could *not* be arranged by order of the King. . . . Or he would abdicate, resign the throne to Frederick, who would be glad enough to take it. The possibility had already been discussed.

Thus, in some such fashion, the heir-apparent may have reasoned on the drive from Brighthelmstone to Windsor, when he went to pay his filial respects.

The King's physicians met him with long faces, and gave him an unsatisfactory, obscure report.

His Majesty's 'disorder' had been induced by water on the brain, caused doubtless in the first place by an accumulation of anxiety. His Majesty had been greatly disturbed by the loss of his American colonies. His Majesty suffered from a chronic condition of overheated blood. Remedies had been applied – purges, leeches, plasters. His Majesty's condition was improving; there was no cause for immediate alarm. His Majesty that day had been distinctly better, refused to go to bed, had expressed the wish to dine with the Family and His Royal Highness, of whose arrival His Majesty had been informed. The King would be pleased to see His Royal Highness. . . .

George with impatience heard them out. He was touched that his father wished to see him. Each previous attempt that he had made to repair the breach between them had been rebuffed. Perhaps under his supreme selfishness he may have had some latent affection for the author of his being, who, ever since the affair with Mrs Fitzherbert had ignored his existence, and openly avowed that he had ceased to be a son in all but name.

The King's welcome was startling and effusive. He took the Prince in his arms, kissed him repeatedly, and babbled all the time: 'You see me now an old man. I am only fifty, but an old – old man. I said to Lady Effingham – "I am all at once an old man" – hey? Am'nt I turned old?'

He had. And George was shocked. For the first time
within his memory he saw the King without his wig:
he was scarcely recognizable; a stranger. His hair, grey
and lifeless, hung in wispy elf-locks over that poor,
harassed, receding brow; his pendulous chin showed a
nine days' growth of beard; his eyes protruded, his lips
were moist and unnaturally red; his face dark-veined
and swollen. Even his voice had changed, it had become
hoarse – almost incoherent. His hands moved incessantly pulling at his hair, huddling himself into his
purple dressing-gown, rubbing his chin in pitiful
apology. 'I itch. I am not shaved. You will excuse – I am
not shaved. They have refused to shave me. I cannot
sit still to be shaved. I am nervous – nervous. You will
dine – you will dine with me? What of your woman –
hey? Have you left her – have you come to your senses?
We must all – we must all come to our senses.' The
restless hand strayed gropingly towards the shattered
George, who, terrified, took it in both his own. 'You
will stay with me?' the dreadful voice continued. 'You
will stay – you will not leave me – my son – my son—'

His son choked back a sob, 'I'll not leave you, Sir.
Pray calm yourself – the doctors—'

'Doctors! Doctors! What care I for doctors? If they
would tell me the truth – but they tell lies – lies. I love
Doctor Heberden the best for he has not told me a lie.
He said that I was nervous: Sir George Baker has told
me a lie – a white lie, he says, but I hate a white lie! If
it will be a lie let it be a black lie. . . . Black. . . . You
have said you will stay – you will dine? We will all dine
– all dine together.' The distorted lips relaxed, the
wandering gaze cleared; the King made a visible supreme effort at control, his body straightened. 'I am glad
to see you, George, my son,' the King said, quietly.

Unable to hold his tears, George bent his lips to his
father's hand, muttered something, and rushed from the

room. And he stood, regardless of the footmen, weeping unrestrainedly with his back to that curtained door.

'Meanwhile,' remarks Miss Burney, 'a stillness the most uncommon reigned over the whole house. Nobody stirred . . . there seemed a strangeness in the house most extraordinary.' And later in the day she tells us, 'Oh, my dear friends, what a history! The King at dinner had broken forth into positive delirium, which long had been menacing all who saw him closely; and the Queen was so overpowered as to fall into hysterics. All the Princesses were in misery, and the Prince of Wales burst into tears. No one knew what was to follow. . . .'

Soon the whole of England knew what was to follow. The news was carried up and down the Kingdom and out of it, across the seven seas.

*

William was in Jamaica when he heard it. His stay in Halifax had been of short duration, but not too short for him. The station, regarded by the Navy as the most unpleasant in the western hemisphere, was by Captain Guelph thought to be an exile, a further penance inflicted on him by way of punishment for breach of discipline. Complaint to higher quarters would, he knew, be unavailing. To all intents he had been banished.

At the begining of the winter, however, he had instructions to sail for the West Indies and arrived there in the middle of November 1788.

The *Andromeda* came to harbour in Port Royal at sundown, with the Blue Mountains turned violet under a sky aflame, and light melting in the shadows on the hillsides, and feathering the tops of palms with gold. It was his third visit to the islands but he never failed to approach them with the same thrill of expectancy that faded as soon as he set foot ashore. He knew too well the dreary routine that awaited him, the celebrations and the crowds, the grinning blacks, the cheering whites, the tedious social round of presentations and palaver.

This time it happened that his arrival at the port was unexpected, and he landed without the customary fuss, accompanied only by his First Lieutenant. It was a new experience to come ashore with none to bow and scrape and follow him and stare. None had any notion who he was or whence he came; only his uniform to mark him and that served as sufficient introduction to the public rooms which was the one club the place possessed. There he played billiards with the Colonel-Commandant, and beat him. He had several drinks and told several yarns, and then staggered the Colonel by requesting him to have his regiment parade for his inspection in the morning. The Colonel thought he was drunk. The Colonel reddened and spluttered in his glass and inquired, with boiling sarcasm: 'And suppose, Sir, I should grant your – hah! – very natural request, will you permit that I should come aboard and inspect your sailors – eh?'

'With all my heart!' said William and, nothing daunted, called for a fresh bottle on the strength of it.

The Colonel had scarcely got his breath when a Captain of his regiment strolled in to make a nonchalant announcement. The *Andromeda* had arrived in port with Prince William aboard as her Commander.

His brief respite was over, the room in a buzz, and the company upon its feet at the salute. The Colonel, scarlet as his coat, muttered his apologies, but William, laughing, shook him by the hand. 'Not a bit of it – not a bit of it! What say you to another bottle, sir – to show there's no ill-feeling? You shall come aboard to see my ship – if you'll let me see your soldiers. Pray, be seated, gentlemen – don't incommode yourselves on my account – and we will *all* take wine!'

All did; and all were merry, till the Captain who had brought the news remembered, suddenly, a letter. . . . It had come from England for the Prince, and been held by him, who acted as a kind of honorary secretary to the rooms, and had been awaiting His Royal Highness's arrival.

William recognized his brother George's feathers on the seal and tore it open. They saw his face change as he read it. There was a moment of tense silence, then: 'Gentlemen,' he turned to them, crushing the letter in his hand, 'The King is gravely ill. My father is – I am told that he is—' there he stuck; he could not say it, but those watching guessed the rest. Rumours had reached them even on that island in the Caribbean Sea.

Their unspoken sympathy was less for the King than for his son whose stiffened lip showed the struggle for control. But the Colonel saw a lad young enough to be his own, and laid his hand an instant on his shoulder. 'God save the King,' said the Colonel, gruff-voiced. And: 'Thank you, sir – and thank you all,' said William, and abruptly left the room.

He immediately applied to higher command for leave to go home. He was refused. He had taken leave without permission once, he must await his orders now, and Authority's convenience.

He chafed at the delay. All were in conspiracy against him. The awful nature of his father's illness preyed on his mind. He must keep a strict observance on himself. He would drink less so that his blood should not become overheated. . . He thought of Sarah and could see the Hand of God in the prevention of that marriage. What a mercy! His poor beloved Sarah . . . To have inflicted her children with his heritage. He would never marry. More than ever now was it clear he must not marry. Henceforth he would be wedded to his ship.

It was about this time that his officers and men observed a tightening up of discipline on the part of their Commander. He would spend hours in his cabin dictating interminable orders, and was a stickler for etiquette in dress.

[1]With the established uniform the officers and gentlemen belonging to His Majesty's ship I have the honour to command are when sent upon all Duties to wear Boots, gold laced Hats, black Stocks, and their hair queued constantly. . . .

Every morning at daylight the Quarter-deck, main-deck, Forecastle and gangways are to be regularly *washed*. The Quarter-deck to be every morning *scrubbed* with the stone. The lower deck and gun-room to be washed with Vinegar.

He then levels an attack on the midshipmen.

From the scandalous and disgraceful behaviour of the Gentlemen, it is my positive orders and directions that the Officer of the Watch at sea and the Officer carrying on the duty at an anchor do at six bells in in the morning send down the Day-Mate to have the Gentlemen's Hammocks lashed up and taken down ready to be immediately brought up when they are piped up.

And finally a singular proviso:

The order requesting and directing the First Lieut-enant or Commanding Officer to see all strangers out

---

[1] Captain's order's, *Andromeda*, 1788, reproduced by permission of Navy Records Society.

of His Majesty's Ship under my Command at gun-fire is by no means meant to restrain the Officers and men from having either Black or White Women on Board through the night, so long as the discipline is unhurt by the indulgence.

Which may account for the unsavoury legend of a charmer from Jamaica who was, somewhat surprisingly, named 'Wowski', and is supposed to have been stowed away in the *Andromeda* on her voyage home to England for the delectation of the Captain and his crew.

If leave was slow in coming, news was slower, and when at last he heard, his trouble was increased. His mother wrote that the King's malady had been augmented by a 'bilious fever'. There was talk of a Regency. The King's affairs were temporarily carried out by the Prince of Wales, herself, and Mr Pitt. There was much debate and intrigue. George as heir-presumptive had first claim to the Regency, but he was at loggerheads with Mr Pitt and the bosom friend of Mr Fox. Mr Fox had been recalled from a holiday in Italy. A total change of Government was to be expected.

George wrote that Pitt was plotting against him and playing for time, that Fox was his staunchest supporter, and that ladies wore Regency caps. . . . Frederick wrote in the New Year that their father was unmistakably recovering. When the Archbishop of Canterbury was reading morning prayers to the King in his room, 'Rex' had interrupted the service suddenly with hunting-calls: ' 'Ware fox! Hey! Tallee-ho! Hark-a-way—' and so on. Everyone had been delighted to see him jovial.

More than ever William worried. It all sounded very ominous, and the signs of improvement indicated by Frederick did not, in his opinion, augur well. He yearned to be at home. He had a deep affection for his father, in spite of the fact that he considered him responsible for the ruin of his own, and, possibly, his lovely Sarah's life. However, as things had turned out now that the King was . . . No! never say it. And he prayed on his knees night and morning for his father's recovery.

At last, after weeks of suspense, he could stand it no longer. He would take the law into his own hands and risk the consequences and Authority's displeasure. In for a penny – in for a pound. At the worst they couldn't hang him!

So once more, without permission, William sailed away. His father's illness served as his excuse.

*

William landed at Spithead on 29 April to learn that the King was convalescent and the question of a Regency suspended. Although in Portsmouth the signs of jubilance were mild, in London, he was told, the decorations were tremendous. St James's was ablaze with coloured lights, all the clubs lit up with stars and Royal monograms, all the balconies festooned with gold and purple, and the Bank of England exhibited, besides illuminations, two pictures of the King and Mr Pitt.

Carlton House alone showed some restraint; a line of flambeaux, simply. The members of White's who had supported the Government and Pitt in the controversy against the Prince and the Regency Bill, stated flatly that the Prince was – disappointed.

Fox and his Whigs at Brooks's kept their counsel, while the Prince's followers in clubland laid their bets and waited to see which way the wind would blow. The doctors had not said the King was cured.

But when on 23 April 1789, the King attended in person a Thanksgiving Service at St Paul's in celebration of his recovery, they were forced to acknowledge hope lost.

In clubland the rejoicings were not universal. The stakes had run high.

However, those who did not give their King a welcome on that day were an insignificant minority. People from all parts thronged the streets to shout their 'Huzzas!' as the King with the Queen beside him drove along the route in his glass coach drawn by eight of his cream-coloured horses from Hanover.

All the ladies wore caps edged with purple, and caps embroidered with 'God save the King' worked in gold thread on white satin – an elegant taste.

From the highest to the lowest all London was *en fête*. The rich gave balls and banquets to celebrate the great occasion; the poor declared their joy no less sincerely in the sharing of a penny bloater in addition to their daily bread. Even the felons in Newgate turned in their chains to cry: 'Long live the King and damnation to the Prince of Wales!' There was not a man – beyond a few – throughout the country's breadth that would not sooner see the King mad on his throne than his son sane in his place before him.

For even in that underworld, as far removed from palaces as Hell from Heaven, there where hunger stalked and man did not so much exist as he fermented in his rags and his starved flesh – even there they had heard tell of the Prince's debts and his extravagance, his grant from Parliament, the wanton waste of money. Money! A word so strange to them in whose sight a fourpenny piece was a less likely marvel than the sight of the Lord himself. . . . Talk they had heard to wonder at in those festering places where such as they were privileged to dwell. Privileged indeed – in gutters and holes where none came to question, or ask rent of the roofless, or raise up his voice among them to speak of the Rights of Man.

That voice was yet to come.

William had missed the procession. He arrived six days too late.

He stayed in Portsmouth long enough to see his ship docked and his officers and men ashore, and then drove up to Windsor. He worked himself into a frenzy on the way, dreading the interview with his father and worrying the question of how best he could explain this second fall from grace. For if the King were now himself again there'd be the devil and all to pay. He'd done it twice – there was the rub! Though surely to God in such extenuating circumstances a son had the right to return to his father – with, or without, permission. He could make no sense of the Admiralty's silence on the subject. He had heard nothing when he landed. Either the Sea Lords were preparing, stealthily, to connive at a court martial or they would let the matter go and hush it up. Finally, everything depended on the King and his attitude, and very largely on his health.

So in this frame of mind, ready to meet and face the worst (the King would rage without a doubt if he were better), William came to Windsor, unannounced. None it seems had any time for *him*.

He had been hurriedly deposited by his father's equerry, Colonel Manners, in the ladies' parlour, and there he sat in a fidget, surveying with disgust Mrs Schwellenberg's collection of live toads. What a hobby! But not inappropriate. They might well – decided William, pensively rubbing his nose – be the offspring of that old reptile with her yellow face, and her fat potato-jaw. . . . And just at that moment when his nerves were on edge and his temper boiling with the imagined slight offered him by Colonel Manners, both in his choice of a waiting-room, and the length of time he had to wait – just at that very moment Mrs Schwellenberg, unfortunately, chose to waddle in.

Seeing William there, she precipitously backed out

again, then, seeming to recollect herself, returned to tell him with a smile that was none the less ghastly for attempting to be coy: 'A t'ousand pardons, Your R'yal Highness, I t'ought it vass der Duke of York.'

'And what if it had been the Duke of York?' demanded William, up in arms.

The Schwellenberg visibly yellowed. 'But *naturlich* – Your R'yal Highness—'

'There's no naturlich about it. Has my brother got the plague then, that you avoid him?'

'No, no! Assuredly, Your R'yal—'

'Go,' said William briefly.

She went, and with alacrity; and according to her story, related in hysterics to the ladies, the Prince was heard to mutter something to the effect that, 'she deserved a good round dozen before the pages of the back-stairs and for two pins he'd give it her!'

One may or may not believe it.

But the incident, though trifling, had further disturbed William. It had shown him forcibly in what low esteem his brother Frederick was held at Court. Not that anybody cared a fig for the good opinion of old 'Schwelly', all the same she ruled the roost among his mother's hens, and it was common knowledge that her word with the Queen was only next to God's.

William saw himself in a predicament – forced to take sides for or against his brothers and at the same time to keep in favour with the King. A pretty coil and no mistake! There seemed to be no end to all the worry. As if he hadn't got enough to combat, with his own.

At last came Colonel Manners. His Majesty would see His Royal Highness.

Back again to all the same performance. Bowing, scraping, like a troop of monkeys in a circus. Who'd exchange the freedom of the sea and the deck of a ship that rides it, for this pantomime, this stuffy smell of

prisoned air and unwashed bodies that had never been
swept clean by the sea's spray – bodies that stank, not of
honest sweat, but of tinselled finery and stale scent? By
God! It was no life for a man – this!

The measured steps of Colonel Manners paused at
the curtained door.

'I'll announce myself,' said William, 'thank ye.'

At the end of the room by the window, the King sat
in his chair staring at nothing, and playing tunes on his
chair-arm with his fingers. He wore his Windsor dress
– the dark blue uniform with gold buttons and scarlet
facings – and his wig.

William had not seen his father for three years, and
he expected from all accounts to see him worse. He was
inexpressibly relieved. The King appeared to be in
glowing health, his face shone like a red sun in a fog.
True he had put on weight, was startlingly fat and had
three chins, and his bulging eyes were almost swallowed
by their puffy lids – but he was well, he was cured, and
reassuringly exuberant.

Never had William been greeted by his father with
such warmth. He was wrapped in embraces, wept upon,
repeatedly and moistly kissed. Then, laughing and
crying in one breath, the King led him to a sofa, and
bade his gentlemen: 'Leave us – leave us – we wish to
be alone. Don't you see that William's come?' And as
the door closed he added with a secretive sideways look,
'They watch me. They think I am still – you know.
They still think that I am – hey?'

William swallowed something in his throat and
looked away from the mild gaze of those wandering
gooseberry eyes, 'I am more than happy, Sir' – he
mumbled, with his head turned to hide the shake in his
chin that he couldn't keep out of his voice – 'to see you
in such good spirits. I only wish that I—'

'Hey? What! What!' The King roused himself from

his smiling complacency. 'Good spirits, hey? Never been better. Never better. And what of you – ye scoundrel!' Playfully the King prodded him in the ribs. 'Runnin' away from the sea again to come back to your old father – what?' And another prod.

This gesture of familiarity, so unlike the King, agonized William into thinking the doctors had been over sanguine in their diagnosis of recovery; but the next minute his father began to tell him of the wonderful scene in St Paul's, and though he spoke with more than usual rapidity, he gave a vivid enough account of it all. William's doubts were again allayed. It was the greatest pity, the King said, that he had missed the celebrations, but William had no right to have come back – no right at all – without permission – hey? Not the first time he had disobeyed – 'But we'll forgive ye – we'll forgive ye. The Admiralty won't though,' chuckled the King, 'but that's for them to settle. I've more to bother me head than— Did ye know your brothers plot against me? My own sons – hey? But I'm supported.'

The loose smiling lips steadied, and in those empty bulging eyes was kindled a sudden spark, 'I'm supported,' the King said strongly, 'by a pack o' me own hounds to run a Fox and his cubs to the kill, with Pitt and myself as joint masters. Keep out o' politics, my son, keep out o' them is my advice to you. Politics and politicians are the devil. Go in for farming.'

'Sir, I would like—' began William, thinking to seize this opportunity to explain away his latest misdemeanour. He did not greatly relish being left to the mercies of the Admiralty – but—

'My farms,' said the King, not listening, 'have been grossly neglected since my illness.' All *that* he said, would have to be changed, now he was out and about again without a troop o' doctors at his heels. There was Keel's Farm at Mortlake. A tidy property. 'You must come around with me – you must come around with me on horseback. Do you ride? Do you hunt? Ye're no rider. We'll make a rider of you – hey? I propose to convert more of Richmond Park into arable land. There's plenty and more to spare. I shall soon be writing my articles again for the Annals of Agriculture. Did ye ever read my articles on agriculture? What? What? There's a lodge between Kew and Richmond – ye'd better go and see it – go and see it—'

'But – Sir – I—'

'Yes, you go and see it.' The King smiled round at him, and patted William's hand. 'I've a surprise for ye, my son – a good surprise. How'd ye like to be Duke of Clarence – hey? I'm going to make ye Duke o' Clarence.'

Here was news!

William left his father's presence much relieved. The doctors surely must be right. The King was well. Talkative, perhaps, but sane, thank God. More sane in this unwonted cordiality than in his brain-storms. . . . Duke of Clarence! He'd been wondering how long he'd have to wait for the Duchy to which he'd been entitled these three years. Still – not so bad – not at all so bad. And a house of his own at last. Not a schoolroom on Kew Green and not a palace, but a home. It was almost worth losing his command to get a home. And he might have both, a ship at sea, and a house on land. And God and the King willing, a wife to sit in it . . . Who knew?

All that now remained was to wait events and the King's official pleasure.

That came a month later, when he took his seat in the House of Lords as Duke of Clarence and St Andrews, Earl of Munster.

He gave a dinner at Willis's by way of celebration. No expense was spared. He was to receive a grant of twelve thousand a year. He could afford to be lavish.

He was.

Roses, red and white, bunched with blue ribbons festooned the walls of the banqueting room, and over the table where he and his brothers sat, the arms of the three were presented, entwined, surmounted by the Prince of Wales's feathers and supported on one side by the colours of the Coldstream Guards in compliment to Frederick, and on the other by a modest flag and anchor. At the base a scroll, bearing the words 'United for ever' in gold.

This display of brotherly affection, however, did not lessen William's own predicament. George and Frederick were openly antagonistic to the King. William, on the other hand, had every reason to be grateful to his father. But his brothers had stood by him when he was in disgrace at Plymouth – he could not very well desert them now when public opinion and the King were all against them.

To run with the hare and hunt with the hounds seemed a sneak-thief's game to William, yet what else was he to do? Offend his father just when he had been restored to favour and at a time when he'd been completely sunk by the Admiralty? His declared adherence to his brothers had heaped injury on insult in the estimation of the Sea Lords, who chose to regard this partisanship as an identification with politics, and a further reason to suggest it were better Captain Guelph stayed ashore than went to sea.

So William, left without a ship, looked round for a house instead.

He found one on the edge of Richmond Park: 'In the middle of the village,' so Mr Walpole tells us, 'with nothing but a short green apron to the river.'

It had belonged to a Mr Hobart, was small, compact, and approached by a modest drive in front with a courtyard and stabling at the back.

William renamed it Clarence Lodge and was as proud of his new home as any bride of hers. He drove over from Windsor every day to superintend the decorations; he bought furniture and curtains, and maybe, carried in his mind the picture of a certain house in Portsmouth, when he chose flowered chintzes for the windows of his parlour, and sprigged paper for his walls.

George offered him a set of gilded chairs that had belonged to the grandfather of Louis of France, and a bureau ornate with marqueterie and cupids, and a table with gold legs. But William would have none of that. Mahogany for him – rich and dark, made in the workshops of Mr Sheraton, and a table large enough to seat two dozen without an extra leaf, and chairs to hold a man's weight – not a lady's.

George was offended and offered no more, but Frederick gave him some china.

In the garden he ordered an herbaceous border to be bedded with old-fashioned flowers, hollyhocks and Canterbury bells, and a plant of the name of 'Sweet William'.

Mr Walpole, his neighbour at Strawberry Hill, came to look, and went to chatter.

The Duke of Clarence has taken Mr Henry Hobart's house, point-blank over against Mr Cambridge's, which will make the good woman of that mansion cross herself piteously and stretch the throat of the blatant beast at Sudbrook [Lady Greenwich] and of all the other pious matrons *à la ronde*; for His Royal Highness to divert lonesomeness has brought with him a Miss Polly Finch. . . .[1]

Here was talk in plenty! And who in the name of

[1] From *Horace Walpole's Letters*, ed. Tonybee. By permission of Clarendon Press, Oxford.

Fortune was Miss Finch? None knew – not even Mr Walpole. And whence had she come? One might hazard a guess and not be far wrong. Straight from the gutters of St James's or the arms of Mr Fox, or his friend the Prince of Wales, or from nowhere.

And did His Royal Highness expect the neighbourhood to shut its eyes to *that*!

His Royal Highness expected nothing and obviously did not care whether eyes were shut or open. A house without a woman could be cold comfort, and Polly was both comfortable and warm. And she was lively with a handsome pair of eyes, and a willing enough body to divert a man from lonesomeness who had been denied a wife.

Soon all the houses up and down the Thames side had the truth of it, and there she was for all of them to see; driving in his carriage, decked out like a playactress or worse, returning stare for brazen stare – the bold-faced thing. A crying scandal!

Thanks to Mr Walpole the affair was floated into legend, but none heard Polly's side of it, unless it were her master, and he may have heard it often, and too much – to send him boiling to his own room to be quit of her and to regret his bargain.

She could bring the roof down with her temper; her tongue was loose as any in the galleys. And what now was *her* complaint?

Life in a village – and looked upon as dirt! And the noses of those lady hags as high in air as though she were a smell. And who were they to draw their skirts aside from where *she'd* trod when all knew they had a man a-piece under each petticoat – making cuckolds of their husbands and bastards of their brats! 'Ods blood! Was *this* what one must suffer as poplolly to a Prince? A fine protector! Had he no sense to see that every insult offered her was one to him?

Although it is unlikely that Mr Walpole was present at these scenes we learn from him that Polly Finch declared: 'Any tempter would make even Paradise more agreeable than a constant *tête-à-tête....*'

With William, we presume. And she had a further grievance.

'He' was as proper in the home as an old maid in her four-poster – or a Captain in his ship. You scarce could sneeze but he was glaring. You mustn't lean your head against a chair-back for the powder. He was forever whisking with his handkerchief and ordering the servants: 'Dust this – sweep that – and polish.' As for *her* she mustn't touch an ornament or drop a breadcrumb on the floor. And if she went into his room, as once or twice she did – without permission – he had the devil in him with a clout to burn her ears.

'This room is mine,' he said, 'and not for – you!' And how he said it – 'you!'

There was more than met the eye in that room of his, papered with sprigs and curtained like a lady's. On the mantelpiece he kept a picture of a girl – without a name. 'And who is she?' demanded Polly pointing.

'A memory,' he said. 'And that's mine, too.' And turned her out by her shoulders – turned her *out* and locked the door, and himself in!

That was her story. He could tell another: of how she made a shambles of the place, spilled wine on the tablecloths and food on the quilts, ate meals in her bed, was afraid of the dark and kept candles burning at her bedside – in constant danger of firing the house. And she was for ever pestering him to go to town – to take her to Ranelagh, to masquerades and balls. There was no peace and never any quiet. She sang. But how she sang! A macaw could sing sweeter – off the note. He was for ever finding soiled caps and kerchiefs on his sofas; garters on the chairs, and her lap-dogs piddling on his carpets. She was a slattern in her dress and dirty in her person. She ordered gowns by the dozen and handed him the bills – silks, brocades, and satins – every colour of the rainbow, yet she'd think nothing of sitting down to dinner in her shift. She had holes in her stockings, and stale powder in her hair. She never washed. Her tongue was ugly. She would shout – he was shamed for the servants to hear her. He was sick of her within a week and hated her within a month, and worked himself into a fever with worry of how best to let her go. He would double her price to be rid of her – without a scene.

So much for that experiment. Never again – no thank ye! Next time he'd be more guarded in his choice, if there should ever be a next time, which he doubted. It was a wife he wanted, or as good. George had a wife – *sub rosa*. Why couldn't he?

Things went from bad to worse; but still she stayed all through that summer. And in the autumn the silent Sea Lords came to life.

William had his orders, never before so thankfully received. He had been appointed to the *Valiant*, held in readiness to cruise the Channel. He must report for duty at Spithead without delay.

The Admiralty had spoken – and relented.

*

He left Polly at Clarence Lodge on the tacit understanding that he hoped to find her gone when he came back.

Such arrangement was all to Polly's liking. She was not now in any hurry to depart. She had 'His' house and not 'His' company. She could spill – and drink – as much wine as she pleased, stay in bed all day, have gentlemen from London to entertain her in the evening, and all the light she wanted for the dark.

Which she did; and to some consequence.

She left candles burning as usual by her bedside, but she had also left her room, and all the windows open with a breeze to catch the curtains, while she acted hostess to a visitor that night.

The smell of smoke aroused the household; Polly's screams aroused the neighbours, and while the servants fought the flames, Polly, under cover of the noise and the confusion, fled with her gentleman; nor did she return.

So, according to the tale told to William, when he hurried up from Portsmouth at the news, to find half his house in ruins, and Mr Walpole on the doorstep – to condole.

Mr Walpole offered a suggestion. There was a house nearby at Roehampton that would comfortably accommodate the Duke while repairs at Clarence Lodge were being made.

To move again? And not three months in the place! A pretty penny it would cost, thought William, gloomily, as he surveyed his blackened walls and tattered curtains, and all that was left of his dining-table and his chairs. His own room, luckily, had been untouched by the fire.

Mr Walpole, sympathetic, stayed to tea, and told William details of other fires that had happened within his recollection. There had been, for instance, the fire at the house of Her Royal Highness, the Princess Amelia, on which occasion she had displayed the utmost coolness and helped the servants, ineffectually, to extinguish it by throwing tumblers of water on the flames. . . . He also gave William a full account of the old lady's last illness – she had died of bronchitis while William was at sea – and of how she had, or had not, left her legacies and some amusing anecdotes of her early life – or as early as Mr Walpole could remember it: of how one Sunday she had gone to church in a green riding-habit with a dog under her arm; and of her rude remarks to any lady she disliked. There was a certain Madame de Mirefoix to whom the Princess said the second time she saw her: '*Madame, vous n'avez pas tant de rouge aujourdhui: la première fois que vous êtes venue ici vous aviez une quantité horrible. . . .*' Until he had William shouting with laughter to forget his troubles and his house and Polly Finch.

And with her departure William seems to have been speedily restored to grace, for we find Mr Walpole writing to the effect that:

My neighbour, the Duke of Clarence, is so popular that if Richmond were a borough and he had not attained his title, but still retained the idea of standing candidate, he would certainly be elected there. He pays his bills regularly himself, locks up his doors at night that his servants may not stay out late, and never drinks but a few glasses of wine. . . .

Such exemplary existence must soon have palled ('and no wonder – at his age!' says Mr Walpole, 'in a situation only fit for an old gentlewoman who has put out her knee-pans and loves cards . . .') for William was now preparing for another move. This time he had seen and taken a fancy to Ivy Lodge, the house at Roehampton, recommended by his ubiquitous neighbour.

Choosing furniture again and staying nights in London at St James's, and back and forth to Richmond superintending his affairs, occupied his leave till after Christmas. Neither George nor Frederick were in London at that time, and with Budé at his elbow William may have found that his resources of amusement were as limited in Town as in the country.

But there was always the theatre. He would go to

Drury Lane to see the Jordan playing Viola in *Twelfth Night*.

So with Budé in attendance, William took a box. Not the Royal box – he had no desire to be recognized; he sat in a stage-box on the lowest tier with the standers in the pit offensively under his nose. Budé held a hand-kerchief to his. William glared. A mincing beau, and sixty if a day, with rouge in his wrinkles, ruffles at his throat, and a waistcoat – God save us! – patterned with green monkeys carrying silver parasols. Most fitting. 'Sit back,' growled William, 'you'll have the whole house staring.'

Budé took his nose out of his handkerchief to say:

' 'Tis your duty, Sir, to give the audience the pleasure of—'

'A sight of you?' inquired William rudely. 'That 'ud entertain 'em, I'll be bound. Take a look at 'em – poor devils. How in hell do they find the pence to buy en-trance to the play when half of them don't get a meal a week inside their bellies?'

Budé almost choked himself. Such shocking talk! It savoured mightily of – never say the word – with the Bastille fallen over there in France and the King's son siding with the people and their – hem!

'Give them an inch, Sir, and they'll take an ell. Already there are secret meetings here in London, shouting treason to the King.'

'You'd shout if you were starving,' William said. 'Yes! There are secrets here in England that will come to light one day – you mark *my* words.'

Budé did, in some alarm. Was H.R.H. as crazy as his father?

'And what,' asked William, 'of this Jordan? Have you seen her? Can she act? Is she another Siddons? *She* rants and raves and bellows. I've not much taste for tragedy, or women with big noses. I'm told the Jordan's a comedienne. Is she young?'

Budé hastened to assure him, thankful for this normal turn of conversation. 'Passably young, Sir – very sprightly – and an excellent good actress. She plays Shakespeare here for the first time. She should be well suited to Viola. She plays the boy, Sir, to perfection. I hear she is preparing now for a new rôle, that of Little Pickle in *The Spoiled Child*, a play written by herself – or so they say. Your Royal Highness has no doubt heard that—'

And Budé presented William with the tale of Mrs Jordan's past and present history. Of Irish origin; born, hem – obscurely, her rightful name, if ever she possessed one, was Dorothy Bland. She had four children by several fathers and was the mistress of a Mr Richard Ford, some kind of questionable lawyer. It had been said she was his wife, but that had been denied when—

William, inattentive and withdrawn into his corner, watched the house. It was packed from pit to gallery high to the painted dome, the four tiers of boxes filled with persons of the *ton*, many of whom he recognized – brocaded, wigged, and glittering, to draw attention from the gaping herd beneath them, who with upturned faces and their eyes a-blink in the glare of light from silver-lacquered candelabra, gazed to have their money's worth before the curtain rose.

It was a long time rising. The pit became impatient, and showed it with cat-calls and booings, and a shower of orange peel at the fiddlers in the orchestra, as they with cool indifference arranged their music on the stands.

Budé whispered on: 'She made attempt to use the name of Ford, but her manager, King, had it struck off the play-bills . . .'

The candles were lighted in the foot-floats. The audience stamped its feet and cheered.

'. . . and Ford – tee-hee! was hoping to be rid of her, he has in fact *crossed* the Jordan!'

The murmurs subsided and swept up again, in a wave of thunderous applause, as the crimson curtains parted, and Dora Jordan dressed for her shipwreck scene with her boy's suit showing underneath her hooded cloak, came down to make her bow.

She curtsied to the yelling pit – the gallery; to boxes right and left. She smiled, she blew kisses; she curtsied once again, and the house, appeased was silent.

William, forgetful of the audience, leaned forward, stood transfixed, with a burning in his sight and a melting in his ears. . . .

What country, friends, is this?

A new country for William, a new life.

BOOK TWO

The Squire

Chapter One

FOR England a new era.

Across that strip of water that divided Britain from the mainland, smoke drifted from the torch of revolution. A howling mob had stormed the Paris streets, with human heads on pikes as symbol of a falling dynasty, an epoch doomed.

A King and his wife were imprisoned, the last scene of the Terror had been staged, and the whole of Europe, petrified, waited for the Grand Finale.

In London news was guarded. Those howls of Liberty, Equality, must find no echo here: yet there were murmurs, secret voices, meetings up back-stairs, and one voice stronger than the rest to strike a clarion note – 'The Rights of Man'.

The whispers that George the King, in his madness, had dreaded, were spoken aloud by a voice that dared more than to murmur. It dictated the written word. The forcible suppression of those unhoused, unfed, unwanted, those hidden starving hordes had found a champion: an Englishman by birth,[1] American by choice, and a citizen of the world, self-styled.

In February 1791, we hear of a pamphlet circulated among tens of thousands, a direct answer to Burke's righteously indignant Tory 'Thoughts on the French Revolution', a Crusader's sword to sever the cloying tendrils of tradition from the sturdy growth of new democracy.

But he, who was destined to set his seal upon that

[1] Thomas Paine.

135

word and faith – he had no thought of it. He took no heed; a word – no more than that, and uttered by a madman, or fanatic. Let him speak – or write: speech should be free, and if he passed beyond the bounds of law and order – string him up! There must be no treason here to Britain's monarchy, even though a King's head fell in France. . . . For Britain's King and Constitution such a fate was as improbable as the dethroning of the Lord Himself in His High Heaven. The King's son might rub his nose and goggle at unspeakable calamities far removed from 'Merrie' England, while for him his England never had been merrier – or at least the only England that he knew – where no voice from its underworld could reach him, a world which would one day with all its land above, and overseas, be his heritage.

Nor did he know that, when from Richmond to Drury Lane his coach drove daily through the first summer of his courtship.

He was making yet another change of residence. Pending the reconstruction of the damage done to Clarence Lodge, he, tiring of the villa at Roehampton, had taken a house at Petersham, and tongues again were busy. For why, if you please, should the Duke require *two* houses in one neighbourhood?

Mr Walpole might have hinted at a reason for such unnecessary expenditure, although a Prince had every right to spend the nation's money – and his own. That aged beau may have uttered, too, a thought upon affairs not wholly ornamental, when called in to give advice in decoration.

'Why not, Sir, choose for curtains here, a Chinese influence? A *soupçon*, merely, for effect to match your charming Chippendale. Chinoiserie is all the rage in Paris – or it *was*.'

Was! 'Eh?' quoth William shying. 'Chinoiserie? I

think not. Too outlandish altogether – for my taste.'
'Was' indeed! With Marie Antoinette and her children
in the Bastille and poor simple Louis dragged there by
a horde of yelling fish-hags in red caps. . . .

'Their poor French Majesties,' sighed Mr Walpole,
watching his effect, 'such a superabundance of woe!
have you heard, Sir, of some shocking mischief the other
night at Ranelagh, when the Revolution Club – can
you fancy the name, Sir? – wished to hold their jubilee
in the gardens and were, very naturally, refused. They
had intended to exhibit flags and three-coloured cock-
ades sent from France.'

'The devil they did!' cried William. 'I'd have hanged
'em.'

Mr Walpole, smiling, offered his snuff-box. William
shook his head. 'No, thank ye – never take it.'

'Your Royal Highness will excuse me, if I—?'

'Yes, yes, pray do! What else?'

'I hear, Sir, that numbers of Paine's pamphlets were
to have been distributed, but equally without success.
Dear me!' murmured Mr Walpole, as he daintily
inhaled snuff, 'what a world it is! And when this
hurricane is blown over, the anarchy of France will be
quoted as worse than despotism. For any attempt to
suppress general prejudice by violence serves only to
inflame and root those very prejudices more deeply in
the sufferers. . . . So *not* then, Sir, Chinoiserie?'

'No,' said William scowling.

'On second thoughts, Sir, I agree,' still smiling Mr
Walpole flicked a grain of snuff from his Mechlin wrist-
lets. ' 'Tis a fashion now exploded. We are fast returning to – shall we say – Cromwellian simplicity? Even
in our dress. We will go unpowdered and short-cropped.
I understand that the *victime* coiffure, with neck bared
as for the block, is fashion's latest fancy. And ladies are
leaving the hoop. An ominous sign of the times, me-

thinks. 'Twould be a sad sight indeed to see our gentles trousered, although I vow there is nothing in the world more bewitching than the incomparable "Pickle" breeched and booted. I hear she comes to dazzle Richmond very shortly.'

The quick blood mounted to the scratch, and Mr Walpole drooped a lid to raise an eyebrow. So! Rumour *hadn't* lied.

'I hear, too,' purred Mr Walpole, 'that the lady is now *acknowledged* Mrs Ford.'

'That,' said William loudly, 'is untrue. She has denied it.'

Oho! From red to white. A skin like a girl's, deliciously transparent. . . . Youth, youth, *l'amour*! sighed Mr Walpole, as he hurried home to write:

Mrs Jordan, whom Mr Ford had declared his wife and presented her as such to some ladies at Richmond, has resumed her former name and is said to be much at a *princ*ipal villa at Petersham, which I do not affirm – far be it from me to vouch a quarter of what I hear. . . .

And a quarter of that may have been gleaned from newspapers, for:

'Little Pickle has been besieged,' says the *Morning Post* of 15 July, 'by a certain exalted youth, whom at present she has managed to keep at bay.'

Thus we have it straight from Mr Walpole's pen and the gossips of society; yet none can tell us how or when they met. It is possible that William worshipped from afar for months before he had ventured to approach her. Time lagged. The *Valiant* had been paid off, and her Commander retired with the rank of Rear-Admiral at twenty-five. Buying and furnishing houses as a hobby soon proved as tedious as the decorous entertainment offered him at Windsor or St James's. To London from Richmond was an easy drive, so no wonder that his carriage might be seen three nights out of every six in Drury Lane.

From his stage-box he watched her critically, aware that foot-lamps lent a softness to harshly painted cheeks, and lustre to eyes grown weary.

Perhaps he feared another disillusionment. Polly Finch had left him cautious; she, too, had been a playactress some time. Between Polly of the gutter and Jordan of the Lane there might be no greater difference than that one was gifted and the other not. Both belonged to that half-world where women's love is bought and paid for on account, and both were young – or young enough; yet according to old Budé's calculations, the Jordan could not be so *very* young; and that was the more remarkable, for her figure in her boy's clothes was a child's, half-girl's, half-urchin's – every movement of her body a delight, with just that awkward grace of adolescence to make one catch one's breath and wonder – is it true she is the mother of a family.

She had a secret that not Sarah Siddons with all her genius possessed, and which would take a sterner critic than William to define. Did it lie in her voice with its faint hint of a brogue, its infinite gradations? Not strong, but a quality that Hazlitt calls 'a cordial to the heart, like the luscious juice of the ripe grape? . . .' Was it her laugh? 'The most enlivening thing in nature.' Or was it the woman who gave herself so openly to gladness that 'to hear the audience laugh at me,' she ingenuously confessed, 'I must laugh with them – at myself'?

There is no reason to believe that the faithful attendance of the Duke of Clarence in his box unduly overwhelmed her. She was used to Royal patronage. She had played before the 'Family' at Cheltenham. The Princesses were enraptured, and Fanny Burney writes: 'Mrs

Jordan played the Country Girl most admirably; but the play is so disagreeable in its whole plot and tendency that all the merit of her performance was insufficient to ward off disgust. . . .'

The 'Royals', however, do not appear to have shared Miss Burney's squeamishness, for a week later they and their entourage – Fanny, we presume, included – 'made a very full and respectable appearance in this village theatre'.

But there were further fields than Cheltenham's to conquer. It is one thing to make your bow to Royalty behind the footlights, and quite another to be personally presented in the flesh. That honour was to come when the Prince of Wales and his brother Ernest, Duke of Cumberland, visited her in her dressing-room at Drury Lane.

And still we have no evidence that William joined them there. He shows, for him, remarkable restraint, until the first production of *The Spoiled Child*.

The play was the poorest farce, entirely redeemed by her as the impish schoolboy 'Little Pickle'. Never had the Jordan been more popular.

'Pickle's' mischievous practical-joking conquered London. It also conquered William, who seeing her may perhaps have seen himself again, as 'Snotty' of the cockpit.

And now at last he ventured nearer than a view from the stage-box.

It is possible that Budé was sent to clear the way, and we can well imagine that Kemble, acting manager for Sheridan – received the Prince's emissary with pomp.

Two members of the Royal Family had already been presented – and now a third! Kemble, bowing head to knees, took all glory to himself and Drury Lane.

The moment could have scarcely been more oppor

tune for Dora. Richard Ford was in her dressing-room, sadistically to criticize, as was his custom. She had been too boisterous; she had over-acted. She had sacrificed grace of posture to the part. To his mind her attitudes had been too rakish altogether. In truth, her figure was a *leetle* portly now for breeches. The time was come when she must take to petticoats. She had out-played the boy. That, however, was a matter of opinion. The gallery was evidently pleased.

She held her tongue and temper, but her fingers itched to claw the grin out of his face. Too well he knew how best to goad her till all control was lost, and she, a maddened fury, would be up and at him, fists and tooth and nail. Such scenes were frequent – but not at the theatre. They were preserved to give flavour to the home.

And how she loathed him in his calm superiority, sitting there judicially before her with that thread of a tight-drawn smile on his lips: he, who once was all her life and had taken the best years of it, whose children she had borne, whose name he had allowed her while she kept him out of debt, he who paraded her before the world as wife just so long as it suited him to do so, and now when it suited him no longer, with a civil appointment pending, which an equivocal relationship would smash, he was driving her to take the first initiative – driving her, till pride and human tolerance – and love – must break.

She released her bitten under-lip with an ooze of blood upon it through the paint.

'You are as ever – my sincerest critic, Ford,' said Dora, high; for Kemble's head was round the door and her part must still be played, so, 'Ecod, John Kemble! Give me leave to change me suit!'

'No time for that,' hissed Kemble with a glance over his shoulder at Budé's quizzing glass behind him in the passage, 'His Royal Highness—' on his breath he mouthed it, swelling, 'His Royal Highness, the Duke of Clarence.'

'Glory be to God!' whispered Dora, saucer-eyed. 'How in the devil can I curtsy in me breeks?'

Kemble frowned. Such levity was out of place. As for Ford, he must go – and quickly. Scant ceremony here. Kemble mouthed again. 'His Royal Highness—'

' 'Ods life!' cried Dora, tearing off her wig to let her hair fall curling on her shoulders. 'Will you say it once more and I'll scream!'

'Hush, pray!' urged Kemble in an agony with his eyes all ways at once, and Budé hemming his throat raw outside in disapproval. 'Mr Ford, sir, I must beg you – leave the room.'

This was little to Ford's liking. 'You request *me*, sir – *me* – to leave the room?'

'Etiquette,' said Kemble through his teeth and almost dancing. 'His Royal High— We've *Royalty*! Pray, sir, will you go?'

Smothering a laugh Dora brushed the tangles from her curls and watched Ford's face in the mirror – black as a boot and longer than a fiddle!

Revenge could never have been sweeter than at that moment when London's future Magistrate unwillingly passed out, to allow the future King of England to pass in.

*

So much for the beginning, and how far it had gone by the time Mr Walpole and the papers had news of it, we can only guess.

His attentions now were openly persistent. She, fulfilling her annual engagement at the Richmond Theatre, was in full blaze, and the Duke in attendance every night. His carriage had been placed at her disposal and waited at the stage door to take her home. It was noted the Duke did not accompany her; nor did Mr Ford, which gave a further rise to speculation.

If Ford had left her, why did not the Duke take advantage of the vacancy? Could it be that the lady had refused him? Or was his admiration reserved solely for her acting?

When the Duke gave parties at his house, *she*, most properly, was not invited. All was as it should be when His Royal Highness entertained. The pious matrons may have wished it otherwise, since not a glimpse of any flagrancy had been vouchsafed to them. The Jordan acted for their benefit behind – and not before – the foot-lamps. Any other performance that she chose to give must be played in private – to an audience of one. And did he pay her – ran conjecture – for the privilege?

All Richmond was agog to know the worst.

Meanwhile the two chief actors in the comedy, indifferent to the pointed tongues around them, met – to meet again.

William went slowly; his approach was cautious. He made no demands. She had captured, not his heart, but his imagination. It was no hot-headed boy who came to her beseeching, stammering his love, but a man, critical of her; and of himself – on guard. He knew that she could not give him half of all he needed. Though he asked little, yet he asked too much. A wife. And that he was forbidden. In all Europe there was not a wife for him. And since he could not marry of his choice, he would, he swore, be never married for convenience.

It must have been the strangest wooing. One can well believe he was direct; that he stated his case clearly, that he examined with her, every pro and con. Discipline had schooled him to be practical. Also, he was decided: this must be no slight intrigue, one of a series, besmirched by repetition. If it could not be a marriage, it could – *must* – be a bond. He was tired of himself; his house was lonely. She too, perhaps, was lonely?

She told him, No. She had her children and her work. Children. Ford's. Or . . . whose? He sheered off that. Children, no matter who their father, were pleasant company to have about a home: but – work. That was another thing. 'Quite another thing,' said William staring.

She, too, could be decided. She would not give up her work. It was her life.

'You mean,' he told her bluntly, 'that you want the best of both worlds.'

She tilted up her chin. 'And who does not?'

'You're honest,' William said, 'at all events.'

'I am; you too.' She looked at him with eyes like stars behind a mist. 'I love honesty,' she said, 'before everything except my children, and them I love before my honour – or your rank.'

William caught his breath. . . . So small she was, he could look down at her. Most women were his height, or taller; and with her smallness she was sturdy, yet soft to touch, soft-lipped, with teeth as white as almonds, and hair rust red and curly as a gipsy's. . . . Children! He wanted children. Hers; with all her gaiety, and laughter, her abandon – and her strength.

'You may keep his children,' William said, 'if you will give me mine.'

And now all cards were on the table, except one that she was saving up her sleeve. Clearly, she was not dazzled by his offer, for was she not a queen in her own right, second to none in comedy, before whom even Siddons must take a second place?

She, too, could hoist her standard, set a price upon herself that was not, however, to be termed in gold. She, whose origin was shrouded in obscurity, who had made her name and yet was nameless, had one ambition dearer to her than success. She wished of all things to be legally inscribed upon the roll of those immortal to the drama. Dorothy Bland, Dora Jordan, or Mrs Richard Ford, she had been called all three, and could lay no claim to one of them. But Ford had made a promise. He would marry her. He had paraded her to all his friends as wife; that, in its essentials she had been for at least five years, and he, though not the first with her, had so far been the last. He had entirely possessed her. She loved and hated him with equal passion. She could not let him go without a fight. If he would marry her. . . .

She went to him. She had no pride; close intimacy had killed it long ago. He was as much her kin, her flesh, as were his children. But he *must* marry her. A crisis had been reached. They must face it now, together – or apart.

That was her ultimatum. Would he take it? She had played her trump card and the stakes were high – too high perhaps, for him with a knighthood and success as great as hers in the near future. The Chief Magistrate of London could pick and choose his wife from England's peerage.

Meanwhile the journalists had scooped up dirt enough to make a story. The *Morning Post* came out with blatant headings.

A celebrated Actress who has withdrawn from her late nominal Spouse, has not yet formed her Princely connection. The lawyers are at present employed in drawing up the settlement. Her terms are £1,200 a year annuity, an equipage, and her children by *all parties* provided for. Her *ci-devant* friend has withdrawn himself from this favourite daughter of Thalia, though no later than yesterday she offered to forego the *Princely* offers, if he would make her his *wedded* wife. This has been refused, and everything is now in preparation to gratify to the fullest the vanity of the mock *Princess*!

These preliminaries may conceivably have chilled what little glamour entered the transaction. The Duke had coolly stated his requirements, so she as coolly stated hers.

' 'Pon life! Am I such an ogre, then?' cried William, growing hot as she grew cold. The shabby dressing-room was a fit setting for the scene; she, who on the stage created romance, might well deny it here among her cast-off trappings, wigs, feathers, tinsel gew-gaws. Every chair was littered; the mirror fogged with powder, and she before it in a careless wrapper that revealed more of her than it was meant to hide.

'What you ask, Sir, must be bought,' she said, 'not given.'

'I ask as much as any man who wants,' said William dizzy.

'Wants! Wants!' she dabbed a hare's foot to each cheek, leaving two bright spots of colour that were not wholly rouge, 'an infant wants – and grabs at every bauble, but a man—'

'Thirsts,' said William, as she paused, 'like Tantalus for fruit above his head.'

'The gods will punish greed,' she murmured, with sweet wryness.

'I'll take what comes to me,' he whispered, burning. 'I'll defy the gods.'

'The gods, Sir, are revengeful. Never tempt them!'

'I'll risk—'

'Your pardon, Sir.' Her mouth was a closed bud, not yet for his to open. 'The curtain rises in five minutes. Will it please Your Royal Highness to excuse—?'

Thus far – no farther.

She kept him waiting, till he was past himself and on his knees.

Such homage must have come as balm to wounded vanity and outraged pride. The King's son was a fair substitute for Ford.

Very well, then: let it be in order, deeds drawn up and duly signed and sealed.

This movement (thus again the *Morning Post* who gave the lead to gossip, had for some time been anticipated, but it was not until Saturday last (8 October) that she quitted the comforts which a private situation could af-*ford*. She has in return all the solace which a new and elevated lover can bestow, with the added hope that history will record her attractions, and that she may be looked on as the Nell Gwynn of her day.

Both now had burned their boats; but Ford escaped the conflagration. He left England in a hurry and William in possession. He left, also, enough friends to present him as the injured party – the deserted 'husband', thrown over for a Prince.

If Ford had friends, Dora had her enemies. There was not a lady in the land who did not envy her, and not one, who loudest in her virtue, did not hesitate to smear her with the venom spewed from the gutter-press.

The humour of the day was Rabelaisian and seldom witty. The majority of comments were crude beyond belief.

'The Duchess in a jealous fit let out a reef of her tongue on Saturday night. The resolute Tar buffeted the storm and produced a calm after giving a broad-side of *Sink me's* that if she did not close hatches he would bear down on every woman he saw for a month.'

'The conduct of a certain pair in their journey to and from the neighbourhood of Richmond, is the daily occasion of a blush in everything except the milestones.'

While from Strawberry Hill to Billingsgate the gossips giggled, Dora laughed. She would laugh last, and loudest. Ecod! She'd give them all they asked and more – and a free view into the bargain.

So, with tongue in cheek and arm-in-arm, she flaunted her Royal conquest in Bond Street and St James's. She drove with him beside her in his carriage, or alone, attended by three footmen. She was received – behind the curtain, by her brothers-in-all-but-law, George, the Prince of Wales, and Ernest, Duke of Cumberland, who looked the very villain of the piece; dark, thin, sleek-voiced, and tall for a son of Hanover; Cumberland, who watched the comedy with narrowed eyes, and allowed his brother William more taste in the choosing of a woman than he would have believed possible, in such a clown.

Ernest shared with Edward a similar contempt for their fraternal sailor, yet William had stepped in and carried off the prize that Ernest coveted – in secret. All of Ernest's life was lived in secret; he walked as softly as a cat, and even his thoughts were guarded, from himself. But he made no secret of his admiration for the Jordan. 'I find it easier to envy than to compliment you on your choice,' he told William with his lip dragged up in his snarling grin.

Not, however, even this support could stem the tide of public opinion turned against the foolish pair, and they certainly did nothing to abate it. She now lived openly at Petersham; he drove her up to London every day, his box at the theatre was empty, the front of the house saw him no more. He sat in her dressing-room behind it. He could be seen any night through a crack in the curtain, laughing and joking with her on the stage between the acts.

The climax came when together they attended a performance of *The Country Girl* at the Haymarket, on which occasion she drew all eyes from the actors to herself – chattered and giggled the whole play through, quizzed him, tweaked his hair to scandalize the audience, and was hissed as she came out.

That pulled her up.

It would never do to lose favour with her public. She realized she may have gone too far. They must retract. Both were popular enough in Richmond to be sure of more friends there than enemies in London.

So in October she retired with Ford's children to the house at Petersham, and William stayed in residence at Clarence Lodge.

But they were not permitted to escape the fusillade without a parting volley from the prints. Peter Pindar had the last word – in a jingle.

> As Jordan's high and mighty Squire
> Her playhouse profits deign to skim
> Some folks audaciously inquire
> If *he* keeps her or *she* keeps him.

*

Let them jeer! He had been given what he wanted. A home to hold a woman as near as possible to wife. In every way she suited him; he delighted in her *gamin* wit, her wholesome frank good nature; he loved the trace of Irish in her voice. True, her tastes were not domestic; her lack of supervision in the household caused unrest among her staff. She was for ever changing servants, would be alternately too imperious or too familiar. She put the men in ornate liveries of yellow plush, gossiped in the kitchen with the maids, and gave

them her old dresses. In return they gave her impudence. She dismissed her cook for calling her 'Your
Grace'. Though recklessly extravagant, and generous
to folly, she saved every guinea William had settled
on her for the future security of Ford's three little
girls.

Perhaps it is as well that William kept his own establishment at Richmond distinct from hers. His inherent
love of order had been increased by his naval training.
He would have found much to criticize in Dora's
methods of housekeeping had he seen enough of it.
That was to come later. Meantime he had a private door
built for her across to his apartments at St James's
which he permitted her to use when she was wished,
and which she redecorated, dreadfully, in royal blue
and silver, with crimson sarsnet curtains.

Still, he was happy. If his first approach had not been
conspicuously ardent, he was fond, and she impulsively
affectionate. His senior on her own admission by three
years, and possibly more than that, for perhaps not she
herself knew the actual date of her birth, Dora admirably played the child, and sought, even if she did not
always take, his advice in her affairs. That pleased and
flattered him – for Dora knew her man. She would discuss with him the interpretation of a new part, and
when word perfect, she would make him 'hear' her,
giving her the cues: that pleased him most of all.

Her retirement was short. December saw her back
again in the theatre, rehearsing for another play – *The
Sultan*. She had made it clear she would not give up the
stage for any man alive – not for the King himself; nor
did he press her, and if he at all resented her absorption
in a life beyond his own, he had sense enough not to
enforce his will to be resisted. She had him in her hand
in those first years of their union, and William was
content it should be so. Women had always had their

way with him and always would. To Sarah Martin he
had given a boy's devout idealism which had left in
memory a shadowed void, unfilled; but if Dora had
not all his heart, she had his confidence.

Until there came an awkward interruption.

It was toward the end of November while he was at
St James's, that he received a visit from his brother
Ernest.

This attention, uninvited, was remarkable enough
to make William suspicious of its good intent. He was
not left long in doubt.

Ernest, suave and elegant in the latest fashion of
swallow-tailed coat, high neckcloth, and striped pantaloons, with his hair cropped and unpowdered, presented
a serene contrast to him, who lay in bed with a streaming cold. The message sent by his man to this effect,
was, however, no deterrent.

Ernest sent word back that he had come on a matter
of importance.

'You come then,' William warned him, 'at your risk.
I may be sickening for an infection.'

'I will keep my distance,' Ernest said, and sat. 'You
have made some alterations in your rooms, I see. A
pretty choice of colour.' His eyes narrowed in a glance
that took in the crimson curtains, the royal blue and
silver walls. 'Very gay,' he added, airily, opening his
snuff-box. 'Your bed-trimmings—'

'Are new. The colour will soon fade. I hope.' William
pulled the covers to his chin and glared above them.
'My head aches most infernally.'

'Belladonna,' suggested Ernest, 'is very efficacious I
am told. I am fortunate that I have never suffered from
the headache in my life. Have you heard from Edward
lately?'

William answered, No – why should he hear from
Edward?

'I have,' said Ernest, taking snuff. 'He writes me from Gibraltar.'

'He may write you from Hell for all I care,' retorted William, reddening.

'Strange,' said Ernest, pensive, 'his letters must have gone astray. I understand from him he wrote you twice.'

'They must,' William agreed, 'have gone astray.' And a faint dew appeared upon his forehead. For he lied. Edward *had* written him – and twice – a year ago. He had ignored the letters. Their purport, he believed, had nothing in the world to do with him.

'You will forgive me,' Ernest said, agreeably, 'if I allude to a delicate and – private matter? The young person concerned—'

'The person, whether young or old,' William interrupted, sliding lower in the bed, 'is none of my affair.'

Ernest raised his eyebrows. 'My dear William, how can you possibly know to what – or to whom – I allude if you have not received Edward's letters?'

William stretched a hand towards the bell-rope. 'I am in no humour for your pleasantries. Will you go? Or must I—'

'Pray,' said Ernest rising, 'do not ring. I would not have your fellow take my news to the back-stairs. I have said the case is urgent. I am here on your behalf. The lady,' and coming to the foot of the bed, Ernest lightly poised his words, and threw them out, 'the lady is in London.' Saying that, he made for the door, and with one hand on the door-knob, turned. 'And so is Hardenberg,' he added.

'So is who?' asked William, his mouth muffled under the sheet, his eyes as round as marbles peering above it.

'I don't know him,' William shook his head; the yellow coxcomb on it seemed to lift. 'No,' he said, 'I never heard of him. Pray shut the door. I'm in a draught.'

'Would Lüneburg remind you?' inquired Ernest

gently. 'A thousand pardons.' And he closed the door, returning.

'Lüneburg?' William in a rare sweat now, raised himself upon the pillows. 'Egad! I *do* remember. Of all the rogues unhung – if it's the man I think you mean. A swarthy, slinking rascal like yourself. Blue-chinned and shifty-eyed. You might be brothers. There's more between the pair o' ye in looks than between you and me, or any one of us – thank God! Well! Hardenberg. I almost slit the fellow, and would have, too, if it hadn't been for Budé.'

'Budé?' Ernest glanced up. 'Did Budé know him?'

'Everybody knew him. The fellow was a shark. And you should know him. Birds of a feather – eh?'

'That,' Ernest said, close-lipped, 'is a remark I do not relish.'

'No more,' said William, gathering a sneeze, 'than I rer-rer-rer – damnation! – relish your slimy interference. Why in hell don't you speak out if you've anything to say? And if you haven't – keep your mouth shut.'

'My intention in the first place was to help you,' said Ernest, with disgust.

'That's uncommon kind, I'm sure. On what consideration?'

Shaken from his calm, 'By God, you are impossible,' snarled Ernest. 'Briefly it has come to my knowledge that you will soon find the prints are once more dragging your – *our* – name through the garbage of publicity. The King has had enough of it – and so have I.'

'King Ernest the First,' muttered William in the sheets.

'And I understand,' proceeded Ernest, ignoring, if he heard it, this remark, 'that Baron Hardenberg – so-called – is at the root of this new trouble.'

'Whatever trouble there may be, it is not mine!'
cried William, rising from the sheets to shout. 'Whatever filth you've found, you've dug it up. The devil
knows what *your* game is – but I could make a guess. If
you think to come to me with your grubby findings at a
price to hold your tongue, then you're mistaken. I'll
thank ye to keep your nose out of my affairs. I can look
after my own business, if you mind yours. You and
Edward – a fine couple!'

'Do I take it then,' asked Ernest, very cold, 'that this
display of brotherly – and gentlemanly – feeling indi-
cates that—'

'Cut your words!' yelled William. 'I tell you I know
nothing of your dirt. Edward wrote me – yes – he wrote
me twice from Lüneburg – if you must have it. I took
no notice. Why? Why should I? Just because some
German mopsy comes with a tale of a brat and calls it
mine? Can you prove it? I knew a hundred girls in
Lüneburg – but not one well enough to lay a bastard
at my door. Edward was ready to believe it – both of ye!
Yes – and glad enough to rub your heads together to
make *me* stink. I'll swear Edward was calling all of
Lüneburg to come to Jesus – savin' *my* soul – by God!
You save your own! And now get out of here. Get out!'

'I will,' said Ernest's lips, his face immovable. 'This
talk has been an edifying revelation. I do not readily
forget – or take – an insult.'

Then head up, nose pointed, out he went, and William dived beneath the bed-clothes, aching hot; burned,
shivered, and was cold, and bade his valet 'Send for
Mrs Jordan.' For he felt ill enough to die, and thought
he would.

The Court bulletins announced next day he had the
influenza.

Dora kept away, and not until he had returned to
Petersham for convalescence did he see her.

Her reception could have scarcely been less cordial. She was not at the door to welcome him, nor in his room. His man brought tea which he took alone, and still she kept him waiting, while he fumed. It darkened.

The candles were lit and the curtains drawn before she came, with a paper in her hand, no warmth in her voice, and no word for his well-being.

'Why – what now?' demanded William when she turned her lips from his. 'A pretty way to greet me! Are you ill, too?'

'I might well be,' she said, with ice, and held the *Times* to him. 'Will you take a look at this, and explain it – if you can.'

'This' was startlingly a paragraph:

We are given to understand that a lady has just arrived from Hanover bringing with her a child, of whom a certain Royal Duke is the reputed Father. Numerous attempts having been made to obtain from His Royal Highness that support for his Offspring, which his humanity should teach him to grant, and which the laws of his country will force him to bestow, and all those attempts having failed of success, the inhabitants of Hanover, by a public subscription, have enabled the injured woman to travel to London, and seek that redress from her unprincipled seducer, to which she is so justly entitled.

Well! Ernest had been busy. William had no doubt but that his brother was at the root of it. He and Hardenberg, his boon companion. He saw it all. The German had used this opportunity as a means of revenge for the unfortunate affair at Lüneburg. Ernest and that pawky rogue were in league together – both to the same end, and the deuce alone could know what that would be. As for Edward – he in his niggling prudery must have written to Ernest as well as to himself. . . . 'Hell's blood!' ejaculated William, stunned. 'It's slander. But why bring it to *me*?' He saw a loophole, since names had not been mentioned. 'There are half a dozen Royal Dukes in England. 'Tis a trumped-up monstrous outrage,' he protested, unconvincingly, with Dora's eye as black as ink upon him. 'I know no more of it than you.'

'Do you not?' said she with the brogue in her voice, and honeyed.

'Damme!' William dug his chin in his cravat that had suddenly tightened. 'I swear—'

'You are not asked to swear, at all. I have my information.'

If that were a random shot it found its mark. William's forehead reddened, and Dora, watching, pounced. 'Can you deny it?'

'Deny what?' Pinioned, he began to shout. 'Deny the existence of a woman I have never seen?'

'No man need see for what's been done to *her*,' said Dora, sharp as knives. 'It can be done as well or better by the blind.'

William groaned. Good life! Was ever man so plagued? Here was Dora in her tantrums, London laughing itself silly, and the *Times* handing him a by-blow in a mare's nest. . . . Then he flew into a passion. He'd prove his innocence of this – he'd have those who dared to slur it on their knees. Sue them for libel – put an end to all these gerrymanders and their tricks.

'Oh,' said Dora, nodding, as he paused. 'So you will prove your innocence. And how, pray, will you prove it? Unless you've lived as holy as a Trappist.'

'I wish to God,' he muttered, 'that I had.'

Confound all women! Everyone of them bred trouble. As for this latest development he could thank Edward for the start of it – of that he was convinced.

Edward had spent three years in Lüneberg. The jade –
whoever she might be – had gone to Edward with her
tale, and Edward would be glad enough to put it to his
brother William's count. The case was clear. Edward's
letters had been full of piety and protestations; besides
which Edward and Ernest were as close as peas together
in a pod. Edward on his last leave had shared a house
with Ernest on Kew Green. Ernest, too, had been in
Lüneberg – the whole pack of them went there for
military training – so, come to that – all Hanover must
be swarming with their seed. As for Hardenberg. . . .
And at that point in his conjectures William halted.
Why should Ernest rake up Hardenberg unless, as
William had suspected, Ernest owed the Baron money?
That was not improbable. If so, the circle was complete,
with Hardenberg in London now, forsooth! And why!
Why now – for the first time in all these years? To
bring the woman over as bird-lime to spring a trap and
share the spoils? A pretty pair o' snakes – and one his
brother!

As for Hardenberg, this time, William swore, he'd
have his blood – if he could find him.

Meanwhile, how in Heaven's name was he to prove
– as Dora had so deftly pointed – that he was *not* the
father of this brat? When in Lüneburg with Frederick,
he had lived something of a life – but so had Frederick.
And, also, Frederick had been more often drunk than
sober. Egad! That well might be the truth of it. Much
more readily could one assume his brother Frederick
responsible for the begetting of a bastard in his cups,
than William in his caution. He remembered he had
always practised caution. . . .

He decided, finally, to consult a lawyer.

It was, however, Dora who took the case in hand, for
though ready to condemn him, she was loyal. His plight

was serious; his name again bespattered – but not with hers, and that was her chief grievance. That another woman had been coupled with her man raised her gall. If Dora had no fear of publicity she greatly feared a rival, and would fight her, if needs be, to the death.

'You say you've never seen the woman. The saints alone know if you lie.'

'I do not lie,' protested William. 'You can believe me if I tell you I do not even know her name.' For the name she gave was none that he remembered.

Through the medium of a Mr Barton, an attorney whose service Dora recommended, the lady had been traced to a house in Soho Square. The author of the paragraph in the *Times* obliged with her address, and Dora accompanied by Barton called upon her with a view to settlement.

Dora's account of the interview, retailed at lively length to William, reported: 'A pock-marked *rousse* with a cast in one eye, and a bosom as big as the dome of St Paul's,' who feigned all ignorance of Baron Hardenberg, but presented Dora to her 'brother' – 'as shifty a rogue as ever dropped from a gallows-tree and dark as the devil—'

'That's Hardenberg!' cried William interrupting.

' 'Twas what I thought, but I held me peace. As for Barton he was scared for his life to be away – after one look at *him*. But glad enough I was to have so much as that peeking sparrow to support me, for if ever a man spelled rape and murder that one did. "My brodder," says milady as bold as you please. "My brodder who comes mit me from Hanover to do me right vat has been done so wrong. . . .' Barton was for putting in his word, but I was there before him. "Wrong?" I says, "will you produce your wrong then, Madam Fräulein? Will you prove it? Bring out the child." '

And Dora spread her arms and rolled her eyes, giving

so droll a reproduction of the scene that William was
convulsed with laughter and pulled her on his knees to
kiss her. 'Wait! I've not half done—' she struggled up
and pranced before him with one hand low to the floor
as though she held a midget. 'Ecod, me love – look you!
The ugliest squint-eyed little monster – if I never speak
truth again 'tis never yours. It might be your brother
Ernest's – black as soot.'

'Or Hardenberg's,' said William.

'Or Hardenberg's,' she nodded. 'If he be man enough
to breed, which I misdoubt. But I would stake me life
it's neither yours *nor* Ernest's – nor yet the holy Bishop
Duke of York's. It hasn't got your eyes – I'd know a pair
o' those Guelph gooseberries in Hell. But milady's
codlin has a pair o' pitch-balls stuck in a lump o' dough
– and its head is round-shaped like an apple – without
the pine! And nothing of your pink and white and
gold to grace it, bless you. And its nose! If ever I saw a
Jew 'tis in that nose. . . . And "Ho!" says I, "Is this a
son of Hanover?"

' " 'Tis the son—" says she, and how I kept me nails
off her face I do not know. " 'Tis the son of *Klarr*-ence!"
Did you hear the impudence to beat it? "And its age?"
I asks as sweet as pie. "Four years," says she, with one
eye at the ceiling and the other on me foot. "Four! A
bonny child for its years," I says, and gives a glance
round sideways at me "brodder" to see him yellow as
a guinea and biting at his lip until it bled. "*Five* years,"
he growls out of his throat. "Mein sister, she is mistook."
Barton takes his cue and steps in quick. "His Royal
Highness the Duke of Clarence left Lüneburg these
seven years. The charge is utterly absurd. You waste
our time." '

'And money,' William added fretfully. 'You paid?'

'Oh, yes, we paid – the woman's return fare to
Hanover. 'Twas worth it to be quit of her. As for

Hardenberg, we've pulled *his* fangs. He'll trouble you no
more. Barton threatened to charge him with blackmail,
and reminded him that the penalty was hanging. You're
well out of it – and cheaper than you hoped,' said Dora,
perching on his knees to stroke his hair.

'I wonder,' William said, reflectively: 'There's Ernest
still to reckon with.'

'Ah, now, my soul! Meet trouble when it comes, and
be thankful for small mercies. For I'll tell you. . . .'

And she told.

Then William knew that if he had not been a father
in the past, he would, without doubt, be a father in the
future.

Chapter Two

In the New Year the tide of horror that had flooded
France swept to its hideous climax with the murder of
Louis XVI. That bloody pageant swarming in the
shadow of the guillotine, had reached its highest pitch
of atrocity when it hurled a King's head in defiance to
all Europe. The British peoples could no longer watch
and wait; the murmurous undercurrent of discontent
subsided in a wave of national indignation, that drew
from every man a spirited response to demonaic chal-
lenge.

The long and desperate struggle between England
and the French republic had begun, to last with one
short interval for more than twenty years.

Immediately after the declaration of war in January
1793, William as Rear-Admiral of the Red offered his
services for action. The Sea Lords gave him no decisive
answer; he was not accepted, neither was he definitely
refused. He was told, politely, to stand by. He stood,
with a burning grievance in his heart, while his
brothers went before him with their armies.

First Frederick with his Guards, accompanied by
crowds, huzzaing. William saw him off at Greenwich,
with his mother and sisters watching from the palace on
the river, and Frederick's young Duchess – a niece of
Frederick the Great, whom he had recently married in
Germany – weeping in his arms to swing public opinion
in his favour, and make the handsome Duke of York the
nation's hero.

Then Ernest, to serve in Flanders in command of the

161

Hanoverian troops; but Ernest went in secret, with no flourish of farewells, for Ernest if a cad, was first a soldier.

Edward, though not at the seat of war in France, was put in charge of an expedition to capture the French islands between Cuba and Haiti in the Western world. And even young Adolphus, aged eighteen, was permitted to serve in Holland as a Lieutenant, with the Coldstream. Of all the King's sons, Augustus only, who was delicate and wintering in Rome, and William with his ten years of naval warfare at the back of him, were inactive. George, as heir-apparent, had no choice but to stay out of it; preserved in safety from all risk.

Perhaps only Nelson knew what it must mean to one who had the sea in his blood and asked no more than to serve his country as a sailor, to be thus ignored: Nelson who when he, too, six months before had been disregarded by the Admiralty wrote to him:

> In what way it might be in the power of such a humble individual as myself best to serve my King has been a matter of serious consideration, and no mode appeared so proper as asking for a ship; accordingly on Saturday last Lord Chatham received my letter desiring the command of one. Still, as hitherto I have been disappointed in all my applications to his Lordship, I can hardly expect an answer to my letter which has always been the way I have been treated. But neither at sea nor on shore can my attachment to my King be shaken. It will but end with my life.

To which guarded appeal William replied: 'Should matters between the two countries grow serious you *must* be employed. Never be alarmed, I will stand your friend. . . .'

He kept his word. It was through his intervention that Nelson was given the *Agamemnon*, yet William could not get a hearing for himself. His rank of Rear-Admiral was a mockery. The Admiralty's vague decree had now materialized. He was rejected. The Navy had no use for him in war.

The blow was the more bitter in that he knew he had none but himself to blame for it. In the past he had defied authority and sailed twice in disregard of orders. He could not now be given a command who had been proved so unreliable: nor could he with his farcical rank of Admiral be reduced to Captain. The Sea Lords had been cunning in promoting him, a mimic sailor in gold lace and cocked hat, to display himself for show and not for action.

And talk again was rife. The prints nailed him – with Dora – to the mast, and jeered, 'The Duke would sooner have one drop of Jordan water than all the ocean's salt,' . . . 'she did not care for rocking in a hammock, on the sea. She would sooner ride her Man-o'-war at Richmond. . . .' All this and more they flung at him unsparingly. He stood alone in his humiliation. Dora was no helpmate to him here. Preoccupied with her work again, after her confinement, she was back in the theatre, rehearsing daily and acting every night, anxious to regain that position with her public temporarily lost by her enforced retirement. Their first child, a daughter, had been prematurely born, and lived only long enough to draw a breath. That, too, for William, had been a disappointment, but not for her, who had three children by another man.

It seemed the whole of life was turned against him. His father, who had heard his case at Windsor, would give him no support.

'What? What? You feel yourself hard done by? As you sow, so must you reap. Your record won't bear scrutiny. If you've been proved unsuitable to control a ship, how can you control a squadron – hey? The first duty of an officer in my service is obedience. You disobeyed. You must be punished—'

'With a life setnence?' put in William, blazing.

'Hey? I'll have no arguing – no – no – mutiny!' Although since his illness the King's brain-storms had decreased, his irate temper was all too easily aroused; the veins upon his forehead swelled as he spoke, the pendulous under-lip protruded, one clumsy red hand opened to fist itself and thump the chair-arm. 'In defying Admiralty's orders, you have defied *me*! Go back to your actress. I hear you keep an actress. What? What? How much do you pay her. What? How *much*?' The King repeated violently, while his son stood mute.

'Twelve hundred,' muttered William.

'Twelve hundred? Twelve hundred a year? Too much – too much. Half that would be enough, more than enough. Go! I'm sick o' the sight o' ye! Go – kick your heels. 'Tis all you're fit for. That – and fornication. Go, I say!'

He went, with blackness, seething. In the length and breadth of Britain, he alone had no place. He who had been in battle in his teens was now condemned to stay ingloriously idle, while from the lowest to the highest, others went before him to give their lives if need be, for their country's cause. In his shame and misery he felt disposed to offer himself in the ranks as an ordinary seaman. Who would care? Who would know or recognize him if he did? He could pass as his own double.

In some such reckless state of mind he received his good friend Nelson, who came to pay him a farewell visit at St James's before sailing in the *Agamemnon* with the Mediterranean Fleet.

The interview was brief for time was short, and Nelson due at Portsmouth the next morning.

'Well, Captain Nelson, you find me with my hatch-ways battened down. I've only myself to thank for it.' So often had he brooded on his wrongs that his recital of them now became a parrot-cry. 'A man or officer who disobeys an order must be punished – eh? That's the first rule of the Navy. A fine punishment. A landlubber in a palace full o' flunkeys on their knees to do my bidding, while those who were my juniors afloat take my command. I've slung my hammock in a comfortable berth, my friend. *J'y suis, J'y reste*. A good long rest for me.'

His eyes wavered from the unspoken sympathy in that steady clear regard.

'They also serve,' said Nelson, quietly.

'Yes, but it's not my way only to stand – and wait,' William answered in his throat.

'I, too,' said Nelson, 'had to wait, and but for you, Sir, I might be waiting still.'

'By God!' William's clenched hand came down upon his knee. 'The senselessness of those that mount us! You!' His glance rested on that frail yet wiry frame that held such force of energy within it. 'Cannot they see – these beldames in Whitehall, that the Navy hides a leader in its pocket who will one day astonish the world?'

'You do me too much honour, Sir,' a thin flush shone through the egg-shell pallor at the tribute. 'I am now only a Captain, but I will – if I live – serve actively and to the best of my abilities. I require nursing like a child,' Nelson added, wryly. 'My mind carries me beyond my strength, though I swear I'll not die in my bed.' And he was on his feet to be away. 'Sir, I must go, or I shall not make Portsmouth in the morning.'

William rose, too. 'Yes, you must go, and I must stay. I would give ten years of my life if I could follow you as your Lieutenant. A sailor without a ship is like a snail without a shell – in time of war. But you'll have my thoughts behind you. And – God-speed, Captain Nelson.' He gave his hand, and Nelson bent to kiss it. He could not just then, speak.

The year dragged on, with intermittent news of battles at sea and on land, but with no great naval or military achievement on either side. The first public enthusiasm waned. William sat glumly in the House of Lords and listened to the speeches, composing in his mind his own. If those in power kept him from his ship at least they could not stop his tongue. And he launched forth for two hours to his astonished peers on the most rambling diatribe ever delivered in that House.

He must enforce, he said, conviction on their lordships that as France had set an example of cutting off the heads of their King and Queen it was not at all improbable that the same system might be adopted in other countries, and Europe might exhibit the extraordinary spectacle of thrones without Kings and Kings without heads. In his imagination, he declared, he saw the demons of anarchy and rebellion stalking his native land, sent over by the revolutionary spirits of France to commit the same havoc in this country as they had done in their own.

The English peoples he knew to be brave, loyal and generous, but when other nations carried their revolutionary spirit to that excess as to cut off the heads of their King and Queen, then indeed England would be highly culpable and deserving of the contempt of all the nations of Europe if she did not interfere and show the regicides that they could *not* cut off the heads of Kings and Queens like so many poppies in a garden. . . .

Behind their hands the younger members giggled; their elders yawned and went to sleep. 'But we have a Navy,' thundered William, 'to hold these murderers at bay. Yes – a Navy – but who have we now to lead it? Our revered Admirals are no longer in their prime – but in their dotage! Where are their successors? I know of one whose skill and knowledge of navigation is un-exampled in the history of naval warfare – one as yet unrecognized whose name unknown to you will live immortal in the history of our country – one who until my intervention was kept retired in a village on half-pay. I commend your lordships to one Captain Nelson. Note the name, my lords – you'll live to cherish it! I commend also to your notice one Napoleon Buonaparte, who has so admirably conducted the siege of Toulon that although he be our enemy we cannot but admit him an honourable foe. He, my lords, is still only a young subaltern in the artillery, but I believe that he will prove to be an enemy whom your lordships cannot ignore. He it is,' shouted William, 'who by virtue of his military genius holds France in the hollow of his hand. *He* is no murderer – he is the saviour of France. France has found her leader. We, my lords, have not!'

He sat down, shaking. The slumbering peers woke up, and tittered, to disperse, and tell each other that the Duke was *toqué*.

William went home to Dora to be soothed, and found her studying a new part. 'Aramanthis' in *The Child of Nature*, with only half an ear for him.

'You waste your breath, my soul, in talking to those cabbage-heads. Will you give me my cues?'

'No, I will not!' roared William, snatching the script from her hand to fling it the other side of the room, 'would ye have me turn play-actor to play your fool? And what do you want with this mummery? You won't be fit to act again for months. You owe your duty now to me. That much I demand of you – and I'll get it, too. You've been brought to bed of an abortion once already by your folly.'

Dora was pregnant again and near her time. She burst into tears and made a fine show of hysterics. She lay on the couch, her little body distorted with impending motherhood, heaving beneath the hoop she wore to hide it. She hammered with her heels on the cushions, pulled at her hair till it tumbled, screamed that he was cruel – had ruined her career – had no thought for her in his gross selfishness. 'Me! Me! who am England's darling – and you would make a brood-mare of me. I want my work – I came to you on that condition. Here's Sheridan with offers at the door, and I'm tied, tied, *tied*!' Her voice rose in a shriek. 'You've forced your child on me! I warn you I'll not suckle it. I'll wean it from its birth—'

'You've killed one child – play-acting,' said William, pale.

'Killed!' Her mouth fell open with the shock of that. 'Killed! You dare to tell me—'

'I implored you to be quiet. You would not. You disobeyed me and the doctors. You worked till the last minute, until for decency you had to quit the boards – or be a laughing-stock. Only public opinion, and not *my* will, made you retire. When have you studied my wishes – or me? I'm less to you than the stage-hands who shift the scenery. I know! I know!' cried William, losing control and boiling, white-hot, for the day had sorely tried him, and his head was full of slights and insults – those peers with their yawns and their giggles – yes! he knew with an inward, hideous conviction that he had been a figure of fun before the House. 'I know,' repeated William smarting, 'that if I'd not been who I am I'd have had as much chance of your favours as – as a pieman. Do you *go* to Sheridan then! He'll keep ye – he'll give you all the play you want. Why don't you go?'

Dora was alarmed. She had overstepped her mark and knew it. She had no desire for a breach in their relationship at this stage. She had more to lose by it than he.

Pulling her ebbing dignity around her as though it were a cloak, 'Pray,' she whispered, 'will you leave me, Sir? What you have said I shall not soon forget.' She had learned a trick of changing colour, could blush or blanch to will as easily as she made tears and turned them off. It was her stock-in-trade. She used it now, with lips drawn back from her teeth and her eyelids closing. 'I've a pain across me heart. . . . Mother o' God! The pain!' And she lay whitening and shook with such a titillation of her limbs and gasping of her breath that William thought her near to dying, and was on his knees beside her in a panic.

'For mercy's sake! I'll take it back. I never meant a word of it. I'll fetch the doctor.'

She shook her head. 'No doctor,' she murmured faintly, 'can heal the bleeding wound you've dealt me. *Killed* – you said. Our child!'

'Now, now!' cried William, in a state, 'I swear I never meant it. I have been worried. I have been put about with troubles of my own.'

She opened one eye. 'Is that excuse enough to trouble me in my condition?'

'I deserve horse-whipping. Are you harmed? If I've harmed you—'

'Time alone will show.' Dora opened both eyes to turn them up. 'Give me the script. I'll learn another part before I die.' She made the greatest effort to raise herself upon an elbow as William retrieved the fallen script and brought it to her. 'Why do I work – you wish to know? Do you think it's for me honour then – or glory?'

'I don't think about it now,' he soothed her, 'nor must you. My love, if you are harmed I'll kill myself.'

'Will you not talk so glib of killing? Wait. . . . I'm

better,' she smiled wanly: 'I feel the colour in me cheeks again.'

'It is,' said William thankfully. 'You are looking more yourself.'

'It is me will-power. Why do I work – when I have you and all your bounty and your love? Am I ungrateful?'

'Hush, pray.'

'No – we will thresh this matter out, never to return to it. Forgive me that I speak of such a thing, me darlin', but I earned last year in salary—'

'Do I care! Why must you bring *this* up?' Hurriedly William turned the pages of the script he held. 'Where do you wish me to begin? I'll hear you.'

'I bring it up because I want you, love, clearly to understand my position. I have my children to support. I cannot come to you for *their* keep – can I? Eh, dear!' And her hand was pressed against her side. 'The pain of it! . . . *Will* you listen to me?'

'No, I won't. You are unwell. I beseech you not to overstrain yourself. You shall have double. I'll double your allowance if you will promise me that when our child is born you will for the first nine months devote yourself to it entirely. I'll give you *treble* for that promise.'

'Sure! I'd never take it,' protested Dora, widening her eyes. 'Am I a rat, to gnaw at your vitals for filthy gain with this treasure of ours under me heart? And would I not work meself to the bone for you – and it? God knows the Government keeps you close enough – you with three households and a retinue of servants in all of them. Treble! 'Twould be manna in the desert with three of my own and *our* little angel coming – to provide for. But no! Never!' Dora declared, heroically. 'Never in the world let it be uttered that I'm a rat for greed. Every penny that I earn I'd hand to you if it were not for me three fatherless, unwanted children.'

'Am *I* a rat then – or a pimp,' William shouted, 'that you should think *I'd* take it? What is yours is yours and what is mine is – is ours.'

'Too good! Too good!' she whispered, 'and I so undeserving. What a saint! D'ye hear him?' Her eyes rolled heavenwards. 'Of all his brothers he should wear the crown. A King of men, indeed. Page twenty o' the script, my soul. Act Two, Scene One.'

*

In January 1794, Dora Jordan was delivered of a son at Petersham, and William named him George Augustus Frederick Fitzclarence.

No father had ever been more proud. In that small red atom of humanity so indisputably his, William saw himself reborn. His son, unhampered by the swaddling clothes of Royalty, should achieve all that had been denied to him. He would be an Admiral by merit, and not by virtue of his high degree.

He was amazed that anything so young could look so old; creased and wizened as a medlar, with eyes that seemed perpetually astonished at the size of this great world after the small dimness of its own. William was seized with a sick dread lest his father's taint should be transmitted. He dared not take his fears to Dora, but he spoke in private to the doctor who reassured him. 'An intelligent, fine child, Sir – turning the scale at seven pounds at birth.'

'But do all infants look so *strange*?' persisted William.

The strangeness would wear off, he was told. And sure enough it did. Within an incredibly short time those miniature blurred features became comically humanized, and bore a distinct resemblance to his own;

the same shaped head, covered with a downy yellow fluff, a skin as white as milk, where it was not pink as apple-blossom. There had never been a more exquisite child, of that he was convinced; and he became almost jealous of its mother who had so much more to do with it than he.

'God sakes!' cried Dora, laughing, 'I believe if you could you'd give it suck.' And William blushed. Such things she'd out with! Never was woman to his mind so shameless – or more dear. He was infinitely tender with her now. It gave him a queer warm feeling to see his son in the curve of her arm, his tiny face greedily hidden against the luscious white globe of her breast, while over that nestling head she held her script, and murmured alternately her lines and love-words to her baby.

For although an admirable mother, she was chafing to be up again and back at the theatre. She had laid her plans in spite of him, and had engaged herself with Sheridan for the whole of the next season. The first production *The Child of Nature* was only waiting for its leading lady before going into rehearsal, and less than eight weeks after her confinement Dora returned to the stage.

William could make no objection to this arrangement, since Dora, amazingly, contrived to keep the balance between professional and maternal duties. She took rooms in Golden Square, and had the child with her.

He throve out of all knowledge, and although she did eventually engage the services of a wet-nurse, she continued, even while rehearsing, to lend herself to her son's needs. It was a not uncommon sight to see her sitting in the wings suckling her baby, and the whole company held up to wait his pleasure; or she would take him with her when she went to order her stage costumes, and might be seen any morning alighting from her yellow chariot at Miss Tuting's – the milliner in St James's Street – with the young Fitzclarence in her arms, to order hats, and change his napkins in the shop. And sometimes on these expeditions. William would accompany her; he was not ashamed to own his son before the world.

Parenthood, however, though a novelty to him, was not sufficiently absorbing to atone for lack of occupation at a time when to be unemployed in service for his country, was a slur on any able-bodied man. True, William had been instrumental in raising a volunteer corps at Teddington during the first summer of the war. He had stood on a platform in the middle of the village green in the blazing heat of an August noon, wearing – not his Admiral's uniform – but a plain snuff-coloured coat and kerseymeres and one of those curious new hats, not unlike a chimney-pot with a curly brim, that were the latest fashion; for Dora kept him to the fashions and supervised his dress.

And there he stood, like any country squire, surrounded by a group of gaping oafs and ploughboys and farmers in their smocks, and girls who came to ogle him and wonder who this rather stout and very fair young man might be, for half of the audience had no notion, and the other half were doubtful, until a whisper flew around and he was recognized and greeted with such resounding cheers that his speech was interrupted, and he had to beg for silence to continue.

The village of Teddington was near enough to Richmond for the local inhabitants to have heard something of the Duke's popularity in his own parish, and of his many unobtrusive acts of kindness to the poor, and of the quiet, domesticated life he lived with his play-actress, who was no less bountiful than he; and although over their mugs of ale in the inns for miles round they chortled of his doings – and of hers – there was not a man who liked him less for that, nor did not vote him the best of a bad lot.

And William, in his element, enrolled more men in half an hour than the recruiting officer had done in a day. He shook hands with each one who came up, chatted with the farmers of the harvest and their crops – the little knowledge on the subject that he had gleaned from his father stood him in good stead – and finally he ended up, stirringly, with: 'Army or Navy – what's the odds, lads, when duty calls us? When my time comes I will go with you, fight in your ranks, and never return without you!' Carried away by his own vehemence, his face shining under his hat, which every now and then he removed, to mop his forehead with his handkerchief and puff and blow – for he was gaining weight and felt it in the heat – he quite forgot in the enthusiasm of the moment that his own services had been refused. He did not in fact believe it, and hoped beyond hope that his suspension was merely temporary. But as time went on, and the war was a year old, and still he had no orders from the Admiralty, he swallowed his pride and wrote a last desperate appeal.

CLARENCE LODGE,
March 15, 1794.

MY LORDS,

I solicit in this hour of peril to my country that employment in its service which every subject is bound to seek, and particularly myself considering the exalted rank which I hold in the country and the cause which it is my duty to maintain. I regard a refusal of that employment as a tacit acknowledgment of my incapacity and which cannot fail to degrade me in the opinion of the public who from the conduct that has been pursued towards me, are justified in drawing a conclusion unfavourable to my professional character. . . .

If the rank which I hold in the Navy operates as an impediment to my obtaining the command of a ship without that of a squadron being attached to it, I will willingly relinquish that rank, and serve as a volunteer aboard any ship to which it may please your Lordships to appoint me. All I require is active service, and that when my gallant countrymen are fighting the cause of their country and their Sovereign, I may not have the imputation thrown upon me of living a life of inglorious ease when I ought to be in the front of danger.

WILLIAM.

But the Admiralty remained inimically silent; he received no answer to or even an acknowledgment of his letter. Exasperated, he then wrote to his father:

March 24th, 1794.

SIR,

On the 15th of this month I addressed a letter to the Lords of the Admiralty of which I transmit you a copy.

To neglect they have added insult, inasmuch as they have withheld from me even that courtesy which is due to every individual who makes a respectful tender of his services at a momentous period like the present.

As in this treatment of the Lords of the Admiralty my character as a naval officer becomes seriously implicated, I am emboldened to make this plea to my Royal father, soliciting from him that he will be pleased to issue his commands to the Lords of Admiralty to grant me that employment which I desire, or *publicly to state the grounds* on which their refusal is founded.

That at least – the letter of a son to his father, and not of a subject to his Sovereign – would, he thought, bring some result. He felt sure the King could not possibly refuse to give him a ship. He had stated his case frankly, and asked for a fair hearing.

He went on tenterhooks, became nervous and irascible with waiting; he lost his appetite, and some of his plumpness. Dora declared he was on a diet to get thin. From her he had no comfort in this crisis. He could not speak of it, for when he tried, she only said that she for one was not anxious he should go.

'What would I do without you, my dear soul? You might be killed, and leave me in shame and unprotected.' And she told him shrewdly a truth he much resented. 'You are always thinking that some Peeping Tom is round the corner pokin' fun at you, me darlin'. You think too much of the opinions of the world and folk that have nought to do with you. 'Tis as much as what the public will be saying of you now, as zest for soldiering that makes you feel so sore.'

'I'm *not* a soldier!' bellowed William, stung.

' 'Ods life, then – sailoring. Lord bless and save us where's the difference when every one of ye's set out to kill? War's murder when all's said – and a godless way to peace. Listen to Shakespeare. "A peace is of the nature of a conquest, for then both parties nobly are subdued and neither party loses." And are we not told to love our enemies, though to be sure,' said Dora, comically, 'I'd burn in Hell before I'd love the French.'

He could not but laugh with her, even while he smarted from the imputation that his wish to serve his country was prompted as much from what the world would say of him if he did not, as from heroics. 'And come to that,' said William, following his thoughts aloud, 'all heroism is mighty near to cowardice – and *vice versa*. The most gallant acts in battle are often

176

performed from the fear of being *seen* afraid. I never was afraid in action, but I take no credit to myself for that. It's because maybe I lack imagination.'

'Yet you have enough imagination,' Dora told him, 'to worry yourself sick over what was or was not said of you behind your back, or if milord Tomnoddy in the House snored during your speeches or if the cat grinned at ye, or if those pesky peers are looking at ye through a telescope from the other side of nowhere and calling you names and God knows what – bad cess to them! And may they burn for bringing you to trouble, me heart's blood! Not but that you don't bring half your troubles on yourself, by thinking them. As Hamlet says, "There's nothing either good or bad but thinking makes it so." Remember that.'

But William was in no mood to remember that or anything except his wrongs, and he went on worrying and fidgeting about those until at last a formal answer came – not from his father, but from the Secretary of State and briefly:

His Majesty has not been pleased to issue his commands on the subject of His Royal Highness's communication of the 24th *ult.*

He stood condemned: there could be no redress.

Chapter Three

THREE years after the birth of William's eldest son, the household at Petersham moved to Bushey Lodge. By the death of Lady North, widow of England's premier, the rangership of Bushey Park had become vacant, and the King having no one else in mind on whom to bestow it at that time, grudgingly gave it to William.

This honour, though insignificant enough, did at least carry with it an establishment proportionate with the almost perennial increase of William's family.

Set in the middle of wooded parkland, surrounded by several acres of garden and approached by the famous chestnut avenue, Bushey House consisted of one main building, two wings, a chapel and a vast number of rooms, but none too many for the demands of the young Fitzclarences, most of whom were born in this retreat, and who continued to live there long after their mother had gone out of their lives.

And in his enforced capacity of country squire, William made the best of a life, which, though not uncongenial, was none of his choosing, and accepted the entire onus of responsibility in the rearing of his young brood. For Dora, in spite of frequent necessary interruptions, continued to act between intervals, with a fine disregard for the unsubdued comments in the newspapers, and the cartoons that spared neither her nor her protector.

William took the duties of parenthood very seriously; he it was who ran the household, ordered the meals, engaged nurses, governesses, and tutors for his own and Dora's children.

The eldest of these, Frances, commonly acknowledged the daughter of Richard Ford, was actually the result of an earlier indiscretion between Dora and a certain Richard Daly, actor-manager, the first to discover and present her at the Smock Alley Theatre, in Dublin.

Although William was well aware that Dora's past would not bear scrutiny, it must have been something of a shock to him when, immediately before the birth of their second child, she gave him gratuitously a full account of herself, and the truth of Fanny's parentage. For, notwithstanding that long habit should have enured her to the natural function of childbirth, Dora had suddenly conceived the notion that she might die in a confinement. 'As a visitation of the Lord's righteous wrath upon me for my sins,' she said, and appointed William guardian to her three daughters, extracting from him a promise not to turn 'the poor innocents out into this cruel world uncared for.'

William, agitated by this divulgence, as unwelcome as it was unexpected, and in as great a fright as Dora, who had successfully transmitted her morbid fears to him, promised all she asked, and at her request took his solemn oath upon the Bible that he would not relinquish his guardianship until all three had attained their majority.

'Now I shall die happy in me mind,' said Dora, faintly, sending William from her room to fetch the midwife, for the labour pains were on her, and she was ready, she declared, to meet her end.

It is not be wondered at that William wept with joy and relief, when a few hours later the doctors announced to him the birth of a daughter, and that mother and child were both in robust health.

By the end of the century William found himself the proud father of five, two girls and three boys, and there were more to come. His devotion to his children amply atoned for their mother's seeming neglect, since even Dora's abundant energy and maternal love could not but be exhausted by the dual role she so persistently was called upon to play; for while with unfailing regularity she went on having babies almost every year, she emphatically refused to renounce her work to their demands, and no sooner was she up from child-bed, than she was back at Drury Lane or off on one of her 'cruises' as in compliment to William she termed her theatrical tours.

And he had no choice but to accept this singular conjugal arrangement. He had learned long ago that any attempt to remonstrate with Dora in regard to her own mode of living her own life, was as useless as attempting to turn the tide or stay a thunderstorm. For peace, he held his tongue. Hers could be sharp, her temper violent, her language shocking; but he loved her, he was used to her and to her ways, he had an enormous admiration for her talent no less than for her courage. He would not readily forget how boldly she had faced the battery of opprobrium hurled at her in the early days of their association.

As for her faults, of which her quick temper was the least and her untidiness to his orderly mind, the worst; her streak of vulgarity that sometimes jarred but more often than not amused him, her wild extravagance – for in spite of the huge salary she earned and the allowance that he gave her, she was continually asking for more, and he was hard put to it enough to meet his own expenses – all these peculiarities, were, he told himself, the natural complement of genius. He who had made such a failure of his own career, could pay generous homage to the success of hers. And when like a homing bird she returned to offer him her lovely little body unimpaired by the ravages of nature, her wit as fresh and sparkling, her laughter as delicious as in those days

when it had brought him to her side – when submissively, without complaint, she bore his many children,
any doubts he might have had of their mutual happiness, or of her love for him, were all dispelled, and he
could respond whole-heartedly to her exuberant affection.

It was inevitable that relations between William and
his family had become a little strained since his open
adherence to a notorious play-actress. He had lost touch
with his brothers. Frederick, at the war, was seldom
home on leave; George had been forced into a marriage
with Caroline of Brunswick, whom he loathed and had
treated abominably, returning, within a week of his
marriage, to his lady at Brighton – and even William
who loved him could not forgive that. Nor in his heart
could he forgive his father for his refusal to grant him
the honour of serving his country. It rankled: a festering sore in his life.

Thus did he enter upon those long years of domestic
retirement, making his rare appearances in the House
of Lords, paying his equally rare visits to his parents,
and ignored by the rest of the world.

Of all Dora's children, Frances, the eldest, was the
only one who caused her mother any anxiety at all. The
young Fitzclarences were healthy, handsome, boisterous,
and devoted to their Papa who knew how to temper indulgence with discipline. The two little Fords,
Dorothea and Lucy, were docile and loving, easy to
manage, well mannered – but Fanny! She was a problem indeed.

Imperious, self-willed and high-spirited, she had all
of her mother's vivacity and none of her looks. At
seventeen she was small for her age, with a shock of
rust-brown hair that never appeared to be brushed, a
greenish pale complexion, and black glinting eyes, like

a gipsy's. Although by no possible stretch of imagination – except perhaps her own – could Fanny be called
beautiful, she had a certain sprite-ish charm. Dora,
however, thought her woefully plain and everyone said
she was 'queer' in her ways if not 'wrong' in her
head.

She had her mother's quick temper, but also she
would sulk for days on end, and that Dora never did.
Her tantrums were up and over in a flash, but Fanny
would brood and glower; dumb. 'Lost in your own badness,' Dora would say, and would tell her, too, she was
a changeling, half-believing it. 'And how in Gemini,'
Dora wondered, 'shall I ever get her married?'

For Fanny was nearing the age when a mother's
thoughts revolve upon that all-important question.
Fanny, however, was so childish and young for her
years that Dora hoped she could continue to keep her
secluded for some time to come. Having presented herself to William as several years younger than actually
she was, Dora did not at all relish the idea of producing
a grown-up daughter who, according to her own account
of herself, could be no more than fourteen. So Fanny
was kept in the schoolroom in little-girl frocks, and her
tutor, the Reverend Mr Lloyd, private chaplain to the
Duke, who taught her and her sisters, the Fords – and
later the Fitzclarences – reported her over-sharp for her
age but deplorably lazy.

Fanny hated lessons, and detested Mr Lloyd. He was
pompous and ugly with warts on his nose and long
yellow teeth like a wolf's. He taught Latin and lectured
drearily upon the modes and customs of the ancients,
which Fanny considered must be tedious beyond com-
pare, until she read in her mother's Shakespeare the
story of Venus and Adonis.

Thereafter Fanny was often discovered browsing in
the library and taking books down from the shelves,

although she knew very well she had no right of way to any of the rooms used by the Duke. Only the little Fitzclarences were admitted to those precincts. But Fanny had no respect for rules, which she considered were made to be broken. She chose her time when she knew 'Our Billy' – as she called him to her sisters and very much 'Sir' to his face – would not be likely to find her there.

Dora and Lucy could never be induced to follow Fanny's lead in any naughtiness; both were a little afraid of her. She had frightening tales to tell of bogeys and witches, and ghosts, and a white lady who walked the terrace at night wringing her hands and moaning, to make your blood run cold. Fanny declared she had seen her; she declared, too, with an awesome rolling of her eyes and hideous grimaces, that she herself had learned the spells of witchcraft, in an old book discovered in the Duke's library; and she vowed she possessed the power to turn Dora and Lucy into toads or mice, or worse, if they did not do her bidding, scaring them so dreadfully that they were ready to follow her anywhere, even in her wickedness, to save themselves from such a fate. And she had more to tell than that. Fanny had a shrewd idea why the Duke went out of his way to avoid her and her sisters. They, poor fools, did not mind if they were passed over like dirt, but she did, for she knew the reason, and stored it in her heart among other grievances on which to brood.

There was no doubt that William *did* avoid her – more than the two little Fords who were charming, and pretty enough, almost to compensate for the fact that their existence was a perpetual reminder of a period in their mother's life that he would sooner forget. Fanny, however, he actively disliked. He thought her not only unattractive, but dangerously sly: also, Fanny was more than half-Irish, and William shared the general an-

tagonism at that time to anything Irish – except his
Dora and her brogue, which was more assumed than
natural.

But in spite of his personal revulsion to poor Fanny,
William was strictly conscientious; he allowed her and
the Ford children precisely the same advantages in up-
bringing and education as he accorded to his own, and
although he had made arrangements at Bushey to keep
Dora's three as much apart as possible from his – giving
them a separate suite for their own use – he did not
enforce this rule when their mother was at home. It was
the custom then for all the family to meet together,
when Fanny would be on her best behaviour, and so
self-effacing and such a proper little nurse to the babies,
that William would be made uncomfortably to feel that
he had been harsh and prejudiced, and that it was ill-
natured in him to exaggerate the poor child's faults
simply because of her origin.

Once he found her posturing before the mirror in her
mother's bedroom, and her mother's newest gown, with
jewels round her neck, feathers in her hair, and paint
on her face like a harlot's.

She stood demurely and quite unembarrassed before
him, while he thundered at her as though she were a
refractory young gentleman amidships.

'But, Sir,' she ventured, when he paused, 'I was only
practising the manners of the Court against the day
when I may be presented.'

When William reported the incident to Dora she
laughed and said, 'That day will be a long time coming
– if ever it comes at all. She must marry an earl at the
least to get *there* – if she gets over *me*. Their Majesties
will come to see me act but they'll not receive me or my
by-blows – nor even yours, my love!'

Besides being a potential débutante, Fanny had also
reached that age when Dora noted with some anxiety

that she must surely begin to question the relationship that existed between the Duke and her Mamma.

She did: and formed her own conclusions that were readily confirmed by the cuttings from the newspapers she found in Dora's bureau. It gave Fanny immense pleasure to rummage in her mother's drawers, and read her mother's letters. Dora was a prolific letter-writer, and half that she wrote was never sent, but would be tucked away in a pigeon-hole, and forgotten. She would often leave her private correspondence open and un-guarded, from which Fanny soon learned all there was to know of the family at Bushey House.

Slight though her connection with Royalty might be, Fanny was extremely proud of it. She was far more proud of her mother's position as mistress to the King's son than of her fame as actress. Fanny wished with all her might that she were the daughter of the Duke, instead of nobody's. When, through her investigations, the truth of her parentage dawned upon her, she har-boured the knowledge in sullen resentment. She stood alone. She was unwanted. Dora and Lucy were full-blood sisters; they belonged to each other. She was only half-sister to them and the Fitzclarence babies. She had no name – but come to that none of them had a name. Since, however, there was no longer any reason why she should be called Miss Ford, she decided to call herself Miss Jordan.

This intention she announced to Dora, who was greatly touched and took it as a personal compliment.

'I declare! A most delicate thought, me darling. And so you *shall* call yourself by the name I've made for you – until, please God – you get another.'

'How old am I, Mamma?' asked Fanny, gently.

Dora was very much taken aback. 'How old? Well – do you know? – I seem to have lost count. There are so many of ye. How old *are* ye now? Fifteen?'

Fanny's eyes glinted elfishly under her lowered lids. 'Shall I not soon be nineteen, Mamma?'

'Nineteen?' shrieked Dora. 'Of what in the name of sin can ye be thinkin'?' For there was no knowing, indeed. An imp of Satan, if ever there was one, standing there so meek, with her sly hidden look that brewed the devil alone could tell what mischief.

'I'm thinking of my age, Mamma,' said Fanny, looking down. 'Because when I *am* nineteen I would like to go to Court and be a lady.'

'Oh,' with the greatest effort Dora restrained her hands from her daughter's ears and placed them on her hips; 'Oh, so you'd like to go to Court and be a lady. May I inquire when you first *courted* the idea? And –' as Fanny opened her mouth to speak again – 'let me never hear another word of this, or so sure as I'm alive I'll give ye a taste of something you've not bargained for. A lady! So! What next? And you a child in the schoolroom.'

Fanny flushed a dark sullen red. Without raising her head her gaze shifted upwards to meet her mother's with defiance, 'I am not a child, Mamma,' she said distinctly, 'and if you have forgotten my age, I may be able to remind you – and the Duke!'

Dora stared speechless, to gather breath, as she received the full impact of this announcement; then – 'The Duke – is it?' she articulated. 'The Duke – forsooth! So that's what you're spinning in your wicked web of a mind. God sakes! That she should be me own!' cried Dora, eyes to heaven, 'or that I should live to see the black-hearted way of her. D'ye hear her threaten me? *Me!* That you should dare.' And with a spring and in a blaze, Dora seized her daughter by the arm and shook her till her teeth rattled. 'You little viper! I'll teach you to threaten me with your dark hints and your wickedness.'

'When – when—' stuttered Fanny, wrenching herself free from Dora's clutches to rub her shoulder and her arm. 'When have I threatened you, Mamma? I only said—'

'Yes, you only said!' And Dora's palm descended smartly on Fanny's cheek. 'And you'll not say again – I promise you! *I'll* stop your mouth – *I'll*—'

Fanny dodged. 'I never threatened you,' she whimpered. 'I never did, Mamma. I didn't mean anything, I didn't – I declare! Oh, dear!' And Fanny burst into floods of tears with boo-hoos and howls enough to raise the roof, and bring William who happened to be passing in the corridor, to put his head round the door to see what was amiss, and seing he would have bolted out again, but that Dora called to him: 'Pray, Sir, will you hear this little villain? She has something on her mind, I think, to tell you?'

'I hah – haven't!' sobbed Fanny.

'Yes, you have, me darlin',' Dora flashed, with smiles. 'Out with it.'

'I hah – have not,' protested Fanny, redoubling her howls. 'Oh, dear! Oh, no! I hah – haven't.'

'Tell the Duke, me darlin, how you want to go to Court and be a lady,' urged Dora winningly.

'Oh, be damned!' muttered William making for the door. 'Settle your nonsense between you. . . . Bother me!'

And out he went, disgustedly, and with a fine contempt for all such feminine disorders.

'So, milady – will you change your tune?' said Dora, hands to hips again, and nodding. 'And don't you ever dare repeat it to me. Court! . . . Come here.'

For Dora's temper never burned for long, and Fanny with her ankle-length, high-waisted muslin dress, her heelless sandals, and her short curly hair tumbling round her face, her tears, and her knuckles in her eyes looked no more than the child Dora would have her be. 'Come here!' repeated Dora, melting.

Seizing her opportunity: 'I only thought,' sobbed Fanny, 'that maybe I mi – hi – hight be allowed to go to London sah – sah – sometimes. I am si-i-ick of living in the mi-hi-iddle of a park and seeing nothing but deer and Mr Le-her-lloyd. I only wa-ah-ant to go to London to see you a-act.'

'So you shall then – so you shall, me darlin',' declared Dora, exchanging slaps for kisses. 'Dry your eyes now – fie! For shame! A great girl like you to cry. Would ye have me believe you're a minute more than twelve?' With her handkerchief Dora mopped up the streaming tears. 'They don't improve ye – wanton little hussy! This day week,' said Dora, 'I play before the King. If between now and then you'll mend your ways – be good – and no more vapours, mind – you shall be there.'

'The King!' Fanny's tears miraculously ceased. Not for nothing had she staged this scene. Her lips widened to a smile; her eyes sparkled; she was almost pretty. Perhaps, sighed Dora, she'll turn out a swan, poor duckling. 'There!' said Dora, kissing her, 'all's well.'

'Thank you, Mamma! *Thank* you. Oh! . . . The King!'

'And you shall stay the night with me at Golden Square.'

'Oh, Mamma!'

A curious, strange child – if you like! thought Dora, as she watched Fanny go dancingly away, out at the french window, over the velvety lawn, waving her arms like windmills, her witch's hair wild in the breeze. Was she, perhaps, not quite . . . accountable? Nineteen! How had she guessed it? Spying, prying, even thieving, one wouldn't be surprised. Her father was bad to the bone. And what in the devil, brooded Dora, shall I do with such a one? Take her to London? Take a house

and keep her there and bring her out and marry her –
please God – to a good husband? It would not be easy
And again, 'twould cost – how much? Too much for
her, who must save and save to give her girls security –
and herself, too. One never knew which way the wind
would blow the fancy of a man nearing his prime.

It seemed to her that lately the Duke had been unlike
himself – off-hand, less loving in her arms; short in his
words. He'd look with a query in his eyes, and would be
at her like a sheriff with his questions when the bills
for this and that came in. As if she could be expected
to keep count of every item with nine children to provide for and another on the way. There had been a
recent argument, not the first by any means. She had
said: 'They must be clothed, and so must I.'

'So I see,' he answered, grimly.

'Well? Do I not pay my way with what I earn?' she
had demanded.

'I thought,' he said, 'that was our first arrangement.
And you have your settlement from me.' There again!
To throw it in her teeth. How could a woman with such
calls as hers upon her mind and body, concern herself
with settlements and bills.

'Bills! Bills!' she told him, flaring. 'You can pay
them, and I'll pay you back from my bare living wage.
'Tis a mercy your old gossiping familiar, Mr Walpole,
is dead and buried – or he'd plaster you as a pimp
before the world.'

She had seen him colour up at that, and fold his lips,
and draw himself to his full, small height, with one of
those rare flashes of dignity to lower her in her own eyes
and his – and loosed her tongue upon him in defence,
with speech that rose from God alone knew what forgotten dung-heap of her past – till he turned heel and
left her.

It had been one of many, that clash of words, and

quickly over, yet it left behind a smear upon the surface
of their pleasure, like the trail of a slug upon a wall.
And like a wall, too, would rise between them, after
such scenes as this, the furtive ghost of their submerged
hostility. And recollecting it and all their many differences, Dora shivered as though a faint, cold breath had
touched her. Sure, the devil is in me at such times, she
thought contritely. And he so good and patient – though
he, too, had a temper, and a tongue when he cared to
use it. But like that impish girl of hers, he'd brood and
store up grievances, so that you could never know which
way he would be thinking.

That he resented her absorption in her work was
common knowledge; that he had accumulated a vast
amount of debts to his account, was knowledge, too;
but that the debts were hers and not his, none could
know *that* unless she told them. And the world was
ready to believe the worst of any spawn of Hanover.

Dora moved her head uncomfortably against the
chair-back. Her eyes, vague and troubled, watched her
daughter's elfish figure recede into the flowering green.
All Bushey was in blossom, the leaves just full, the
meadows brazen with buttercups, the deer knee-high
in the grass. This lovely home, should she not cherish it
– strive to keep it, renounce, as he would have her do –
her name, her fame, her genius? . . . By heaven, no!
Dora raised her chin. She from nowhere, who had
carved her niche in immortality – would hold it. For I
shall live, she said, when those who stand beside me
now, and all our children, and their father, too, have
been forgotten. *He'll* not be King, but *I* shall be a
Queen – in my own right.

It was a great thought, a great and noble thought.
The shade of the bar sinister cast upon her dear ones
would be lightened by their mother's lasting glory. And
he'd have her give it up. 'Never!' she declared aloud,

and with a gesture. ' "Shine out, fair sun," ' she quoted
deeply, savouring the words, ' "Shine out, fair sun, till
I have bought a glass – that I may see my shadow – as I
pass!" '

*

For a whole week Fanny had counted the hours till
the day when she would go to London to see her mother
play before the King. Certainly the pleasure of anticipa-
tion had been a trifle dimmed by the fact that Dora and
Lucy were permitted to share in the treat, for they, in
Fanny's estimation, were far too young to appreciate so
momentous an occasion. She deemed it wiser, however,
to keep these reflections to herself and to say nothing
that might give rise to argument.

Accordingly, she and her sisters accompanied by their
governess, Miss Turner, started off in the early morning of 15 May.

The day was warm and sunny, the chestnuts lighting
the long avenue with candles of pink and white were
still in their first splendour; small fleecy clouds scur-
ried across the fervent blue of the sky, the air smelled
of hawthorn and the joyous springing green; the deer
stood flank-high in the sun-dappled grass under the
trees, lifting lovely antlered heads to gaze unafraid at
the chaise as it rolled by, and to bend daintily again
to their cropping as it passed. They were tame and fed
sweetly from your hand.

'The darlings,' cried Lucy, whose especial pets they
were, but Fanny had eyes for nothing so stupid as deer.
She regarded her sisters with lofty disdain, and wished
her Mamma had thought fit to allow her to wear a gown
distinct from theirs.

All three were dressed alike in childish frocks of
India muslin, so high in the waist that their rose-
coloured sashes were under their arm-pits; they wore

twilled sarsnet pelisses to match, and close-fitting muslin caps tied with pink ribbons that made Fanny, although the elder of the trio by five years, look about thirteen.

It was for all of them a great event, if for Miss Turner fraught with some anxiety. There had been talk of highwaymen along the road to London; a coach and six had been held up only the week before, and the occupants, a lady and gentleman, robbed of their jewels and all their money. If a coach with a gentleman inside it, to say nothing of a coachman and outriders, could be set upon, what dire calamity might not befall a defence-less lady – Miss Turner never described herself or any other member of her sex as 'woman', unless she belonged to the lower orders – a defenceless lady and three little girls. Still, she consoled herself with the reminder that they were well attended, with two footmen, and John, the Duke's coachman, on the box, who could be relied upon, Miss Turner hoped, to offer some protection.

'One would think,' said Fanny, saucily, 'that we were making a journey to the Indies – such a fuss!' And when mildly reproved for her impertinence, of which she took no smallest heed, she added, 'I should have worn breeches and the Duke's cocked hat, and then I would have been mistaken for a gentleman and none would dare attack us.'

She thought it would be a wonderful adventure to be held up, maybe by someone young and dashing – a nobleman in disguise – who would rescue her from her miserable existence in a big house in the middle of a park, where nobody, not even her mother loved her. She would tell him a pitiful story about that, and how her stepfather was a wicked Prince who hated her and wished to do her wrong. She sat composing a fairy tale in which she played the heroine, who married one of the Royal Dukes – Edward of Kent, perhaps, or the

brave Duke of Cumberland (who they said had been
shot in the face and was handsome one side and ugly
the other, and had lost an eye), while Miss Turner
strove to divert her own fears by a dissertation on the
habits of the wild fauna of Great Britain.

At the inn at Twickenham the party halted for refreshment. At the sight of the elegant equipage and its
liveried servants, the landlord, with a white apron tied
across his middle, came bowing to the door to receive
the quality; the chambermaids, flicking dusters from
the windows, leaned out to watch, and drew back disappointed to see no gentlemen but only a pinch-faced
lady and three children. No tips or amusement from
such!

A young lad in his shirt-sleeves and a yellow waistcoat
who was grooming a horse in the yard, stared at the
cavalcade, and at Fanny, who, on the heels of Miss
Turner, gave him an impudent look – and another over
her shoulder, to poke her tongue at him.

That piece of naughtiness behind Miss Turner's
back compensated somewhat for the tedium of the
drive. Besides, he had no right to stare so brazenly at
her – a common stable-boy! She would let him know
who she was – if she had half a chance.

The beaming host conducted his guests to a parlour
overlooking an orchard splashed with waves of flower-
foam and resonant with bird-song. Fanny declared she
did not want a bite to eat, but would walk in the garden. Then Dora and Lucy must follow her lead and
say there were not hungry, Miss Turner, indeed, they
were not. Might they not all walk in the garden? . . .
By no means! There was no time for dawdling and
their Mamma had given orders. They were to partake
of egg-flip and a boiled fowl at Twickenham.

'I do detest egg-flip!' cried Fanny pouting. 'Can we
not have syllabub?'

'Yes! Yes!' agreed the chorus. 'Syllabub.'

'Egg-flips for all,' Miss Turner commanded. 'And, Frances, pray, do not act so contrary. You set your sisters the worst possible example.'

Frances, scowling, held her peace, hating Miss Turner and wishing to see her pickled in brine. Such a scarecrow in that dowdy grey cloak, with the ugliest brown velvet bonnet – to dare to take so much upon herself as to dictate to Fanny *Jordan*. One day, *I* shall teach *you* your place, ma'am, Fanny promised inwardly. A mere penniless, dependent, old maid! . . .

The lad from the stable-yard waited on them, with a lordly air. He had put on a bottle-green coat and a clean neckcloth. He looked, thought Fanny, almost – but not quite – a gentleman. He had dark wavy hair, a face as brown as a nut, and narrow black eyes that tilted slightly upwards at the corners.

Fanny regretted she had poked her tongue at him, and endeavoured to prolong the meal by eating very slowly, for the pleasure of having him at her elbow with the dishes. Miss Turner, however, bade her hurry, as already they were late and must on no account arrive at the theatre after the King. Then she whispered to each discreetly. Dora and Lucy said, Yes, if you please, Miss Turner, but Fanny said, No – for she saw here her opportunity, and took it.

Left alone in the parlour while Miss Turner led her charges to the privy, Fanny darted to the bell-rope and pulled. As she hoped, the boy who had waited at table answered the summons. Fanny stood in the middle of the room, opened her mouth to speak, and for a moment or two said nothing; for her heart was beating so strangely under her broad ribbon sash, she could scarcely get her breath.

'Oh – I – I – made a face at you. It was very rude – I should apologize.'

'I did not see you,' answered the boy, coolly. His thick black eyebrows almost met over his nose, which was small and hawkish, sharply curved. *Not* so handsome after all, decided Fanny, blushing with mortification at this cavalier acceptance of apology.

'Then you should have seen,' she retorted hotly. 'Who are you – what is your name?'

Thomas Alsop, she was told.

'Do you live here?'

'This is my father's house.' His eyes boldly raked her face, and searchingly her childish figure, and, 'Is there anything you want?' he said, with a twist of his lips.

'That is not the way to address me. You should say *Miss*. What do you mean – this is your father's house? Is your father the landlord?'

'He is.'

'And so he makes a servant of you. You don't talk like a servant – you don't *look* like a servant. Have you ever been to London?'

'I have lived in London.'

Fanny paused a moment to take this in. 'Oh-oh! So *that* is why you speak like an educated person. What did you do in London? Did you work? Were you a footman? Have you been associated with gentlefolk?'

'You ask too many questions.'

'Well, I declare!' Fanny almost lost her breath again – the coolness of him! 'What age,' she demanded, 'are you?'

'Seventeen – *Miss*.' He flashed a grin at her. 'And what age are you?'

'What business is it of yours?' But she bit back a giggle, not wholly displeased at this *tu quoque* retort. 'I am older than you by a year or more – but I am supposed to be fifteen. I look younger than my age, do I not?'

'I don't know. I haven't looked at you.'

'That's a lie! You are looking at me now.'

He was, with that raking look of his, that seemed to see right through her clothes to her nakedness – a look that whipped the blood into her cheeks.

'I—' she said, high-voiced and in confusion, 'I am going to London now – to see the King.'

He seemed not one whit impressed.

'I've seen him many times,' he said. 'He's mad.'

'You have no right to speak so. 'Tis treason. You could be hanged for saying it. Do you know who *I* am?'

'How should I know?'

His tone implied that he cared less.

'I am Miss Jordan,' said Fanny, haughtily. 'Do you know the name?'

'I may have heard it.'

'*M*ay have!' He was too provoking! 'Don't dare to tell me you have not heard of the greatest play-actress of all time – my mother, Mistress Jordan.'

She threw this at him with her chin in the air, and he tossed back to her crisply:

'She is by no means the greatest. Siddons is that.'

'Oh!' Fanny clapped a hand to her mouth and stared at him, blazing. 'Your impudence! What right have you to pass an opinion?'

'As much right,' he answered carelessly, 'as you – to criticize me and give yourself airs.'

She could scarcely believe her hearing. The blood rushed in a torrent to her cheeks, and words to her lips.

'You – you monster! I'll have you flogged. I'll have you put in the stocks. I'll complain of you to my step-father, His Royal Highness the Duke of Clarence – *he'll* send you to jail – quick march!'

He laughed at that, a silent laugh behind his eyes, and said, offensively, 'You rang. Did you want anything?'

'No – only never to see you again!'

'Very good – Miss.' He bowed, in mock politeness, and turned to go. She called him back. 'Come here!'

He came, and stood before her, so near that she could smell him, and the scent of horse and hay upon his clothes.

'Would you—' she asked him, breathless, 'would you like to see my Mamma act – before the King?'

'I wouldn't mind.'

'You wouldn't *mind*! You should be honoured. Listen,' she spoke in a rapid whisper impelled by some queer sudden urge outside herself, and hastened by the sound of Miss Turner's voice in the room above, hurrying the children. 'Have you a horse? I saw you grooming one. Is it yours?'

'My father's. I ride him.'

'Then,' whispered Fanny in a rush, 'do you follow our chaise and come to London to see the play!'

His eyebrows lifted. 'What!'

She gave a noiseless stamp of her foot. 'I am telling you! Have you any money to buy yourself a seat?'

'Not a groat.'

'Here!' She unfastened her reticule, searching frantically among its contents for her purse. 'That should buy you a seat in the pit.' She handed him a crown piece.

'Yes, but,' he objected, with his eyes on hers, slanting, 'it will not buy me stabling for my horse and board and lodging for the night.'

'Very well. Here is a guinea besides. I have plenty more. My Mamma is very rich. She earns a fortune. I shall be in the stage box. And,' said Fanny, impishly, 'I will poke my tongue at you again for a reminder. Where shall you lodge? I lodge in Golden Square.'

'I will find my way,' he said, with meaning.

'Hush! . . . You will come?' And for the benefit of

Miss Turner who was by this time on the stairs, she added loudly, 'Bring me a glass of water – and make haste.'

Thomas Alsop pocketed the money, gave her a quick nod and a long look, and went.

For the remainder of the drive Fanny was in the highest spirits. She chattered incessantly, giggled to herself, and seemed so excited and capricious that Miss Turner thought she must be sickening for a fever. 'You are overwrought, my dear. Pray sit still.' For she was for ever jumping up to put her head out of the window.

'To see that we are safe from highwaymen,' she said. 'There is a horseman following. Do you think he is likely to overtake us?' And saying it she laughed immoderately – for no reason at all.

Quelling simultaneously her own alarms and the timid squeaks of her younger charges, Miss Turner firmly said it was foolish to suspect every inoffensive horseman on the road. The King's highway was free. 'Once we are past Barnes Common we shall be safe. Besides, in broad daylight there is little chance of an encounter. I really must beg you to compose yourself, Frances, and sit quietly. You jump up and down like a jack-in-the-box.'

'I *feel* like a jack-in-the-box,' declared Fanny. 'I feel as if I were on springs.'

Dora and Lucy crowed with laughter at that. Fanny was *too* droll!

After which Fanny subsided, and sat hugging herself in her corner, and smiling into space. If they could but know – those little sillies, and long-faced prim Miss Turner – that she had manœuvred so cunningly behind their backs! True, it had cost her a crown and a guinea, but her Mamma was generous, and gave her as much pocket money as ever she could spend in a dead and alive village.

To think that for the first time in her life she had talked alone with a young man! For even if he were only seventeen he had all the *manners* of a man, and a gentleman, too – although he *had* been provokingly rude, but this rudeness was part of his charm. He was like – Fanny had read her Grecian mythology, with Mr Lloyd – like the young Pan. He needed only goat's feet to make a satyr of him – chasing *me* – thought Fanny wildly, his nymph! . . .

As the coach entered the village of Kensington, progress was delayed by a stream of carts, wagons, and droves of cattle returning from Smithfield's market, and at Piccadilly turnpike came another stop. This was caused by a crowd of people in a great stir: artisans, farmers, women of the town, but mostly beggars, who habitually congregated at the toll-gate to collect pence thrown at them from the carriages of the gentry. All these and all sorts, straggled in groups across the road and blocked the entrance to Hyde Park.

'What is it? What is it?' demanded Fanny of the coachman. 'Why don't you go on? We shall be late.'

Miss Turner thought there might have been an accident and sent a footman to inquire of the turnpike keeper. He came back to report that while the King had been reviewing his troops earlier in the morning, a musket had unexpectedly been fired. 'The ball,' he said, 'passed through the coat of a Frenchman, and hit a boy in the chest standing not a dozen paces from His Majesty.'

'Dear! Dear! How very shocking!' Miss Turner murmured helplessly.

'What has that to do with us?' cried Fanny. 'The King was not hit. Tell these people to move aside. Tell them we shall be late for the play.'

A woman half-naked in her rags, with a skeleton baby

at her breast and a dreadful face covered in sores, sidled up to the carriage window to thrust a skinny hand through it, under Fanny's nose. 'For the love of Jesus – pretty lady—'

Fanny drew back in horror.

'I vow and declare I shall be sick! Go away – *go away*. John! Whip this creature off!'

'Hush, pray!' whispered Miss Turner. 'Do you want them to throw stones at us?'

But that ragged herd, whose pale gaunt faces were turned toward the carriage, not to threaten, only to gaze, like patient beasts from behind their bars of poverty, at beings who inhabited another sphere and were their masters – they had no thought beyond the hope of alms, no resentment in their stifled hearts, no murmur in their throats. Those voices that spoke for them and for their needs – as God might speak in Heaven for the damned – had not yet reached their ears, though it was there, a low, far-distant thunder, not yet to break in storm.

At the crack of the coachman's whip, the beggarwoman and the mob behind her slunk submissively aside to let the gentry pass, who, in consequence of these delays, arrived at Drury Lane only a few minutes before the Royal Family.

The house was packed, not so much in compliment to Mrs Jordan and the play, as to the King, who had expressed a wish to see *She would and she would not*, by Colley Cibber.

Everyone of note was present, all eyes fixed expectantly upon the Royal box with its crimson velvet drapery, and garlands of fresh flowers. Fanny, leaning out of her seat, anxiously scanned the sea of faces surging in the pit, but it was impossible to distinguish anyone among that mass.

Scarcely had she and her sisters taken their places and

removed their wraps, when a muffled roar swept through the mob below, to be echoed by a polite rustling whisper from the tiers above. Gentlemen in the latest fashion of cut-away coat and high cravats dodged their ladies' feathered turbans, the musicians in the orchestra tucked their fiddles under their chins, and suddenly the Royal box was filled.

Beneath the velvet canopy and half-concealed by the curtains, stood the King in his scarlet Field-Marshal's uniform, peering at the house with his glass to his eye, his red face shining under the cropped unpowdered wig he now affected. Behind him, at the entrance to the box, appeared the Queen, atrociously gowned in heliotrope, and rippling with smiles, while like a flock of fluttering white birds the Princesses followed her, and the whole house rose to its feet drowning the first strains of the anthem in a tremendous noise of cheering and clapping for the story of the King's escape earlier in the day had been already circulated.

Delighted at this friendly welcome, the King came forward, bowing right and left, well in front of the box, when in a flash a man sprang up from the second row of benches in the pit, levelled a horse-pistol at that genial red-coated figure and fired.

For a moment the audience stood panic-stricken in a tense and breathless silence, then, as the neighbours of the man seized and held him, a great cry tore through the vast theatre. 'The King! God save the King! . . . And saved he was, still bowing, still smiling, seemingly cool and undisturbed, with his eyeglass searching the yelling house, while in an undertone he soothed his terrified Queen – 'A squib, my dear – nothing but a squib. They have been firing squibs.'

Slowly the curtain rose, and 'God save the King' was played again accompanied by a full-throated, full-hearted chorus, and all the actors on the stage.

Fanny, who had been well to the fore when the pistol
went off, and had nearly tumbled over the edge of the
box in her fright, soon recovered herself to find her
sisters in the giggles and Miss Turner in a faint. Here
was a to-do! . . . Fanny was in no mind to attend to
Miss Turner and her vapours, but when a search in that
lady's reticule revealed a total lack of any kind of res-
torative, and as the poor lady emerged from her stupor
to fall into laughing hysterics, there was nothing for it
but to go and seek an attendant in the cloakroom.

'And miss the play, I suppose,' grumbled Fanny, as
with some enjoyment she slapped Miss Turner's hands
and tweaked her nose and bid her: 'Hush, you ridiculous creature! Aren't you ashamed?' to no avail.

Bidding her sisters, 'Watch this sickly fool till I
return,' Fanny left the box and ran down the deserted
corridor straight into the arms of a tall gentleman who
was hurrying along it.

'Oh!' gasped Fanny disengaging, 'I beg your pardon,
sir.' And raising her eyes to his face, she almost fell at
his feet in astonishment as she recognized – the Duke
of Cumberland!

She had seen him only twice before in her life when
he had visited his brother at Bushey, but although
Fanny had been presented to the Duke by her mother
on one of these occasion, it seemed evident that now he
had no notion who she was, not even though she swept
him a curtsy to the ground and murmured rapturously:
'Sir! . . . Your Royal Highness.'

With the barest acknowledgement, a jerk of the head
and a glance from his unimpaired eye – he had lost one
in the war but the other was keen and assured him the
girl was not worth his attention – the Duke hurried on.

Fanny gazed after him, flustered and pouting. How
rude! But how splendid he looked in his elegant plum-
coloured coat and white breeches. How much more

distinguished than 'Our Billy'. Such whiskers! To start
a new fashion, they said – because he'd been shot in the
face.

Where could he be going in such haste?

This was not Fanny's first visit to Drury Lane
Theatre, and she knew that the way he had taken led
to the back of the house. Why should the Duke go to
the back of the house, unless perhaps to cancel the performance on account of the shooting? If so, he would
surely visit her Mamma. . . .

She could hear that the tumult in the auditorium had
by no means subsided. The people were clamouring for
the traitor to be brought upon the stage. She could
hear howls and hoots and catcalls. Fanny wished she
could find Thomas Alsop, who must have seen the incident if he were in the pit – but it would be impossible
to seek him out in that mob. Besides, she would attract
attention to herself if she tried to force her way among
the common folk. As for the Duke of Cumberland, he
no doubt was flurried. That was why he had not recognized her. . . . If she went behind the scenes she would
soon know the truth of what had happened.

Her curiosity aroused and her errand all forgotten,
Fanny retraced her steps to follow, discreetly, in the
wake of the hurrying Duke.

Meanwhile, the King with great presence of mind,
had commanded that the play should go on, in spite
of the Queen's protestations and the plight of his
daughters, all of whom, with the exception of Princess
Augusta, were in a state of collapse. But the performance was a complete fiasco, the actors were continually
interrupted by shouts and questions from the pit and
gallery, and the demand that the assassin – whose name
it seemed was Hadfield – should be exhibited before
them – 'drawn and quartered'.

Finally, Dora took it upon herself to come forward and assure the house that: 'The miscreant has been perfectly secured and properly attended.'

He was; bound hand and foot and guarded by four stage-hands and a lad in a bottle-green coat, who had been the first to leap at him and knock the pistol out of his hand, and hold him struggling and kicking till others came to his assistance.

Young Alsop had certainly not bargained for such excitement as this when he accepted Fanny's invitation and her bribe. Although he had missed the play he had become the centre of attraction. He and those who aided him had hauled the fellow over the palisade into the orchestra, and down the steps to the music-room beneath it. There, yelling like the maniac that later he proved to be, they detained him until the constables arrived; and there, too, Alsop and his assistants were complimented by the Duke of Clarence and amply rewarded for their gallantry.

Although William had not witnessed the outrage it had greatly disturbed him. Twice in one day! There was no doubt in his mind that a similar attempt on the King's life had been made during the review of the Guards in the morning. That first shot, he was sure, had been no accident. Both balls had gone wide, but the next time, perhaps, his father might not be so lucky.

And what could such a murderous attack portend and from what poisoned root did it spring? They said this fellow Hadfield was mad.

Watching him held, bound, and screaming, with foam on his lips, his face hideously distorted with terror William could well believe it. Still, an act of such sinister violence, even if perpetrated by a lunatic, could not be disregarded.

There is no effect, thought William gloomily, without a cause. And what cause was here? What dark resentful grievance lay coiled like some malignant growth at the roots of Britain's constitution? Monarchy and all it stood for, kingship and the forms and pieties of English life, the familiar backwash of age-old custom and tradition – were these to be exploded by some new, destructive force? Destructive – yes – but by destruction, one might perhaps rebuild.

William had no special quality of insight; he was not gifted with imagination, but, even to the most embodied spirit, at some time or at some crisis in its journey, there may be shed a dim reflection of a purpose to light it on its way.

By which same token, at that moment in the half-lit room beneath the stage of England's national theatre, while above he heard the rich, lilting voice of his mistress soothing the clamorous house – in that moment when he stood before the pitiful fanatic who had so nearly killed his father and his King, it seemed to William that a shutter opened in futurity.

What if he should be the chosen pivot on which a whole new social freedom would revolve? What if he by some unlooked for, fateful intervention should be empowered to champion the cause of a great people toward enlightenment and liberty, and hope? . . . And like a breath on glass, as swiftly fading, it was as if in that one second's pause, he saw himself dissolved in his own destiny.

Chapter Four

As a stone cast upon calm waters will leave its trace in ever-widening ripples, so did events in an obscure concerted sequence diverge from that fifteenth day of June in 1800, to effect the lives of Dora Jordan and William, Duke of Clarence; and other lives than theirs.

The remarkable self-control and indifference to danger exhibited on that occasion by the King, had won the admiration and fervent loyalty of all who witnessed it; but who could tell how far such self-control had strained that crippled mind, or what aftermath of shock intermittently resounded through the hazy corridors of his subconscious?

The methodical examination of those who watched him, revealed no visible sign of any untoward relapse, yet it was observed that he had become more incoherent in his speech, that his memory for words would fail him, and that he seemed more than ever easily aroused to violent fits of temper.

The doctors sent him down to Weymouth for a 'rest', accompanied by the Queen and the Princesses. The people of England waited apprehensively for the guarded reports of his condition. Their elderly, affable King with his simple amiability, his eccentricities, his kindly red face, and above all his monumental courage when madmen attempted to kill him, had, in his declining years and for the first time in his reign, become universally popular.

On the 26th of the month following the incident at Drury Lane Theatre, the man Hadfield was tried and condemned as a criminal lunatic. Young Alsop, called as a witness, was brought very much to the fore. For the innkeeper's son no less than for His Majesty, that command performance had been memorable.

For Fanny, too, whose adventures on that day had far-reaching results.

The full tale of her escapade was never told. None knew the truth of it, save Fanny herself, and she appears to have created the impression that she had suffered from a loss of memory. So according to Dora, who poured into William's unresponsive ears a rigmarole that left him none the wiser. Nor was he at all concerned about the case. He had troubles enough of his own, and debts to meet that overwhelmed him.

But Dora was persistent – for some reason – to bother him with her account of Fanny's misdeeds. From her he heard how after the shooting incident, the girl, on some pretext or other, had left the box and the vapouring Miss Turner – and had not come back.

One can well imagine Miss Turner was distracted, and that she and her young charges had seen nothing of the play, for, sooner than leave them in the box to be kidnapped or murdered by ruffians with blunderbusses, she had insisted that the little girls attend her in her search for their sister.

So, along that red-carpeted corridor had fled Miss Turner with a child attached to each hand; into the ladies' cloak-room to inquire of the attendant if a young lady had been there within the last quarter of an hour. No young lady had been seen. Back again to their box – to find no Fanny. Dora and Lucy set up a hullabaloo. Could they not see the play, Miss Turner? Fanny was sure to return. Oh, please to let them see the play.

Convinced that a blood-stained corpse was concealed behind the curtains, or at least a pistol under a chair, Miss Turner, although on the verge of collapse, resolutely continued her search. Nothing would induce her to leave her pupils alone in the box unguarded. She hurried them round to the back of the house and to their mother's dressing-room.

Mrs Jordan, they were told, was on the stage. Her dresser, exhaling a pungent smell of Hollands, declared there had been no visitors – to her knowledge. No *lady* visitors – she laid some stress on that, though she had, she fancied, seen a gentleman go into the room before Mistress Jordan was called to make her speech. She could not have told you who he was. He might have been Mr Sheridan if he had not been so tall – he was not His Royal Highness, being of a greater height, but as for a young lady – she was positive sure as she could be in such a taking, with all the noise and shouting and to-do, that not a sight of one had passed her way – and she only hoped the varmint would be hanged as he deserved.

Which enigmatic information did nothing to lessen Miss Turner's alarms, and almost rendered her prostrate again. And how to break the news to Mrs Jordan, she did not know.

Further inquiry elicited the fact that a young lady answering to Fanny's description, had been seen by stage-hands talking to the lad Alsop in the wings while the preliminary examination of Hadfield was taking place in the music-room, and in the presence of the Duke of Clarence and his brother Cumberland. They, it seems, with Sheridan had formed part of the escort who accompanied the prisoner to Cold Bath Fields.

As to Fanny's whereabouts between the time when she left Miss Turner and her sisters in the box, and her reappearance in Golden Square at ten o'clock that night, there was no telling.

She had returned in a daze, flushed and dishevelled, with dirt on her rose-coloured pelisse; refused to eat

any supper, laughed and cried when she was scolded,
complained of a headache, and sat shaking in a corner
with the giggles. So strange was her deportment that
Dora sent for the apothecary to have her bled. But
Fanny would have none of that. She vowed she would
stab herself sooner than take to the leeches, and was let
off with a purge.

Next day she was brought up in judgement before her
Mamma. She could not – or would not – give a satisfactory account of what she had done or where she had
been. She had found herself alone in the street in the
dark, and was frightened. She had hired a chair. Her
memory had gone, completely – so she said; and said no
more.

'But you can't,' screamed Dora, 'have forgotten. Good
God! You might have been outraged.'

Fanny lowered her eyes.

'And why did you go behind the stage at all?' her
mother questioned. 'What possessed you to do anything
so brazen and foolhardy?'

Fanny didn't know.

One might as well, thought Dora, get blood out of a
jellyfish as a word of truth from this one. There was
more than met the eye in such forgetfulness. True, the
apothecary had said that a sudden shock – the firing of
the pistol – *might* have induced a temporary disorder.
The Princesses, it seemed, had been greatly affected.
Princess Amelia had passed from one fainting fit to another – but, Fanny, to Dora's knowledge, had never
fainted in her life.

'What induced you,' repeated Dora, 'to go behind?'
For that much Fanny had admitted.

'I think I must have gone, Mamma – to see if you
were safe. If I went at all. I don't remember—'

'But you *must* remember – unless you're crazed. One
of the carpenters saw you talking to that boy.'

' 'Tis all confused, Mamma. I must have fainted.'

'That I'll swear you did not,' retorted Dora. 'You are lying in your teeth. I'll be bound you've something hidden that you'll not disclose. What have I done to be so cursed with such a devil's brat, I'd like to know?'

Fanny gave her mother a slow, sidelong look. 'I think I tried to find your dressing-room, Mamma.'

Said Dora sharply: 'My dresser tells me that she never saw you. I had no visitors that day except the Duke.'

'Which Duke, Mamma?' inquired Fanny, showing the whites of her eyes.

'The girl's bewitched!' whispered Dora with a paleness beneath her rouge, and loud she said: 'There's but one Duke comes to *my* room, remember that!'

'I'll remember it, Mamma,' Fanny answered, in a little voice and downcast. 'Yes, I will remember that – if I forget all else.'

So now! Dora's hands were fisted at her sides, but she restrained them. 'I'd love to break your jaw for ye—' she muttered on her breath, 'but even that 'ud get no word from ye but lies. *And* you'll not repeat them – understand? For so sure as I'm your mother – for my sins – I'll have the skin off your back and the eyes from your head if you go working mischief.'

This horrid threat spoken with hisses on a rising crescendo, caused Fanny to burst into tears and to declare with howls and sobs that she had meant no harm – indeed – indeed! And she would kill herself if her Mamma spoke so unkindly. What had she done? Oh oh! What misery was hers? Was she not si-ick from shock? The Princesses and Miss Turner were permitted to ser-huffer from sh-her-hock – but not herself. Oh no! Oh cruel!

'I'll give ye cruel,' her mother promised her un

softened. 'You may go. And if 'tis to the devil – I will speed ye!'

Which maternal sentiment, and the growing conviction that so equivocal an influence should be removed from the vicinity of her younger daughters, may have hastened Dora's decision to take a house in London.

William encouraged the idea. He would have gladly held himself responsible for the upkeep of the whole establishment to be well quit of Fanny.

*

Although since taking up his residence at Bushey, William had been careful to avoid publicity, the daily prints were ready enough to seize on any current gossip that might be circulated to his disadvantage.

The frequent additions to his family had become a standing joke. The caricaturists were as busy with their pens as the rhymesters with their jingles. Gillray and Rowlandson spared neither Dora nor the Duke; one famous cartoon presents him as a goggle-eyed farmer mopping his over-heated brow as he wheels a perambulator, containing three hideous infants, through the leafy glades of Bushey Park. At his heels, dressed in the scanty garments of the period and grown enormously fat, trails Dora, studying a part from an open script.

There was no mercy shown to him, who, when public spirit moved, was forced to see his children pilloried and the privacies of his own life dragged out and exposed like a naked trollop. More than ever did he seek obliteration in the green solitudes of Bushey, only emerging at intervals to deliver his rambling, but not always unimportant speeches in the House of Lords.

The most enlightened of these, which called forth a perfect hurricane of abuse, was delivered in 1800, when he attacked the Adultery Prevention Bill that sought to prohibit the marriage of divorced persons.

His speech, if not wanting in courage, was certainly wanting in tact. He shocked the bishops and startled the peers when he pleaded for the rights of the woman taken in adultery.

None who heard him knew, or could ever know, that he had championed the cause of women's suffrage a hundred years before the very thought of it had been conceived. 'Let us not assemble here,' he roared, 'to forge the galling chains of prostitution and degrade the English fair sex.'

In view of his own position, straight from the arms of Mrs Jordan, the speech and the sentiment it voiced were regarded as a shameless outrage, not only against the proprieties, but against the superiority of man as opposed to the inferiority of woman – and of one woman in particular whose pernicious influence was attributed the head and front of the offending.

Apart from these occasional appearances he avoided any contact with the outside world. He entertained once a year on his birthday, but even those innocuous festivities were ridiculed and exaggerated and reported in the papers at great length.

The most spectacular of these when he had, for once, launched forth with some extravagance, brought about a virulent offensive from the Radical Cobbett in his *Weekly Political Register*.

The whole performance certainly was lavish, and conducted on a grander scale than any previous affair. William's brothers, who were always invited but who seldom appeared, turned up in full force. Frederick and Edward brought their Guards bands to play choruses in the shrubbery and marches on the lawn. The Prince of Wales and Cumberland were there, the Lord Chancellor, and a host of notabilities of the very highest *ton*. The public, too, had been admitted to behold the banquet, to partake of free refreshments and to wander unmolested in the grounds. The daily journals sent representatives who duly gave account that: 'The Grand Hall had been entirely refitted with bronze pilasters, the ceiling very correctly clouded, and the whole illuminated by some brilliant patent lamps suspended from a beautiful eagle.'

Dora, who had put her men-servants into new liveries and herself in a court gown, was half hysterical with so much honour, and aching stiff with curtsies.

But the crowning feature of the day was a procession of young Fitzclarences headed by the white-headed baby, Augustus, in the arms of his nurse, who with his brothers and sisters was formally presented to his admiring uncles, the Lord Chancellor, the Attorney-General and the whole lot of them.

Cobbett, who seems to have regarded this celebration as one more example of Royal depravity, took considerable exception to this parade of the young Fitzclarences, which, not inappropriately, was heralded by a fanfare from the Duke of Kent's band playing the Oratorio from Handel's 'Creation'.

'We all know that the Duke of Clarence is *not married*,' Cobbet emphatically if superfluously states, 'and if he has children those children must be *bastards*, and their father guilty of a crime in the eye of the law as well as of religion.'

Nor was this the least of the attacks to which William was submitted. The fantastic rumours started by 'Peter Pindar' in the early days of his association with the Jordan, had taken root and flourished. For years afterwards folk audaciously continued to inquire 'if she keeps him or he keeps her?'

And so it became the accepted theory – if not fact – that the Duke of Clarence increased his own exchequer from his lady's salary.

There is no doubt he lived beyond his means. The

yearly governmental grant on which he had to maintain his establishment at Bushey, his growing family and his Royal status, was totally insufficient. Apart from his one spectacular entertainment of which Cobbett so strongly disapproved, he spent nothing on himself; and that he was compelled at some time or other to borrow from Dora is certain, for he wrote to Coutts, his banker, that she had lent him four thousand pounds, 'which I have promised to repay as I think proper'.

Dora must have needed every penny of that sum when she took a house in Golden Square for Fanny.

The furnishings and decorations were luxurious to a degree, for Dora was determined to present her daughter with a flourish.

'It will be,' she said, 'either marriage or Bedlam for you, my girl, before the year is out – one or t'other – and I don't mind which, so long as I'm quit of the sight of ye!'

Fanny, having won her heart's desire – by fair means or foul – submitted to her mother's scoldings with unparalleled docility. She accompanied Dora on expeditions to the mantua-maker and the milliner, stood meekly by while gowns and bonnets, pelissses, gossamers, tiffanys and cambrics were commandeered for her adorning. Never had the change in fashion been more marked than in the first decade of the nineteenth century. Gone were the elaborate balloonings, the monstrous hoops and farthingales, that with slight variations had endured since the time of Elizabeth. Gone, too, were the heavy and often verminous towers of hair, sticky with pomade and powder, to which for almost a hundred years women had uncomplainingly submitted; gone the brocade, the gold and silver *galon*, the garish colour and rich embroidery; ladies went veiled in pastel tints of sheerest muslin, damped to cling in classic folds, with their hair boyishly cropped or carelessly curling, a tyle that was happily becoming to Fanny's elfish locks.

There might still be hope, and Dora prayed for it, hat Fanny would not be long upon her hands.

She gave parties, balls and banquets; Fanny should be given every chance; and if these assemblies were not attended by ladies of the *ton* there were gentlemen enough to compensate for any lack of fairer company.

But in spite of all her mother's efforts, and the number of eligible young noblemen who left their cards and showered bouquets – not on Fanny but on her Mamma; in spite of the line of cabriolets and chairs and carriages that blocked the Square and bore on more than one the Royal crest; in spite of all her mother's lavish hospiality, Fanny's first season, and her second – and her third, brought not one offer of her hand in marriage.

All these unsparing efforts on the part of Mrs Jordan roused much comment among her dearest friends who questioned – why? Why this vast expenditure and blatant prominence of that odious, half-witted Fanny? *Not* so half-witted neither, it was said. There might be method in *her* special kind of madness!

Whispers floated, light as thistledown, to fall at last in seed.

Mrs Jordan's daughter, Fanny, held a *secret* connected with her mother's private life, a secret most unsavoury and shocking; one that if divulged would bring disgrace not only upon Mistress Jordan but on *others*, more exalted: a secret, that if it reached the ears of – You Know Who – would create the greatest scandal that had ever yet descended on the Royal Family.

Small wonder then that Dora, England's 'Pickle', England's 'Romp', was spending all she had and more in Fanny's silence. Young actresses, as superstitious as any old wife in a village, who regularly cut the cards and read the tea-cups, and crossed their fingers at a squint-eye and would not for love or money quote

'Macbeth' aloud inside a dressing-room, for that spelle[
dire misfortune as any mummer to this day will know – a[
these young ladies had the whole truth of the matter t[
pass it to their gentlemen, who in their turn cackled i[
St James's to spread poison, until Dora, to escape th[
taint of it and all the talk, removed her daughter out o[
town to Gifford Lodge at Twickenham. The house an[
the vicinity were Fanny's choosing. . . .

And still the poison spread, until its virus seemed t[
permeate the blood-stream of William's life to produc[
in him a slow, invidious malaise like a canker at th[
roots of all that he had cherished.

He had seen himself the nation's butt, his love de[
filed. And most truly he had loved her. He was ma[
enough to be essentially dependent on a woman. Onc[
anchored, there he stayed; even those who most abuse[
him admitted he was faithful, long after any tie beyon[
the outward form of partnership had ceased.

None knew, and none will ever know what sordi[
arguments, what underflow of mutual antagonisr[
widened to a chasm the merest fissure on the surface o[
their lives.

'Money! Money! – or the want of it,' wrote Dora t[
a friend in the aftermath of separation 'has I am cor[
vinced made *Him* the most wretched of men.'

But money – or the want of it – was only one grain i[
the quicksands of disillusionment.

*

On a morning in late October, 1805, a messenge[
arrived at Bushey post-haste from London, craving a[
interview with the Duke. He was received by Dora t[
be told that His Royal Highness was unwell and coul[
see no one.

The matter being urgent, Dora took it upon hersel[
to read the letter the man delivered, to find with reli[

that the news it contained, though of vital portent to the nation, had no personal significance to herself.

These days she went on tenterhooks not knowing what calamity might fall like a rock from precarious heights to destroy her. . . . She breathed again. This news could be conveyed to 'Him' in her own time. She must watch her opportunity when he would be in better humour to accept it. His gout, from which he suffered periodically and which for this past week had laid him low, was not conducive to a mood of resignation.

She too, recovering from her latest confinement, was in low spirits and bad temper. Her mirror told her that the ravages of child-birth had at last taken toll of her figure. She was fat. Not plump and not well covered, but indubitably *fat*; and though she starved and performed all manner of physical contortions to reduce her size, though she skipped each morning with a skipping-rope to the delight of her family, and the disgust of her spouse, though she practised fencing twice a week with an *émigré* duellist from France, her weight showed no sign of decreasing.

It would not now be possible to play the boy, and not for long, the girl. Her looking-glass too ruthlessly betrayed those sagging contours, those unmistakable two chins, the cushioned shoulders, the spreading hips and breasts. She had no height to carry her ponderous solid curves. And the critics had observed it. Though the incomparable, seductive voice, the sprightly gesture, the puckish gaiety were spared to her, and won time-honoured eulogy even if faintly tinctured here and there with damning praise, the comments on her growing bulk were unkindly frank.

'Her form,' remarked one critic after a performance of Viola, 'is as broad as it is long, and when clothed in white breeches – it would be unjust to call them *small-clothes* – is very affecting to the whole house.'

She who with laughter had defied the venom of the journals that attacked her virtue, her children, her lover, and her life, had no laughter left for this. She saw herself as others saw her, a fat and ageing woman who preposterously aped the tomboy, with calves the size of hams.

How long – oh, God how long – she asked her looking-glass, will I last out? How long before the vigorous applause with which she still so loyally was greeted, would turn to boos and hisses? I'll retire, she vowed to her poor, blurred face, before they stone me to it.

That, however, was only one of all her troubles on this October day in 1805.

Having returned the messenger to London, Dora was in a rare case now to explain the broken seal upon a letter addressed to the Duke.

It was the first time, though she had frequently been tempted to do so, that she had deliberately opened a letter not meant for herself. But latterly she had been more than ever uneasy, never knowing from day to day which way foul winds would blow some ugly evidence to blight her. She was beset with enemies, and that Old Bitch at Windsor, reflected Dora savagely, not the least of them.

The Queen's influence with this third son of hers could do a power of harm, as Dora knew already. His mother, who for years had chosen to ignore him, accepting his respects to her not more than twice a year, had now, for some God-forsaken reason that Dora could not see, opened her arms to him. He was in highest favour with Mamma – *and* with the King, poor soul, who, it was said, was off his head again. . . . Very well then. As Dora saw it, Mamma was on the coat-tails of Sweet William, talking *marriage* with a wink and nod. Some plain-faced Jane from Germany no doubt, or better still in view of all his debts, an heiress. If the King went permanently crazed, as it was rumoured would be not at all unlikely, then George, God help us, Dora reasoned, would be ruling in his place. Prinny would repeal that Royal Marriage Act, for his own ends, when once he was rid of his wife. And there was no doubt, too, that the Queen would give her eyes out of her head to marry William off, if not to German Royalty, then to some commoner with money – if only to be rid of Dora Jordan.

As for enemies – if they began at Windsor, the Lord alone knew where they'd end, or how near her own worst enemy might be.

For she went shadowed. Her dreams were nightmares, disturbed by haunting visions of herself exposed before the world as guilty of an execrable sin. Dora had not much religion, but she believed firmly in an after-life, and saw herself already damned in hell. Yet, in her heart, she may have argued, where was the sin of it, if, by self-abasement she could buy security for her three unwanted daughters? A tigress will fight for its cubs. . . . Given long enough, she prayed, she would lay by sufficient for their needs against the day when she was done. The Fitzclarences were well provided for, but her three little miseries, none of whom saw any hope of marriage, might well starve in the gutter for all the care *they'd* get. She loved them fiercely. Even her queer wicked Fanny who brewed her devil's work, poor witless thing, she loved her. All the love of her life went to those three. The Fitzclarences were his – *all* his. They did not need her. Dora gave where she was needed – even if she gave her soul.

Her calculations told her she had already stored a goodly portion, but not enough – not yet enough to meet the ever-lasting drain on her resources, the increased demands from *one* source that must at any cost be met.

It seemed as fast as she augmented her bank balance on one side, it was paid out on the other. The Duke owed her four thousand, and that she swore she'd have from him – with interest. Meanwhile she must play her part before – and behind – the curtain, until such time as she had no part to play.

With the letter in her hand she sought the Duke.

He, propped up in a chair with his swathed foot on another, and his favourite spaniel for company, sat at his open window overlooking the park. The day, unusually warm for the time of year, was golden with October sun and splendid with the bronze and amber bounty of the trees that stood unstirring in the windless noon, against a sky unclouded. In the pearly distance, like bright darting butterflies, William could see his young at play, could hear the shrill, sweet sound of them, muted, like voices in a dream.

Sophia – his eldest girl – her voice was clipped and dainty like herself. He could see her tossing golden head and swelled with pride. The little beauty! Blood in every inch of her; tall too, for her age, and full of grace. Nothing Hanoverian in those long limbs and delicate small bones. A throw-back somewhere – but to whom? The Stuarts, or some obscure Celtic root of Ireland? His son George, taller than she, rosy and shock-haired, was flying a long-tailed kite with more patience than success. Not enough wind. . . . The kite came flopping down upon his head to shrieks of laughter; George, who would never to his father's sorrow be a sailor. George had already decided he would serve his Uncle Frederick to the wars. But there were other sons, thank God, and any one of them might be a First Lord. A son of his should lead the Fleet if he could not. . . .

And suddenly he heard a roaring and boohooing – one, a toddler, had fallen, and Sophia went to lift and comfort him.

William raised himself in sharp alarm. Any damage? No. He was up and toddling again – but where in hell were those damned nurses? He seized a hand-bell on the table at his elbow and vigorously rang it. The movement caused a twinge of agony to his big toe, and brought his dog to his side to thrust a loving cold nose in his hand.

It was not his servant but Dora who came in answer to the summons.

'Where are their nurses?' demanded William, pointing to the window. 'They should not be allowed out unattended. Not a woman within sight. Where are they? Do I pay three nurses to swill porter in the kitchen while my children fall and break their heads? Why don't you see to it?'

'Lord sakes!' she scoffed, 'would you have them soft as dumplings? Let them fall. A bruise or two will make 'em grow. Was it for that you rang?'

'Where is my man?' rasped William.

'I intercepted him,' she answered smoothly. 'Can I not be your woman?' And a trifle too coquettishly she curtsied.

William looked at her, unsmiling. She was very carefully gowned. An artful muslin fichu concealed her exuberant bust, long sleeves of gauze veiled her arms. Under the high, youthful sash that bound her waist she was corsetted in whalebone. Gilded powder sprinkled on her hair hid straying silver gleams; her cheeks were a thought too highly rouged for that merciless clear light, her painted lips were crude and harsh beneath it.

'What have you put on your hair?' he asked her, bluntly.

She coloured, frowning. 'Gold – that I can't put in me pocket.'

He moved his head impatiently. 'Is that all you've come to say?'

'Not all, my soul, nor half of it.' She drew a chair to
the side of his, and sat. The news that she had stolen –
news that had struck a blow to the heart of England,
had been by her forgotten in more personal affairs. The
war, to Dora, and to a million others, was too far removed to affect the lives of those who stayed at home.
Always with Dora, that which sprang uppermost to her
mind must be spoken, unless there were a reason to
withhold it. So, 'That girl of mine,' she blurted, 'and
young Alsop.'

'Young who?'

She could not see his face for he had turned it to the
window, but she heard his voice, and that was not
encouraging.

'Do you not recollect the name?' she asked him,
sharply. Indifferently he told her 'No', with his eyes on
the romping group in the echoing distance. His lips
smiled. He had no ear for her. She tapped his chair-
arm to recall him.

'You surely *must* remember. He saved your father's
life. Listen – will you? For I vow I have me worries.
Much you care! I now know,' said Dora, nodding, 'why
my lady was in such a case to move to Twickenham. At
what expense to me! But I know why.'

And though he heard not half of it, she told him.

Gifford Lodge at Twickenham stood within a furlong
of an inn – a certain inn. The landlord who owned it
was the father of some fellow who was paying court
to Fanny – 'And *has* been,' Dora said, 'for years. It
dates back to that night at the Lane when we lost
her—'

'Wish we'd never found her,' muttered William.

'Eh?'

'No matter. Well?'

' 'Tis anything but well. Turner reports to me that
there's no holding her. The whole of Twickenham is

talking. Milady takes to riding, now – forsooth! A horse she *must* have, so she says to me—'

'And so you buy her one. Of course,' said William.

'Cheap. A spavined raw-boned brute, knocked down at Tattersall's for fifteen guineas. It's not *that* I mind. The exercise is good for her – but what does she do but take this Alsop out with her as groom.'

'I have no doubt,' said William sourly, 'that all this is of vast interest to you – but—'

'Wait! I'm coming to the point. That's only the beginning. Would to God it were the end. Will ye listen now?' coaxed Dora to the back of William's head. 'This Alsop writes to me, if you please – can you fancy the impudence? – writes to *me* a begging letter – will I use my influence with you, not daring to approach you himself, to give him a post in the Ordnance Office of the Tower. Have you heard a word of what I've said, my soul?'

'Is this roundabout,' William cautiously inquired, 'your method of approach to drag a government appointment from me for your daughter's paramour?'

That put her out. She reddened and flung back: 'I'll not take insults to her – from you – or any other. I'm telling you – he saved your father's life. He was the lad who seized that madman Hadfield. If he'd not been so quick the King would most likely not be here today.'

William rubbed his nose. 'I do remember something now,' he murmured. 'He should have been sufficiently rewarded. If not – and if that is what he's after he can have it as far as I'm concerned. Always providing,' William added sourly 'that any governmental office will take note of a request from me.'

'Bless you!' Dora bent, rhapsodically to kiss the back of his hand that rested on the chair-arm. 'A heart of gold! Did I not always say so?'

''M. You seem mighty anxious to curry favours for

this fellow,' remarked William with a straight look.
'Why?'

'Why?' She drew back from him to stand, fingering
the muslin folds across her breast. 'I'll tell you why,' she
said, her gaze avoiding his, to stay an inch or two above
his head. 'If you *must* have it – 'tis because I see a
chance to get my poor girl married.'

'To a groom?'

'To a sweep – to a pig – to the hangman!' cried Dora,
throwing wide her arms, 'to anyone who'll take her –
and I'll pay him for it. But *he's* no groom. That young
man has brains. He may go far. His father has made a
mint of money at that inn. She could do worse, even if
she'll not do better. Now you know!'

'I wonder—' William caught her lifted eye and held
it, 'I wonder if I know – or if I'll ever know what's in
your mind.'

'And what,' she flung back hotly, 'do you insinuate?
That I'm a liar? False?'

'Key Suckuse,' he murmured.

'How gallant! I vow you do surpass yourself in court-
liness. 'Tis the gout in your toe, my love, that turns
you acid. *Qui s'accuse – mai foi!* Your accent!' She
dropped beside him on her knees with a pretty show of
wheedling, to rub her head against his arm. 'Be kind to
me. Be loving. Do you love me no more, at all?'

He stroked her hair; her tricks held memories. He
saw the shadow of her youth behind them, and the pity
of its passing in the silver threads among the gay gold-
powdered curls. The nape of her down-bent neck was
still as white, the tendrils that clustered there as soft
as ever he remembered. He touched them with a finger-
tip. She took his hand and laid it to her breast and
looked up at him with melting eyes.

'They're full of tears,' said William.

She shook her head as though to shake the tears away,

and was on her feet with amazing young agility. The letter she had tucked into her fichu fell to the ground. He saw it – and the broken seal.

'What's that?'

Like lightning she was on it. 'Nothing. A message sent to me.' Then she checked herself. No need to deceive him over this. 'I'm lying,' Dora said. 'It was meant for you. I opened it.'

There was a second's pause before his voice lashed out at her: 'You opened it?'

'To spare ye,' she told him, lamely. 'I thought you were in no fit state to hear—'

He snatched the letter from her. She watched the colour drain from his face while he read, and all the actress in her rose to the moment's drama.

'Nelson dies!' she uttered in ringing tones, 'for England's glory!'

He turned on her a long, unseeing look.

'He was my friend.' The paper fell from his slackened hand. 'My only friend,' said William.

Chapter Five

THE whole nation stood aghast. Nelson, the hero of Trafalgar, was dead in the greatest battle ever fought at sea. The enemy, who for hundreds of years had threatened England's shores, had been incredibly and gloriously defeated. Yet, in the height of exaltation, Britain mourned.

His destiny, prophesied for him by the King's son long before the force of his genius had been recognized, was now triumphantly fulfilled; and not a man from the King on his throne to the meanest of his subjects, who did not feel in his passing a personal loss.

In the capital, in every town and hamlet, there was a strange cessation of normal life. Voices were hushed; shop windows exhibited funeral urns and hideous funeral trappings. Black drapery festooned the houses; carters tied black ribbons to their whips. Nothing else was talked of in London clubs, in Mayfair drawing-rooms, in every cottage on the road to Portsmouth, in every tavern on the coast.

Young gentlemen drove to their tailors in St James's to order new suits of black broad-cloth to attend the memorial service at St Paul's. Ladies wore black scarves and black sashes. No other subject was discussed over tea-cups or at dining-tables, or even in the gaming-rooms in the intervals of play. And then suddenly in the midst of it all came out the Union Jacks, the gay bright buntings, bonfires, and illuminations, to commemorate immortal victory to England.

But the King's son in his loneliness, had no heart

for celebration. He had lost his friend. 'My only friend' the one in all his life who had stayed faithful. The one, by whom for five and twenty years he had set his standard, whose counsel and whose loyalty had been his anchorage in the wreck of his hopes and ambitions. All through the war, since the day he had bade God-speed to Nelson in the palace at St James's, the two sailors had kept up a regular correspondence, with only two gaps between – one after the Battle of the Nile, when the delivery of mail was delayed, and after Teneriffe, where Nelson lost his arm and had not yet learned to write left-handed.

Every letter from Nelson William cherished; and in the quiet of his room, he read and re-read them till his sight was blurred.

One request was granted. The foremast of the *Victory* against which Nelson fell, was brought to him. He kept it in his dining-room at Bushey under a bust of his friend.

The capture of vessels at Trafalgar having brought to His Majesty's Treasury an enormous increase of capital, the King, in an unwonted fit of generosity, handed a share of the spoils to his sons. Each received a moiety of twenty thousand pounds, a godsend to William, who could now repay the greater part of his liabilities and his debt to Mrs Jordan.

For the first time in years he had some surcease from financial difficulties; and now more than ever was he determined to induce Dora to leave the stage. He knew her popularity was waning, and he banked on her personal vanity to give her sense enough to acknowledge it and return to him and his children. He still hoped, forlornly, for a reconstruction of their breaking lives, and for a while it seemed that the shadow of unrest between them lifted. She had made no promise to give up her theatrical work, but on the other hand, she had made no further contracts, and though she still retained her two houses – the one in London, and the other, Gifford Lodge, at Twickenham – she spent more time at Bushey now, with him.

But after the birth of their tenth and last child, Amelia, it was evident she had no serious intention of making a permanent retirement. Unknown to William she had signed an agreement to appear in a new play, not ineptly entitled, *Something to do*, and before her baby was six weeks old she was back again in Golden Square for rehearsals at the Lane.

This open defiance of his wishes came as a shattering blow to William. He could see no justification for it, so he argued, in a vain attempt to stay her. There was no necessity now for her to work. She had all she asked of him, she shared to the full his increase of income.

'All is not enough,' she told him sullenly, 'I have calls on me that you know nothing of.'

She plunged into a list of her expenditures – the same old story – and it sickened him. From the beginning, from the very moment that he had signed a settlement in her interest it seemed there had always been this continuous talk of money. He loathed the sound of the word, and when she spoke it, he could almost have loathed her. All their quarrels were based on that one theme; it had bored its way into his life, like a worm into old wood, and from that dry-rot there spread another grievance.

'You have no thought of calls on or duty owed – to me,' he answered, burning with a sense of his own injury. 'Always with you it is what *you* want – regardless of me or my wishes – or my children's needs. You are public property. Any Tom, Dick, or Harry in the pit has as much right to you as I – or more. You give *them* your bag o' tricks, and hand to me your leavings. Do you think I love to stand by and look on and ape the

mountebank at your heels for favours – like any whor-
ing, lady-mouthed sod at the stage-door?' the stored-up
resentment of years that beneath all his easy-going,
stolid outwardness he had hid from her leapt up at last,
released. 'But I'm not tied to you!' he shouted. 'There's
no law in the land to hold me – beyond the tie of our
children and they're more mine than yours. *All* mine!
Who's nursed them, reared them – mothered them? Not
you!'

She was alarmed. His words were a barb to her pride.
She was proud of her capacity for motherhood. He had
wounded her deeply. Her tears were not entirely
assumed. He could not mean what he said, she weep-
ingly protested. He *killed* her with his vile, cruel in-
sinuations. She had not deceived him – never, never in
this world had she deceived him into thinking that she
would renounce her life's work for her life with him.
. . . Yes! She *was* a public servant. He knew that. As
for her beloved children – had she not destroyed her
health, her body in the birth of them to his demands?
When, in the name of God, had she denied him his
natural rights?

'Leave God's name out of this,' William said; and
said no more. For always she managed to secure the last
word to give him wrong. He supposed there was some
justice in her reasoning.

But dimly he felt that greater issues were at stake
than the repetition of countless other scenes that would
start on a whisper – a breath to raise a storm which left
them both a little more depleted. He was seized with a
fierce inarticulate desire to guard her and himself from
some awful crisis that instinctively he knew was pending. Like a hovering cloud it had menaced their fair-
weather, brief respite, but the forces at work against
them had yet to gather strength.

He heard with relief that Fanny was at last to be

married, and to that fellow Alsop, who had through William's influence obtained an appointment in the Ordnance Office of the Tower.

The position, though it carried nothing of a salary, did at least bear a certain social status, but Dora would still have to keep them. She had taken a house in Park Place, St James's, for her daughter and future son-in-law.

And Fanny was elated with her triumph. She had got what she had wanted in her own time and at her own price. Through years of waiting, she had won him. Not only had she won him, she had *made* him, and was always ready to remind him: 'But for me you would still be in the tap-room.' They were for ever quarrelling. There seemed to be no love in this queer distorted union. She would be possessive, imperious, and wildly passionate in turn; he, full of scorn, repelled by and disdainful of her outbursts, yet between them there existed some sort of strange affinity.

On a day in the early spring of 1808, a week or so before the wedding, Alsop and Fanny rode out together in Richmond Park. It was a boisterous March morning with a pre-taste of April in the alternation of sun and storm, cut by a whipping wind that brought colour to Fanny's pale cheeks and a sparkle to her eyes. In her long red habit and black velvet hat with its sweeping white plume she looked her best, although she still retained her air of awkward adolescence that she seemed never to outgrow. She rode well and fearlessly, but today she was in the worst of ill-humours and not in the least enjoying her ride.

'It is hateful—' she complained to her betrothed, who sat his horse in a glum, brooding silence, possessed by his own thoughts, and with no ear for hers, no eye for the eager freshness of the day, its hint of green in the faint tracery of trees against the clear white sky. Spring's yearning ecstasy, its gleam and song, blossom and cloud, found no response in him – 'It is hateful of Mamma,' whined Fanny, 'not to give me a proper wedding. I want a dozen bridesmaids and a full choir with a banquet afterwards. But no! She says *two* bridesmaids only – those whey-faced sisters of mine – and not *one* of the Fitzclarences, and no guests except a few of her most intimate friends to the breakfast. Her friends! That old horror Siddons, I suppose, and that drunken sot Sheridan, and all her low company from the Lane. Thank you! I thought at least to have one or other of the Royalties.' Fanny stopped and giggled with a sideways glance at her scowling swain, 'I thought at least if she wouldn't invite dear Uncle *Ernest*, she would bring our Billy to give us *ton*. But she says there has been too much publicity already over me, so I'm to be married like a pauper – *to* a pauper!'

To this taunt Alsop made no reply beyond a look of concentrated fury that Fanny returned with a burst of laughter. 'Lord! A pretty bridegroom – you! So gallant. So loving. I should be proud to be so loved!' And with a sudden cut of her whip on his wrist, and a kick of her heel to her startled horse, she was off in a wild, mad gallop, through glades, over fallen tree-trunks, under low-hanging tree-branches, and ground rotten with rabbit-burrows, crouched on her horse's neck with her habit streaming behind her like a witch's crimson cloak.

Alsop spurred after her and came alongside to catch at her rein and pull her up with a strangled curse. 'You fool! Do you want to break your neck?'

'Much you would care if I did – after we are wed!' she retorted. 'For then you'll have my money.'

'I've yet to see it,' he answered curtly. 'Promises are not enough – unless they're made on paper.'

His hand was still on her rein, curbing her dancing

horse. 'I brought you out to talk to you,' he said, 'and not for a circus ride.'

'To talk! And you as silent as the grave – and as cheerful. Talk! Of what? Of *secrets*?' She showed her little childish teeth in a grin with her upper lip shortened, like a dog that will bite in fun.

'Get off your horse,' Alsop said abruptly.

She pouted. 'Am I your slave?'

'You will be before I've done with you,' he muttered, and slid from his saddle, holding out his arms to her. 'Come.'

She shrugged her shoulders and dismounted, without his aid.

They tethered their horses to a tree, and found a place they knew in a sheltered hollow at the foot of a grassy slope, where last year's bracken was splashed with the fresh green of young fern-fronds, and the turf was soft as a bed. The sun had struggled through the wind-swept clouds again and shone warm from a drift of blue. A lark soared upwards, loud with song.

Fanny took off her hat and sat hugging her knees to watch that small mounting speck, to hum beneath her breath a tuneless tune – 'I am happy,' she broke off to say. 'Are you?'

'I'll be happier,' he answered surlily, 'when you're mine – tied up by law and deed.'

A dark flush crept into her cheeks.

'You vile beast!' she whispered. 'God knows why I am taking you when I hate the sight of you.'

'At least,' Tom Alsop answered coolly, 'we understand each other. Hate, they say, is akin to love.'

'Do you love me?'

'Yes,' he answered, with a smile that was the merest stretching of his lips, 'as one loves a vixen one has tamed.'

'You've not tamed me, and never will!' Her slinking

glance wandered over his face, cherishing each feature – that small hawk's nose under the straight black brows, that hard immobile mouth, the squared chin with its hint of a cleft, out-thrust above the high velvet collar of his riding coat. She nodded complacently. 'You're very grand in your new suit like a gentleman – a fine gentleman, too – thanks to Fanny Jordan. You should be grateful to poor Fanny who pays your bills and gets no grace for it – only insults and black hate. What a sweet pair we are to be sure.'

Alsop's curved nostrils quivered slightly, but he showed no other sign that he was stung. 'Have you,' he demanded, 'done what I asked you to do?'

'What was that? You are for ever asking. You ask too much.' She plucked a grass and nibbled it, looking all ways but at him.

'You know.' He took her chin in his hand and dragged her face round, forcing her eyes to meet his. 'You know,' he repeated, tight-lipped.

'I don't,' she insisted sullenly. 'I don't know what you mean.'

'Don't lie to me.' He dropped his hand. 'And don't trick me at the last, for by God,' he muttered, 'if you do I'll kill you.'

'And then you'll hang,' said Fanny lightly. 'I think you'll hang in any case. I've always known that you were gallow's meat. Maybe we'll hang together. . . . How bad – oh, God, how bad I am!' She gave a sudden shiver. 'But you are worse. You are the devil incarnate, I do believe – or if not you go hand in hoof with him.' She turned her eyes upwards till the iris almost disappeared. 'When I think how I have bartered my soul's salvation for the sight and touch of your body—'

He cut in shortly with: 'Keep your dramatics for your mother – or the stage.'

'Ah! The stage!' She sat up, alertly. 'Yes, the stage

will be my hope when all else fails. I am a greater actress than Mamma. And young – I look as young as when I was fifteen. Why should I marry *you* – a low-born cur who for all his fine new clothes that I have bought him, and his office in the Tower, and his clerk-ship and his learning – *still* stinks of the stable and knows better how to coax a mare than touch a woman. Why should I marry *you* – I ask myself. Why? Why? I know you – *all* of you – flesh and mind and wickedness – as you know me.' She caught her breath on a sob, and flung herself against him. 'Hold me!' she whimpered. 'Hold me, Tom! Don't let the devil take me.'

He loosened her clinging childish fingers that were entwined in his, and said, 'You're crazed.'

'Maybe I am. My Mamma tells me so.'

'Your Mamma,' he sneered the word, 'is right. I'll need a handsome portion to smooth our marriage bed. It will be no bed of roses, even if well-lined. Have you spoken to your mother as I told you? Answer me.' He gripped her arm.

She wriggled. 'I – I – have had no chance—'

His grip upon her frail forearm tightened till she yelped. 'I'll break you,' said Alsop quietly, 'if you fool me over this. We have made a bargain and I'll keep you to it, or –' he paused, '– there'll be no marriage for us.'

'Let me go!' screamed Fanny. ' 'Tis *you who drive* me crazed with your tormenting.' She wrenched her arm away from him. 'Look how I am bruised!' She showed him two red angry marks on her soft skin. 'You monster! Devil! Beast! What can I do? What *more* can I do? I must bide my time. Oh – mercy me! If I had foreseen the consequences, I never, never would have told you—'

'You have told me nothing that the world does not suspect,' Alsop interrupted. 'But I want further proof.'

He dropped his voice. 'If I could buy such proof I would not need to scrounge after you, my little darling.'

She rounded on him in another gust of rage, her nails ready for him, but he caught her wrists and held them. 'No, you don't! There – there,' his voice caressed her. 'Do you not want to be my love – my wife – my sweetheart? Then come – No! That's enough.' For with swiftest change of mood she was as ready with her kisses as her claws, 'I have this to tell you. Will you listen? I have seen—' Alsop paused and Fanny looked up sharply, 'I have seen this fellow Sellis.'

'Sellis?' repeated Fanny, puzzled.

'Yes,' said Alsop with impatience. 'Do you tell me you have never heard the name?'

'If so I have forgot it.'

'Then you had best remember it,' said Alsop grimly. 'For I have learned that Sellis plays his own game – and that's not mine. Our gentleman—' he smiled, his thin, tight smile, 'our gentleman toys with his valet's wife. Did you know that?'

'How should I know?' Fanny twisted in his grip that tightened. 'And how can that affect us either way?'

'Because,' said Alsop steadily, 'if Sellis has information he will keep it, and will use it for his own ends – that are not ours. Would it not be shocking,' said Alsop slowly, his eyes still holding hers, 'if some ugly evidence were found by anyone – but her own daughter?'

'You rat!' breathed Fanny while the colour fled from her cheeks and lips. 'You gutter-bred rat! You scum! I'll hang you first – and I will hang myself before I'll be a party to—'

He laid his hand on her mouth: 'Idiot! Hold your noise.'

'I won't! I won't. Vermin! Rat! Rat!' With each repetition of the word she lashed herself into a whirl-

wind of hysteria, beating at his face with a red cloud
before her sight and a torment in her finger-tips to tear
him till blood spurted.

But long custom had enured Alsop to her fits. He
could deal with them. While she struggled like a mad
woman, he pinioned and held her fast, and soothed her
with his voice until he laid her sobbing, limp, exhausted
in the bracken, silenced to his will.

*

Although Dora had insisted on a quiet wedding for
her daughter, slanderous comments leaked out and continued to drift around the name of Alsop.

He was in the news, coupled with his wife – 'that half-
wit, Fanny' – on whom, so it was whispered, her mother
had settled a marriage portion of no less than ten thousand pounds. Some gave it as twenty. Moreover, according to the original agreement made between Dora and
the Duke of Clarence, it appeared he was in part
responsible to contribute to this sum, and that he had
point-blank refused to abide by his word and deed, had
been the cause of the most violent quarrels on the part
of the Squire at Bushey and his lady.

Already the prints had issued warning of a separation.
There had been a serious outbreak of fire at Drury Lane
that year, fortunately at a time when the theatre was
closed.

Pending repairs Dora went off on another of her long
provincial 'cruises'. Gossip, hot on her track, gave it that
the household at Bushey had been broken up and the
final parting staged, while Mistress Dora wrote round
robins to her friends in vehement contradiction.

'It would be painful to me and unnecessary to you to
mention the cruel and infamous reports that for some
time have been in circulation, and to the extent of
which I was really a stranger till last week. . . .'

'With regard to the report of my quarrel with the Duke, every day of our past and present life must give the lie to it. He is an example for half the husbands and fathers in the world, the best of masters, and the most firm and generous of friends. . . .'

Her pride as much as her loyalty upheld him, and while she saw her whole world crumbling beneath her, she clung pitifully to his support, his name, their long association. Whatever the future held for them both, her head was high: she still hoped that an entire dissolution might be prevented. She feared the talk, the pointed tongues, the gloating triumph of her enemies, the veiled pity of friends, more than the loss of him, who, since the birth of their last child, had been a stranger in all but name.

The fact that William had recently bought a house at Maidenhead, may have embellished reports of the 'quarrels' which Dora so persistently denied. William had taken the house as some provision for his daughters, since in the event of his death they would be homeless. He had no home to leave them. Bushey was Crown property, and he had sold his house at Petersham in part payment of his debts. His boys he could provide for. The services were open to them, under the patronage of their uncles York and Kent – but his five little girls – the eldest of them not fifteen, neglected by their mother who provided solely for the three that were not his, presented a sore problem that rankled.

He had nothing much to leave his daughters from his personal estate. True, his brother George had promised to make each one of his nieces an allowance while she remained unmarried and in the event of their father's death, but promises from George, William realized, though made in all good faith were seldom kept.

Frederick was head over ears in debt already, no help could come from him. Moreover, Frederick had taken under his protection a young woman – one Mrs Mary Ann Clark, with whom he was completely infatuated and obsessed. He kept her in Royal style in a house in Gloucester Place, with half a dozen maid-servants, a butler, two footmen, two chefs, three carriages and eight horses. Nor was that all. He had bought a country house for her at Weybridge, within a mile of Oatlands, his own residence, where his unhappy little Duchess lived in solitude, and for distraction paid visits to the poor. So Frederick, William realized, had his hands too full with Mary Ann to dispense largesse to his nieces.

It must therefore have been particularly galling when William realized he was bound by deed to provide a maintenance allowance to Dora's three daughters in event of their marriage, since he had no means of providing for his own.

The purchase of the house at Maidenhead plunged him into debt again, and he borrowed from his brother George who could ill afford to lend. His own riotous extravagances at Brighton, and the vast fortune spent upon his garish new Pavilion, was causing trouble enough in Parliament and more brain-storms to the King.

And the King was slowly breaking. He had borne enough to break him long ago. He was old and going blind. His country was at war with the greatest military genius of all time, whose giant shadow now bestrode the whole of Europe.

Nelson was dead. Pitt and Fox were dead. National affairs were in the hands of a group of bungling mediocrities. He had one strong man at the head of his expeditionary force in the Peninsular – one Arthur Wellesley – who had won a victory at Vimeiro only to nullify it by the signing of the convention of Cintra, and that put the poor old King into a panic. Again and again he assured his ministers that he 'knew of *no* excuse a

British officer could make for the signing of such disgraceful conditions to the nation. . . .'

And he had his family troubles besides. He had three old-maid daughters who now would never marry, and one, his beloved youngest, Amelia, dying of consumption. He had a wife who nagged him, and an heir to his throne who disgraced it.

But the whispers that floated like blow-flies from Brighton to torment the King's sick, bemused mind, were scattered in the blaze of the most appalling scandal that had ever yet attacked the Royal Family. The Duke of York, the King's second and favourite son, was charged with corruption and bribery. He, Commander-in-Chief of the Army, stood accused of receiving a fifty-per-cent bonus from Mrs Mary Ann Clark, as his share in the sale of commissions in the Guards.

There was no smothering it.

The King's son was brought to trial, not in private, and not before his peers, but in Parliament before a committee of the House of Commons – before six hundred Members, to have his maudlin letters to his mistress read aloud, while the whole House roared with laughter at the 'Darling this' and 'Angel that' with which they were bespattered.

In his quiet room at Windsor King George sat and listened. . . . It was noted that he always seemed to listen, while his dimmed eyes peering into blindness strove to *see* the voices that continually murmured at his side, and in his head, and all about him – like a whispering cloud.

Once before that cloud had come to take and comfort him, and soothe him into sleep and a forgetting. If he could sleep again, he prayed to God that he might never wake.

Frederick!

His handsome, gay, affectionate kind Frederick, had

been accused of a dreadful dishonour. What was the news? 'Hey! Colonel Manners! Give me the news. What have they done – what have they done to Frederick? It is an insult – an insult to *my* person to bring my son to trial like a – like a felon. My son – my son is blameless,' he assured his gentlemen. 'You will remember that? Lies – all lies. All of you tell lies. My son does not tell lies. He is a good son. An honourable son. He loves me. . . .'

It was perhaps as well that Frederick, who as a youth had entertained his toadies in St James's to imitations of his father's babbling, was spared his parent's fond appreciation.

It was evident to all that the King was on the verge of a relapse. Although his physical health was mainly good, he began to show ominous familiar symptoms: failing memory, insomnia, and stumbling incoherent speech. He lost weight. His jaw hung pendulous and flabby, his face had a purplish tinge. He discarded his wig. 'Too hot – too hot for my head.' His hair strayed in silvery white wisps about the puckered forehead. He walked with a stick, his faltering steps guarded by two attendants. He was firmer in the saddle than on his feet, and rode each day in Windsor Great Park, his horse led by a groom, and at all times he wore his 'George', his Star of the Garter pinned to his royal-blue coat.

William, who had heard with alarm the guarded reports of the doctors, was constantly at Windsor.

'You,' his father told him, 'have never been so good a son as Fred. You have defied me. Obstinate. You were always obstinate. You had no right – no right to sail without orders. You lost your ship and your command – hey? Wasted. Wasted life – hey? Your own fault. As we sow – you have sown – to reap. I hear you have made a soldier of your eldest boy. I can hear if I can't see. A cornet, hey? Your brother Fred is a fine soldier . . . or was . . . or was. He has resigned his appointment as

Commander-in-Chief. But he is blameless. Blameless. Exonerated, hey? You've heard he is exonerated?

William nodded, speechless. He had been profoundly shocked at the awful charges made against his brother, but had vigorously upheld him. The whole thing, he was convinced, and stoutly maintained, had been promoted by the woman Clark who had everything to gain and nothing to lose by creating a sensation. He was more concerned at the effect of the deplorable affair upon the King's health than at the cause of it.

His father's red-rimmed protruding eyes peered at him mistily. 'Bad sons – bad sons—' he mumbled. 'I am too old for this. Too old to face the shame of . . . He has shamed me.' A slow painful wetness trickled from the tired eyes. 'I have lived too long. I have outlived . . . my grey hairs . . . in sorrow. . . .'

'Come, Sir, come! Mustn't say that,' broke in William hastily. 'This is the year of your jubilee, you know. Such a celebration as you'll have – eh? Fifty years a King. The longest reign of any King of England.'

'Fifty years,' his father echoed, nodding. 'Come closer. I can't see you.' He waved his hand uncertainly before his sight as though a fog had dimmed it. 'Everybody now – my wife, my sons, my daughters – all these bowing fools around my chair – all of ye – all – you look like ghosts. Grey as . . . Is *your* hair grey?'

'It will be soon,' said William. He took his father's hand and stroked it. 'We none of us grows younger.'

The King nodded thrice. 'My hair was . . . yellow once.' The loose lips parted in a toothless smile, and something slid in William's chest. He looked away.

'How many sons have you by that play-actress?' the King asked suddenly. It was as though the hovering spirit that controlled the feeble mind had all at once returned to master it. 'How many – hey?' the King repeated.

'Five,' muttered William, 'and five daughters.'

'Ten grandchildren, and I've not seen one of 'em. It won't do,' said the King with a shake of his head, 'for me to entertain your bastards. Ten – hey? And not one that can come to the throne. Have you ever thought that a son of yours *might* come to the throne?' queried the King, shrewdly.

William started. 'No, Sire. George has a daughter.'

'Yes, and she may never marry. And if she does she may not bear a child. Or she may bear a dozen – or she may not live. Who knows? There's Fred's wife – she's childless. And you have ten. One 'ud be enough if it were born in wedlock. One. *You'll* not be King, but a child o' yours – who knows? What? What? You ought to marry – ought to marry. You're the only one o' the whole bunch that has bred men. George's daughter . . .'

There was a long silence. The King's head dropped; his lips moved as if in secret calculation. 'Not since Anne – a Queen. England wants Kings. . . . Women no good. No good. She may not breed. *You* will . . . I . . . I'm tired. Leave me now. Perhaps I'll sleep.' He turned his forehead in the direction of his son who mutely bent and kissed it; then, on tiptoe William left the room.

The King's words had struck home. Marriage! And a son who . . . well? Why not? Three lives only stood between him and the throne, and although England would never know him as a monarch, there was more than a remote possibility that a legitimate son of his might indeed be King. But marriage. . . . How could he marry, who, although free, was yet imprisoned by moral obligations as binding as any legal tie.

He was well aware of the current rumours around his name and hers, that public opinion credited him with living on her money; and that in the event of a separation he would be pilloried and she upheld as a martyr, abandoned by him who had been her protector for almost twenty years. The odium attached to his brother Frederick in the recent Clark affair had rendered every one of the King's sons more vulnerable to attack. There would be no escaping the accusations hurled at himself should he make the first – and final – gesture for release. But it was not so much the world's opprobrium from which he shrank, as the admission of his own life's failure to secure a peaceful anchorage – a harbour. He had brought his ship upon the rocks through unskilful navigation, so he saw it, and for that he wholly blamed himself, not her.

*

The King's jubilee, that 'ill-timed farce', had come and gone with all due celebrations. The buzz of scandal was temporarily extinguished in dutiful rejoicing. Old though he was, and blind and slightly mad, he had been their King for fifty years, and the vast majority of his people had never known a time without him.

He still walked on the terrace at Windsor, sightless, enfeebled, with a daughter on either side of him holding his arm. He babbled happily. He could see the sun, a dim red fire in his darkened eyes, and a blur of green that was his garden; he could still smell the scent of flowers and he knew the voices of his sons, and he liked to listen to the music of his fiddlers who played to him while he walked. He was sinking slowly into a blessed calm tranquillity that hushed the screaming tumult of his mind, and enclosed him in a muted world wherein his lost bewildered spirit could rest revived, untroubled. But not for long. A few month only, and his curtained peace was shattered by another fatal blow.

Once more a son of his had been dragged into the glare of publicity. His son – the King's fifth son – Ernest,

Duke of Cumberland, had been attacked and almost murdered in his bedroom by his confidential valet.

Like fire spread the news, licking up every titbit to make the story blaze. Sellis, the valet, had been systematically blackmailing the Duke, and threatening to expose some shameful secret of his private life. The Duke had paid vast sums of money for his silence, and because at the last he refused to pay more, his man had attempted to kill him. Thus, one account of it; but the most popular and the spiciest, was that Sellis had found Duke Ernest in bed with his wife.

Much embellishment was given to the tale. The woman in her shift, had rushed screaming from the room as Sellis, brandishing a sabre, had rushed in. A second valet, Neale, had wakened to a cry for help. 'For God's sake come! I'm murdered—' He had found the Duke on the floor in a pool of blood surrounded by every evidence of a violent attack. Chairs overturned, the Duke naked, the Duke's sword on the floor, bloodstained, the Duke's head sliced down the middle and his brains exposed, the Duke's left thigh stabbed to the bone, and the Duke himself as green as a pea, gasping before he passed into a faint: 'Sellis! Find Sellis – find Sellis!'

And Sellis was found – in his room that communicated with the Duke's apartments – and Sellis was dead, with a gash in his throat from ear to ear, and razor by his hand.

He was still warm and fully dressed. There appeared to be no sign of any struggle, but his slippers marked in his name were found in the privy leading from the Duke's chamber. And the question rose on every lip – had Sellis committed suicide or been murdered by the Duke in self-defence?

If so, why was Sellis not found with the Duke? Had he dragged himself to his own room to die? That was unlikely for he had bled profusely, and blood-stains would have surely marked the way from the Duke's apartments to the valet's. No trace of blood-stains had been discovered in the passage between the rooms.

The Duke's own story in a feeble statement taken at his bedside was, to say the least of it, fantastic. He had been to a concert and returned at midnight, and was in a deep sleep by one o'clock. He had been violently awakened by a blow on the head that almost knocked him senseless, and which being accompanied by a hissing sound made him believe a bat had flown through the open window. His room was dimly lit by one lamp only. He could see nothing. He got out of bed to call for Sellis, and at the same time received another blow on his head and a sword-thrust in his thigh. Then he had seen a face – a face of terror, white and dreadful. He remembered calling for his valet, Neale – and he remembered nothing more.

The tale of the bat seemed most unlikely. Why a bat? Could any creature so small and inoffensive as a bat strike a blow on the head to knock a man almost senseless? And do bats hiss? . . . The jury sat considering. They considered for some hours before they brought in a tactful verdict against Sellis for attempted murder of the Duke – and suicide.

The public were disappointed. They had it firmly in their minds – the wish no doubt was father to the thought since of all the Royal Princes, Cumberland, 'the Dreary Duke', was the most hated – that he had killed his valet and raped his valet's wife, and everybody hoped to see him hanged.

It seemed he still might die.

At the request of the Prince of Wales, Cumberland had been removed to Carlton House, where he lay in a high fever visited by no one but his doctors. William hurried up from Bushey at an urgent summons from the Prince of Wales, who met him with a long face and longer tale. Ernest's condition was critical. The blow to the head had struck through to the brain. The doctors had said that only a miracle could have saved him from instant death. There had been some extraordinary divulgences from the second valet Neale, about which George had deemed it necessary to consult his brother.

'Me? Why me?' asked William in alarm.

'I'll tell you in good time.'

Importantly George took him by the arm, and led him to his private chamber that overlooked the lawns of Carlton House – the small bow-room leading from the library that had recently been decorated with a sky-blue ceiling, doors painted black and gold, and cherry-coloured walls almost entirely covered with pictures of the Dutch School that were the Prince's pride. Here, too, he had brought and placed the overflow of his Oriental treasures from the Pavilion at Brighton.

William gazed round him, in bewilderment at the nodding mandarins, the golden Buddhas, the ivory elephants, dragons, vases, swords, and grinning masks that crowded every corner and hung in every space beneath the warm, precise interiors of Pieter de Hooch, the miniature fish-stals of Gerard Dow, and Jan Steens and Vanderveldes, the rich and glowing Rembrandts.

'*Pro tem – pro tem,*' explained George with a wave of his hand. 'They will be moved when I can find a home – a temple for my gods. They frighten my beautiful cows.' And tenderly he lifted an unframed picture that leaned against the wall, and beckoned the startled William. 'I bought it yesterday. A Cuyp. The sweetest – the most gracious thing. Do you see the gentle curve of this rump against that golden sky? Do you feel the stillness? No master can so exquisitely render the peace of summer fields and grazing cattle. I flatter myself I have discovered Cuyp.'

246

'Cow – eh?' said William, goggling.

'Yes,' George smiled. 'Cows.' And reverently he replaced the picture. 'Sit down, my dear – and help yourself to wine. 'Tis an excellent good vintage.'

Bottles and glasses stood on a Buhl table.

'No, thank 'ee,' William said. 'Red wine don't suit my gout.'

'Nor mine,' said George, 'but it suits me. You look well,' he added grudgingly. 'Damme, Bill, you're twice the man I am. How d'ye keep your figure?'

'I walk,' said William bluntly. 'I suppose you never walk?'

'Walk? No.' George refilled his glass and drank its contents at a gulp, and leaned back in his chair with his pale ringed hands crossed on his paunch and his puffy lids drooping. 'No,' he repeated, but it was evident his thoughts were away from his words, 'I never walk.'

The two brothers presented a striking contrast. The Prince of Wales, now nearing his fiftieth year, had grown grotesquely stout and florid; his hair was dyed and frizzed in curls, his face rouged and powdered to the eyebrows. He wore a suit of his own design fastened with silver frogs, and diamond buttons on his waistcoat. But in spite of his absurdities, his ponderous flesh, his effeminate, affected voice and gestures, he still retained that evasive charm, the swift irresistible smile, the sudden gust of laughter like a boy's, and the graceful turn of a phrase that stayed with him to the end.

'You're too fat, George,' William said, 'you're much too fat. 'Tain't healthy.'

He noted with satisfaction that he had worn better than George. He at forty-five could pass for ten years younger, thanks to the retired life he led, his moderation in food and drink, his careful exercising. His hair, still youthfully blond, sprang virile and wiry from his cone-shaped head. In his subdued well-tailored suit of navy blue, with his high fresh colour, stocky build and sturdy shoulders, he looked nothing of a Prince, and nothing of a dandy, but all of a sea-captain, retired.

'Fat – eh?' George took it in good part. 'You've been tellin' me I'm fat since I was seventeen. But I'm healthy enough to out-live you, my boy. Nothing wrong with me. I enjoy life here, even though I burn hereafter.' He poured himself another glass of wine. 'Ernest's bad,' he added, 'Heberden tells me it's a case of touch and go.'

'Dying?' murmured William, in a suitably hushed voice.

'It looks uncommon like it. What's your opinion of this shockin' business?'

'I know nothing but what the prints give out,' said William guardedly, 'and they can't be believed.'

'As you should know,' George nodded, his flabby lips melting in a grin. 'They've raked up muck enough round you and yours and me and mine – and all of us. Egad! We'll stink through all posterity. Who cares? We shan't be here to savour it. Isn't it Rochefoucauld who says 'tis the right of the great to have great vices? It would be interestin' to read our history a hundred years from now.'

'If the prints and journals of today are preserved,' said William surlily, 'we'll be presented as the lowest, vilest, most dissolute horde of Yahoos that ever polluted the Blood. Here's Fred who resigns his command to the trick of a whore – that'll look pretty in history, and myself with no wife and ten bastards. And now Ernest – half-murdered for rape.'

'You don't believe *cette histoire*, surely?'

'I'd believe the worst of Ernest,' muttered William, rubbing his nose.

'You would, eh?' George gave him a dubious look. 'Then that makes what I've to tell you easier to say, though nothing less unpleasant.'

248

William stared. 'Unpleasant? What – for me?'

As though to fortify himself George drank another glass, leaving a trickle of wine like a smear of blood in the corner of his mouth. 'There have been,' he said, his speech becoming more noticeably careful as the drink took its effect, 'some ugly doings of which you ought to know, and of which if you do *not* know I feel it my bounden duty to inform you.' He fumbled in his pocket and produced a crumpled rag of paper. 'This was found on the body of the man Sellis by Erness' – by Ernest's second valet Neale – who read it. And having read it he very properly refrain' from – refrained it—' George cleared his throat, 'he very properly kept it from the constables and handed it to me. None knows of issex – it's ex-istence besize Neale – who can be trusted – and *you* whom it concerns.'

And having got this out, George with much solemnity offered the letter to William, who snatched it from him. He had recognized that large untidy scrawl; and as he hurriedly smoothed and scanned the page, his breathing quickened.

'This—' he raised his eyes to meet his brother's focused hazily upon him. 'This—' a spasm that he could not for the life of him control, caught at his throat. He swallowed.

George, with an effort, heaved his vast bulk from his chair, and stood, ever so slightly swaying – 'Is one,' he said, 'of many. Neale took Erness' keys and made a search. He brought me everything he found. A packet – all f'om same source. I destroyed 'em. But I kep' this because I thought it would interess' you to know *why* she paid ten thousan' to her precious daughter. A clear case of blackmail, my dear – on *both* sides.'

'You're drunk,' said William stonily.

'Yes, a trifle.' The first gentleman of Europe lifted his head. There was that in his brother's face, a queer fixed look, a greyness, which touched his fuddled sense and sobered him.

'But not so drunk that I cannot see – straight. And as I see it – Alsop – her son-in-law, has used his knowledge – she admits as much – to his own advantage, while Sellis steals incrim – incriminating evidence to sell it back to Erness' at a price. But when the fellows finds his master flagrantly delighting in his wife – he turns from blackmail to murder – and then suicide. *Quod erat demonstrandum.*'

From William's lips issued a strangled sound. He took his handkerchief and wiped his forehead, saying hoarsely: 'She – and Ernest! And that tape-worm Alsop – knew. He knew!'

'Yes, and others knew – or guessed.' George set down his empty glass upon the table, and with an uncertain glance at William, returned to his chair. ' 'Twould make strong melodrama – eh? All the ingredients. Blackmail, attempted murder, suicide – and rape. That's a pretty score to add to Erness' name and yours – and the tale of Mrs Jordan in the future.'

William sat in silence, still as death.

Who shall tell of what in those moments he was thinking? Of himself and the crushing-out of twenty years of life, and of his own life's failure, and the irony of this most sordid last humiliation? Or did he think of her and of all that he had cherished, those deep encircling fibres that had their roots in the very essence of his being – in her children and his. If all *were* his. . . .

It may be that from some shadowed corner of his mind, the slow suspicion, poisonous and formless, un-coiled like a snake upreared to strike, and fled before his spirit's staunch denial. Or he may have seen in this most bitter force of circumstance the inexorable work-ing of a scheme, which while all else dissolves and melts away, moves slowly on in the resistless ebb and flow of change and forms and energies towards some lifted, new horizon. Or it may be that in his shocked, dumb bewilderment he had no thought at all.

So with his brother's heavy-lidded gaze upon him, William faced his revelation. And presently he rose from where he sat, his eyes turned to the grate, where, though the day was warm, a small wood-fire smouldered.

'There'll be no tale,' William said, 'to tell of this.' His joints creaked as carefully he knelt, and held the letter to the flame that leapt to meet it. 'No tale,' he repeated grimly, 'and – no lies.'

George leaned forward, staring. Suddenly he spoke. 'Let go – you fool! You may need that.'

But William held the blazing paper till it shrivelled, black, in ashes, and only then did he withdraw his hand, aware of pain.

'God damme! Here,' he said, 'I've – burned myself!'

BOOK THREE

The King

Chapter One

In the dusk of a July evening in the year 1818, a travelling coach laden with luggage drove up to Grillon's Hotel in Albemarle Street, and deposited three ladies at the door.

These were evidently visitors of the least importance, since they were received, not by Monsieur Grillon, but by the boots. He, in no hurry to detach himself from the contemplation of a news-sheet, lethargically approached the foremost of the three – a portly middle-aged party in a magenta shawl and a formidable turban, surmounted by a towering aigrette. It was this lady, or more correctly, the lady's turban, which seemed to dominate her presence and drew the boots' regard aloft, as to a magnet, that he, with shocking nonchalance, addressed.

'Beg pardon, mum, but 'tain't no use your applyin' for rooms 'ere. We're full.'

'Full?' echoed the lady, loudly incredulous. 'Full? *Doch! Das ist schrecklich!* Haf you then no roomss for us reservedt? Haf you not of our arrival been informdt?'

'What name would it be?' inquired the boots with the caution due to foreigners, and a sliding glance in the direction of a small, slight girl whom he took to be the maid, and who stood retiringly in the background, dressed in a dove-grey pelisse and a plain chip bonnet that almost entirely hid her primrose pale hair. And having decided that she was not worth looking at twice – 'We ain't,' announced the boots conclusively, 'expectin' no more today.'

This intelligence created a distinct stir among the

255

three. The lady in the turban folded her lips and her hands simultaneously, and drew herself up to her very full height. The girl in grey painfully blushed. The other, a rosy-cheeked, pleasant-faced young woman, inclined to plumpness, but fashionably attired in a grass-green Wellington mantle and high befeathered hat, made a sharp movement forward as though she would have spoken, but was silenced by a gesture from the leader of the trio. She, fixing the boots with a commanding eye, bade him:

'Fetch de *maître d'hôtel.*'

'Fetch 'oo?'

'Tell,' pronounced the lady in a voice that thundered through a second's awful pause like the booming of a gun, 'Tell der master of der house dat I – der Duchess Regent of Saxe-Coburg-Meiningen and my daughter, der Princess Adelaide – haf *komm.*'

And twenty-four hours too soon!

Never in the history of Grillon's had such a dreadful *contretemps* occurred. The boots, roused from his phlegm, precipitously scattered to convey the news to Monsieur Grillon, who at that very moment was giving orders for the red carpet to be laid at dawn. He, poor man, half-demented with shock, almost prostrate with bows, and quite incoherent with apologies, came hurrying.

There had been some error, some most terrible, inconceivable, unfortunate mistake – but as Monsieur Grillon hysterically assured Her Highness, he was not to blame for it. He had received his orders from the Lord Chamberlain, who in his turn had it from His Royal Highness the Prince Regent, that Their Highnesses were not expected till the morrow. All – all was now in process of preparation. 'Such a menu!' cried Monsieur Grillon, well-nigh in tears and ticking off the items on his fingers. '*Le cygnet rôti. Les petites canetons de volaille en haricot vierges; les filets de perdreaux à la Grande Duchesse; la suprême aux fraises à la Princesse Adelaide* – I have four chefs who all through the night they will be cooking.'

'I hope not,' replied the Duchess, 'for I am starving. I do not care to wait until tomorrow for my dinner.'

'*Ah! Le bon Dieu!*' Monsieur Grillon wrung his hands. 'Your Highness! If I had known! There are no flowers – no red carpet—'

'Carpet! But we cannot eat the carpet!' screamed the Duchess.

'*Non, non!*' wailed Monsieur Grillon. 'Assuredly, *Madame, non!* Your Highness miscomprehends – a thousand pardons, *Madame*. If Your Highness will but give herself the pain to follow me she will be served *à l'instant* but not as I would wish.'

And having thoroughly exhausted his hearers, himself, and his apologies, Monsieur Grillon, backing, led the way along the corridor to a suite of apartments on the ground floor. But even in the throes of his contortions, delivered with remarkable finesse in his backward journey to the entrance of the suite, Monsieur Grillon had, as if by magic, collected an army of assistants.

The lethargic boots, galvanized to action, brought the luggage from the coach. A housekeeper almost as regal as the Duchess, came with three handmaidens to unpack it, and three footmen to attend the Royal party, while a messenger had been despatched to Carlton House.

If the Duchess, scarcely waiting to be relieved of her wrappings and her turban, did full justice to the admirable meal that Monsieur Grillon, in spite of this eruption to his household, had managed to provide, the younger ladies made no attempt to follow her example.

'You eat insufficient, my dear child,' said the Duchess, 'to fill the stomach of a mouse. Fräulein Von Humboldt also. This good man will tear his hair to see the dishes go untasted. I insist, my dear Fräulein, that you eat this smallest possible wing of a fowl.'

'Dear Mamma, we are too tired to be hungry,' ventured the Princess in response to an agonized glance from her maid-in-waiting.

'I did not address my last remark to you, my love,' replied the Duchess, holding in her fingers and crunching to its marrow the leg of a chicken. 'I think only of this so excellent *hôtelier* who is in tears. I cannot, naturally, force you or Fräulein Von Humboldt to eat, but I can at least appeal to a sense of courtesy due to our host for whom,' said the Duchess, as silently she belched, 'my heart most truly bleeds. Try, my dear, this morsel of chicken breast – as tender as a baby's.'

And selecting a titbit from her plate, the Duchess passed it on her fork to the Princess.

'Indeed – indeed, Mamma, I cannot,' protested Adelaide, shrinking. 'I have been sea-sick.'

'What of it? So have I. All the more reason for an appetite. Bring me,' commanded the Duchess, 'some rossbiff. I hear much of your Englischer rossbiff. . . . T'ank you. Enough. Adelaide, you will eat of this rossbiff of England. It is the national dish.'

'Pray, Mamma, if you would excuse me, I can truly eat no more.'

The Princess looked so pale, wan, and drooping that the Duchess, in the act of shovelling into her mouth a large portion of roast beef and vegetables, paused.

'If you are unwell, my dear, I will certainly excuse you. You may leave the table. Fräulein Von Humboldt, do you take the Princess to her room. I will visit you later, my darling – with soup.'

The Princess very thankfully retired.

It was not without much gentle persuasion from her

daughter, that the Duchess had permitted Gabriele Von Humboldt to accompany the Princess on her journey to London, and then only on the understanding that Fräulein Von Humboldt paid her own expenses.

In her capacity of Regent to her young son, Duke Bernard, the Duchess, since the death of her husband fourteen years before, had practised at the Court of Meiningen the most rigid economy. A woman of immense resource, practical, and determined, she had remained firmly at her post throughout the war that for a generation had thundered to and fro across the face of Germany.

Adelaide had been reared in the shadow of bloodshed and invasion. While Europe swayed in a death-struggle with Napoleon, she had seen the tiny state of Meiningen terrorized and mutilated, its inhabitants subjected to the merciless rule of might, until the die was cast at Waterloo, to bring triumph to the allies and peace to the oppressed.

Through all the troubled years of her Regency the Duchess had faced with courage her reverses, submitting to the iron hand in outward acquiescence, and when the menace was finally dispersed and she once more held the reins of governance, she was wise enough to follow the enlightened traditions of the husband she succeeded.

He had been that *rara avis* in Germany, a liberal-minded sovereign. When his son was born, he invited all his subjects to be godparents, and named the child Bernard Eric *Freund* – as an assurance of the heir-presumptive's future friendship towards the people. He permitted entire freedom of the Press, and reinstated those writers who had been exiled for too loud a proclamation of their revolutionary principles. He interested himself in education. He founded schools. He was a connoisseur of art and something of a poet. He invited Schiller and Paul Richter to his table. Adelaide had sat on Schiller's knee when she was two.

She loved her father deeply; scarcely eleven when he died, she cherished the memory of a kindly scholar, tall and stooping, pale-haired and pale-faced, who, peering short-sightedly through spectacles while she sat in rapt attention on a low stool at his feet, would read aloud to her his poems from immense sheets of parchment

None knew what his death meant to the lonely, reserved child who grew up under the all-enveloping wing of her Mamma. If the Duchess followed the example of her husband in the ruling of his state, she had her own ideas in the rearing of her children. Ida, the younger of her two daughters, had been happily endowed by nature with more than her share of good looks, of a type that appealed to German taste. A highly-coloured, sprightly blonde, sufficiently domesticated, and not overburdened with wit, she had no lack of suitors, and was married in her teens to Duke Bernard of Saxe-Weimer, who, if not a reigning prince, was at least the son of one.

But no such luck came to Adelaide. She was her mother's despair. She had no *verve*, no repartee, no conversation. She had – her Mamma admitted it – no beauty. Her figure was a child's, slight, small-boned, her skin so waxen-white, one would think she had not blood enough in her veins to tint it. Her eyes, almost too large for her face, were wide-set under faint brows, perpetually raised in the sweet, surprised look of a young girl, half-awakened. Her heavy crown of hair, the colour and texture of spun glass, seemed too great a burden for the small head to carry. So Beechey has painted her. He may or he may not have flattered.

She read – but how she read! And *what* she read! The Duchess could make nothing of her daughter's choice in literature. A blue-stocking – surely! Philosophy. The Socratean dialogues in Greek, with the aid of a professor of classics. Shakespeare in German. Voltaire and Racine in French. Certainly her daughter was accomplished, in all but the charm of a woman. And she was for ever visiting the art galleries, she had actually expressed a wish to study art. To study art with paint-brushes and a canvas and an art master? Never in this world! She might, if she wished as becoming to a lady, even of one of high degree, dabble in water-colours on silk or ivory – but as for oil-paints and palettes, the notion was absurd. To paint! The Duchess was genuinely horrified. Paint what?

When, very timidly, Adelaide said portraits, the Duchess shrieked. *Gottes Himmel!* Would her daughter be suggesting, then, to paint the human head from human models? Such a notion must be instantly suppressed.

So Adelaide turned to her tambour frame and embroidered portraits of her friends in wool, instead. Was ever girl more difficult? Marry her soon, dear God, the Duchess prayed, to some good man, even if he be a burgomaster, one would most earnestly be grateful – and one always could create him Baron after all. . . .

When finally Adelaide began to visits schools, and offered her sponsorship to the founding of an orphanage, in which she herself proposed to take a class in French, the Duchess gave up hope. Born in another sphere of life it was evident her daughter would have made an admirable schoolmistress. Born a Princess and lacking all essentials in the sight of would-be suitors, it was evident that she must stay a spinster. The Duchess was resigned.

And then from Heaven, so the Duchess was persuaded, came a message. From Heaven, through the medium of the aged Queen of England and her son, the Regent Prince of Wales, who intimated that an alliance between the Princess Adelaide and the King's third son, the Duke of Clarence, would be graciously considered.

The Duchess thanked her God for this good fortune. The Duke of Clarence! What a match for her poor, plain Adelaide! In all Europe there could not be a better. Naturally, there was talk about these English princes, but one laid not much account to it. With the past history of this middle-aged, bankrupt Duke, the Duchess was not at all concerned. It was the prerogative of Princes to have their *amourettes*. As least the Duke of Clarence had the good taste to have been the protector of only one and not half a dozen like his brother, the Prince Regent. True, he had ten children, but they would have no recognition. To all but their own parents they were non-existent. As for the mother – she had been disposed of long ago – and with a handsome pension. Too handsome indeed for this impoverished Duke's exchequer, or the Duchess of Saxe-Meiningen's approval. It meant four thousand a year less to her daughter. However, the British Government would doubtless prove accommodating, and provide a grant sufficient to maintain his married state.

It had been rumoured that the Duke had contemplated marriage with a commoner – a Miss Tilney Long – an heiress, in order that the debts incurred by him during his unfortunate mésalliance with the notorious Mrs Jordan, might duly be dispersed.

Happily that rumour had not materialized. The Duke was still a bachelor at fifty-three; and though his prospect of an ultimate ascension to the throne was negligible, an event of great significance had recently occurred.

A sad event indeed, the Duchess cheerfully allowed, when in her privacy she reviewed the situation, but one that considerably augmented the status of the Duke of Clarence.

The Prince Regent's daughter was dead of a still-born child. Too sad indeed. Calamitous!

On heavy black-edged paper the Duchess penned condolence to the bereaved Prince Regent and his mother. Dead, she who was the heiress-presumptive to the throne of England, when at such occasion in the probably near future, the Regent would ascend it. The poor King was nearly eighty and incurably insane. His death would be a merciful release. And when at such time it should come, since the Duchess of York was long past child-bearing age, the Duke of Clarence would be second in succession. Although *he* might never ascend to the throne, there was more than a chance that his legal child would.

'How you, my love,' the Duchess said, 'should give thanks to the good God for this beneficence. What an honour! What a mission – to be the mother of the future Sovereign of Great Britain!'

If marriage to a man whom she had never seen, who was more than twice her age, and the father of sons and daughters older than herself by a woman who had never been his wife, did not present to Adelaide quite so glorious a prospect as it did to her Mamma, she kept her counsel. She, in the ordering of her life was not con-sulted. . . . She knew her place, and that was to obey.

Gabriele Von Humboldt, impulsive, warm of heart, and hot of tongue, did not hesitate to speak her mind on that first night of the arrival in London of the un-wooed, unwelcomed bride. Not since they had left Meiningen had the two girls been alone together un-relieved of the presence of the Duchess, until the moment when Gabriele closed the door of Adelaide's room and turned the key in the lock.

'Princess! There is yet – even *yet* – time to retract!'

To those words uttered in a strained, urgent whisper, Adelaide made no reply. She stood with head down-bent, absently fingering the articles upon the dressing-table that had been unpacked and placed for her disposal. The gold-backed jewelled brushes, a wedding present from her sister Ida, the cameo brooch with the head of Mars wrought in ivory and coral, a silver vinaigrette, a pin-cushion studded with pins cunningly arranged in some sort of design.

She picked it up to examine it more closely. Somebody, the housekeeper, perhaps, or one of the maids, had contrived a message, 'God bless the Princess Adelaide,' in red, white, and blue pins under a golden lion rampart. Adelaide's lips trembled. It was kind of these good people to offer her a welcome. She laid the cushion on the table and going to the window pulled aside the curtain and looked out.

A still breathless evening, heavy with heat and the promise of rain. A misted moon had risen and shed a ghostly radiance on roof-tops and chimney-stacks, huddled dark against a lavender sky. In the ill-lit street below, a group of link-boys, their lanterns glowing like dim orange flowers in the dusk, stood waiting to lead chance pedestrians on their way. Their muted voices mingled with the clear clip-clop of horses' hoofs on cobble-stones, the wheels of a passing coach, the tread of the watchman on his rounds, and his monotonous cry, 'Nine o' the clock and a fine warm night,' droning into the distance.

'Warm indeed,' murmured Adelaide, 'and damp as a city under the sea. I was told that London houses were built of red-brick, but I see nothing but stucco and plaster. Perhaps this is the new style of architecture.'

To this not very successful attempt at conversation

there came no answer save a small suspicious sound. Without turning her head, 'I can hear your tears,' said Adelaide, low-voiced. 'They hurt me.'

'Madam!' Mopping at her eyes with her handkerchief Gabriele blurted, 'I must speak. I must! The slight to you! Even suppose that we arrived a day before they expected us, though God knows how such a mistake could have occurred – but even suppose! That is no excuse for not sending an escort for you. To let you come alone! They should have sent the Royal yacht at least. Such lack of common courtesy! What sort of boors, then, are these English?'

'Hush, Gabriele.' Adelaide closed the window and leaned her forehead against the cool pane. 'You forget your promise.'

'My promise! Yes – I promised – but how can I be silent even at the risk of your displeasure – even though you dismiss me – *hate* me—'

'Hate you, Gabriele?'

Adelaide turned to take the girl's flushed face between her hands; the candle-light shone on her glistening hair and showed a sudden moisture in her eyes, 'Do I give hate for love.'

'And—' Gabriele mastered a sob. 'And I love Your Highness, that I would sooner see you dead than the wife of this – this dissolute—'

'Gabriele!' A note of authority crept into the gentle voice. 'You are speaking of him who is to be my husband.'

Cried Gabriele passionately, 'Yes! And if I never speak again I will speak now. For God's love I pray you, Madam, hear me. I speak not only from my heart – but for your brother. The Duke implored me, Madam, the very day we left to dissuade you even at the last minute – from this deplorable – this impossible marriage. His Highness has no power to forbid it, we

265

know that. Not yet. But in one year he'll be of age –
and then—'

'Would you have me dishonour my given word,
Gabriele?'

'Madam! The dishonour is in the acceptance of your
word. To take you – a young girl – younger than his
daughters – you, so innocent, who know nothing, nothing
of the world—'

A faint smile like the gleam of sun on marble
quivered on Adelaide's lips. 'Do you know more of it
than I? Has Baron Von Bülow taught you so much
already?'

Gabriele blushed. 'No, Madam. He treats me as a
child, but I am of the earth and you – you are of
heaven!' Her face crumpled up, tears coursed un-
checked down her cheeks. 'You cannot possibly conceive what horrors lie in store for one so sensitive as
yourself – wedded to that uncouth monster who for
years has consorted with a vulgar play-actress whose
name has been a byword in all the gutters of this
country!'

'Poor soul. And yet she may have loved him,' murmured Adelaide.

'Love! These creatures never love. And how could
any woman, no matter how low, love him?'

Adelaide raised her steady eyes. 'Do you know him,
Gabriele?'

'I know *of* him, Madam. Baron Von Bülow says he is
uncultured, coarse, and utterly plebian. He is – or *was* –
nothing but a common sailor.'

'It is a common sailor who won the battle of Trafalgar, Gabriele.'

'Oh God! Madam! Can I not make you see?'
Despairingly Gabriele sank to her knees, clasping one
of Adelaide's slim hands in both her own. 'This
marriage – it is the mating of a gazelle with a – with a

rhinoceros! Pray – pray consider it, Your Highness. Wait! If you would only wait. If even now at this last minute you would ask for a year's grace – in a year the Duke will be of age. He could then forbid the marriage. *He* will be in power then. Wait just this year, my darling – insist that you have time to make your own decision. It is *your* life – *your* future they dispose of. In all Europe there is not a family of brothers so loathed, and so detestable as these. And think! You are to be tied to one of them – for life!'

Adelaide's hand in Gabrele's turned to ice; she did not move but behind that softness and immobility, a look, desperate, resolved, crossed her face to make Gabriele cry out, 'It is a crucifixion!'

'My dear,' gently Adelaide drew her hand from the girl's feverish clinging fingers, and laid it on her head, 'you are fatigued and overwrought. You do not know what you are saying.'

'I do! I do! I would die to save you from—'

At that moment a great clatter and commotion in the street below halted the torrent of words on Gabriele's lips, and brought her to her feet. She flew to the window and opened it. A coach and six, with postilions and foot-men in scarlet and gold, had drawn up outside the hotel. The raised lanterns of the link-boys threw a glare of light across the figure of a fat man in a curled, coquettish yellow wig, who with the assistance of two flunkeys was got out of the coach. A man whose painted cheeks bulged over the wings of his immensely high cravat, and whose enormous bulk was ineffectually disguised in a coat of royal purple with overlapping capes.

There was a moment's horrified silence, then, 'Good God!' breathed Gabriele, 'is that—?'

A knock at the door and an impatient rattle at the handle stayed Adelaide's answer. 'Open! Open!' came a screaming whisper from the Duchess through the keyhole. 'Why is the door locked? Open it! Do you hear me, Adelaide? The Prince – the Prince Regent has come!'

But not the bridegroom.

The messenger who was riding hell for leather along the road to Maidenhead, did not get there till long past midnight to rouse the household of the Duke of Clarence with a racket of hoofs and holla's in the courtyard, that brought the Duke from his bed in his nightcap, and his man in a fright to his room.

The news of the untimely arrival of his future bride threw William in a torrent of anxiety and fuss. He must travel to London at once. He would be there in under four hours with six horses – but there were not six horses in the stables. The establishment at Maidenhead was modest. Very well then. Horses must be hired. Or – make a circuit and pick them up at Bushey – or no! that would not do at all. Too much delay. Go to the inn. Send at once to the inn. It was now two o'clock. 'God damme!' He shouted to the flurried servants. 'What are you all about? I am asking you for horses. Horses! Have you never heard of horses? One would think by your faces I was asking for winged pigs!'

While this and that one hurried to his bidding, his daughter Sophia, who like everyone else had been awakened, came to her father's room.

'Now, Papa, pray don't work yourself into a fever. There is no necessity at all to leave here until the morning. The Princess will still be sleeping by the time that you arrive if you start now. You can travel at your ease and be there by ten o'clock if you leave here at six – in the carriage.'

'I know what I'm about,' replied her father testily. 'Don't fluster me. You fluster me, Sophia – I must go first to St James's and get into Court dress. Then I shall breakfast—'

'But, Papa, darling, you *can't* appear in Court dress to pay an informal visit in the morning!'

William flushed a deep brick-red. 'Informal! Do you call it informal when I've to meet a woman I've never seen and am going to marry in a week?'

With the tassel of his night-cap falling over one eye, while he clutched round him the dressing-gown he had hastily flung over his shoulders and tied under the chin by the sleeves, and with a good half-yard of plump bare leg showing from beneath his night-shirt, he presented so droll a spectacle that Sophia in fits of laughter ran to hug him. 'Dearest! What *have* you done to yourself? You are tied up like a cocoon and you look a cross between a cherub and the Furies. Now let me advise you. Go back to bed.'

'No, no, no. *No!*' reiterated William, forcibly, and disengaging. 'Leave me be, my dear, leave me be. I know what I've to do. I will dress immediately. Pull the bell. I start at once. Tell – Ah! There you are!' to his valet who had unobtrusively re-entered. 'I start at once – at *once!* Pray, Sophia, let me speak. I start at once – you understand? I will take breakfast here. Yes. I think that would be best. I will take a hurried breakfast while I dress. A light breakfast. Coffee and – Sophia, *who* is giving orders, you or I? And one small mutton chop. It is the most unheard-of – disgraceful – I cannot possibly imagine – and some fruit. Bake me an apple and you had better shave me now. The Lord Chamberlain is to blame for it without a doubt – or my brother George. Yes. I can well believe your uncle George, my dear – trust *him* to make a damned infernal muddle – I distinctly understood from him *tomorrow* which already is today – and in my case I should be starting. The Lord Chamberlain wrote to me himself. I have the letter somewhere. He said – yes – *one* mutton chop and two horses from the Bear. Now where in Hades did I put that letter?'

While from this coherent monologue his valet sorted his own orders and obeyed them, and while the whole household willingly bestirred itself with the exception of the two youngest Miss Fitzclarences aged respectively eleven and fourteen, who slept through the din undisturbed; while William endeavoured to do a dozen things at once – to get into his small-clothes while he ate a mutton chop and while talking all the time submitted his chin to be shaved, and through the lather damned to hell his brother George, the Lord Chamberlain and all the British Government; while maids and men were scurrying in the kitchen and the stables, Sophia, armed with scissors and a basket, stole out into the garden.

The moon had waned to the ghost of itself, and a chill had crept up from the river that lay languid and glassy under a whitening sky. Shadows had fled and colours were slowly returning; a cock crew through the shrouded stillness, and the blurred hedgerows and silent trees were suddenly awake with sleepy sound.

Sophia went light-footed over the dew-silvered lawn to cut roses. She knew where to find the best of the half-opened buds. It had been a splendid blooming, and although some were over, there were beauties enough left to fill her basket with crimson, gold, and white – long-stemmed and heavy-scented.

When she came back to the house, the chaise was at the door and her father on the doorstep in his blue surtout and his grey beaver hat, buttoning a pair of very yellow gloves, all ready to depart.

Sophia darted forward with her basket.

'Papa! Take these. I thought you might forget to give her flowers.'

'Flowers, eh?' He smiled into the eager upturned face as she stood on the step below him. 'Thank 'ee, my darling. Very thoughtful of ye. I should have certainly forgotten. It's so long since I went courting.' He gave a tug at his cravat. ' 'Pon life! I feel as scared as when I boarded my first ship.'

'Poor Papa! Never mind. 'Twill soon be over. *She's* probably just as terrified as you.' Sophia gave his hand a reassuring pat as she thrust the basket into it, closing her father's fist upon the handle. 'There! I send her all my lovelies – with my love. Only you mustn't tell her that. They're from you. And don't go in Court dress. You look very well as you are. And don't talk too much – you always do when you are nervous. Don't talk about yourself or the Navy or politics – and above all, *don't* talk about *us!*'

'Then what *am* I to talk about?' exploded William.

Sophia giggled. 'Gracious, Papa! You surely don't need me to teach you how to go a-wooing! Tell her – oh, tell her the only thing a woman ever wants to hear.'

He pinched her cheek. 'And what might that be, hussy?'

'What no man,' Sophia said, 'has yet told me.' And pulling his face down to hers to kiss, she whispered, 'And *don't wipe your nose on your finger!*'

With these injunctions in his ears, the basket on his knee, and the first sunbeam of the day lighting his daughter's golden head as she waved him good-bye from the doorstep, William started off to meet his unknown bride, in a stuffy hired coach that smelled of mice.

He felt utterly ridiculous. Here was he, a man well past his prime – though he didn't look his age – (or did he?) – about to wed a girl scarcely older than Sophia.

In the cracked mirror let into the dingy padding at his side he stole a glance. Not so bad for fifty-three. He removed his hat. A good head of hair – no need for a wig. He'd never be bald, and the white in it didn't show – much.

But this girl – more than young enough to be his daughter. He replaced his hat and pulled down a dubious lip. June and December. How would it answer? A bit late in the day to ask that! She'd have the worst of the bargain, poor child, for at least she was giving him youth. More than which, he knew nothing about her.

George said she was hopelessly plain and full of book-learning and pious, and couldn't say Bo to a goose. But George could know that only from hearsay. George hadn't seen her. Nobody had seen her. And if she were ugly as sin, then so much the better. She'd not be so likely to want to go gadding about. A nice thing if she should be flighty and expect him at his age to take her dancing and whatnot. . . . A gentle sweat broke out on his forehead. And why shouldn't she? A girl didn't have to be a beauty to go dancing. Young women today cared for nothing but pleasure – or so it seemed to judge by his own. Here was Sophia – crazy mad about this new-fangled waltz brought from France by Lady Jersey who had the whole of Almack's on the whirl. And would *he* be expected to go monkeying around at the heels of a young lady wife? Not for me, thank 'ee, said William. Leave that to George who, in spite of his seventeen stone, was making a jackass of himself with his pirouetting down at Brighton.

Well! she'd have to find another dancing partner if that was what she wanted. His son George would have to take her on, along with Sophia. Yes! And that's another thing, thought William, removing his hat again to mop his face. Whew! . . . Quite another thing. He was prepared for trouble with her over his four girls. Would she accept 'em? Be damned to that! She'd have

to. He'd be firm on *that* point. He'd put his foot down –
he'd show who was master in his house. Thank God
Mary was married and Beth about to be if young what's-
his-name – Errol's son, came up to scratch. But Sophia
was harder to please. She'd refused half a dozen already.
Still he was in no hurry to lose her, and the others were
children as yet. As for the boys – they were all doing
well and didn't need him. George and Fred both in the
Army – Adolphus at sea – a Commander. Augustus a
bookworm – *he'd* take holy orders. And she who had
borne them was dead.

His mind jogged back, scanning the years since he
had seen his life torn across in one merciless blow, his
faith broken. Yet, through it all, he had spared her. . . .

A shutter in forgetfulness slid open and William
peered into the past. What did it give him? A shadow
show lost in the clouds of distance, a queer, insistent
tugging at the rigid knots and seals which he had closed
the doors upon her memory through all these years of
utter separation. And now she was gone beyond recall.
Or so they said. . . .

Her death had not been proved. Boaden, who was
writing her biography, swore he had seen her in the
Strand, looking in the window of a bookshop. Her – or
her shade? William had no belief in hauntings, for
surely if the dead could come again, she would have
come to him. He would sooner know that she was dead,
at peace, than hiding in some foreign town, an exile.

She had fled to France, that much he knew, to escape
her creditors. Alsop, who should by all rights have been
hanged, but that the raking up of evidence would have
reflected too strongly upon her – Alsop had bled her to
the last. Alsop and others. Debts on every side. But she
had not been left without provision. He had seen to
that. He had settled enough to keep her in luxury for
life, if she had not been so consistently imposed upon

and victimized by the incessant whinings of her daughter.

What a coil! And he entangled in it, shamefully betrayed by his own brother!

William's hand in its yellow glove involuntarily clenched on the handle of the basket he still held. God! . . . That anything so evil should be allowed to live! Yet Ernest lived, and wormed his foul destructive way into the lives of men, into the hearts of women, into the throne itself, or the good graces of him who sat in the King's place upon it, holding the reins of Regency in his gross paws. Ernest, to whom in all these years, William had never spoken more than lip utterance in public, at Court functions, and to whom, he vowed, that while he lived he would never speak again.

And she? . . .

At least she had shown courage. For that his hidden thought of her applauded. There had been no flinching at the last and no evasion. He remembered how in answer to his summons, she, travelling all night from Cheltenham where she had been playing, had come to meet him, unhesitatingly to take what he must tell her. She had not even troubled to change out of her stage clothes. She was still in her paint, breeched and booted for the boy. Strange that his first and last sight of her should have been as Viola. . . . The cloak she wore over her doublet had been gracious to her over-ripe maturity. And she had stood unbowed and unafraid before him. Almost it seemed as though she welcomed the discovery. She had walked in darkness, fearful of her shadow, but she had met her sentence bravely in the light.

The world condemned him while it made of her a martyr. She had been ruthlessly abandoned, left to starve. He had thrown her over for an heiress, a Miss Tilney Long to whom he had proposed a dozen times:

so they said. Once again the humorists were busy. 'Man wants but little here below, but he wants that little Long. . . .'

St James's found it comical. Actually there was no more in it than that Sophia and Miss Tilney Long were bosom friends for one short season. Quite inseparable in fact. Miss Long with her Mamma came to stay at Maidenhead where William played the host. Sophia was invited to stay at fashionable Ramsgate where the Tilney Longs had taken a house for the summer.

And while William, with a bandanna handkerchief upon his head and Mrs Tilney Long beside him, sat and roasted in the sun and watched his Sophia and Miss Tilney Long go bathing in great wide-brimmed straw hats, long-frilled pantalettes, and skirts ballooning on the ocean as they bobbed to playful shrieks; while Mamma Tilney Long (who may or may not have encouraged rumour to couple her daughter's name with the Duke's – for even the richest heiress in all England would not be such a ninny as to turn her nose up at a Prince, be he fifty or fifteen) – while Mamma, then expatiated on her daughter's beauty and her virtue, her accomplishments, and wealth – 'Two hundred thousand as her portion! None knows of this but you, Sir. My girl must be married for love – not money.' And, 'Eh? No – quite, egad! Yes,' mumbled William, stifling his yawns and a strong desire for a pint of shrimps offered by the vendors of such, bawling their wares on the beach; while William chaperoned his pretty Sophia here, there and everywhere – and no dragonish Mamma could have kept a stricter eye – talk linked him every season to this one and to that, but in spite of it he had remained a bachelor. . . . Till now.

And at this point in his meditations William's head began to nod, his eyes to close, shutting out the memories that came about him like a mist. His sense

bemused and drowsy, went sliding down the avenues of
sleep, to dream and very strangely: of a tall ship and
himself at the helm of her, steering his course through
narrow streets of water with cheering crowds along the
way. All the flags of the world were flying, and at his
side stood a girl with the sun on her hair like a crown.

And her face as he dreamed her shone out of the past,
the face of the young Sarah Martin. . . .

*

'At least we can be sure,' said Gabriele, 'that however
dreadful he may be, he can't be *worse* than his brother.'

She spoke in a whisper, for the door of the Princess's
bedroom was ajar, and in the room beyond the Duchess
sat at breakfast. Although not seen she could be heard,
and while Gabriele at the dressing-table brushed
Adelaide's hair – her fine silken hair that hung long
and straight as rain almost to her knees – the Duchess
maintained a running commentary on immediate
events.

'I find the Regent the most charming – most cultured
of men. Please – another helping of this so delicious
ham and eggs. Is ziss also a national dish? . . . Adelaide!'
The Duchess raised her voice. 'Did you have ham and
eggs for breakfast?'

'No, Mamma. I had coffee and rolls.'

'Tcha! You have had coffee and rolls every day of
your life. When in Rome – or London – one does as the
Londoners do – is it not? I suggest that you wear the
striped *gros de Naples* and the Wellington cap – or no!
I think *not* the cap. The Duke will want to see your
hair. We must not hide your one passably good feature,
poor child.'

Facing her mirror her daughter sat, so white and
motionless it seemed as though every drop of blood in
her body had ceased to flow. Dark circles lay beneath

her eyes, whose pupils had widened till the eyes themselves looked black. It was evident she had not slept all night.

'My poor darling,' whispered Gabriele, 'let me tell the Duchess you are ill. Have this day to rest and be composed. You are in no fit state to meet the Duke and bear any more horrors.'

'As for the Regent,' boomed the Duchess, 'it is a pity you could not appreciate his witty conversation, Adelaide. What a *ranconteur*! Perhaps now you will regret that you have given more time to the study of French than English. How often have I told you that English might be of more importance to your future life than French? You will now have to take lessons in English. I confess I was disappointed. What the Prince must have thought of you I cannot imagine. Even when he spoke to you in French you answered like a charity-school child. I have never been so bitterly ashamed. . . . God send these servants do not understand our language. . . . *Sprechen Sie Deutsch?* Do you speak German?'

'No, Your Highness.'

'Dat is good. . . . Your beloved father, Adelaide, would have been enraptured at his charm. Do you not think he is charming?'

'No, Mamma, I think he is odious.'

The effect of this rejoinder, so clear, so cold, so unexpected, was sensational. Gabriele, eyes rounded, stayed her brush in mid-air. From the next room came a choking sound. 'You – said?'

'I said, Mamma,' repeated Adelaide, turning if possible, paler than before, 'that I think the Prince Regent is odious. It is not necessary to understand English to see that he was drunk.'

'Drunk?' screamed the Duchess, 'that you should *breathe* such calumny! Have you taken leave of your senses?'

K

'No, Mamma. I have found them.'

Gabriele bit back a giggle, but her eyes grew rounder still. She was almost inclined to believe that the Princess was indeed suffering from some mental aberration due to the strain of the last few days, for surely nothing else could account for this defiance?

'I know,' pursued the Princess quietly, 'that it is inexcusable in me, Mamma, to venture an opinion, but did you not observe—'

'Be silent! What are you saying?'

A chair rasped on the polished floor, there was a hiss and a rustle of petticoats, a ponderous step, and the half-opened door was flung wide. The Duchess in a fearsome *négligée* of shot green and amber silk, her turban replaced by a frilled cap perched high on a monument of puffs and curl-papers, appeared upon the threshold. Between the folds of her wrapper, distributed on every available inch of her bosom, pinned to her nightdress and circling her arms, jewels glittered – hers and her daughter's. She had worn them throughout the journey, she had slept with them under her pillow, she had hid them in calico bags beneath her petticoats. She went in mortal fear of being robbed.

Said the Duchess, piercingly: 'Let me hear no more of this. You understand? You will keep your opinions to yourself. You will not air them. You see nothing you know nothing, you *breathe* nothing that can be carried on the air to the detriment of the Family to whom in honour you are pledged. Have I to tell you this? Should not your instinct – your own loyalty command you to hold your tongue?'

The Princess, who had risen at her mother's entrance, dropped her eyes. Gabriele dropped her brush. The Duchess with superb restraint, continued: 'You are evidently unbalanced, my poor child. The fatigue of the journey has proved too much for you. Fräulein Von

Humboldt, have you *sal volatile* at hand? Adelaide, I insist that you rest upon this couch until the Duke arrives.'

He had in fact arrived that very moment, and waited in an ante-room and an agony of apprehension, while the Duchess, cancelling all previous commands, hustled Gabriele aside and her daughter from her cushions. There was no time to rest.

With the air of a high priest officiating at a sacrificial rite, the Duchess selected and discarded gowns for this momentous toilette, including the *gros de Naples*, which was pronounced too elaborate. She chose finally a vestal white jaconet muslin with a scarf and sash of *eau de nil* crape, and no jewels but the Princess's pearls. These were twined in the plaits of the pale gold hair. 'And now,' said the Duchess concealing a sigh, for, though exquisitely gowned – no expense had been spared on the trousseau – the girl was the colour of dough and as lifeless. 'And now, do you, my love, go down to the Duke. I will follow. It may be unconventional that you meet your betrothed for the first time alone, but I think on the whole it were better we do not stand *too* much on ceremony.'

Also, the Duchess was fully aware that Adelaide did not show to the best advantage in the presence of her mother. Last night before the Prince Regent she had sat like a block of wood, hands folded, eyes lowered, with nothing to say. 'He must have certainly thought her a half-wit,' murmured the Duchess, speaking aloud as was sometimes her habit when ruffled. 'And she is utterly lacking in feminine appeal – but God knows I have done my best. . . . And so you go down, dearest heart, and make my apologies and entertain the Duke until I come. If he does not speak German you must speak French or Greek or Latin or Chinese – but you *must speak*!'

. . . . .

In the ante-room William waited – and he waited. Had he come too early? She was probably asleep. Sophia's roses were wilting in their basket. They'd be dead before she came. Should he send out to the florist's for a fresh bouquet? There appeared to be flowers enough already. The room was chock-a-block with bowls and vases, filled to overflowing. And from whom? From George, no doubt. George could always be relied upon to play the cavalier. He knew all the tricks. I don't, thought William gloomily, and what I used to know I have forgotten. . . .

He peered at himself in a mirror and passed his hand over his hair, that in the flurry of departure he had omitted to smooth with pomade. It stood *en brosse* like the tuft on a pineapple. The pressure of his hat had left an angry mark upon his forehead which deepened to the sudden red that dyed his cheeks. Egad! What a sight to go a-courting! He buttoned his coat over a slight protuberance above his waist-line, adjusted the folds of his neck-cloth to hide his second chin, and turned – as the door slowly opened.

She stood in the doorway, a slip of a thing, with eyes like great frozen pools in a face as white as the pearls in her hair that gleamed gold with a sunbeam upon it.

William's glance hovered an instant and stayed – startled. Those eyes and that pure pale brow, that hair like a halo to crown it. . . . Where in his life or a dream had he seen that fleeting shy resemblance which lay, not in form or in feature, but in the very spirit of the past? . . . *I am not worthy of a flower to my name.* . . . It was as though a dead orchard had blossomed in the wintered ashes of forgotten youth.

But William was not given to whimsies, and if some such in that moment came to him, he stifled them. 'Princess?' His intonation lifted in a query, for this meeting was, to say the least of it, irregular. He wondered if this girl, this child – could be a maid-in-waiting.

Her eyes were lowered and her lips set in a proud determination to control their trembling. 'Sir, my mother bid me to present her apologies. She will—' Her soft, broken voice trailed off to a whisper, scarcely heard, and his heart absurdly drumming against his shirt-front, William bowed.

'It is for me to present my apologies, Princess. That I was not here to receive you is unpardonable. There must have been some error in the arrangements.'

A poor enough excuse. He was lamentably aware that the Royal yacht, or at least an equerry, should have been sent to fetch her. He would have gone himself to Meiningen to bring her over, if he had not all the previous week been laid low with asthma. He had left the final arrangements to his brother George, and *this* was what had come of it! No use making matters worse by explanation. To greet her with a tale of himself as a wheezing dotard was not the most tactful introduction to a courtship, so: 'I hope,' he mumbled, lamely, 'that I may be forgiven?'

'Pleass . . . yes. It is with us also the same. I thank Your Highness.'

Her hand, engulfed in his, fluttered like a captive bird; woefully embarrassed he released it. 'Pray be seated, Princess.'

There was a painful pause. He looked at her downcast face, the pale curve of her cheek, the white slender throat in which he could just discern the faint throb of a pulse. . . . She was palpably nervous, and he had nothing to say, cursing himself for a tongue-tied fool until he remembered the basket of roses that he had placed on the table. That made a diversion.

'From my garden,' he said, 'picked this morning – at dawn. You'll find they'll freshen up in water.'

She thanked him in her precise, careful English. At

least, he observed with relief, his ears would not all the rest of his life be offended by guttural croakings. His mother's voice was like a corncrake. Her accent, he remarked, had more of French in it than German. But what a mere child she looked. Had they lied to him about her age? He had understood that she was four or five and twenty. And seating him carefully beside her on the sofa. 'How – young – exactly are you?' he inquired. 'You look about sixteen.'

'Pleass?'

'Never mind.' He eyed her quizzically. 'Better leave the question of our ages.' And suddenly he sensed that she was shivering. Scared out of her wits – of what? Of him?

'This,' he blurted, 'must be a damnable ordeal for you.' He laid his hand a moment on hers. 'I've daughters of my own, y'know, so—' He stopped abruptly. Confound his jabbering tongue! Just the very thing that Sophia had warned him *not* to say. Ruefully he watched the swift colour mount to her cheeks at his words – or his touch. Both were misplaced – and distasteful. He withdrew his hand quickly. Her colour died down. She'd a skin like a shell, or a flower. . . . William cleared his throat and changed his tactics.

'You and I, Princess, are servants of the State, and as such we can't pick and choose our wives or husbands. If we could you'd not choose me, that's certain. By all the laws of nature you should be married to a boy of your own age, and if I had my way I'd tell you to go straight back to Meiningen and find him. And that,' he added, with a comical look, 'might have been better expressed. They call me the most tactless man in England.'

For the first time her closed lips unfolded in a smile; her shy glance swerved to his and drooped again – but still, she had smiled, and that was at least a concession.

'You mustn't mind my blunt ways,' he apologized,

'I've lived so much inside myself and so long outside the world, that I've forgotten my manners if ever I learned 'em. All my boyhood was lived in a ship and the rest of my life in the country. But I expect,' and his tone was defensive, 'you've heard all about me, and if you haven't you soon will when you come to our cackling Court. There's none who'll give me any quarter there.'

The faint brows lifted, puzzled. She made a small helpless gesture. 'Pleass?'

It was then that the truth dawned upon him. She spoke, save for a few parrot phrases, no English. He'd been wasting his breath. 'Do – you – not – understand?' pronounced William distinctly.

She shook her head. 'Not ver-ry, Sir.

'I see.' He twinkled. 'And I've forgotten all my German – so what are we to do? If I were twenty years younger I should know what to do. There's one language we'd both understand.'

And, saying that, his heart gave a startled dive and then leapt up again. . . . To relive spring in autumn, to know, to feel, to rediscover youth's magic with this young tender thing so soon to be his bride, was a prospect to turn the head and light the blood of any man – past fifty. And as if she read his thoughts he saw her shrink.

A sudden hot resentment flared in him. Why – why should all that he had missed in life have come at last – too late? 'And why,' he almost shouted, 'do you look at me as though I were a – a cockroach? Do you find me so repulsive? I know I'm a battered old hulk with the gout in me foot, and I'm nearly thirty years older than you. You don't have to remind me of that – but God help me! I'll make you forget it! Do you think,' he added wryly, 'that I can?'

She said apologetically, with that shadow of a smile: 'If it pleases, Your Highness – not to spik so quick.'

'I see,' said William, staring at her soft bewildered eyes, 'that I shall have to teach you more than English.' Again that queer emotion held him, a poignant longing for all the years that he had lost; an aching sweetness at the thought of those to come. 'There's a deal I'll have to teach you – but there's more for me to learn. And so' – he took her hand and turned it palm upwards to his lips – 'we will learn from one another . . . my Princess.'

284

Chapter Two

In his darkened rooms at Windsor, a shadow among
shadows, dwelled the King. His life was limited to
padded walls, to soothing hymns and prayers, and the
little tunes he liked to pick out on his pianoforte with
one finger. At his window, in his purple dressing-gown,
day in, day out he sat, staring at the sky he could not
see, at the sun whose warmth he could feel upon his
face, at the green gay earth that he could smell, and the
flowers whose scent came to him sweetly, with comfort.

He was blind and almost deaf. The only voices that
he clearly heard were those from Heaven. A celestial
choir sang to him; sometimes he talked to God. And
sometimes he wept for loneliness, and would tell those
who waited on him, 'Bring me my mourning clothes.
The King is dead.' And sometimes in his darkness he
came to life again and spoke with them that lived for
him, in memory. . . . 'Lord North! My good Lord
North! Hey, now, I have been exceeding wishful to
see you. They tell me some preposterous shocking news.
They say I have lost my colonies, my American colonies.
What? It's false, hey? Lies. . . . They tell me lies.
All – all tell lies. You'll not tell me lies, my good Lord
North.'

Sometimes in his muffled ears he heard a voice he
knew. 'That's my son George. Hey, George, I'm glad
to . . . glad to . . . But I cannot *see*!' His clenched
hands would be lifted in impotent rage, to fall limply
as he bowed his head. 'God's will be done to me even
as to Job. . . . They say you sit on my throne and

walk on my grave. . . . They say we've beat the French at Waterloo. . . .'

He had a hobby-horse, and would mount it and go gleefully capering up and down his empty rooms with hunting calls, while his unresponsive keepers played at dice.

The years slid by and he was young again, a boy who drove in state through the shouting streets beside his bride, to be crowned King. There had been much talk of brides. His wife came, wizened and yellow with age, hiding her fear of him but not her grief, for he could never see her tears, to tell him brightly: 'William is married and Edward also – he is married. Both were married yesterday at Kew. A double wedding. Can you not hear me, dearest heart?'

He could hear nothing, for even in his lucid moments he did not care to hear. He lived in a world of mysterious dimensions where earthly sense can never penetrate, a world where sound of smallest things becomes significantly great, and where all sight is boundless. He could hear the whisper of the clouds and the laughter of the gods; he could hear the grass grow, could see the birth of a star and the colour of the wind, and the faces of the dead who never die. And he was happy in his world of exquisite imaginings where mortal affairs have power neither to dismay nor to delight – happy until the gentle fever lifted and he came to life again, and knew himself an old man, blind and mad.

But beyond the walls of his vast palace where he sat islanded, the stream of life flowed on, gathering impetus as the tide of change engulfed the nineteenth century in the dawn of a new age, a new morality, a newer creed. It was an age of transition, of social and political revolt, of young leaders who dared to speak their minds, not in Parliament, but on hustings, at street corners, sponsored by such godfathers as Owen, Cobbett, Huskisson, Burdett; pioneers who paved the way for the builders of an Empire to follow.

The spirit of Reform stalked fearlessly abroad, while throughout the country came news of rick-burning and riots, the breaking of these new-fangled machines that ousted honest weavers from their work and spelled destruction to mankind.

There were those who visioned in this menace of machinery a danger, not only to the individual, but to the whole community of life. A hydra-headed monster had sprung into being with far-flung tentacles to crush and to despoil. There were those who spoke of what might come if this iron-girded, Christ-defying Thing were permitted to breed until it would annihilate the soul of man. It would conquer the elements and all of nature that was noble, fair, and true. It would make wars hideous that the very skies would shake, and the peoples of the earth be sunk beneath a force that is almightier than God's. . . . The iron age of Progress.

And over and above the murmurous thunder of unrest, the ceaseless throb of the machine and the voice of the dissenter, was heard the poet's song. But its theme was revolution, a new Utopia, a new ideal.

'Everybody attacks me for my detestable principles,' wrote Shelley before he retired to Pisa, 'I am reckoned an outcast.'

Byron had loosened an outburst of revolt in 'Manfred', and the men of the workers were learning to read. They read Godwin's *Political Justice*. Very soon all men would read. There was talk of education for the masses. A Welshman named Owen had founded a school for infants; more than that, he had built a model factory north of the Clyde which provided for humane and intelligent supervision of mind and body. Thousands of visitors drove from the Thames to Scotland to see this wonder and the man who worked it, and to return with grim forebodings. What did this democracy portend? A state controlled by working men who had not only learned to read, but to think for themselves in this strange new world that had won wars to gain peace, and scream for plenty.

And while the champions of the new age shouldered the burdens of the weak and scattered the seeds of Parliamentary Reform, the King's sons lived their lives apart, remote, untroubled.

At Brighton, 'Prinny', emblazoned with orders, wearing a new suit of Brummell's design, still drove his yellow tilbury along the Steyne, bowing right and left to his cronies and his ladies. His Pavilion grew more crowded and more curious; more Bacchanalian his orgies, more extravagant his debts. He over-ate and fattened, he entertained, he drank. More than ever did he now acquire priceless furniture, old masters, and new mistresses, and talked of divorcing his wife.

As for Edward of Kent, he had hurried his Duchess to England just in time for the birth of a baby princess, of whom none took the smallest account. Of much more importance was the expected child of the Duke of Clarence, who would one day be heir-presumptive to the throne.

He, immediately after the wedding, had taken his young bride to Hanover, and there, in those ensuing weeks, with bluff chivalry if clumsy insistence, he pursued his married courtship.

Of that incalculable honeymoon little is known, but Gabriele Von Humboldt, whose services Adelaide retained until her marriage with Baron Von Bülow, writes:

I would not have believed that he [the Duke] could show so much delicacy and restraint. I think she is not insensible to his consideration. It is evident to all of us that he is falling in love with his wife. What an agreeable surprise to find him so amenable and gracious! I did indeed misdoubt this marriage which now I think will prove happier than I had ever hoped. . . .

The Duke's equerry, Colonel Wilbraham, was also writing home:

You would be surprised at the Duke if you were to see him. His wife has entirely reformed him, and instead of that *polisson* manner of which he used to be celebrated, he is now quiet and well-behaved as anybody else.

And she, who all her life had been suppressed and dominated, now found herself upon a pedestal, adored. Her tastes were studied, her whims gratified. William, whose exchequer had, after his marriage, been replenished by the Government, was generously lavish with his gifts. Not the least of these was a surprise for her, a box of oil-colours. 'You say you've always wished to paint – well, now you can.'

That almost won her; almost, but not quite.

Not until the birth of her first and still-born child, did he succeed in breaking her defences. Then of her will she turned to him for comfort. She did not find him wanting.

'You are so young, my darling. You will yet be the mother of many.' So young. . . . That for him was both a joy and a regret. He determined that she should never feel the disparity of age between them. They had some tastes in common and these with pathetic eagerness he stressed. 'You like a country life, my dear, I know. And you will love Bushey – eh? And the charming, simple folk of the parish who know me as their squire. You will like that. And you will like to ride.

There's grand riding in the Park. We'll bring over a couple of the stud from Hanover – when you're well enough to travel. . . .'

He was impatient to be back in England, to show her his home. One thing profoundly moved him. He had carefully avoided all mention of his daughters, until the day when, in her halting English, that he insisted she should always speak to him, she said, 'I would like to know your little girls.'

'My . . . ?' The gooseberry eyes protruded and he mumbled, reddening, 'They're not so little. Even the youngest – Amelia's bigger than you.'

'I would – like,' said Adelaide firmly, 'that I know them. They are yours. So all are . . . mine.'

He had no more to say to that. Something came into his throat to make a fool of him. He could only take her face between his hands, and gaze dumbly down into her eyes, and:

'You are,' she said, 'so kind. I have to thank you.'

Three months later William was excitedly writing from Lichenstein to Lord Liverpool, the Prime Minister:

It is with real satisfaction yet it is also with an anxious mind that I now address your Lordship to request you to inform the Regent that there is every reason to believe the Dutchess is once more with child. It is now a fortnight since Dr Halliday and myself had our suspicions. . . . Things being thus I should be uneasy if I did not address these lines to your Lordship for the information of the Regent. My anxiety to see the Dutchess safely landed in England must be very great. I lament I cannot leave this place till the Fifteenth inst. I trust to arrive with this excellent and admirable Princess at St James's on the Tenth of September. . . .

Once again was he doomed to disappointment. The journey proved too much for the frail Adelaide, who collapsed at Dunkirk and lay ill there for weeks after a miscarriage.

As soon as she was fit to travel he hurried her home to England. It was now apparent to the whole nation that the birth of an heir to the Duke of Clarence must be of paramount importance. The King at last was dying. The death of his wife a few months after William's marriage may have penetrated to his dimmed consciousness, for thereafter he visibly began to sink, and in the New Year came the merciful end.

Only two lives now stood between William and the throne, and there was no possible doubt whatever that even if Clarence did not survive his elder brothers, his child would be King. He was convinced that he would have a son. He wanted a son, he prayed for a son. But at Bushey in December 1820, was born to Adelaide a daughter.

*

They gave her the magic name of Elizabeth. In his joy and relief at his wife's safe deliverance after twenty-four hours' agonizing labour, he had forgotten that he had seen his son a sailor. Now his universe was centred in this whimpering atom who represented the future Sovereign of Britain. And she throve. She was sturdy, strong; she turned the scale at eleven pounds at birth. Her lusty emergence almost killed her mother.

In her bedroom overlooking Bushey Park, Adelaide lay at peace. In this very room she knew that other daughters had been born to him who fathered hers, but that knowledge brought no bitterness and no resentment. Not in vain had he so diffidently wooed her to draw their lives together in closer confidence and trust. The extraordinary influence she wielded over her husband has been noted by various commentators, to be briefly summed up by George the King, who told his Lady Conyngham: 'The fact is, my brother Billy is mad in love with his little white mouse of a wife.'

The spectacle of this elderly Duke's infatuation for the insignificant Adelaide was a source of endless entertainment to the Court. But though the ladies giggled, they allowed the Duchess a pretty taste in clothes. Plain she might be, colourless, small, and absurdly undeveloped in her shape, it was admitted that she did know how to dress. On one of those rare occasions when the homely pair could be induced to leave their retreat at Bushey for the frivolities of Brighton, Lady Granville recounts that, 'The Duchess of Clarence has *nine* new gowns – the most loyal of us not having been able to muster more than *six*,' and generously concedes, 'she moves very gracefully and enters and leaves a room *à ravir*.'

The household at Bushey had been entirely transformed. Starry-blossomed chintz and fashionable striped wallpapers replaced the garish shabbiness of former years. The ghosts of the past were laid gently; there was no insistence, no intrusion of new governance. So quietly did his little 'white mouse' settle in his home that her husband scarcely realized a change, beyond the deep pervading peace of it. The days seemed all too short for all there was to do with her beside him to share the life he loved.

He, more accustomed to walking than riding, would set out with his dogs for a tour of his estate, and meet her on her cream-coloured pony at some prearranged spot for a picnic luncheon under the trees. Then together they would visit a cottage in need of repair, or pay a call on a country neighbour, for she was as ready as he to dispense with etiquette, even so far as to startle the world and the spinster Princesses at Windsor, by extending her patronage to the Duke's illegitimate family.

It was said that his unmarried daughters now lived with her and their father at Bushey; that they drove with the Duchess wherever she went, sat at her table and attended her to church. . . . Eyes were raised to heaven. Who had ever heard the like? The elderly Princesses Augusta and Sophia, declared that Poor Mamma must surely have turned in her grave.

But very soon they came to accept this singular state of affairs along with the nephews and nieces whose existence they had hitherto ignored. William was delighted, the neighbourhood was charmed, and George Fitzclarence told his cronies at Boodle's that his step-mother was 'the best and dearest creature in the world.'

Meanwhile public interest was, and had been for the past twelve months, focused on the new King and the scandal attached to his Consort. Never since Henry VIII had a King brought a case of divorce against his wife. Was she innocent or guilty? And who the devil cared, so long as garbage enough could be served to feed the appetite of the rag, tag and bobtail who avidly savoured the spice offered by the pens of the lampoonists.

Queen Caroline was well supported by her 'Party'. She drove to her trial through cheering streets in a state carriage drawn by six of the cream-coloured horses. She was dressed in black and a curled girlish wig, and painted to the eyebrows. Loathing as they did their pre-posterous fat King who had squandered the nation's money on himself, his women, his houses, and his drink, the bulk of the people were for her, and: 'By Jove, my dear,' wrote Creevey, 'we are coming to critical times.' Which did not unduly trouble William.

He was far too engrossed with his life and his only legitimate child to take much to heart the predicament of George. Although he may have felt in duty bound to support the King in this abortive crisis, he also must have thanked his stars that he who had again and again been put in the pillory, spat upon, jeered at, and ridiculed by the Press, was, for once, out of it. He may, in fact, have been a trifle sanctimonious in his new-found respectability, the virtue of his wife, and his privately professed disgust of George 'and all these antics'.

Then, scarcely had the noise and the excitement sub-sided, than the preparations for the coronation went apace. Parliament voted a grant of a quarter of a million for the purpose, which was eventually raised to four hundred thousand. The King, it seemed, would make his country pay for his long delayed accession to the throne.

On a blustering day in early March of the year 1821, the Princess Augusta drove over from Frogmore to Bushey to visit 'dear Adelaide' – now in highest favour – and to give her the latest news of the Court, the King, and the Government grant. Augusta loved to gossip.

The years shadowed by her father's illness and her implacable mother's demands, had robbed Augusta of all her sportive humour. She had stoutened; her complexion was a mottled mauve, and time had set its damaging marks under her eyes in a network of lines and creases. Careless in her dress and downright in her manner, she hid her warmth of heart beneath a sharpened tongue. She held decided views and impulsive likes and dislikes. She either 'loved' or she 'detested'. She 'adored' her brothers George and 'dearest' William. She bitterly mourned the death of her brother, Edward of Kent, whose fatal chill had been caused by walking in the rain without goloshes.

She was still wearing heavy black for him when she arrived that afternoon at Bushey Lodge, to find William in a rare fuss, the doctor's carriage at the door, and Adelaide invisible.

'She's with the baby,' said William, very agitated. 'Such a morning as we've had! I've ate no luncheon. I've sent for Halford. This local man's no good.'

'For gracious sake! Who's ill?' cried Augusta in alarm.

'Elizabeth. As you know – or perhaps you don't – pray do sit down. May I offer you a glass of wine? Madeira? Sherry? As you know it is our custom—'

'Madeira,' said Augusta.

'As you know – pray, my dear, be seated, you fidget me. It is our custom to have Elizabeth brought to our room in the morning before breakfast. The most charming, intelligent child, already so companionable. Well, the nurse brought her as usual this morning with a face as long as your arm. She'd been screaming all night—'

'Good heavens! The nurse?' interrupted Augusta.

'No, no! Our poor little angel – with pain. We thought at once – the colic! Sent for our man here, who purged her. She appeared to be no easier, so then I sent for Halford. He should be here any moment. That other God-forsaken idiot is with her now.' Taking his gold repeater from his pocket he glanced at it and then at the clock. 'That,' he said, 'is five minutes slow. I can't imagine why Halford doesn't come. He should have been here an hour ago. It is too monstrous cruel that anything so young should be allowed to suffer. Poor Adelaide's distracted and I'm helpless. I—' he dropped into a chair. 'I can do nothing – but wait.'

'Come, come!' exclaimed Augusta briskly, 'you mustn't give way. All babies have attacks of something – sometimes.'

'Much you know of babies,' growled her brother.

'That,' replied Augusta dryly, 'is less my fault than

my misfortune. And since you *are* so pressing I will, I thank you, take a glass of wine.'

'Dear me! A thousand pardons. Sherry?'

'If you insist. I *said* – Madeira.'

With a shaking hand William filled a glass from one of two decanters on the table. 'She means so much to us,' he murmured. 'To us and to the nation. You realize, of course – she will be Queen?'

'My dear Wililam, are you not a little premature? Our beloved George is not as yet crowned King. And if one may judge by precedent you may yet be the father of half a dozen boys.'

'True,' William permitted his harassed features the relaxation of a grin, 'you never can tell. I'm still spry. I never walk less than ten miles a day and that's good enough for my age. Adelaide, bless her, rides. The finest horsewoman in the county. She'd hunt if I'd let her. She's absolutely fearless. You'd never think that such a midget of a woman could sit a horse so well. I'm told her hands are perfect. I've bred a couple of ponies for Elizabeth from the Windsor stud. I'll have her taught to ride as soon as she can walk. Wish I'd done more of it in my time. Nothing like it for shaking up the liver.'

'Yes, you ought to ride,' agreed Augusta dryly, 'instead of so much walking. It would reduce your weight.'

'Weight? What d'you mean weight?' retorted William in a huff. 'Let me tell you I've lost ten pounds since Christmas. No one,' he added, pushing out his chest and pulling in his stomach, 'would ever take me for almost thirty years older than my wife. Now George *looks* his age – and more. And so does Fred. I'll wager I'll out-live the pair of 'em. What's all this about George and his grant? Is it true the Government are handing out a quarter of a million for the coronation?'

Augusta nodded. 'And more than that if I know our brother George!'

'Damned stiff!' muttered William. 'That'll raise a hullaballoo. He ain't all that popular that he can afford to throw the nation's money away on a circus. He's storing up trouble for himself and those that follow him, mark me.' But not for long was William's mind away from his own anxiety. 'I wonder—' Once again he consulted his watch. 'I wonder if I ought to send another messenger. The man left here at nine this morning. . . . Half past four. Halford should certainly be here by now. I can't think what can have delayed him, unless he's been held up. There were highway robberies at Barnes last week. Do you think—'

'I think,' put in Augusta calmly, 'that I hear a carriage in the drive.'

All that day, all through the night, the stricken mother sat by her baby's cot, while the doctors battled for the small precious life, that not their skill nor a mother's prayers could save. Science had not taught enough to operate.

She died in the dawn of the second day, William's daughter, the Princess Elizabeth.

*

One Royal baby more or less meant nothing to the nation. The nursery at Kensington guarded another child, and the Duchess of Clarence was young. She might yet be the mother of many.

Their shared sorrow and their aching hope long after hope had gone, forged between William and his wife a closer link, a deeper understanding. Each was more dependent on the other in the isolation of their grief, and in the fruitless years to come. For William who had fathered ten, was the father of none to his name.

But the hand of fate was moving in this dynasty of Kings.

In 1827 Frederick of York died an inglorious death of the dropsy, and for the first time and at the age of sixty-two, the life of William, Duke of Clarence, became of paramount importance to his country.

He, whose offer of service thirty years before had been slighted and rebuffed, must now, as heir-presumptive to the throne, perforce be recognized.

It was an end to his peaceful retirement.

They dug him up, ironically to honour him with the office of Lord High Admiral of England, in abeyance since the time of Anne. He had come into his own – a trifle late.

Transplantation from his quiet home at Bushey to function as a figurehead in Whitehall, was the last thing that he at his age would have wanted. If only this had come to him, twenty – *ten* years earlier, he would have welcomed it, but not now when he had lost touch with the world and the Navy.

There was, however, nothing for it but to accept and to remove himself, his wife, and his two unmarried daughters from Bushey Park to Admiralty House.

It was not without regret that Adelaide relinquished her gardens and her country charities, to preside over dinners and receptions in a company that, to say the least of it, was mixed.

The new Lord High Admiral issued invitations right and left with more regard for old acquaintance sake than discriminate selection. The crowded rooms swarmed with resuscitated shipmates and their wives. William, in his element, would be found in boisterous confabulation with some elderly gentleman in an old-fashioned uniform of forty years before, excitedly beckoning his wife.

'Come here, my dear! Here's Commodore Storey, who was with me in the *Prince George* in 'seventy-nine. D'you remember when we played *The Merry Wives of*

Windsor, and ducked you in the muddy ditch? Egad!
But those were days—'

It seemed he was determined to revive them. The
dockyards of Portsmouth and Plymouth received their
Lord High Admiral with loudest demonstrations.
Covered with orders and medals he reviewed the Fleet,
conducted manœuvres, and handed out appointments
to old friends from the past, to the unutterable confusion of his Council.

Nor was that all. His activities were as limitless as
his enthusiasm. He electrified the Board by hurling at
them questions that had never been discussed since the
days before Trafalgar. He swung from past to present,
and attacked the council for the shocking conditions
still prevalent among the naval ratings. On either side
of him at that long table in Whitehall, where generations of Admiralty Lords have sat and are still sitting,
his perturbed officials heard him out, too startled to
protest.

'I intend to be no figurehead,' roared William, banging his fist on the mahogany to make the ink-pots jump.
'I am a sailor – and most of you are not. I know the sea
and I know seamen and I've lived in His Majesty's
ships. Many years ago, before some of you were born,
and before the rest of you can well remember, I saw
much in the system of life afloat that I deplored and
had no power to reform. My investigations since I took
up office here have shown me that this same system still
exists in this so-called "enlightened" age of steam and
new inventions – a system that has no right to *be*! I
declare to you, my lords and gentlemen, that certain
systems which have too long existed to our shame are
about to be abolished!'

The trick of repetition had grown still more pronounced, his speeches more verbose and more untidy,
but the message he conveyed was clear enough. His lords

and gentlemen might look along their noses and snicker in their hands, and think him crazy, yet he won his way. He forbade the use of the 'cat' for a start, except in cases of mutiny. Medical supervision became a daily routine. He extracted from the Treasury large sums with which to pension off old officers, and promoted younger ones to take their place. He finally bellowed for steam.

'Must we waste this new discovery – the greatest invention of all time? Railways will soon replace the coach and speed up transport. Must shipping stay behind? Let the Navy take the lead!'

Such startling demands were not received with favour. It was thought he took too much upon himself. No figurehead, forsooth! A figurehead he was and would remain if the Lords in office had the right of it.

They had – when the imbecile administration under Goderich was dissolved, to make Wellington the leader of the Government.

All unconscious of the storm behind him, William steered his course along the Admiralty highway in blithe defiance of his council, even as years before he had defied supreme command.

It was a case of history repeated, since under the terms of his appointment, his orders were subject to the decision of his Board. But this he disregarded when in his flagship, the *Royal Sovereign*, he led a squadron out to sea upon manœuvres with none in charge of it except himself. He had done it again, and this time once too often. And when the Lord High Admiral brought his flagship into port he was asked by the King to resign.

There were many who regarded his collapse as a stroke of ill-luck for the Navy. During his short term of office he had been unceasing in his efforts to instil into traditional administration a new spirit conformable with the new age. In defiance of all obstacles presented, he had put into commission the first steamship. But that alone had been enough to damn him in the opinion of the die-hards. Steam! Which though yet in its experimental stage had been the first cause of industrial riots. Did he want a repetition of machine-breaking afloat? He'd have to go.

He went, subdued.

The continuous badgering and bullying of those who were subordinate to him in nothing more than name, had told upon his spirits. It was good to be back in the quiet of Bushey after all the excitement and bother; good to have his wife to himself again to rub the chalk-stones from his fingers and to sympathize and soothe; good to hear the laughter and chatter of his girls, and to go tramping his own land on his ten-mile walks to inspect a new herd of cows, a new cottage. It was good, indeed, to be back in his home. He hoped to God he'd never have to leave it.

His boast of out-living his brothers was not now so often heard. If he should out-live George he would be faced by staggering, immense responsibilities that loomed ahead with no promise of pending glory, but with ever-increasing gloom. His brother George was ailing. What did that portend? A temporary indisposition or decline?

William heard the reports with deepening concern and was for ever pestering the doctors: 'Is he likely to live? Surely he's good for another ten years. Maybe he'll see me out yet.'

The motive of these queries very naturally was misconstrued. The King's heir seemed mighty anxious for the Crown. But in that they did him an injustice. More and more did William dread the climax of his destiny. He was too old. . . .

Soon it became clear to all of England that the King's condition was grave. He had grown so alarmingly fat that he looked like a feather bed. In constant pain from gouty inflammation and almost blind in one eye, he put up a valiant fight to save himself. Life beckoned; life could still be sweet if he had strength enough to live and to enjoy. He still drank cherry brandy before break-fast, and maraschino before lunch. Women were still and always would be beautiful. He had his pictures, his Pavilion; and his horse had won the Craven Stakes at Epsom. A good omen. He would win through yet, he swore. He'd still be King.

He sent for William, who hurried to his bedside to find him sipping chocolate in a slightly soiled night-shirt, which, half-buttoned, exposed a bulging hairless chest, white as a woman's. Round his shoulders was flung a gorgeous dressing-gown. Without his rouge his face had a greyish tinge; his features, hands, even his three chins, were hideously swollen. The change in one week since William had last seen him was shockingly apparent. Fearing the worst William prayed for the best, and uncomfortably took his seat beside him.

'Did you go to Epsom yesterday?' asked George. 'I'd have tipped you the wink about the "Colonel". Won by three lengths, egad! D'ye see these?' He spread his sausage fingers. 'Gout, my dear. I'm riddled with it – so are you. That's all it is – the gout. Or is it dropsy? These infernal doctors tell you nothing.' The hazy eyes, still blue, still boyish, widened in a sudden wave of fear. 'Poor Fred! It was the dropsy did for *him*.'

'Dropsy? Stuff!' said William stoutly. 'You're looking better than when I saw you last.'

'Liar!' The loose lips parted in a flash of the old smile. 'I know – and *you* know – that I'm not.'

William blinked. 'I've seen you looking worse,' he growled. 'Here – let me take that cup.' For the poor distorted hand could scarcely hold it.

'Thank you, my dear.' That enormous bulk moved

uneasily beneath its coverings; from under the tasselled night-cap strayed one bright yellow curl, the sight of which brought, unaccountably, a stone to William's throat. He swallowed it and looked away. George had always been a dandy.

'Well,' said George, his one sound eye upon the ceiling, 'I've always done my best. I've injured no one – but my wife. And you.'

'Me?' William's head jerked up. 'Why me?'

'I'm leavin' you a heritage, my dear,' George told him solemnly, 'of worse than debts. I'm leavin' you a slur to monarchy. Our poor "Rex" used to tell me I'd disgraced him and the Throne. But this I'll say. I've given something to the country that no other of our forbears yet has done. I've given art to England. Architecture. I've made Brighton beautiful. It was I discovered Nash. For that alone in time to come I'll be remembered.'

'Now, now, George!' blurted William. 'Don't be morbid. You're good for another ten years yet. You'll outlive me.'

His brother smiled.

'God's will be done. The future of my people rests with you. . . . *All* will rest on you. And heaven knows – I leave a mint of trouble. It's too bad that you should face it.'

'I will not,' said William loudly, 'countenance such talk. This depression will soon pass. It is all a symptom of the gout. For myself I find that nothing loosens mine but exercise. I've always told you that you never walk enough.'

'And I shall never walk again. My dear, I'm not a fool – even if my doctor is. I've done my best, although my people think . . . but they don't understand. I've been an egoist, supremely. It should be written on my epitaph – "this man knew how to live".' Tears welled behind the puffy lids; the grotesque chins began to

shake. 'And I hope that I'll know how to die,' said
George, the King

*

On the morning of 26 June, William, who latterly
had not been sleeping well, rose at daybreak, and without disturbing his valet or his wife, dressed and went
down to his study. He found the housemaids busy with
brooms and dusters, and bidding them: 'Get on with it
– get on with it. Never mind me,' he sat down at his
desk.

With hurrying efficiency the maids finished their
work and left him. Then began the daily ritual of
exercise. First his fingers must be stretched and slackened. This laboriously performed, he signed his name
not once but a dozen times. At the last 'William' his
quill paused to add an R which with heightened colour
he hastily erased. Tearing the paper into pieces he got
up from his chair, removed his coat and marched over
to the open window. Then, expanding his chest he
stretched his arms above his head, and his body forward
and downward in an attempt to touch his toes. He was
still perseveringly engaged in this endeavour, when Sir
Henry Halford, the King's physician, drove up in his
carriage to the door.

His arrival at that hour when none but the master of
the house and his servants was astir, brought William to
the hall in his shirt-sleeves, and one arm in and one out
of his coat.

The doctor's face was grave and William's pale, as,
stammering, he questioned: 'Why – what – Sir Henry!
What news of the King?'

'Sire—' And as bare-headed Halford knelt, an icy
hand was closed on William's heart.

So it had to come, the dreaded moment, and in
silence William faced it, while Sir Henry told of the

King's passing. The end that for five days had been hourly expected, had been swift and sudden at the last of a burst blood-vessel.

George IV, fully conscious, had died in his chair, gasping: 'O God! This is death!' as he expired.

William's first coherent thought was for his wife. She must be told at once, and none but he must do it.

He hastened to their room to find her still asleep, nor did she wake when he came and stood beside her. She lay, absurdly small in their great four-post bed, her little body curled beneath the covers, her head turned sideways on the pillow, one hand beneath her cheek, her heavy pale hair falling round her shoulders like a schoolgirl's. For him she had not altered since the day he saw her first. The faint coin-like markings time had traced on the fair fragile skin were smoothed in sleep. As he leaned to touch with his lips that calm untroubled brow, she stirred, and her eyes opened to find his.

'You are already dressed? Have I overslept then? Is it late?'

'No, my darling, it is early.'

Her eyes, widening, read the words he would have spoken in his face as all colour fled from hers. She raised herself upon an elbow. 'What,' she whispered, 'have you come to tell me?'

Kneeling he gathered her into his arms. 'That more than ever do I need you now. . . . My Queen.'

She drew his head against her breast and held it there.

Chapter Three

At the gates of St James's Palace a small crowd of people had collected, not to mourn the death of their King, but to watch for the arrival of his brother. London had the news that he was on his way from his retreat in Bushey. Few of his subjects had ever set eyes on him; to the vast majority he was nothing but a name. Those of a decade earlier who had enjoyed to the full the scandal of his private life, had soon forgotten it. He was now to all intents and purposes a stranger, but one who might with any luck be better, he certainly could not be any worse than he, for whom the flags were at half-mast.

The King was dead, long live the new King William.

There were some who may have genuinely hoped he would live long, for if he didn't they would have a child on the Throne, and the loathly Duke of Cumberland for Regent. They'd had enough of Regents. This new fellow, according to the club-men of St James's, whatever he might prove to be, would at least save them from the 'Dreary Duke'. All the world knew that Cumberland was greedy for the Throne, and would stop at nothing – even murder – to attain it. It was rumoured that he or his paid assassins had tried to shoot the young Princess Victoria. Who knew but what he might not shoot the King?

The books were sent for, entries made. 'A thousand to one that Billy will be winged before the coronation.' 'Five thousand to one there'll be a Regency before the year is out.' 'What's the odds he'll die as dotty as his father?'

And while with some such jocularity the bets were laid by the blue-blooded goats of St James's, the sheep outside the palace waited, mildly inquisitive but with no intense excitement, for their King. They knew what to expect; no bewigged painted old rip, but an amiable, elderly gentleman who had lived most of his life in the country and all his young manhood at sea. One who had fought in the wars but had never distinguished himself as a sailor, and who as Lord High Admiral had been forced out of office by his extraordinary behaviour.

Perhaps he was a lunatic, but still he was their King, and one who for the first time in living memory was not a George. For that, obscurely, they were thankful. They had not been lucky, so far, with their Georges. The best of them was mad and the worst of them lay dead inside his castle.

So, while his people waited to receive him, the new King drove to his capital unheralded, in no state coach, with no fanfare, no pomp. He came in a carriage and pair, and – since he possessed no suit of black – in navy blue. His concession to mourning was a crape streamer on his hat, and this he doffed to right and left through all the villages along the way, to the wonder of the natives, who had no notion who this beaming gentleman might be. Through Twickenham and Putney and Hammersmith, he came to Knightsbridge and the Piccadilly turnpike. There the gate-keeper approached to take his toll. William, broadly smiling, paid it with a crown-piece, and 'Keep the change,' he told him, airily. 'There'll be no more shillings now with George's head.'

It seemed this sudden glory was mounting to his own . . . So to St James's where no soul raised a cheer. He passed unrecognized by them who had waited there since dawn for a first sight of him.

Other carriages had passed before him through the gates, bearing more familiar figures. The Duke of

Wellington in a barouche and four, the Duke of Cumberland, with his dyed whiskers and his snarling grin, his hat pulled askew to hide his scarred eye-socket. The two old-maid Princesses: Augusta, stiff as a ram-rod and smothered in black veils, full of woe; the gentle, blind Sophia, her sightless eyes turned up, tears from them running down; and the Duchess of Kent looking happy as a grig, with her podgy little daughter beside her obediently kissing her hand to the silent crowd, and obviously scared. All these had come, and some had gone, before the King arrived.

Who can tell of what he thought along that lonely drive? What aspirations and what hopes, what fears upheld or shattered him?

Such stupendous elevation after sixty-four years of insignificance was staggering enough to turn a stouter heart than his. Not even when Frederick died had William dared to reckon on the Throne. In spite of his unhealthy fat, George had always been robust. His spirit had been strengthened by his zest for life and living to outweigh the weaker flesh. Only in the past few weeks had William realized that 'all', as George had said, 'would rest on him'. Would the burden prove too great? He prayed he would be given strength to take it.

In the third drawing-room of St James's, ninety Privy Councillors, black-coated and suitably solemn, were assembled, awaiting their King. They grew impatient – he was late; watches were consulted, chins stroked, whispers passed from ear to ear. What would he be like? The great majority there present knew no more about him than the crowd outside the gate, and though the remainder might claim acquaintance, there were scarcely three among them who had in all their lives exchanged one word with him or even been presented. Time dragged and faces grew longer. It was well past midday when the great doors were at last flung open and the King hurried into the room.

Sturdy, red-faced, silver-haired, immaculately neat in a well-tailored suit – no mourning it was noticed beyond a crape band on the arm – he marched between the line of bowing Councillors with the brisk, alert tread of a sailor. There was no mistaking it, that slight roll in his gait, the keen steady glance that swept the watchful faces as he took his stand at the table before them, as though he stood on the bridge of a ship.

His speech, delivered in a rich fruity voice without pause or hesitation, was impressive enough and emotional.

'In addition to that loss, which,' he said, 'I sustain in common with you all, I have to lament the death of a beloved and affectionate brother, with whom I have lived from my earliest years on terms of the most cordial and uninterrupted friendship. I am now called upon under the dispensation of Almighty God to administer the government of this great Empire, and I rely with confidence upon the advice and assistance of Parliament and upon its zealous co-operation in my anxious endeavours to promote the prosperity and happiness of all classes of my people. . . .'

It was generally agreed that he had spoken well but had rather spoiled his effect at the end by remarking, when he signed his name to the declaration: 'This is a damned bad pen you have given me!' The whole room heard it and though half were scandalized, and half amused, all were of opinion that he was a distinct improvement on his brother, and might make 'a very decent King – if he didn't go mad'.

Some people thought he would. His hearty downright manner, his hail-fellow-well-met attitude to all, his naïve delight in his exalted eminence which soon succeeded his first reaction to the shock of it, were anxiously regarded as symptomatic of his father's taint. There was plenty of gossip. At Bushey, where he still spent his week-ends, he refused to put his servants into mourning. Worse than that, he sent for the officer of the Palace guards to take all the muffles off the drums.

'My revered brother,' William said, 'would have disliked that dismal sound – and so do I.'

His brother had not been dead twelve hours before the King countermanded an order for new uniforms – 'to spare the officers an unnecessary expenditure'.

He went to Woolwich to review the gunners and preside at a dinner afterwards, with, it was reported, a great to-do of toasts and hip-hurrahing three times three, which he led himself.

Very jovial indeed, and not much harm in it – but odd.

At the King's funeral he behaved in the most extraordinary fashion. The attendance was not very numerous, and when all were gathered together in St George's Hall and with exception of the tearful Lord Mount Stephen, a gayer company beneath that roof had never been beheld.

King William, as chief mourner in a long purple cloak and the Star and Garter twinkling on his chest, entered the chapel directly behind the coffin. With his face wreathed in smiles, his head nodding here, there, and everywhere as he recognized old friends, he passed breezily up the aisle, and at one point actually left the procession to dart across to an elderly peer – Lord Stratheven – and shake him warmly by the hand. It might, they said, have been a coronation.

He began to alarm his Ministers and astonish the world. Here was a new idea in monarchy. All very well to be affable and democratic, but he surely was going too far. His sayings were stored up and repeated. His brother, the Duke of Sussex, had urged him to

receive the Freemasons with a solemn address, but this
he refused. Instead, he greeted them with, 'Gentlemen,
if my love for you equalled my ignorance of everything
concerning you, it would be unbounded.'

And at another and more important affair when he
held a reception in honour of the King and Queen of
Wurtemburg, he made an amusing speech, on conjugal
fidelity.

As the King of Wurtemburg, who had married the
King's sister, Princess Charlotte, was notoriously un-
faithful, with half a dozen mistresses in all the capitals
of Europe, the subject of his speech might have been
better chosen. All the company rose with the King, but
he airily bade them be seated. Then, still standing, he
said that he had been so short a time upon the Throne
that he didn't know whether etiquette required that he
should speak sitting down or standing up. However, he
had long been used to speaking on his legs and he would
continue to do so now. But the *pièce de résistance* of his
doings was recorded after a reception to an address
from the universities, at a Court full of academic grey-
beards. Having divested himself of his robes, and
instead of resting quietly, the King told his wife that
he would take a walk alone.

'Alone?' the startled Adelaide repeated, 'without an
equerry?'

'Yes, without an equerry. With no one. I have never
yet walked through the streets of London by myself – as
King.'

She begged him to be careful. 'It is not safe, my love.'

'Not safe? A pretty sort of King I'll be if I'm not safe
among my subjects. In any case I shan't be recognized.
I'm not yet known – none of them has ever seen me.
Don't you fuss, my dear, I'll soon be back.' And out he
went in his suit of navy blue, his grey beaver at a jaunty
angle – the Citizen King.

Up St James's Street he ambled, staring into the faces of the passers-by and peering in shop windows. In a jeweller's he saw a brooch that took his fancy. Turquoise and small brilliants set in the shape of a heart. He went in to inquire the price. Thirty-five guineas. 'Make it pounds,' he said, 'and I'll buy it for my wife.' The salesman began to haggle. 'Take it or leave it,' said William. 'It's not worth *twenty*-five. These stones are only splinters.' In the end he had his way; the brooch was wrapped and placed in a case, then clapping his hand to his pocket, 'Why, damme!' he exclaimed, 'I have no money with me. You'll have to take a bill.'

The salesman was dubious. 'As a rule, sir, we don't take bills from strangers.'

'You don't, eh?' William chuckled. 'Quite right – quite right. Then do you keep it for me and I'll send the cash tomorrow.'

'The name, sir, if you please?'

'William Henry – at your service,' with a twinkle, said the King. And he left the shop, and the man wondering.

As he turned into Pall Mall he saw an old friend, a Mr Watson Taylor, on the opposite side of the way. Raising his stick he hailed him, 'Hi!' and dashed across the road, dodging a barouche under the heads of the horses. Mr Taylor, a hearty old Whig with a paunch and a sense of humour, was greatly tickled at the situation. They fell into step together and arm-in-arm strolled along past the windows of the clubs, up St James's Street and down again.

But this time the King was recognized. The jeweller's salesman had spread the story, and a cheering mob collected, led by a harlot who ran to the King, flung her arms round his neck and kissed him, amid a thunder of bawling and applause that could be heard from Piccadilly to the Palace.

The horrified members of White's, seeing and hearing it all from their windows and misinterpreting the friendly row into a riot, rushed out to drag the King to safety. William in the struggle lost his hat and Mr Watson Taylor. Two peers who had come to his assistance, were buffeted and shoved about till they were black and blue. Accompanied by yells of 'Let him be! We want the King – he's ours!' he was escorted to the Palace by an hysterically delighted crowd – 'Our Billy, God bless him! The King!'

At the gates of the Palace under the eyes of the gaping sentries, panting, perspiring and grinning all over his face, he turned to thank them.

'Your loyal demonstration, friends, has made me proud and very happy – but now I must ask you to disperse. Or if you like you are welcome to take a quiet stroll in the gardens here.' And waving his stick in a cheery farewell, while his audience yelled themselves tired, he turned and marched into his house.

He found his wife, who had been watching the scene from behind a curtain, stretched upon a couch, surrounded by her ladies and a great smell of burnt feathers. The Queen they told him had all but fainted, thinking His Majesty was mobbed.

William gave a grunt of laughter. 'And so I was, by Jove! But we mustn't mind this sort of thing. When I've walked about a few times they will get used to it and won't take any notice of me.' And dismissing the fluttering ladies he knelt by the couch to take the Queen's white little face in his hands. 'What! Tears and vapours? I told you that I'd come back safe and sound – and here I am.'

'Thank God!' breathed Adelaide. 'I thought it was a revolution.'

'Revolution, why, 'pon my life! They love me. I'll be the most popular King,' he excitedly assured her, 'who has ever sat upon this Throne. Yes! There'll be a revolution – but not the kind you think. There'll be an end to tyranny and the isolation of the Sovereign. They'll be my friends. You wait! This is only a beginning.'

Yes, but where, his wife refrained from asking, would it end?

Everyone else was asking the same thing. 'I tremble for him; at present he is only a mountebank, but he bids fair to be a maniac,' said Greville. Though while they watched and snickered they allowed that he had plenty of common sense. He went too fast but he had not gone too far – as yet. Public opinion veered like a weather-cock, blowing hot and cold for him according to the latest tales of his doings. He had 'made a *perfect* speech'. His deportment had been 'all that was most dignified'. 'Every new thing that I hear of him raises him higher in my estimation,' says Creevey, who had not much good to say of him before.

He told gleefully in clubs, the story of how when the aged Derby, creaking in every joint, was about to kneel upon being sworn a Privy Councillor, the King shot out his hand to raise him up. 'I beg you won't kneel, Lord Derby. I know you have the gout.'

'Your Majesty must allow me—'

'No! No! I won't hear of it. I suffer from gout my-self. You should take exercise.' Very amiable indeed.

On another occasion at an informal Court reception, a lady brought her débutante daughter to present her to the Queen. To do so they had to pass the King. It so happened they had been neighbours of the Clarences at Bushey and used to visit there. The girl, following her mother, was so terrified that she took no notice of the King as she passed, upon which he laid hold of her and pulled her round to face him, 'Oh ho! Is this the way you treat your country friends when you come to Court!' and gave her a kiss and let her go.

The Court was still in mourning but the season went

with a swing. The King dutifully attended the opera in full Admiral's rig with a 'cock-a-pinch' hat and accompanied by the Queen, who, as passionately musical as he was not, followed the whole performance from an open score while William slept. The audience with one eye on him and the other on the stage, roared to the roof as the curtain fell, to bring the King from his doze and take more calls than Grisi.

In an opposite box, Ernest of Cumberland, his face wolfishly pointed in his brother's direction, and not at all relishing the cheers, sat with the Duchess of Kent and diminutive daughter, of whom nothing save the top of her head was visible until she stood for 'God Save the King'. Then, 'she looked,' Creevey said, 'a very nice little girl. I was sorry not to see more of her.'

The King, too, was sorry not to see more of that 'nice little girl', whose mother kept her sternly away from Windsor and the household at Bushey. The Duchess of Kent had long ago determined that her saintly child should never come within sight and touch of those 'dreadful Fitzclarences'. The nurseries at Bushey were filled with bouncing babies – a second generation, the mothers of whom invaded the rooms, handed tea to visitors, were all attention and sweetness to Adelaide, fussed over their 'darling Papa', and had all been raised to the rank of the daughters of a marquess.

At Windsor, at Court, the invasion persisted. George Fitzclarence, now Earl of Munster – he had been given one of his father's former titles – was, with his brother Lord 'Dolly' Fitzclarence, an equerry.

That they treated their illustrious parent with the scantiest respect was common knowledge. They came down late for breakfast, for the King, whether in his Palace or his country house, insisted on punctuality at meals, and always rose at seven. It was said there had been a fearful row with 'Dolly', who had staggered into breakfast in his dressing-gown, still drunk from the night before. Small wonder that the Duchess kept her daughter to herself.

But the King was getting restive. Except on state occasions he never had a chance to see the child. Adelaide made dresses for the little 'Drina's' dolls, and received prettily worded letters of thanks from her niece, but that was all – and not enough. William, who had begun by being hurt, ended by being furious. He'd put a stop to all this nonsense. The child was his heir and he her uncle. He insisted on her presence at the Court.

So now a feud had started between the Duchess and himself, that tended to grow more and more embittered. In the event of the King's death the Duchess of Kent had been appointed Regent to her daughter, as a result of which her self-inflation knew no bounds. Her airs and her pretentions, when gorgeously attired in velvet and feathers, the plump rosy-cheeked widow paraded the heiress of England before enthusiastic crowds, must have been excessively galling to him who had lost his only legitimate child. When he read in the papers of the Duchess's latest exploit, a tour of the industrial centres, with the demurely ringleted 'Drina' in a white bonnet at her heels, he boiled and fumed, that not even his wife could placate him.

'That woman,' he bellowed, 'is a nuisance! I'll take the child from her and have her live with us. God damme! Who is it wears the crown I'd like to know? That baggage Kent – or I?'

He didn't wear it yet. The coronation could not take place before the year was out. Meanwhile he had more than family annoyance to provoke him. The political atmosphere was thunderous at home; and a succession of disturbances abroad threatened to set Europe in a blaze. The July revolution in Paris had driven the

French Royal Family flying to England in rowing-boats, and over and above the noise of that could be heard the upraised voice of the people, no hidden murmur now, but a powerful outcry that there was no ignoring – the demand for constitutional reform.

'Their future rests with you,' George IV had solemnly adjured his brother William. Little did either of them guess how significant that prophecy would prove to be.

He who, buoyant and stout-hearted, had eagerly set out upon his voyage with high hopes of a smooth passage, sailed into the storm at the start.

He had not been three months on the Throne when Wellington's Ministry resigned with the Tories, and Grey with the Whigs came in.

This was no great loss to William. He liked Grey, and he disliked Wellington, whom he had never forgiven for having urged his resignation from the Admiralty.

'With you embarked in the same boat with me,' the King told Grey, 'we'll steer her safe to port – I have no fear.' He was charmed with his new Premier, who, the soul of tact, perceptive, keen, and quick to seize upon advantage, exploited this patriot King for all he was worth.

The task that lay before him was stupendous. He knew that all depended on the King's acceptance of the proposed plan for Reform, that since the days of Pitt and in spite of all obstruction, had been moving slowly, inevitably but so far bloodlessly, towards its climax, to determine now in the reign of King William, the casting vote that would establish for all time, democracy for Britain.

And if he failed – or if the King should fail him – Grey realized that a convulsion as great as that which ravaged Cromwell's England would be the grim alternative.

The time had come to strike.

It was with this in his mind, and the plan in his pocket, that Grey journeyed down to Brighton for an audience. A ticklish operation for a Prime Minister who had not been in office a month, to lay before his Sovereign a proposal that would reduce the power of the Crown and transfer control of Government from the upper to the middle classes; a proposal that would create a redistribution of parliamentary seats and re-form the electoral system by the Ten-pound Household franchise; above all, and undividedly, it would strike at the 'borough-mongers' who from the start of time had stolen the birthright of the nation.

But would such a proposal, coming from a Cabinet of Ministers drawn from the highest aristocracy in Eng-land, win the confidence and co-operation of the work-ing man? Would he in his sullen blindness see that the life of the community, *his* life, was about to be re-modelled according to the new enlightenment, towards a newer faith? That was the doubtful question and one that could not be disregarded. Would he turn and lick the hand that stretched to help him, or would he savage it?

The answer lay in the word of the King and the lap of the gods. . . .

Grey found himself well met.

'Billy,' who was in ecstasies with his Prime Minister, his people, his glorious new life and everyone concern-ing it except 'That Person', the Duchess of Kent, re-ceived his Premier with open arms in poor George's Chinese sitting-room at Brighton.

And very strange indeed did that room look, half divested of its mandarins, with sporting prints displayed to hide the patches on the walls where grinning masks had hung, and English Sheraton replacing blood-red lacquer; while jostling shoulders with some priceless

jade or rarest porcelain, stood simple cottage Stafford-
shire and Chelsea ware, as fresh and wholesome as a
milkmaid. There was little left of George's taste at
Brighton.

The King full of asthma, but in excellent form and
clear-headed, listened intelligently to all Grey had to
tell him, going over every point of the plan submitted
with conscientious care. It was not easy to take it in for
William was no politician, but he was pathetically eager
to please.

So there they sat, either side of the Sheraton table,
Grey, his beautiful thin face suave and calm, his gimlet
eyes probing, his mind commanding the King's decision
with a prayer in his heart. . . . Would he win? And if
the King gave his support would he stand by it? Or
would he jib at the last – or go crazy? And what of the
Queen? He had heard she regarded Reform and the
devil as one and the same, and the King wouldn't move
an inch without her.

Knotting his lean fingers till the knuckles paled, Grey
watched William's face bent over the paper – that
dubious lip, those flaxen-white eyebrows drawn fiercely
together in the effort at concentration, while furtively
the King rubbed his nose; then a deep wheezing breath
and he raised his head and himself in his chair with a
thump of his fist on the table.

'By God, Lord Grey, I'm with you! But—' His lifted
hand quenched the 'Ah!' of relief that broke from
Grey's tightened lips – 'But I'll not give you an un-
qualified assent. My chief objection to Reform is a fear
of introducing a measure that would be likely to cause
a breach between the Commons and the Lords.'

'The Lords, Your Majesty,' Grey said, 'are for it.'

'Not all by a long chalk, and only half by word of
mouth.'

'The Cabinet, Sire, is composed entirely of—'

'Hereditary peers, and the sons of such. I know! I know! But you're in the minority. Laws are not passed by Cabinets of a few picked men with brains. The mere fact that the voice of the people is asking for this thing, demanding it – *commanding* it – will make those ice-bound noblemen sit tight as oysters. Don't I know? I ought to. I've sat in the House of Lords myself, remember, for over thirty years. You'll have to get complete accord in this from *all* parties – and the Lords'll make it hard for you – mark me!'

Grey did, and jogged back to London, jubilant. The Lords! He'd settle them. As for the King – so far so very good, that he felt he could soon press for a general election. The King was evidently anxious to please everybody.

Matters moved apace and to a head. In March little Lord John Russell introduced the Bill into the Commons for its first reading. It was passed unchallenged by the Tories, and the country flamed from one end to the other while it waited for the Bill to be printed ready for its second reading. Never had there been such political excitement. In all classes of society from the darkest hovel to the Palace of the King there was no word spoken but Reform. And he who had been hauled into the maelstrom, he, too, was infected, and talked of it to Adelaide until she could have screamed.

'We shall win, my dear, we'll win! I'll go down to history as William the Reformer. This is a crusade. My Ministers are Knights Templars crushing the Saracen of Tyranny.' He waxed poetic. He read Shelley. '*He* was a Reformer. Here you are. Just listen here, my love. What a mind! And what a loss to us that he should die so young. 'Whom the gods love' – eh? We've none to touch him these days. I'd have made him Poet Laureate. What verse! What genius – take this.'

With swelling eloquence he read:

' "To defy Power, which seems omnipotent,
   To love and bear; to hope till Hope creates
From its own wreck the thing it contemplates;
   Neither to change, nor flatter, nor repent;
This, like thy glory, Titan, is to be
Good, great, joyous, beautiful and free;
   This is alone Life, Joy, Empire and Victory.'

'Yes! Prophetic!' William cried, banging down the book. 'Victory! Empire! This Bill will make of Britain the greatest Empire the world has ever seen. It will be far-reaching. It will extend beyond the seas. It will build colonies.'

'Pray God,' murmured Adelaide, too low for him to hear, 'it will not break them.'

*

Grey's initial success with the King had so far encouraged him that he was determined to strike for a dissolution of Parliament without delay. The decisive die was cast, but the future of the Bill depended entirely on the whim of a retired Admiral. At the second reading the Bill had been passed by one vote. Grey realized that a general election was imperative. Although the opposition of the Lords had not been violent, a majority of one was no criterion that at the next reading the Bill would not be killed stone dead. He must strike while the iron was hot.

Once more he sought an audience. This time at St James's.

He was ushered into the small library where the King, with the Queen beside him, was busy signing papers. On the table reposed a basin of warm water, and while with his right hand the King scribbled his William R's on the pile of letters before him, he dabbed the fingers of the other in the water. When sufficiently soaked, the Queen carefully proceeded to massage his finger-joints. On seeing Grey, William sprang to his feet almost upsetting the bowl in his greeting.

'My dear Lord Grey! I did not expect you for at least another hour. I beg you to excuse this very domestic scene. My fingers are full of chalk-stones and only the Queen's gentle persuasion can soothe them away. My right hand has already undergone its morning treatment. Pray, my love, continue' – as Adelaide quietly rose – 'we have nothing that cannot be said before the Queen, Lord Grey.'

The Queen sat down again, her eyes fixed on Grey's masked face, her own immovable. She did not share her husband's love for his Prime Minister. She feared his ruthlessness and above all she feared Reform. Though her father's sympathies had been entirely with the people, he had never relinquished the reins of government to them. For a King to hand over political power to the *bourgeoisie* seemed to her a desertion of hereditary duty. While fully appreciating the conflict with which her husband was confronted, she hoped against hope for a compromise. On the all-important question she dared give no advice. Time and again had William urged her for her views upon the crisis – not, he insisted, that he would allow his judgment to be swayed by any woman, not even by his wife – that would not be right. Still, he would like to know the woman's point of view. Women in his opinion were not permitted, in our present scheme of things, enough prerogative. She, as the first woman in England, should be consulted.

She had told him firmly: No, she would never wish to be consulted. The subject was beyond her understanding. Besides, it had been already said that she opposed the Bill.

And that had startled him. 'Who,' he wished to know, 'had said—?'

She smiled. 'Perhaps not to say, only to whisper.'

'To hell with that!' If such whispers reached his ears, he'd deal with them. As to the case in point – for he was never far from it. He was burning, he said, between two fires. He wished to do what would be right for all. He wished to *give* to his people freedom of thought, a humane tolerance one to the other. He wished to establish the true doctrine of Christianity by which all men might live in brotherhood, but the risk that such a measure would entail was tremendous. Was the working man sufficiently intelligent to use his freedom wisely? What foundation was he laying for the future? The responsibility! Was ever Sovereign faced with one so great?

His first enthusiasm had begun to wane. He realized that the perilous task before him needed more than ecstatic fervour to carry it through. The cold judicial light of reason had penetrated the mirage of an impulsive idealism, to the desert wastes beyond that stood for failure. If posterity should prove that he had set his seal on Britain's downfall, then not for the present nor for one century ahead, but for all time would he be damned.

And Adelaide, his wife and helpmate through the years, in this predicament, could give no comfort. For his distress, his sleepless nights, which as the crisis mounted were becoming sadly frequent, for his reliance on her sympathy, she gave herself as always; yet, from the all-absorbing problem which only he might solve, she remained aloof and guarded. It must rest with him alone. . . .

But all her heart was in her eyes when she looked from Grey to him. 'It is your wish then, that I stay?'

'Do we talk secrets, my lord?' asked William bluntly.

Grey's sauve lips tightened. 'All that I wish to say, Sire, will be repeated to Your Majesty's Government between which and the King there are no secrets.'

'And the King and his wife are one, so you can stay, my dear.'

She stood.

'I would prefer,' she said with gentle emphasis, 'to go. I would not wish it imputed' – and she looked full at Grey – 'that I have used my influence with the King against this measure.'

Grey's eyes narrowed. For all her self-effacement the Queen was not a fool. Still waters – thought Grey grimly, while gracefully he bowed. 'Your Majesty! Who would dare the imputation?'

'Have you read this morning's *Times*, my lord?' Her eyes, wide-set and steady, challenged his. 'If not, I will have a certain cutting sent to you.'

Grey's face expressed correct astonishment and consternation. 'Indeed, Your Majesty, I would be grateful. Your Majesty can rest assured that I will take immediate steps to put a stop to any injudicious or improper statements.'

'Improper what?' ejaculated William, who, still busy signing letters, had not heard half of this.

The door closed soundlessly; the Queen had left the room.

'I missed that,' said William frowning. 'My hearing isn't what it used to be. My poor father was almost stone-deaf at the last. And my old Great-aunt Amelia – long before your time. Runs in the family. I shall have to let Halford take a look at my ears. They're always a-buzz as though I had bees in my bonnet. Still! That's better than bats in my belfry – eh?'

Grey joined his politely appreciative chuckle to His Majesty's guffaw. 'And now,' said William fussily, 'to business. Sit down, Lord Grey, and let me have your ultimatum. I understand the Lords are getting ugly. You can't say I didn't warn you.'

'You did, Your Majesty.' And sitting, Grey smoothed an invisible crease from each knee of his buff pantaloons. 'But I was counting on a Whig majority and Your Majesty's agreement, to dissolve the present Parliament without delay.'

William's head went up as his fist came down. 'I have told you I'll concede you anything but that. Good God! You've only been in a few months and now you push for a general election—'

(The trouble with him, thought Grey, watching the King's mutinous lips, is that he can only take in one point at a time. He'll gnaw at it and worry it and let the larger issues slide . . . Talk of straining at a gnat! God send me patience.)

'– Or an alternative,' he said aloud. 'My resignation, Sire.'

At that statement, cool and cutting as a whip-lash, the ready blood flew to William's forehead. The silver tuft that crowned it seemed to rise. 'So! you threaten – with a pistol to my head?'

'Sire,' Grey got upon his feet, 'I would turn a pistol to my own if by so doing I could serve you better. A crisis is upon us that can permit of not one moment's indecision. The opposition Lords are even now preparing to offer an address in protest to Your Majesty against a dissolution. If we give in now we're lost. Already the Tory leaders are regretting they let the second reading pass without sufficient fight – they'll never let is pass again unchallenged.'

'I see no reason,' persisted William doggedly, 'to dissolve Parliament at this juncture unless I can be persuaded that the Commons no longer represent the country's views. My position here is in capacity of umpire – I have to see fair play. I can give you my private approval of the Bill, but I cannot have it said that I truckle to the Whigs. The King must have no party politics. He represents the nation as a whole. As for your peers – let them *bring* their protest and I'll throw it in their teeth. The Commons govern us and not the Lords.'

'The mob will govern us,' Grey murmured, 'if this Bill does not go through.'

'I have no fear of mobs,' said William glaring. 'And I'll not be hustled. I must have time to think, until . . . tomorrow.'

Grey bowed and backed, and gave himself a smile. The King was hesitating. He had won.

Yes, he had won – the first round, and sufficient for the day which already was – tomorrow. At eleven o'clock Grey and Brougham, the Lord Chancellor, again besieged the King. He, dizzy with want of sleep. He had not closed his eyes the whole night through. His ruddy colour faded, his face, haggard with the conflict of indecision, looked for the first time an old man's, and very weary, but his greeting lacked nothing of heartiness.

'My lords, I realize I am no state skipper. I cannot sail a ship on dry land. From now on you take command. I'm your lieutenant.'

The two Ministers exchanged a glance. Brougham, dark and saturnine, his long upper lip drawn down, and heavy eyebrows lifted, released a startled breath. Grey knelt.

'Your Majesty—'

'Get up,' said the King curtly, 'and get on with the next move.'

Grey played his ace.

'The House is sitting, Sire, will you go down to them – now?'

'So – I'm to walk the plank,' the King retorted with sardonic humour. He raised his head: 'I'm ready. Will you oblige me, Lord Grey, by pulling the bell-rope? We will order the state coach.'

But there was no time to order the state coach. Officials hurried from the stables with apologies and explanations. No time to plait the horses' manes and polish the equipment. . . .

William cut them short. 'The equipment should be polished daily whether in use or not. Very well then. Leave the coach and horses and if you can't find a carriage for me, I'll go in a hackney-cab.'

As always, when his mind was fixed there was no holding him. A messenger was sent post-haste to the Tower to fetch the crown. Such attendants as could at a moment's notice be found to wait upon His Majesty, were routed from their clubs; the robes taken from their wrappings. 'I'll put them on when I get to the House,' William said. 'I'll drive there in the suit I am wearing.'

He did, and in a closed chaise with no outriders and only one footman, while from the Palace to Thames Strand and all along the route, ran the noise of the King's latest exploit. To go down to his Houses of Parliament in a jarvey! Not in England's history had ever been the like of it – and not in England's history such a King!

His progress was triumphal, if tinged with disappointment for the swarms of excited onlookers, who had come to see the show and saw nothing but the swiftly bowling carriage drawn by a pair of black horses, no postilions, no trappings – and after all, no cab! Still, he'd been willing to do it and they cheered him full blast for that, even though they had no sight of him for he sat well back with his hat pulled down over his eyes, arms folded, his chin in his stock, and the Prime Minister beside him.

In the Commons the fun ran fast and furious. Peel using every sort of violent invective attacked the

Government for incompetence, recklessness, and folly, to the accompaniment of a bellowing and interruptions of calls to order, in such a pandemonium as had never in that House been heard before. Suddenly, and in the midst of it, a great booming of guns announced the arrival of the King, and at each explosion the Government raised a cheering and hullaballoo to drown the voice of Peel, who proceeded manfully although unheard, until the usher of the Black Rod came to summon the Commons to the Lords.

There the proceedings were even more outrageous. Lord Wharncliffe, who was to have moved an address to the Crown against the dissolution, was roared down by the Whigs every time he opened his mouth. The Duke of Richmond endeavouring to keep the peace, moved that the Lords should take their regular places, for everybody seemed to be sitting regardless of rank, and in the greatest disorder. This protest had the unhappy effect of putting Lord Londonderry into such a rage that he rose and threatened the Duke with his whip and a storm of expletives, while four or five of his peers held him down by the tail, his supporters yelling and booing and the guns thundering away outside to shake the rafters.

William, hearing the uproar from the robing-room, wished to know 'what in hell it all meant?' Brougham, his Lord Chancellor, who had hurried down before him and was skipping from the House to the robing-room and back again, making extraordinary speeches to which nobody listened and could never have heard if they had, hastened to assure him: 'They are cheering with joy, Your Majesty.'

'Joy be damned,' snorted William. 'Sounds more like Bedlam to me,' and turning to Lord Hastings, he asked for the crown. 'I'll put it on myself,' he said, and did; grinned in the faces of the staring peers, and, 'Now, my lords,' he told them with a chuckle, 'the coronation's over.' With that last word and the crown for the first time upon his head – a trifle crooked – his ermined robes trailing behind him, his Prime Minister sedately at his heels carrying the sword of state, he marched into the chamber.

If the crowds who had watched the King's progress from the Palace to the House had been enthusiastic, their demonstration when he drove back again was unsurpassed. His popularity, that had already been enhanced by his unconventional behaviour, now reached its climax when by this latest gesture he had publicly declared himself in favour of Reform and would evidently stop at nothing to procure it.

All along the way from Westminster to St James's, the crowds swarmed, black as flies, on lamp-posts, railings, the tops of hackney coaches, wherever they could find a foothold, hysterically to applaud their King. 'Well done, Billy! Well done, old boy!' waving tricolour flags and yelling their doggerel: 'The Bill, the whole Bill and nothing but the Bill!' while the King, his face scarlet with excitement, leaned from his carriage window to join his cheers to theirs.

The 'Peelers', in their dapper new uniforms and shining top-hats, were hard put to it to prevent a cordon of enthusiasts from taking the horses out of the shafts and harnessing themselves to draw the Royal carriage. So, thoroughly exhausted, and shaking with fatigue and strain but none the less proudly elated, the King returned home to his wife.

To her who had heard the noise and had been anxiously awaiting his arrival, William from his couch, while he sipped a mild brandy and water to revive him, recounted the reception of his speech.

'Take it by and large, my dear, I had a good majority of peers, and if I hadn't our supporters yelled down any opposition. Naturally there were no interruptions during my speech, but it's no good saying it was unanimously well received because it wasn't. Though considering,' he added with pardonable complacence, 'that I'd made no preparation – that I had not one single note – and that I spoke on the spur of the moment and entirely extempore – I think that on the whole I acquitted myself with some credit. And,' said William swelling, 'my speech will be remembered. Do you realize, my love, that I've made history?'

'I wish I could have heard you,' murmured Adelaide who had heard from her window alarms enough to make her think the revolution that she was convinced would come, had already started. 'What,' she asked, for she knew he was longing to tell her, 'did you say?'

Delightedly he plunged into detailed repetition. 'I began by saying that I had come there for the express purpose of proroguing Parliament with a view to its immediate dissolution – that I had been induced to resort to such measure for the purpose of ascertaining the *sense* of my people, in which it could be most constitutionally expressed on the expedience of making such changes in the representation as circumstances appeared to require – and so on – and I stressed my determination to uphold the rights of the Crown, but at the same time to give security to the liberty of the people, etcetera, etcetera, and I expressed my desire – a good touch that – to maintain a *paternal* anxiety for their contentment and happiness. That brought the House down. I was greatly moved. There never was such cheering.'

'I am sure,' his wife agreed; and she took his hand and held it. 'You mean so well, *mein Herz*, you are so good – I only hope – I pray—'

'Now, now!' William interrupted briskly. 'You must

not, my love, have any doubts or fears. You always are inclined to be too cautious, and if I may say so – child though you are—' he added gallantly (and that never failed to please her, for he knew she was the least bit vain of her youthful appearance and figure) – 'though you are,' he repeated smiling at her blush, 'you still live in the early years of the century when the whole world and its thoughts ran on revolution. You were brought up in that atmosphere and had the horror of it exploited by your very excellent Mamma until it became a bogey – an obsession with you. What we are doing now is to *prevent* any such calamity descending upon us.'

'I know,' sighed Adelaide, 'but it seems to me very shocking to give in because the people scream.'

'If the French Government had given in because the people screamed,' said William grimly, 'poor Louis Capet would have kept his head.'

'I pray God,' murmured Adelaide, 'that I may have the courage of Marie Antoinette if I am to lose mine.'

But fortunately her husband did not hear her, for she spoke in his deaf ear.

'Yes! A good day's work,' beamed William, as he drained his glass, 'although we've yet to wait events and watch the issue. I've still to reckon with the peers.'

Grey too had still to reckon with the peers, but he had his trump card up his sleeve and would hold it to the last. Having forced the King so far he called a halt pending the general election. He had no fear of the result of that, with the King at his side, the country at his heels, and the order of the Garter in his pocket. And most truly did he feel that he deserved it.

*

In the temporary lull that followed, the preparations for the coronation came as a welcome respite from political crises. The season was at its height, the weather glorious, and the King in residence at Windsor appearing at Court functions, dinners and race-meetings. Although he had no interest in the turf, he dutifully ran a horse and attended Ascot with a cortège of eight coaches, two phaetons and a retinue of sons and daughters.

Their presence in so blatant a family gathering may have accounted for the singularly chill reception accorded him on the first day, and though he professed to care nothing for the squeamishness of a society composed chiefly of the opposition lords and their good ladies, there is no doubt that he was chagrined.

He retired early after seeing his horse break down, to the barely concealed satisfaction of all the racing peers, and commanded Lord Grey to accompany him in his carriage to the Castle, while Adelaide under her parasol sat in frigid silence. And here was another to-do. For the first time in their married life he ventured to reprove her.

'You should not, my dear,' he said when in the privacy of their own apartment he rested on his couch before dinner in a blue brocade dressing-gown patterned with gold anchors, 'you really should not show your dislike of Grey quite so obviously. You did not address one single word to him the whole way home. We must be politic, my love.'

'Politic!' She flushed angrily. 'It is not politic for you to show such favour even to the leader of your Government. To invite him to drive in our carriage without consulting me! I was amazed.'

And he alarmed. This, the nearest approach to a quarrel that had ever yet occurred between them, that had flashed like summer lightning from their cloudless domestic sky, seemed one with the day's imperfections, and a presage to gathering storm. He hastened to divert it. 'I admit I was sadly remiss in not preparing you, my dear, that I had invited him. It was done on the spur of the moment.'

'But to put him in *our* carriage,' she protested, 'for all to see – and stare. And to make jealousy. Already you have given him the Garter – that is enough honour for one week. His head—' disdainfully she raised her own – 'is so big now he will be asking for a ducal coronet to fit it.'

With great anxiety William rubbed his nose and resorted to his favourite catch-phrase: 'That is quite another thing – *quite* another thing! And I am sure, my love, if I have caused you such annoyance, I apologize. But what with the heat – and my horse breaking down – and those damned hell-fire Tories—'

'Please not to swear,' said the Queen icily, 'you speak too often these so shocking words. It has become a habit.'

'Why, God dammit, what have I said now?' demanded the King loudly.

'What you say and always say. I do not like it.'

'And I don't like,' retorted William, 'your high-handed attitude with Grey, my dear. I must beg you to be more amiable to him tonight.'

'Tonight? I do not see Lord Grey tonight. You will dine with him alone.' And with that and with one frozen look she left the room.

William sprang from his couch to rush after her, to have the door that communicated with her own apartment shut in his face, and the key turned in the lock. Scarlet, hot and speechless, as much with astonishment as indignation at this spirited rebuff from his 'white mouse', he stood gazing blankly into space. That she should dare do this to him – his Adelaide, his wife! Was all the world gone mad, and she included? He thumped upon the panels: 'Let me in!' No answer.

Very well. Be damned to everything and everybody. He strode to the bell and pulled the rope with such violence that the silken tassel came off in his hand as a footman came hurrying in.

'We will dine in the small octagon chamber with Lord Grey. Her Majesty is indisposed and will not appear.'

Hostilities between the Queen and Grey were now openly declared. There was no hiding it. The whole Court knew. Moreover the Queen had staunch supporters in her sister-in-law Augusta, her stepsons, Munster and 'Dolly' Fitzclarence, and all her ladies whose husbands sat in judgment in the Lords.

If William sensed this veiled rupture in his own home circle, he chose wisely to ignore it, and rigidly avoiding any political discussion with his wife, hushed the dreaded word 'Reform' when it came upon his lips, and worried himself sick.

While he fully appreciated Adelaide's determination to preserve a strict neutrality of political opinion, thus avoiding all possible accusation of undue influence with the King, the blow was none the less bitter in that he missed the support of her who until now had never failed him. In this great crisis now he knew that he must stand alone, and in a house divided

The result of the general election brought in a good majority for Reform, and at its second reading in spite of the most heated opposition it was carried by 136 votes. It passed through the Commons that summer and was thrown out by the Lords.

Then popular enthusiasm, brought up against an obstacle so stubborn, exploded in a series of outrages unparalleled since the days of the Civil War. In London's Mayfair, the mobs ran riot, far beyond control of Peel's new police force, smashing the windows of those peers who had voted against the Bill – the Duke of Wellington's at Apsley House included. In the manufacturing centres men were drilling and arming to fight the Lords; while from north to south through industrial centres and farm-lands, the repercussion thundered. Night after night the sky burned red with the light from the blazing ricks. Starvation and unemployment turned men desperate, to rage in all the violence of bloodless revolution.

But how long would it be bloodless? In clubland ominous stakes were laid. 'A thousand to one the King will lose his crown before the coronation.' Five thousand to one his head will be inside it!' While Macaulay spoke to a hushed House the memorable words: 'I know only two ways in which society can be governed – by public opinion or – the sword.'

The whole future of Britain hung in the balance to make of democracy the most colossal blunder in the history of politics, and which soon or late must reap its own destruction or – to emerge triumphant, the living symbol of a brotherhood eternally united in faith and hope and liberty, for the good of mankind.

*

The morning of 8 September 1831, dawned chill and dreary with a heavy downpour of rain, that did not, however, damp the enthusiasm of the great multitude who had set out the night before to secure front-line places all along the route of the procession.

There were many who had been present on a similar occasion ten years before, but all knew that the extravagant parade demanded by George IV and which had cost the Government close on half a million pounds, would be absent on this day. Word had gone out to be passed from mouth to mouth, that King William had insisted on a minimum of expenditure; no pageantry, no peers in coronets and coaches to precede him through the streets. This was no time, he said to burden the nation with unnecessary expense.

He, with his ridiculous antics, his defiance of all courtly and Royal etiquette, who surrounded himself and filled the halls of Windsor with *canaille* – so many of whom had been created knights that they were dubbed the 'Thousand and one Arabians' – this vulgar buffoon who would go to any length to curry favour with the masses, seemed determined to deliver shock upon shock to the lordly. They, furious at being done out of a prominent part in the show, were for boycotting the King's 'Half-Crownation'; but the masses to a man were with him, and turned out in full force for his crowning.

William, who had slept uneasily, rose with a headache at the dawn of that day, and, careful not to waken Adelaide in the bed next to his own, went on tiptoe to his dressing-room.

There, pulling aside the curtains to let in the struggling light, he stood looking out at the rain-grey lawns of his park, the Green Park of St James's.

His mind swung back into the past. . . . He was a boy again, filled with the vague tumultuous longings of youth, waiting in the snow for his first love. . . . Here in this very park! He could see the sullen sheen of water where behind the holly bushes they had vowed their children's vows, with their first kiss. . . . There had been other loves, and one so early lost, whose shy sweet ghost had followed him through his young manhood into middle-age, to dwell reincarnate in her who was his wife and love of loves.

But memory shrank from that long interval of aching disillusionment when in the heat and stress of life he had surrendered sense and heart and reason to a shadow, which none the less had left to him a goodly heritage –

a continuity of heirs to his blood if not to his name. For
that and to his death he would be grateful.

Far away, through the muffled silence of the morning,
he could hear the stir and heart-beat of the city, the unceasing muted tread of countless feet – his loyal citizens
who came from the bowels of the metropolis, from dark
and fetid hovels beyond all power of a King's imagination to conceive; from dens of filth, disease and poverty
unspeakable; from street upon street of solid mansions,
where, each a king in his own right, in his own castle,
the city merchants reigned; from the clean wholesome
cottages that ringed the rural suburbs of Bayswater
and Brompton's market gardens; and from high Hamp-
stead's village, from Kensington and Knightsbridge beyond the turnpike gates; from north, south, east and
west of his city came these hosts of unseen people
to do honour to their King.

And while his strained ears listened to that ceaseless
muffled tramping, that subdued buzz of a myriad voices,
and the far-off inexorable mutter of the waking town,
his heart went out in a fierce love for them who were
the very arteries and pulse of his existence. What right
had he to all his great possessions, for which his people
paid in labour, in taxation, in blood and sweat and
toil? What right save that of accident, since all of life
was accident?

I, he mused, who stand here King, but for the accident of birth that made me Royal, would be standing
now among them who come to see me crowned today.
What am I but the figurehead upon my ship? I'm not
the captain of her. A figurehead? By God, no! More
than that, for I can think, can feel, can speak. I have
a mind, a soul to give to those whose souls are
crushed. And I can do. . . . What can I do? I want to
do!

It was then, that looking out upon those rain-soaked

lawns and pastures that stretched as far as eye could see, and where no man but he had right of way, that the thought came to him startlingly – the parks, the Royal parks! Windsor, Richmond, Kew, St James's, and beyond the guarded boundaries of Hyde to the gardens of Kensington, all should belong to the people. . . . Kensington. Those charming glades and avenues where little Drina rode on her white pony, would be the happy playground of London's boys and girls throughout the generations, for as long as London lived.

And to himself, complacently he smiled. What would Madam Kent, he wondered, have to say to that? Let her say! He'd do it. . . . He would give these grassy spaces to them who had no space in which to breathe. The green lungs of the City of London would be the King's gift to his people today.

At half-past ten the roar of cannon announced that the King had left the Palace, and from that patient multitude there rose a deep convulsive murmur as though a monster stirred. The long night's vigil was at last rewarded and the King on his way to be crowned.

Through beflagged thronged streets, black and bobbing with umbrellas, past houses were the limp red bunting hung draggled and rain-soaked, past shouting thousands whose massed voices thundered out their welcome above the boom of the guns and blare of brass to hit the sky, he came. . . .

Before him rode his Life Guards and Scots Greys, followed by liveried barge-men and watermen, marching. Then the *aides-de-camp* on horseback riding two and two, and a hundred Yeomen of the Guard on foot. After them ten coaches of the Household and the state carriage containing each a Royal brother. The Dukes of Sussex and Cambridge were greeted with cheers, Ernest of Cumberland with cat-calls and scowls, and a stone at his head which he dodged and sat crouched in his seat all the way. Not an impressive procession.

But if the rain dulled the glittering uniforms and the bright-coloured fragments of pennons, it could not deaden the mighty tumult that soared to shake the air as the King in his golden coach swept by, while women laughed and screamed for him and men growled in their throats, 'He's first and last a sailor.' For he wore his Admiral's uniform and he was jovial, proud, and nodding familiarly right and left with his little wife beside him: she, smiling, half in tears and all in white with some gold gauze stuff about her, and a glint of diamonds in her hair.

As they alighted at the Abbey to such a storm of cheering as not in living memory of the city had been heard, the sun, for the first time that day, burst through the clouds; and while from every steeple far and distant pealed the bells, the boys of Westminster choir sang:

> I was glad
> When they said unto me
> We will go
> Into the House of the Lords.

Chapter Four

THE last of the summer was spent between Windsor and
Bushey, there to recover and rest; for though William
had youth in his heart, he had age in his bones, and the
excitement of the coronation had undone him. With
all the will in the world he could not now walk ten
miles a day; he reduced it to six. The attacks of asthma
had become more frequent, more swollen the joints of
his fingers, more laborious the signing of his papers
while he stoically denied the pain. ''Tis nothing but
the cramp. It will soon pass.'

He had his daughters and their children with him at
Windsor, for the house at Bushey was not large enough
to hold them all – and one faithful old friend, Admiral
Lord Amelius Beauclerk, with whom arm-in-arm,
William paced the terrace of his Castle, as fifty years
before he had paced the deck of the *Prince George*.
Heads together, wheezing and chuckling over the rags
and tags of memory that bobbed up from a shared past,
they relived their cockpit days.

'D'ye remember that brawl at Gib when those poxy
Spaniards turned on us?' . . . 'Yes, and poor old
Sturt was all but knifed and the three of us were
jailed!'

Of that trio one was missing. Sturt, who had gone
down in the *Isis* in action off the Danish coast in 1801.

William and Beauclerk were of an age, but Beauclerk, William noted – not without a certain relish –
looked a great deal older than himself. To be sure,
Beauclerk had seen longer service and had a game leg

from a wound he had got at Trafalgar, but it had not kept him out of the Navy. Beauclerk had stayed his course.

So, all through that golden September, set fair from the time of his crowning, William rested. It was pleasant to bask on the terrace watching the summer blaze to its death in the fire of autumn glory. Never had his Great Park looked more gracious with the sun as thick as honey in the burnished red and bronze, and a second blooming of roses in his garden: pleasant indeed to drive out with his wife to inspect the building of a quiet little house on the Royal estate – Adelaide Cottage – his coronation gift to her, and a new model dairy. Or together they would visit the labourers' cottages that, under the King's new housing plan, had since his accession been reconstructed to give more space and sanitation – earth-closets and a wash-house in the yard.

And as they passed from door to door, out came the children running. One had a pat on the head, a kind word from the Queen, and all had the King's bright new penny, straight out of the mint and none had the least fear of Majesty. This jolly old King with his beaming red face, his grey beaver hat, his blue coat and white nankeen trousers, his gold watchchain with the big gold repeater on the end of it that played tunes, and was held to the ear of the very young and most favoured – he with his wife at his side and his dog at his heels, was as familiar a figure and far less alarming than the farmer whose orchards they robbed.

His gift of the parks to the public had been received with much disapproval and clacking of tongues in St James's. The masses, however, applauded and were not slow to take advantage of the King's generosity. Within a week of the announcement, Windsor Park was over-run. The King could not walk out but he was mobbed, could not breakfast in his private room that overlooked the terrace without an audience to clamber up the balustrade to stare, to trample down the grass, tear the leaves from the orange trees, and scratch their names disgracefully upon the marble seats.

Then did William rise in wrath and come out upon the terrace – cup in one hand, table-napkin in the other – to harangue them. 'You cannot share my property unless you can respect it. I see that you will force me to do as my brother did and bar the gates.'

Thereafter park-keepers were everywhere installed to deal with malefactors. The grass was fenced, the flower gardens of Hyde Park guarded behind spiked railings and marked 'Private'. Presently from Kensington came reports that urchins swarmed the avenues and had possessed themselves of that little lake known as the 'Round Pond' in full view of the Palace windows, to sail their toy boats and make hideous the air with their noise, that the Duchess of Kent would not permit her daughter outside the Palace grounds lest she be brought in contact with the gutter.

'And why shouldn't she?' the King demanded. 'Why shouldn't she have sight and sound of 'em – whose Queen she'll be – one day?'

There were times when he believed that day was not far distant, when he wondered – would *he*, like Beau-clerk, stay his course? He would need all his will, all his strength and energy to meet the buffetings of life ahead; more turbulence in Parliament, more unrest and rioting among his people, more ominous mutters that had only been hushed, not silenced, by the shouts of acclamation for the King on his way to the Throne.

He was also obsessed by a grievance. 'Madam Kent' – that thorn in his flesh – had pricked him again. It was the talk of the town. The Duchess and Princess Victoria had not been present at the coronation.

Was the slight deliberate? Who could tell? Apologies

and excuses had been offered: very suave. The Duchess craved her august 'brother's' pardon. Little Drina had been 'poorly' – of the mumps. Her 'Mama had carried her off to recuperate in the Isle of Wight. *The Times* came out with guarded reference to the Duchess's 'maternal tenderness' that had naturally enough been alarmed at the prospect of the ordeal and excitement the young Princess would have to undergo in her delicate state of health, and in the course of her attendance at the ceremony.

'Maternal tenderness be damned!' growled William when he read it. 'I don't believe a word of it. Mumps! It's the first I've heard – or anybody else that Drina's had the mumps. And if so – why wasn't I told? That woman's an abomination. She keeps my own niece – poor Edward's child, from me as though I were a leper, and insults me in the face of the whole country – and the Court.'

It rankled, and he brooded, and worked himself into a fever when the crowning injury to insult came, with the news, that down in the Solent that woman was sailing her yacht, and insisting on Royal salutes from the forts and the King's men-o'-war. Royal salutes, indeed! To steal, without a by-your-leave, a King's perogative. Was there no end to this impertinence? These ridiculous poppings must cease. Parading her daughter, as future Queen and usurping the King's Royal right! 'Does she think I've one foot in my grave – then? I'm not dead yet and by God! I'll disappoint her. *She'll* not be Regent. When I go my niece will follow after me – as ruler. That I swear!'

But 'Madam Kent' and her doings were sunk in oblivion when, after his brief sojourn at Windsor, the King returned to London to be dragged once more into the whirlpool of political eruption.

*

The last round in the fight for Reform was begun, the forces on each side arrayed in respective positions, when the decisive year that set the seal upon democracy, dawned in 1832.

To those, who neutrally observed the convulsion in which the country was embroiled, the prospect looked dismal enough to bring conviction that the end of the world was at hand, and the universe about to emerge on a new state of existence.

While up and down the country the war-cry 'Reform' resounded; while still the skies were lit with the red fury of rebellion wreaked upon the harvest ricks to bring famine to the homeless; while maddened insurrectionists inflamed by new-found lust for power yelled 'Liberty – Equality' – as the people of France had yelled murder to the tyrants half a century before – while passions raged as conflagration spread, the priests and preachers spoke of these disruptive shocks, in warning. 'All the moral and physical worlds appear so exactly to announce the coming of a great day of the Lord,' wrote Dr Arnold, 'a period of fearful visitation to terminate the existing state of things, but whether to terminate the whole existence of the human race, neither man nor angel knows. . . .'

To add to the terror of fire and famine came plague. From the low river marshes of London, from the fens of the eastern coast, from the squalid haunts of filth, crime, and starvation, stalked a dreadful mysterious visitant, to lay thousands low, to kill hundreds. Few could escape it who lived in those burrows where dirt and putrescence bred horrors.

The wise men of medicine could make nothing of a disease so obscure. 'And if it had not the name of cholera,' wrote Greville, 'nobody would be alarmed, for many an epidemic has prevailed at different times, far more fatal than this.'

It was fatal enough, however, to spread fear. The people were dying like flies, and showed an invincible repugnance to avail themselves of any attention to cure them. The King was alarmed. In his own household he issued all manner of orders. Windows must be kept sealed lest the air should bring contamination from the river; pillows and bedding must be sprinkled with vinegar each night before retiring. His apartments smelled, 'like a pickle factory', murmured 'Dolly' Fitz-clarence, with a handkerchief to his exquisite nose. The Queen and her ladies were soaked in lavender water and eau-de-Cologne. William gargled his throat every morning, took snuff for the first time in his life, and received Lord Grey in his sanctum with pouring eyes and sneezes.

'My dear Lord Grey! I beg you to excuse – ah – ah – ah – I'm told that snuff is the best – ah – ah – damnation! – disinfectant.'

But with the country at a pitch of madness and a possibility of another defeat of the Bill in the Lords, Grey was not there to discuss the preventive qualities of snuff. Papers in hand, he stood ready for action and waited for the Royal spasms to subside. There must be no wavering and no concessions. Not one jot or tittle would Grey concede – no, not if it came to blows – or civil strife.

'As, Sire, so assuredly it will,' Grey with cautious emphasis adjured his master, 'if we find a further majority against us in the Lords.'

William replaced his snuff-box in his pocket and rising from the table went over to the window. The dust of the winter afternoon was beginning to creep up between the trees in the Park of St James's. Down in the courtyard stood the scarlet-coated sentries guarding the King's Palace, and in the opal-coloured distance across the wet green lawns and intersecting paths, pedestrians hurried or sauntered, each bent on his own mission, each a unit of one great community whose core was centred in the heart of him who ruled them. . . . William turned to his Prime Minister. 'Come here, Lord Grey.'

What now? His pale domed forehead, anxiously creased, Grey warily advanced.

'Look!' William pointed to the window.

Grey strained his eyes and could see nothing more than the flat misty spaces of the park, and the ghostly fog from the river wreathed in the bare branches of the trees that stretched their skeleton arms against the sky.

From that uncompromising vista Grey swept a puzzled glance to the King whose brows were lowered and whose lips were pursed. 'Out there,' said William, and his hand went again to his waistcoat pocket to fumble for his snuff-box, 'out there in my gardens – in my own *private* gardens,' he repeated with solemn insistence, 'walk my people. It is their right of way as much as mine. Do you suggest that they will turn against me and my Government? That no matter how they fight among themselves they will dare fight *me*? I have given them so much. I am sure—' and inhaling vigorously a pinch of the spicy powder on his fingers, 'I am sure,' he said, 'that they are grateful.'

Behind the tightened muscles of his jaw Grey ground his teeth. Was ever Sovereign so simple? His kingdom exploding at his gates and he talked of – gratitude!

'Quite so, Sire. Your subjects' confidence in Your Majesty's good will has never faltered – yet.'

At the stress he laid upon that word William turned to stare. 'Yet? What d'you mean – yet? Ain't I popular?'

'No King has ever been more popular – more loved,' Grey replied with unction. 'But, Your Majesty – there are forces now at work, that like the elements blow from most unlikely quarters.'

William sneezed. 'Don't—' and with his handkerchief he mopped his streaming eyes – 'der – don't talk to me of elements, because there you're out of yours. I'm a sailor. I know the winds. I know which way they're blowing – and they're set fair for me.'

'Pray God!' Grey murmured on a breath.

'And let me tell you, my good Lord Grey,' (confound the fellow with his croakings! As if this hellish cholera were not misery enough, without having to be driven half demented over this everlasting Bill. God damn the Bill! He was sick to death of it.

So, 'Let me tell you,' William said, holding himself in, 'that I have no fear of those graver issues which you, my lord, unpleasantly suggest. And if – as I doubt – you *are* correct in your supposition that my people will dare to rise in strife against my person, *or* yours, may I ask—' and again he pointed to the window, 'may I ask why they do not rise against me now? What's to prevent them from firing a gun from behind those trees out there? Do you know what *will* prevent them? My trust in them – and theirs, my lord, in me! And now—' the King's rosy face crinkled in a smile – 'and now Lord Grey, sit ye down and take a glass of wine with me and let us have no more of these – ah – ah – ah – (pardon me! I have never been used to taking snuff, but Dr Halliday assures me of its excellence) – these suggestions. What is the latest news of the cholera? Are there any signs of it abating?'

Grey, however, was not to be so easily put off. He sat; he dutifully accepted and drank a glass of wine. He gave the total of deaths from the epidemic reported in the last two days, and then:

'Your Majesty. It is my humble duty to inform you that the necessity has arisen – and is of the utmost urgency that I present to Your Majesty the suggestion—'

'There you go again!' growled William, drumming impatient fingers on his chair-arm.

Grey doggedly ignored the interruption.

'– suggestion, Sire, that we look first at the danger of losing the Bill. On calculation there is likely to be a majority of twenty votes against it in the Lords. There is no disguising the fact that the administration and – God forgive me that I utter it – and perhaps the King himself, will be involved in the common danger.'

'You exaggerate the danger,' William muttered. but Grey's insistence was making its impression. His eyes roved uneasily from the room's shadowed firelit corners to the uncurtained window; his hand reached for a silver bell on the table to ring it sharply. 'My servants will not intrude upon us when we are in audience,' he explained, 'until we summon them. . . . Bring candles,' he bade the footman who instantly appeared, 'draw the curtains – and then go.' This done. 'Proceed, Lord Grey, and let us have what's on your mind.' And Grey, summoning his forces, let him have it.

'Sire, painful though it is to resort to so drastic a measure, I submit to Your Majesty that since we have not a majority of peers to carry the Bill – *we must create them.*'

So it was out! And through the long pause that followed, Grey in his silence offered up a prayer. . . . All his life he would remember that curtained room, the dark red damask flowers on the wall, blossoming, glowing in the light of fire and candle, the glints of flame-points in the winey deeps of polished wood, and the bronze figure of a young Pan supporting a lamp behind the King's carved chair. On the rug at the King's feet lay an aged cocker spaniel, grey muzzle on its paws and one bloodshot eye adoringly upon his master; while the King, his ruddy face turned pale, his jaw a little dropped, and the light from the lamp on his silver hair, sat still as stone.

'You—' and the silver head was lifted – 'you are asking me – *me* to stoop to bribery – corruption?'

'Sire.' Grey stood: his lips had whitened, 'I crave for myself and my colleagues the right to vindicate that accusation.'

'What else,' asked William loudly, 'can it be? I call a spade a spade. You can't pass this Bill by fair means so you tell me you'll pass it by foul. That's how I see it, and that's how it is. The Bill has had its chance – has run its course, and the Lords have thrown it out. Very well, then! D'you think that I'll agree to create peers from the Bill's supporters to save *my* skin? No, my lord!' He drew a breath and his old dog rose and came to him; his hand went down to pull the silken ears. 'I told you once I stand at the head of my Government – as umpire. And as umpire in this fight, I call – a foul! I cannot pass it. You may return to the House, my lord, and tell the Government – the King does not consent.'

Grey moistened his dry lips that almost soundlessly moved to say: 'The Government shall be informed of Your Majesty's decision.'

He bowed; he backed and left that room and the King in his chair, his chin sunk on his chest, and his dog on its feet beside him.

*

The crisis had reached a deadlock. Through the spring of 1832, Grey stood, sword in hand, ready to strike the blow that would force the King's word from his mouth. But though Grey drove his steel to the hilt with threats of resignation, that word had not yet come.

All of England waited in another lull before the storm, while night after night the skies reddened and the mutter of thunder hung in the air, and desperate men gathered their arms in secret; spade-men and barrow-men and those that sweated underground in mines, and the ragged hordes who slaved for less than a bare living wage in factories, in pits – they and all the workless from the underworld stood ready, led by a common cause.

Great to the eye loomed the prophecy of a life and death struggle, of mind eclipsed by reason and smouldering hate, rekindled to its final pitch of execration. None should escape it who barred the path of freedom, not the lords in their mansioned seclusion, nor the King on his throne – the Citizen King who walked among his people as their friend. . . . Friend? What friend was he who stayed the word that would break down this hide-bound resistance? No friend – he! A traitor who had played them false, raised high their hopes with lavish gifts and greetings, who drove through the streets of his capital with hand-wavings, hat-doffings, and smiles – a showman who knew all the tricks, that his dupes might come crawling – to be stabbed in the back on their knees!

Grey had lost no time in letting it be known that the King was alongside the 'Waverers'; a weathercock who blow cold as the Whigs blew hot, who had refused the one measure that would make the Bill law. How long would the country endure indecision – how long? Already half Bristol was burned to the ground by the rioters; and the King's popularity waned.

Grey watched, like a cat at a mouse-hole, his followers lined up behind him to harry the King from his fastness – and pounce! Would he budge? Would he come to a compromise? Yes. Word flew. The King, poor muddled fool, had sent for Grey to suggest a half-measure. He would give Grey his peers – drawn from the courtesy titles – heirs of the dukes and the marquesses, but he would not create peers from the Commons.

And up and down the country rang the jingle:

> What though now opposed I be
> Twenty peers shall carry me
> If twenty won't, thirty will
> For I'm his Majesty's Bouncing Bill

Thirty? Grey asked more than that. Fifty or none. The majority against the Bill had grown, spurred by the King's indecision.

He, who had pledged himself, mind and heart and soul to his people, was now alone, outcast. Not one to fight beside or for him. The smooth-tongued Tories, his so-called supporters who cared for nought but vested interests and hereditary rights, who had served him with ridicule, his speeches with yawns, they fought for themselves, the 'Haves' against the 'Have-nots'.

The patience of the country was exhausted. On every side rose the tumult of popular fury sweeping all before it in a roar of revolt, that was heard in the house of the King. . . .

'A week since,' wrote the *Sun* of that day, 'only a short week since, the King was in full possession of the greatest popularity any earthly monarch could enjoy, and now – behold the change!

A change indeed!

He was slow, in his faith, to believe it. His faith in them he had trusted, who had hailed him to his crowning with a welcome such as surely no Sovereign had ever known before, held fast.

The first inkling he had, to strike cold in his heart, was an attack on his wife – not on him. That was the first of it, when on a balmy spring evening, Adelaide went to a concert with her friend, Baroness Von Bülow, whose husband had been recently appointed Prussian Ambassador in London.

351

They were late in returning, and William grew uneasy.

In his private room he waited with one eye on the clock, his mind busy with the harassing events, that, since January, had closed around him fearfully to change the face of his life. His entire universe was spinning, his peace gone, his sleep haunted with devilish nightmares in which he saw himself, his wife, his country swallowed in earthquake, blood, and fire; a glimpse of Hell that warned him of impending doom – to wake him sweating, and demon-ridden to meet another day.

He was too old for this, his strength could never stand it. He felt his years and with the weight of them a burning fierce resentment. The injustice of it! That he should be brought to this unhappy pass by injudicious leadership. For in his harassed bewilderment he turned to blame those nearest him: his good Lord Grey, whose honeyed speech had led him to complacent blind acceptance of This and That – until his eyes were opened and he saw. Yes! He saw – that each side played his own game, each man for himself, even Grey, his trusted Chief, with his hand on the public pulse to mark the beat of it, and throw in his lot with the stronger. . . . Grey! William wondered. Grey. . . . Was he of the faithful? Was Brougham? Brougham who raged through the shires and all the industrial centres with impassioned speeches, begun in liquor and ending in prayer. He'd been told Brougham couldn't speak at all till he was drunk. Speeches! What good could words do now? The time was over for speeches. The country was arming – for deeds.

God help him! Was ever King, unless perhaps Charles his forbear, confronted with such a cataclysm? Would his end be the same as that of poor, misguided Charles Stuart – or Louis Capet? Never! Not for him ignoble death, who had no wish, no will, no thought but for his people – to see justice in his ruling – to play fair.

And sitting there in his quiet room overlooking his Palace gates, where his sentries stood to guard him, the phantoms of past horrors receded. His people were not regicides. My people! Pitifully he clung to the repetition of that word, 'My People'. For all the threats of Government, for all Grey's ghastly hints, there was no sign of discontent against *his* person. Their discontent was rooted in existence – in a state of things, in those obstructive forces that in the course of time and nature must be battered down to make way for new ideas – rebirth, regeneration. That was the law of life.

Where then in this deadly crisis was he to blame? He had been brought up, point-blank, against a wall of opposition. Again resentment flared. Grey, who demanded peers – that *he* should wave his sceptre as a wizard waved his wand and so create them! A scurvy trick, a low-down grubby business – that. No gesture of a King to sway the law to suit his ends and save his crown. If he lost all – and his life with it – he would stay firm.

The ormolu clock on the mantelshelf struck eleven. Late! And Adelaide not home. . . . She should have been back an hour since.

He rose from his chair, and the dog at his feet rose with him, looking up into his face, his dimmed old eyes alert, his feathered stump of a tail expectantly a-wag. 'Come on then – walk,' said William, and out they went together, along the red-carpeted corridor, past bowing footmen to a side entrance, followed discreetly by a lord-in-waiting, who had emerged, magically, from nowhere, like a genie, to be told: 'I don't want you. I'm only taking the dog for a stroll.'

'Your Majesty—'

'Go,' said the King briefly, 'I wish to be alone.'

Never a moment's privacy, except in his own room, and even there, they guarded him with servants at the keyhole, equerries at the door. This spying had increased of late – he supposed they had to do it. Part and parcel of their duties. . . . Did they think, then, he was frightened of his shadow?

He stepped out into the night, a calm, still night of stars and moon with a pale, faint glow in the sky from London's lamps. There was talk of installing this new-fangled gas in the wealthier districts. That would cost a pretty penny. Well! The State would have to pay – if it existed.

With his spaniel shuffling behind him he marched across the moon-white courtyard, past the sentries in their boxes, who presented arms, to receive a nod, a smile, the ghost of a salute – and so through a gate in the wall that led to the gardens overlooked by windows. These belonged to the rooms of the Household, where behind drawn blinds, lights blazed.

He heard the tinkle of a pianoforte, voices, a burst of laughter, song. Some carousing there. He thought he recognized the drawling baa of his son 'Dolly'. His sons! One dead – four living, and no heir of his loins to succeed him. But away over there beyond those trees, not a mile as the crow flew, deep in her dreams lay a child, on whom the future hope of Monarchy and Britain would depend. She, of his blood, who was withheld from him, and whom he could have loved as his own, had That Person ordered otherwise. . . . His head in the clouds – (what a night! The Milky Way was blazing) – he brooded on his wrongs and 'Madam Kent'. Some day, he vowed, he'd have it out with her, take her daughter from her, and teach her how a country *should* be ruled which was not by an autocracy – or Mrs Kent.

And to the winking stars he gave a grin.

Somewhere in a room with an open window, a clock

chimed the half-hour – and Adelaide not home yet! Or if she were, he had not heard her. Snapping his fingers to call the dog, he turned, and at that moment on the quiet air there sounded a guttural murmur which rose in volume with an undertone like the snarl of a wild beast.

At his side in the dark, his dog, nose pointed, quivering, growled low. The sound rose higher, shriller, nearer, with the noise of wheels and horses' hoofs, and voices multiplied on one long-drawn howl, that there was no mistaking '–Queen! – the Queen!'

With a gasp in his throat, and a sickness in his stomach, William hurried back across the courtyard past the sentries, to the Palace gates, as the Queen's carriage swept under the archway, pursued by a hooligan mob.

*

She was half fainting when he took her from Gabriele Von Bülow, who in scarcely better case, gave William a graphic if hysterical account of the affair.

The Queen's carriage had been set upon as it left the concert hall, when, driving along Regent Street, a mob of 'dreadful men' had formed a cordon across the road, holding up the horses. The footmen had leapt from their stands to guard the carriage, but since they were unarmed except for their canes, they were soon overpowered, dragged aside, and trampled underfoot. The coachman had used his whip to some purpose and the 'Peelers' had come running to render a tardy assistance, but they were only four to four hundred. They did, however, lay heavily about them with their truncheons while the coachman drove his horses through the mob, to scatter those nearest and effect an escape.

'But their faces!' shuddered Gabriele, 'their devilish faces – pressed to the window threatening the Queen, howling and gibbering like maniacs – half starved they looked and awful. One threw a stone and broke the window, but, thank God, it did not harm her Majesty.'

And Gabriele, overcome, sank down upon her knees beside the Queen, who took her hand and raised it to her lips. 'It was you who saved me, Gabriele. Look, William!'

Gabriele's hand was bleeding from a cut.

'It is but a scratch,' Gabriele hastily interposed.

'She held her hands before my face,' said the Queen faintly, 'and received the full force of the splinters. I shall not soon forget your courage, my sweet friend – your wonderful presence of mind! But this hurt must be bathed now and bandaged. Go – fetch a basin of warm water and fresh linen. I myself will dress it.'

Her ladies hurried to her bidding; William hurried from the room to send a gentleman to fetch a surgeon. The whole Court was in a tumult of concern and curiosity to know the worst.

The Queen, who, after her first collapse, had made a valiant effort at control, and had been assured by the surgeon that the Baroness's injury was trivial, dismissed her ladies, sent Gabriele to bed, and called her husband to her.

'You must go to bed, too, my love,' insisted William. He, although greatly shocked, had managed to hide his alarms from his wife. 'Good God! That this should have happened to you! However – all's well that ends well – eh? You're no worse for the adventure. Are you?' he added anxiously.

She smiled. 'No – no worse at all. And yes – an adventure, but no surprise. I have seen this coming. They are like wild beasts – like wolves – these desperadoes. It is but a prelude to worse.' Then reading his face, she cried: 'But you will not give way? This attack on me has been deliberately made to force your hand – I know that it has treachery behind it. These people would not dare to strike without a leader.'

William stared at her in distressed amazement. She seemed to be transformed. A flush burned in her cheeks, usually so pale; her eyes were bright and eager as a girl's, her lips quivering, but not with fear. It was as though she had rallied all her latent powers of determination to meet blow with counter-blow. 'You must not give way,' she repeated with an almost violent emphasis. 'I am not afraid – and if *you* are – it is on my account.' She rose from her couch and went to him, her bosom heaving, her small head high, her eyes compelling his. 'I know who is at the root of all this trouble. You know it too. He hates me – he thinks I use my influence with you against the Bill. I have not done so yet—' She paused, her colour deepened. 'But now – *now* all is fair – in war.'

'War!' William started; the blood rushed to his face. 'War!' he echoed hoarsely, 'you can say that to me? Do you *know* what you are saying? Do you know whom you accuse?' He threw a protective arm around her, drawing her close. 'You must not,' he muttered, 'breathe such accusation. I'll swear that Grey is—'

'Hush, no names.' She laid a finger on his lips, glancing at the door that communicated with her bedroom. 'The walls have ears. It was not I who said his name. But if,' she spoke in a vibrant whisper, 'if he thinks to weaken your resistance by striking at your wife – he is mistaken. I am not a coward – nor, *mein Herz*, are you.'

That roused him. 'No, by God, I'm not!' His arm tightened round her fiercely. 'And you don't move from these gates without a bodyguard. If there's treachery at work it shan't touch you – that's certain.' He was shaking with strain and exhaustion. Although he did not in his heart believe that this night's outrage had been premeditated, he could not entirely ignore the suspicion of

357   N

foul play. From what internal source he knew not, nor did he care to know. His mind, sick and dizzy with the confused babel of his thoughts, stumbled at the problem as a winded horse falls at a fence. 'I'll see to it,' he feverishly declared. 'I'll see to it tomorrow. Meantime, do you go to bed.'

'You too,' his wife's lips smiled. 'I will order you a soothing draught. Some hot milk – yes?'

'Hot milk!' exploded William. 'Good God! I don't want milk.'

'Please,' said Adelaide quietly. 'I do not like that you take so much the Almighty's name in vain. You know that hurts me so to hear.'

'I apologize, my love, I apologize – a monstrous ugly habit, I admit. We – we must calm ourselves. Pray let us calm ourselves,' he mumbled, who was looking anything but calm. 'I'll follow presently. There is something I must do.'

'Not now, surely! It is almost morning.'

'Yes, now. I shall not sleep.'

'But what is there to do at this hour of the night?'

'I know – I know what I'm about.' He took her firmly by the arm and marched her to the bedroom door, scattering, as he opened it, a group of ladies who may or may not have been in close proximity to the keyhole. 'Take Her Majesty to bed,' he bade the waiting-women, and – 'Good night, my Queen.'

He returned to his own apartment to find his son, Lord Munster, there before him in an arm-chair, his feet upon another, and a bottle on the table at his side.

'This, Sir, is a sorry business,' stated George, not rising when his father entered.

'Who gave you permission to come here?' demanded William roughly.

'It is my duty, Sir' – George carefully refilled his

glass – 'not only as your son, but as your servant to – attend you.'

William crimsoned. He was in no mood to cope with this cool insolence that drove him to a pitch of exasperation, when he might at any moment lose command of himself and his temper. 'Leave the room!' he shouted. 'I do not need your service.'

George, still sitting, drained his glass. 'I crave Your Majesty's indulgence. I would like to know, Sir, that you have' – he hiccupped – 'taken the necessary precautions for your protection and the Queen's. These swine are gettin' ugly.'

'So are you,' growled his father. 'Get up – and get out. You're drunk.'

'An unjuss' accusation, Sir.' His son heaved himself from his chair to his feet, where he stood with the light of the candelabra on his handsome face, exquisite as d'Orsay in elegant prune-coloured coat, his chin sunk in a satin cravat, his hair oiled and curling. He smiled, an impudent flash of a smile – and William's heart gave a twitch. How like – how like that other George in fleeting expression and feature! But there resemblance ended. That grace of limb, that hair so thickly curling, the irresistible gay laughter in that voice which, even though wine-slurred, held echoes to awaken ghosts – these lived beyond forgetting.

'An unjuss' accusation,' George repeated, his teeth gleaming through that smile. 'I was never more sober. You are upset, Papa. No wonder. Her poor sweet Majesty! How is she?'

William shook his head as though to shake away a memory; his eyes glared, his lips opened to speak, but no words came. Instead, his son spoke for him.

'Of course you realize, Papa, that there is more in this night's affair than meets the eye. The Whigs and their leaders will stoop at nothing to get the Bill through. Thish 'tack upon the Queen is a try-on to see Your Majesty's reaction. I hope, Sir' – George's eyes, very blue and bright, solemnly widened; he made a great effort to control his tongue – "I hope you won't allow yourself to be threatened into s'rrender. If it means a fight – then let 'em fight us, Sir. I'm ready.'

William's bushy brows, in which some faded gold still mingled with the white, were lowered; from under them his frowning glance, not leaving his son's face, softened but his voice was hard.

'I do not ask – nor do I want your gratuitous advice upon affairs of State. Nor do I like your company. I've told you once and I tell you again – you can go!'

George shrugged his immaculate shoulders, and languidly moved to the door. 'Don't say I didn't warn you, Sir,' he drawled. 'I entreat you, Sir – stay stout!'

There was a moment's silence, while his father drew a choking breath, then, 'Hold your impudent tongue, sir!' spluttered William; and fury loosened, blazed in a red mist, consuming sight. A vein swelled on his forehead. 'I've had enough – enough—'

More than enough. Frayed nerves were strained to breaking-point. His hand groped blindly, found and gripped the bottle on the table, lifted it above his head to send it crashing in a hundred glassy splinters, as his son in terror dodged and fled, with a slam of the door behind him.

William stood staring at a slow trickle of wine that dripped like blood down the painted door-panels; he heard footsteps, muffled on moss-soft carpet, hurrying. . . . Whispers, a knock, a voice.

'Your Majesty! Is anything amiss?'

'Nothing, nothing. Go!'

A silence, more whispers, and footsteps on tiptoe, retreating – to stay near, on guard.

Spent, shaking, the King looked around him. Why

360

was he here? What to do? There was something – still something to do. . . . His eye wandered to his desk, and the quill in the ink-stand upon it. He moved forward, weakly, and sat. His brain cleared; fortified, resolute now, he drew paper towards him, dipped his pen and wrote:

The King to Earl Grey.

ST JAMES'S PALACE.

In consequence of what has occurred this night His Majesty is induced to communicate to Earl Grey his sincere hope and expectation that all difficulties may be erased without resorting to any change of Administration by passing the Bill with *such modifications* as may meet all differences of opinion on the subject.

Any such arrangement to this effect would relieve the King from the embarrassment under which he has been placed by the proposal to make an extensive creation of peers and would be highly satisfactory to His Majesty.

A last appeal – a last cry from the heart. His pen faltered as he signed and dated it.

He shivered. A cold finger of dawn crept through the crimson curtains; one candle guttered in its socket and went out.

The pen dropped from his spiritless hand. He laid his white tousled head on his arms, outstretched on the table before him. . . . An old man and very tired.

*

Three hours later, not a mile away as the crow flies, a fair-haired plump little girl in a checked gingham frock, and wide-brimmed straw hat, ran out from a Palace in Kensington to look at her garden – a small plot of ground tucked under the wall where the peach-blossom clustered. Her own most lovely garden, planted with flowers, all her own.

Never until this, her thirteenth year, had Drina possessed anything to call her *very* own, except her dolls and her doll's house and the presents her uncles gave her, and those from good kind Aunt Adelaide, and Lehzen, and her darling half-sister Feodora – and of *course* her dear Mama. But all the presents in the world were not the same – not *quite* the same – as owning ever so little a tiny piece of the earth. That was something different. Something that made you feel important.

Inside the Palace where you lived you did not even have a bedroom of your own. To be sure it was very wrong indeed to wish – (but ever so privately) – for a bedroom all to yourself when you had the privilege, which many poor little girls had not, of sharing a bedroom with the best and kindest of Mamas. Still. . . .

And Drina sighed; then very sternly told herself she ought to be ashamed. Such thoughts were wrong, were wicked, they must be repressed. What was it her dear Lehzen always said? 'Humility. . . . Humility is the foundation of all virtues.' 'So never let me hear you think such thoughts again,' Drina whispered, for having no little friends of her own age to talk to, she did sometimes talk to herself.

It was so early that the birds were still busy with their breakfasts, chattering and rustling in the shiny green light of the trees, hopping and picking on the lawn, not in the least concerned with her who stood so still to watch them.

The last of the dew lay heavy on the grass like a fairy's grey gossamer blanket. Diamond dew-points sparkled in misty spiders' webs, drowned the snow of scattered petals under the apple tree, and trembled in laughing tears on the velvet cat faces of pansies.

'*Just* like little cats,' murmured Drina, kneeling, regardless of dew to peer closer. A weed! Oh! mercy. How shocking! She pulled it and felt the damp soaking through to her knees. She jumped up, brushing the drops from her dress. Now Lehzen would scold. . . . Never mind. She had pulled out that weed – and oh! there was a horrid red worm in its place. . . . The ground was still moist enough not to need watering yet. When the sun went down this evening, she would water.

In the centre of her garden grew a rose tree full of the most delicious baby buds. And there were tulips – tall and straight as soldiers in gold and scarlet uniforms. Those bulbs – the best of all Dutch bulbs – were a present from her dear, *dear* Uncle Leopold. Maybe it was wrong to love one uncle more than another, but Drina certainly did love Uncle Leopold better than anybody else – (except, of course, Mama) – in the world. More, much more than her Uncle Sussex, who lived in his own suite of rooms at the Palace and who stumped about the grounds very red in the face, and followed by a hideous little black page whom he funnily called 'Mr Blackman'.

Drina had a particular and private horror of Uncle Sussex, perhaps because when she was very young – and sometimes naughty, she had been told that Uncle Sussex would Come and Fetch her Away, which dark threat had the effect of making her scream whenever she saw him. . . . That was many years ago. She was thirteen now – or at least she would be very soon – and almost a young lady, and no young lady ever screamed. Nevertheless, she could not altogether rid herself of the thought that Uncle Sussex, and the glimpse she sometimes had of him at his window in a black velvet cap and a bright blue satin dressing-gown, nodding and smiling at her and singing at the top of his voice up and down the scales (he had a very good voice, and Mama said he would have been an opera singer if he hadn't been a Prince) and what with that and the chiming of his hundreds and hundreds of clocks, all of which not only struck the hour, but played tunes and military marches – there was no denying that Uncle Sussex *did* appear to be a little – not frightening – but odd.

Odder still was Uncle William.

Drina was old enough now to know that relations between her dear Mama and Uncle William were a little strained. This hurt her very much, for she had it in her heart to love good Uncle William, who in spite of his loud voice and louder laugh that made his face so purple-red one could almost think that he was choking – and in spite of the way he pinched your cheek so *very* hard by way of a caress, and uttered (never say it!) a *swear* word in almost every sentence – in spite of all his peculiarities, which for a King were very peculiar indeed, Uncle William was *very* good-natured and kind – too kind, Mama said, when she saw the poor dirty children playing in the gardens where Drina used to ride her darling sweet little Rosy. But all things considered Drina was really very fond of Uncle William, and had cried most bitterly on the day of his coronation, which, owing to some misunderstanding between the King and Mama, Drina had not been allowed to attend. . . .

All these and other thoughts and recollections were in Drina's mind on that May morning, a week before her thirteenth birthday. . . . Thirteen! A great event to be entering upon her teens. She remembered that day a year ago when she had found in the pages of her history book the genealogical tree of the Kings of England. At first she had not at all understood the meaning of her own name – Alexandrina Victoria – at

the end of it. But, when Lehzen had explained so carefully and kindly . . . then she *did* understand, and
she knew that never, never while she lived would she
be quite the same Drina again.

'I *will* be good!' It was a promise made, and hidden.
Not to forget, for the knowledge of what Uncle Leopold
called 'that most eminent station which by the dispensation of Providence you are destined to fill—' was something that could *never* be forgotten. But one could drop
a curtain on the thought of it and hold that promise,
veiled, in your heart.

A shadow that had fallen on the honest homely little
face, lifted: the soft lips parted in a smile showing
slightly protuberant teeth. She was a child again, untouched by Destiny, with the sun on her hair, dirt on
her hands, and a wet green smear on her checked
gingham. Ruefully she rubbed at it, her eyes on an
open window, where the ever watchful Lehzen stood to
call 'Drina! Drina! come in – come in at once. You
will haf your feet wet!'

She went obediently, her shoes squelching, to leave a
trail of small footsteps in the grass. Her stockings were
soaking, and Lehzen would scold. She knew it was
naughty to go out in the garden without goloshes so
early in the morning.

Lehzen, however, was in no mood to scold. She had
news. 'Welcome news,' she emphasized with nods, as
though to impress on Drina there must be no doubt at
all on that point. A letter of invitation had just been
received from Drina's dear Aunt Adelaide inviting her
niece – at His Majesty's request – to stay at Windsor
for her birthday.

'And Mama, too?'

'Naturally, my darling.'

'And are we – are we going?'

Lehzen's dark parrot-face was inscrutable as she

answered: 'Her Royal Highness is accepting for you –
and herself, my dear. Are you not delighted?'

Drina dutifully said she was.

But as it transpired that visit, after all, did not
materialize. The Duchess of Kent who had surprisingly,
for once, accepted His Majesty's invitation without
immediate excuse, heard with relief that the visit to
Windsor was cancelled. The King had greater matters
to concern him than the birthday of a niece.

The King's letter to Lord Grey and his determination to see the Bill through intact by any means short
of creating peers, had brought the House to the verge
of combustion. The critical moment for Grey to risk
his all for peace – or war, had come. The people were
armed and waiting for one word from the King to determine the future not only of the Throne, but of Democracy. One word. And if he still withheld it then his
blood be on his head. . . .

But Grey kept his.

Coldly and swiftly he struck the last blow, with no
more palaver, no soft words or hesitation. Adamant, un-
moving, he demanded fifty peers (he had raised the
minimum to fifty now – or the alternative; his resignation. And this time there would be no compromise, no
quarter granted.

None was asked.

The King, harassed beyond endurance, heard the
final ultimatum with mingled alarm and relief. Nothing
could be worse than the present situation. A change of
Government might save it. Yet who could tell what
further complications might emerge with a new man at
the helm, a new crew?

As a last expedient the King wrote personally to a
number of peers entreating them to withdraw their
opposition, but received no tangible assurance. Nothing

for it now but to accept the resignation of the Whigs and Grey – with Wellington appointed his successor.

Those were black days for William. The attack upon his wife had shaken him more than it affected her. It is possible that had she not stood behind him – all professions of neutrality dissolved in exhortations not to relax an inch – he would have been saved that last humiliation which was to cap the climax.

The mud-throwers were itching to spatter the King. 'Our beloved Billy cuts a damnable figure in this business,' wrote Creevey, who went out with the Whigs and was bitter. 'I regret certainly the loss of position and doing agreeable things to myself with my official resources. . . .'

Nothing could have been more unfortunate than that Wellington, at this juncture, should have been called upon to take the lead. The country had long ceased to regard him as a spectacular hero. The new generation cared nothing for wars and famous victories which they were too young to remember. The 'Iron Duke' was better known for his great hooked nose, his crotchety temper, his senile and rather disgusting affairs with ladies of easiest virtue, than for those exploits that had linked his name with Waterloo.

How could 'that damned tiresome old bitch' – as Lord Lyndhurst, one of the younger members nominated for his Cabinet, after a three-hours' interview at Apsley House, described him – lead the country through a crisis that had proved too much for the invulnerable Grey?

It is possible that William shared these sentiments. He still nursed a long-matured grievance against Wellington for having engineered his dismissal from the Admiralty. But any port in a storm was better than none, and the Duke could be relied upon for stamina and fearlessness – he hoped.

He lived on hope during those dark 'Days of May'.

In the short interval that followed the retirement of Grey and the forming of a new Government, he hoped to snatch a few days' rest at Windsor. He needed it. The anxiety was wearing him down. There were times when those about him believed he would collapse under the strain. He had aged ten years in as many weeks.

The Queen had gone to Windsor some days before, when on a Friday morning, the King left St James's in his coach to join her.

Although he had insisted that the Queen should never drive through the city without an armed escort, he would have no bodyguard to attend himself unless on a State occasion.

His entourage consisted of two gentlemen-in-waiting who followed in another carriage, and his eldest son, George, as his equerry, to attend him.

George was not in the best of humours – he was, in fact, furious at being dragged away at a time when London offered much more amusement than the dreary Court at Windsor, and the Queen's hideous collection of old crows. Those interminable evenings – when after dinner one would sit, bursting with yawns, playing whist politely with the King's gentlemen, while the Queen and her frightful ladies netted or tatted – or whatever they did at that table – never talking above a whisper for fear of waking the Old Man, who sat snoring, to open an eye now and then and say – 'Exactly so, ma'am – exactly so,' and go to sleep again. What a prospect! How even for a *week* could one endure it?

George thought nostalgically of a certain young person in Queen Street, Mayfair, whom he till now had found particularly 'tough', and who had suddenly turned tender – on pretty high terms, too, George gloomily considered, with uneasy recollections of an overdraft. The bank would never meet it. And there was that matter of five thousand lost to d'Orsay at Crocky's – and not yet paid. To say nothing of his tailor's bills, and Tattersall's and this and that, God help him! He wondered, with a sliding glance at his father, who sat as glum as he, his chin in his stock, his cheeks flaccid, shoulders bowed – he wondered if the Old Man could be touched – for a tale. Nothing venture, nothing have. He could but try.

'Sir' – George cleared his throat – 'there is a slight matter with which I am loth to trouble Your Majesty at such a moment—'

'Eh? What?' William's head jerked round. 'Speak up. You're on my deaf side.'

'I said, Sir,' George raised his voice approaching his lips to his father's ear. Confound it! This was not a subject one could shout. 'I said, Sir, there is a matter of some urgency which I should like to bring to Your Majesty's notice.'

'You stink of stale brandy,' remarked his father sourly. 'Been drinking all night as usual – eh?'

'No, Sir.' The petulant curved lips pouted. 'I went to bed at ten o'clock.'

'This morning?' queried William, with the suspicion of a grin.

George's fine nostrils quivered. He favoured his parent with a haughty stare. 'If Your Majesty doubts my word—'

'I don't doubt your smell,' retorted William, bristling. 'I know what I know! You're a nuisance, sir – a damned infernal nuisance. You take advantage of the position you hold at Court and as my son, to—'

'As your son, Sir,' George interrupted hotly. 'I hold *no* position – save that of sufferance.'

The thrust went home. The colour flooded his father's face, and receded, leaving a queer mottled pallor. So! William drew a breath – his son reproached him. Never before in his life had this son of his reproached him for the circumstances of his birth. The implication was undeniable: and bitter. He sat in silence, wounded. How sharper than a serpent's tooth . . . but was *he* blameless? A stab to the heart to send thought reeling in a confused sense of the cruelty of life's devices. William raised his gloved hand in a hopeless, weary gesture, and let it fall limp on his knee. 'So! You hold *that* up against me,' he muttered. 'I've made you a peer of the realm. You have my name – or one o' them.'

'And the law and the world give me another, Sir,' George said. Then at the look his father turned on him, a strange aching look, he blurted impulsively, shaken for the moment from the all-absorbing centre of himself – 'Father! Forgive me! I'm behaving like a cad.'

'You behave like a cad, you look like a cad – and you *are* a cad,' said the King slowly.

George reddened to his beautiful arched eyebrows. Damnation! He had queered his pitch. He dared not now approach the Old Man for the needful. He cursed his slippery tongue for leading him so tactlessly astray, and leaned back against the padded leather, arms folded, eyes sullenly lowered.

His father, ignoring him, turned to gaze out of the window with something of a dimness in his sight.

The coach, a modest equipage that bore no indication of importance other than the Royal arms upon its doors, was nearing the Piccadilly turnpike.

A heavy downpour of rain had left the roads muddy. The horses' hoofs splashed in the puddles, bespattering pedestrians, but none looked twice at the elderly gentleman in the grey beaver hat, whose face, if vaguely familiar, passed unrecognized, until – outside Apsley House where a great crowd was gathered, the coach slackened speed, and halted.

'What now?' cried William, bristling. 'Why don't he go on?'

His son sat up. 'Anti-reformers, Sir, having a shot at the Duke again – I'll wager. The damned swine! Shall I tell them to turn back? There may be trouble.'

It was too late to turn back. The mob, having sighted the coach, with its coat of arms and that face at the window, seemed suddenly to have multiplied itself threefold, surrounding the Royal carriage and forming a blockade from one side of the road to the other.

The King, mistaking this reception for one more amiably disposed than that with which of late he had been greeted when he drove through the London streets, raised his hand to his hat in a cheery salute. But the jovial smile froze on his lips as a low rumble rent the air: 'The King! The King!'

It was no voice of acclamation, but an ominous growl from five hundred throats that rose to a wolfish yell of – *'Traitor!'*

'Shall I give the order to turn back, Sir?' breathed George through gritted teeth.

'I will not turn back,' William answered grimly.

'Then *sit* back!' cried his son. 'For God's sake, Sir, don't let them see you!'

A look fiercely resolute crossed the King's face. 'Shall it be said that the King is afraid to show himself to his people?'

And there for all to see he doffed his hat, revealing the white crest of hair on his pineapple head and leaned out with the smile returned to his face, his hand still cheerily waving.

There was a second's pause, then a cry like a signal note, and heavy, resistless as a tidal wave, the mob flung upon the coach, seizing the heads of the horses, while the coachman's whip lashed frenziedly to right and left, and the footmen leapt from their stands to grapple with those nearest.

The coach swayed from side to side as though the ground were cracking in an earthquake. The King was jolted back into his seat. 'Now *stay* there, Sir!' George, white as death, gripped his father's arm. 'Your Majesty! I pray you guard yourself – these vermin are mad – they'll *kill* you!'

'Get away – get away!' muttered William savagely. 'Let me be – I know how to deal with 'em.'

He jerked himself free and staggered to his feet, head and shoulders half out of the window, arms uplifted. 'People!' His ringing voice challenged that bedlam of sound. 'It is your King who speaks—' but his words were lost in a roar of 'The Peelers! The Peelers are coming—' the piercing, terrified shriek of a woman, and then a fearful cry: '*Down* with him! Down with the Traitor-King!'

And still he stood, his pitiful dazed eyes on that crowd-moiled confusion. Were these the same who not a year since had hailed him with joy and love and welcome to their hearts? Were these demoniac faces that seethed before him in a living cauldron of hate, the faces of his own beloved people, changed, transfigured as the damned might be, in Hell?

Nightmare glimpses flashed in that inferno: a man's awful face, hollowed with hunger, one empty eye-socket that oozed red; a harridan, bare-breasted, hair wild, her rags torn and fluttering, her mouth a toothless cavern that screamed curses: 'May you rot! You and your German Queen – may you rot on your thrones together! You who live to see us starve! You – who take our children to *murder* them in factories—'

Other voices took it up: 'Child-murder! Who sanctions child-murder? Give us justice – give us the Bill that we may *live* – not die!'

'Who backs the Lords to stop the Bill?'

'The *King*!'

A tattered scarlet banner with 'Reform' lettered in white upon it was held aloft by a brawny giant.' 'You!' he yelled. 'You! 'Tis *you* who 'old us back – you with your promises! *You* with your lies! We want the Bill, the 'ole Bill and *nothing but* the BILL!'

One sprang forward, threatening arm out-thrust, something hurtled through the air and hit the window-frame, glancing off to shatter one of the carriage-lamps. The coach rocked more violently to the terrified plunging of the horses, the coachman's whip was wrenched from his hand, he was seized and dragged down. Suddenly a shot rang out, there was a mist of smoke, a cry of: 'Break! Break! the red-coats!'

The mob stampeded wildly in all directions, while a hail of mud and stones beat upon the woodwork of the coach, the roof, the maddened horses . . . 'Father!' screamed George, and flung himself before the King – too late. A stone whizzed through the open window straight to its target and struck.

But still the King stood, while the blood dripped from a gash on his temple, to blind his sight – stood, with one trembling hand upraised as though to stay that human hurricane, until the mist of gun-smoke gathered round him, and a darkness fell. . . .

Chapter Five

A HUSH descended on the Palace of the King. No word, no whisper must steal out to spread the tale of this. The newspapers were guarded in half-truths.

'The King when driving down to Windsor yesterday was met by an angry mob who saluted His Majesty with yells and execrations of every description. Dirt was hurled at the carriage, and if the military escort who arrived on the scene had not kept close to the window it is possible His Majesty might have sustained some personal injury.'

That was all, but enough to keep rumour at bay. Even Creevey makes no further comment than: 'Upon leaving the Palace on his return to Windsor, Bill got rather roughly treated by the people at Hyde Park Corner. . . .'

In his room, the King lay with a bandaged head, thankful for the blessed peace and quiet, interrupted only by visits from the doctors and his wife, who had hurried up from Windsor to his side on receipt of a private message.

He was content to lie in a stupor of silence, glad of his wife's cool hand on his aching forehead, her soft voice to soothe and comfort him. '*Mein Hertz* – my poor love! There is nothing now for you to thing of but to be well. All will be well. . . .'

All indeed was well, with her eyes so lovingly in his, with the sweetness of her touch upon him and a scent of lavender. . . . The peace of it! His room, his great downy bed, facing the window where a glimpse of lively tree-tops tossed their branches like green hair against the sky, or stood of an evening, very still and golden. . . .

Peace – and his wife beside him, his dog on the mat by his bed. 'So old, poor fellow, as old as I. No, older if each year of a dog's age is multiplied by seven to every one of ours. That makes you seventy-seven, old man, ten years ahead of me. I ought to know – I bred you, didn't I? From the Bushey strain that'll never die while Bushey lives. . . .'

He had suffered little pain after that first shock when he woke to find his son's pale face bent over him, the carriage at the Palace gates, and a hammer beating a tattoo inside his head.

'Let me be.' He told them firmly; there were more faces than one. 'I can walk. I know what I'm about. Don't make a fuss. Pray – pray don't make a fuss!'

And he walked, supported by his gentlemen, up the staircase to his room, where for the second time that day – and in all his life – he fainted.

Yes, a shattering experience, on which it were better not to dwell. One could almost think, lying there in his blue and gold bedroom, with the pictures of his ships upon the walls, that it had been another of those nightmares which he had so often dreamed of late. Peace. . . . That was what he prayed for, an end to this long agony of indecision and alarms. But would there be an end? His poor exhausted mind and body could not endure a further prolongation of suspense. He was less ill than sick at heart. The slight external injury he suffered had done no hurt that would not soon be healed, but the wound had struck deep – to his soul.

He had nothing of fight in him, when a few days later he received the Duke of Wellington in audience.

The interview was brief. The Duke, that man of indomitable will and iron courage, admitted himself beaten. In grave, measured tones, his face a rock, his nose a jutting fortress, his eyes like steel, unmelting, he shot his bolt.

The Throne, the security of the country was breaking; the storm of popular fury had reached its apex with this last attack upon the King's most precious person. His own desperate efforts to form an administration were clearly doomed. Civil war was imminent. None but the King himself, his word, his seal, could now avoid it.

Et tu Brute! . . .

'Why did you lead me into this?' was the King's sole reproach to Wellington who had left him to decide, alone and unsupported, the most terrible crisis in England's political history. 'Why – why did you not tell me the truth?'

What truth was there to tell that had not flared across the sky, red-hot from earth to heaven – had not resounded in the trumpet-cry of those who rent aside the shackles of tradition, to march fearlessly towards a new enlightenment and freedom? A younger generation, impelled by a young faith that would move mountains; a faith to build upon the dying symbols of the past the immortal glory of an Empire in the future – that the nation shall be master in its house.

So, in the reign of King William IV, the first page in the first chapter of Democracy was irrevocably turned. The great Reform Bill became law.

The final episode staggered the community to its foundations by the sudden and comparatively mild collapse of the opposition.

Grey, recalled to wrench a promise from the King that he could have his peers – unlimited, had won his victory without a further fight. The threat sufficed.

The King, against his judgment, in the face of all he cherished for justice and fair play, baffled, humiliated, had by force, surrendered. . . . From that moment, power passed from the House of Lords to another assembly. The oligarchy of the peerage ceased to be.

'That this should have been accomplished,' Creevey deliriously writes, 'as it has against a majority of peers, without making a single new one, must always remain one of the great miracles in English history. . . . I was in at the death . . . and the triumph.'

*

The long struggle was over, the long day of cloud and tempest drawing to its close; peace descended on the country like a sigh.

But the King was broken. He was tired. The years weighed heavy with the added burden of those memories that could never be erased, memories that had wounded, that had left a scar, 'My people. . . .' They, to whom his heart was pledged, who through strife and torment, through long-suffering endurance, had won to victory in triumph – that was no triumph for him.

He had lost touch with them, his people. As a ship homeward bound, ploughs her course through perilous seas with the track of the storm behind her, so these were phantoms that receded in the unreality of distance, to fade in darkness upon a dim horizon.

And because time was getting shorter, each year, each day that gathered to its twilight was charged with wistful dreams, wherein an old man's fancy might go straying in the shrouded valleys of the past.

Who shall tell what yearnings stirred the echoes, what visions came and went like colours in the sea, like shifting clouds, like a white sail sinking in the circle of the sky, under the last glow of sunset?

It may be that drowsing in the golden evenings on the terrace of his Castle, his thoughts slid back along the shadows to dissolve in the silvery mist of breaking waves, to hear again the voice of the great waters, to tread once more the heaving deck of a ship with the taste of salt on his lips, or a song . . . or the kiss of a girl.

It may be that his ears were full of the sound of sea-shanties, when the faces of friends who had passed before him on a longer voyage thronged ever nearer, though they stood divided by a boundless ocean on a further shore.

And as the last summer dawned, the days' perpetual motion seemed mysteriously to halt, as if the past were merged into the present and there was no life but memory.

Those about him saw that his step had faltered, that his strength, for all the spirit's will, was slowly ebbing, but he stoutly refused their aid. 'Walk? Of course I can walk. Not ten miles a day, maybe – but I can still take the dog for a stroll.'

Another dog, a younger dog, of the same breed, the same devotion, followed at his heels up and down the terrace overlooking the gardens at Windsor.

There he sat with the sun on his head, and his thoughts like bees at work, inside it.

Well! He'd had his day, a long day, that had seen many changes and strange happenings in his journey from cabin-boy to King; great wars, great victories. . . . Trafalgar, Waterloo. He hoped he'd live to see another Waterloo, another anniversary of the day that had freed Europe from the tyrant's stranglehold.

Yes, he had seen strange things and wonderful in the giant stride of progress that had set the tempo of the world to steam – and speed.

The iron horse had replaced the horse of flesh upon the road, and the snort of an engine the sound of hoof and horn. The ocean's highways smoked with the belch-ings of man-created monsters of the deep. Sacrilege to William in his heart, though he had been the first to

swing open the harbour gates to ships of steam – ugly
sisters of those proud beauties who followed the fun-
nelled boats with disdainful spread of canvas, as for
ever they would follow, so long as a sailor lived.

And he who had steered his ship through seas un-
charted, to the shrieking winds of tempest, through fair
weather and foul, still stood on the bridge, and when he
left it there'd be a girl at the helm to bring her safe to
port. A girl, begad, as Captain!

His nose twitched; he rubbed it, chuckling, and
stirred the dog at his feet with his toe. A good dog that,
but not so good as its father. . . . 'No, not walk. Not
now . . . we can't walk . . . now. Lie down.' The wag
of a feathery stump of a tail, a sigh, and the soft silken
body flopped again to the sun-warmed stone. . . . Yes,
he'd stayed the course, he'd kept his word, he'd seen to
it. There'd be no Regency, no Madam Kent in office
with her fine feather, preening herself in her prospec-
tive glory, and keeping her little canary of a daughter in
a cage. No Regency, not if he knew it. Not on his life!
His life had lasted long enough, thank God, to put That
Person in her place, and his niece on the throne when
he went. . . . Eighteen, just turned, but still – eighteen.
She'd come of age.

A smile of reminiscence that had something young,
something of mischief in it: a gleam, a twist of the lips,
and a deeper chuckle— Yes! He had put That Person
in her place as for years he'd itched to do. In front of
them all, at a banquet given for his birthday – his last
birthday – before a hundred guests. What was it he had
said? . . .

'I have been insulted, grossly and continuously insulted by the behaviour of a certain person now near
me—' or words to that effect. He had bellowed them
that all should hear and know that while he lived his
authority as King should be respected. . . . (She and

her Royal salutes!) He hoped, he prayed, that he would be spared another nine months until the Princess, his heir, should come of age, so that there might be no danger from, 'This person, whose behaviour towards myself has been systematically offensive, in that she has kept this young lady, my niece' – (the blushing Drina was in tears by this time) – 'has kept this young lady, my niece, from my Court, and from my Drawing-rooms, when she should in duty bound have been present at my side. I am fully resolved that it shall never happen again. . . .'

And it hadn't happened again.

So much for Madam and her play-acting, those damned infernal poppings that followed her from one end of the Solent to the other. That would teach her to keep the King's heir from her place. . . . What a scene! It had upset him. He had been taken badly with the asthma after that. And he'd shocked Adelaide. They'd almost quarrelled. She wouldn't speak to him for the remainder of the night.

The Duchess in a white-hot rage called for her carriage and went. Poor little Drina was almost hysterical, and the guests all retired, aghast. . . . Yes, a bad job over and done with. It had been festering for years, and now like a boil it had burst. And he felt better.

As for Drina, he had seen to her, had given her a goodly portion, an income of ten thousand a year – settled on her, too – that her mother shouldn't touch it. He'd seen that all was shipshape, the decks and galleys cleared for action. . . . The tide was on the turn.

A pang shot through his side under his heart where it hurt him, a little, to breathe. Settling back in his chair he closed his eyes. The sun had made him sleepy and that pain . . . just there. . . .

Word went about the Court – the King was ill, alarmingly ill; yet his spirit rallied. Although he could not now sit on the terrace in the sun, he refused to go to bed, but sat always at his window gazing out at the summery green, the curve of the low-lying hills, the trees of his Great Park, and the orchards, where the last of the blossom still lingered.

Movement, light, and colour, the great white clouds, the smell of the good earth . . . this beloved island with its myriad offerings, its glory of field and meadow, its woods, its hills, its moorland heights, its cliffs, its low-coast marshes, and the long slow river winding down to the eternal sea, this land he loved, his land, was the more precious now, perhaps because so soon the dark would come to steal the sight of it.

On that last day he rose at his accustomed time of seven.

'I shall get up at once to do the business of the country,' he told the Queen, who all the night had never left his side. He was so weak that they had to wheel him in his chair from his bedroom to his dressing-room, where at the threshold of the door he turned to wave his hand to his weeping daughters, and tell them: 'Bear up! I'm not gone yet. . . . God bless you!'

There was so much to do, and so little time to do it.

'And why are there no newspapers – and no post? What day of the week is it?'

'It is Monday, Sire. There is no post today.'

'True – I had forgot.'

But he had not forgotten that it was the anniversary of Waterloo.

'You must tinker me up,' he told his doctors, 'you must tinker me up somehow. I want to see this day of all days – through.'

'I hope Your Majesty will see many more.'

He grinned in their long faces.

'Eh? That's quite another thing – quite another thing!'

Till twilight fell, and dusk veiled the fields and the meadows, he sat in his wheeled chair by the open window, with his wife beside him, and her hand in his. He knew no pain now; but his heart was busy with an eager, strange excitement. . . .

And presently he turned to her whose arms went round him to draw his head against her shoulder, and lay her lips upon his closing eyes; and in his ears was the beat and hurry of waves, the wind's gallant song in filled sails, and the rush of the tide on a nearing shore, to bring a brave ship home.

*

Dawn broke over Kensington Palace to the sound of hoofs and carriage wheels in the courtyard, and the peal of a bell.

A young girl, sleeping, stirred in her dreams . . . and woke.

BIBLIOGRAPHY

Life and Reign of William IV. Robert Huish.
Life and Times of William IV. Percy Fitzgerald.
The Patriot King. Grace Thompson.
Journal and Letters of Sir T. Byam Martin.
                                    Navy Records Society.
Horace Walpole's Letters. Toynbee Edition.
The Royal Dukes. Roger Fulford.
George IV. Roger Fulford.
The Greville Memoirs. Edited by Henry Reeve.
The Creevey Papers.
                    Edited by Sir Herbert Maxwell, Bart.
Royal George. C. E. Vulliamy.
Journals of Mrs Papiendiek.
                    Edited by Mrs V. D. Broughton.
Madame d'Arblay's Diary. Edited by Austin Dobson.
Life of Nelson. Robert Southey.
Hanoverian Queens. Alice Drayton Greenwood.
The Story of Dorothy Jordan. Clare Jerrold.
Mrs Jordan. W. P. Sergeant.
Life of Mrs Jordan. James Boaden.
Queen Victoria. Lytton Strachey.